Daintree Denizens

A Tropical Thriller

Josef Peeters

DEDICATION

To my daughters and grandchildren.

ACKNOWLEDGMENTS

I would like to thank you, the reader, for taking the time to read my books. I hope you enjoy reading them as much as I enjoy writing them.

CHAPTER ONE

It was one of those mornings that made him feel great to be alive. The sun was just beginning its ponderous ascent over the Coral Sea. The soul-sapping humidity of the north had yet to make its presence known through the cool breezes that wafted gently up the shore into Barry (Bazza) Ottoman's face as he stood on the dunes at the top of the beach. He listened to the gentle susurration of the waves lapping on the shore and the birdsong emerging from the tropical rainforest behind him, the only sounds to be heard.

He scratched at the long beard he had been cultivating for over ten years, ever since he first came north. The salt had taken over the pepper in that beard years ago and his skin was so brown that he passed for a native easily. He stretched his bulky frame to his full height of well over six feet in the old scale. He didn't take to the decimal system introduced into Australia many years ago, never had. Never was able to picture metric measurements in his mind. If someone had told him they caught a Barramundi measuring fifty centimetres, he'd be damned if he knew how long that looked! Tell him it was just a shade under two feet long, and he knew immediately.

He peeled off his threadbare shirt and shorts to stand naked on the top of the dune, feeling the breeze tickle his bare torso and genitals with its feathery touch, causing tingles down his spine. He wanted nothing more than to launch himself down toward the inviting water with every ounce of energy his old body could muster, but he knew it could spell the end. The north was no place to be foolishly careless. At the top end of eastern Australia, with his nearest neighbour an unofficial Aboriginal camp nearly two hours of rough travel away and no decent medical care within cooee, one wrong step could see him in a world of hurt.

In truth, stingers were probably the least of it. They were bad enough, though, and the bloody Irukandji could sting you without your knowledge. You'd keel over from a heart attack and nobody would know. If the jellyfish didn't get you, the bloody crocodiles might. Not that he'd ever seen one on the beach in all the years he'd been there. *You never did see the rotten bastards until they were chewing on your leg. Craftiest reptiles that ever roamed the earth.* He'd never come across one on his stretch of beach but he'd seen plenty in the rivers, the estuaries, and the mangroves; especially the mangroves.

No, Bazza didn't give in to the impulse of running down the beach to dive head first into the cool water for his morning clean up. Instead, he ambled down to the water's edge where he scooped up a few handfuls of relieving freshness to throw over himself, washing off the morning's labours and night's sweat. He lathered himself generously in homemade soap scented with eucalyptus. Soap-making was a lesson he had learned at a workshop years ago. It came in very handy when the nearest store was close to a day trip away. As the crow flies, Cooktown was not too far away. But on the treacherous roads, especially in the Wet, and from where Bazza's stretch of beach was located, Cooktown was a full day's journey away in a four-wheel-drive custom-built vehicle for the north.

Bazza washed away the environmentally-friendly suds, watching them seized by the outgoing wave to mingle with the salty froth of the ocean. As the water retreated he saw the many sea worms' heads poking from the sand, attracted by the flavour of the suds. His brothers would never believe he had invented the perfect worm bait. He remembered how they had toiled at the water's edge for hours with a dead fish as bait, trying to lure the worms up out of the sand, squeezing their slimy heads and pulling hard to get them all the way out swiftly before they retreated.

Bazza winced as he raised himself to full height once more. He lifted his bare foot to view the underside. Unfortunately, it all looked blurry without his reading glasses. He knew he had a splinter in his foot, but he wasn't able to see it clearly. Getting old was everything it was cracked up to be as far as Bazza was concerned. He would have to check on it back at the shack. He was meticulous about all things medical. He had to be, in order to survive in such isolation. If not attended to in short order, something as small as a wood splinter could easily become infected. There were no antibiotics to be had down the road at a chemist. He couldn't even remember the last time he had seen an actual doctor.

Most times, he just went to the Aboriginal camp a few hours away for bush medicine from Boinga Bob. Boinga was a gnarly old

Aboriginal elder with traditional bushcraft knowledge. There wasn't much he didn't know, and even less his aunts couldn't fix with something brewed up from nature. Tasted like shit every single time, but more often than not, the stuff worked. The worst of all were his aunt's tinctures, which she dabbed on open wounds. *Fuck knows what she put in those evil-smelling things.* It was probably best that Bazza never knew.

He ignored the minor discomfort of the splinter as they were an occupational hazard. Not that he actually had a full-time occupation, as such. He felt duty bound to spend some hours each day dedicated to his vocation, though those hours varied greatly depending on numerous factors like; if the fish were biting, if the weather was favourable, if he wasn't too hung-over, or if he actually *felt the fuck like it.*

Bazza owned about one hundred acres of rainforest land, aptly named *Euphoria*, by him, abutting the ocean a little over half way between the Daintree River and Cooktown in Far North Queensland. He owned an idyllic ocean frontage with a mountainous backdrop of impenetrable jungle. He used the hostile environment as a buffer between him and the world. A treacherous, muddy track, known only to Bazza and Boinga Bob, provided access from the only identifiable road to his secluded hideaway. Bazza went to great pains to camouflage the entrance of his track whenever he returned from a trip away; an infrequent occurrence.

At the top of the dunes, Bazza donned his clothes before continuing along the sandy track to his shack hidden under the deep green canopy of the rainforest, where the air turned to a deeply-scented, humid, pungency of rich earthiness. His shack lay nestled beneath towering Hardwoods and Strangler Figs obscuring the rays of the rising sun, bedecked in a botanical profusion of ferns, orchids and bromeliads decorating each and every limb strong enough to bear them. Much of the tangled undergrowth had been cleared by Bazza at great cost to his body and ego. When he first came north he had little knowledge of the land, the flora or the fauna.

Much of his knowledge, he had been forced to learn the hard way, like *the bloody Stinging Tree, and fucking Wait-a-while.* There is a very good reason why Rangers in the north wear long-sleeved shirts all year round. When you get stung by a Stinging Tree (*Dendocnide moroides*), or Gympie-Gympie, the first time, you soon learn to protect yourself in virgin rainforest. Even the dead leaves of the Stinging Tree on the ground carry the fine hairs eager to embed themselves in bare flesh. Their excruciating sting can be experienced repeatedly for months to a year afterward.

Bazza remembered vividly the tale of a tourist taking a trip to the Daintree for the first time, who needed to wander off into the bush to relieve himself. He found a little open area where a tree had fallen and new growth had yet to enclose the canopy again. Unfortunately, he forgot to take his dunny roll, (toilet paper), with him, so he used the closest, large, leaves he could find. They reckon they heard that bloke howling for miles. He never stopped howling until they knocked him out with a morphine shot back at the nearest hospital in Mossman.

Usually, bush treatment consisted of a coil of sticky tape applied to the affected area to remove as many of the fine hairs as possible, but no one was game enough to touch his smelly, shitty arsehole. Bazza could not imagine the pain affecting that fella's arse and hands when all he had suffered was a slight brush against one with an elbow, *which stung like fuck for a year*. Every time he got the area wet, the same pain struck with equal intensity. It is known as the Daintree's most poisonous plant. *Most* tour operators will warn their clients of the potential hazard *before* they wander off alone.

The forest floor in the clearing beneath Bazza's shack was littered with sawdust and wood chips. He knew it was silly to walk around barefoot, but he had misplaced his rubber Crocs somewhere, probably in the shack, and he did not feel like climbing back up the long chain ladder to retrieve them once he was down. It was another lesson to teach him not to be so lazy in future. As he walked over to the basket he used to lower and raise goods to his home, he spied the ubiquitous Crocs hiding in a carton that had been obscured by his bag of composting materials, mainly vegetable left-overs and peelings. Cursing himself for not having taken the time to search the basket, he slipped on the rubber beach shoes lest he attract further splinters.

Later, Bazza climbed the chain ladder to his tree-home for a morning cuppa. Brewed from fresh Milanda Tableland coffee grounds on his combustion stove, Bazza savoured the aroma while he prepared a breakfast of fruit and cereal. His girls had been lax in supplying him with fresh eggs of late, so he had to make do. He chastised his Australorps severely for slacking off before lowering their cage to the ground so that they could forage for the day in relative safety.

He had tried keeping chooks in a cage on the ground but it was next to impossible to keep them alive with the number of feral animals like cats and pigs foraging around the forest at all hours, even the odd crocodile. The bloody pigs could chew through the thickest wire to get at them. He decided that if he built his own home up off the ground to keep himself safe, he may as well do the same for his girls. He had lost only one to a snake in all the years since doing so.

The shack was a very simple affair. Split-level with an elevated sleeping area and hinged walls that raised on all sides within the wide, screened veranda. This layout made the most of any breezes whispering through the dense forest. Strong aluminium mesh kept the insects and their predators at bay…mostly. It wasn't uncommon for Bazza to find gargantuan spiders roaming about his home at times and he was as yet unable to discover their path of ingress. He had no electricity to speak of other than solar panels erected high in the canopy, so no air-conditioning. He used all methods available to trap air currents within the lofty structure which was built almost entirely of bamboo.

It had taken a few years of cultivation to reach a stage where his bamboo plantation was of harvestable size. It was an extremely light-weight, incredibly strong material to use for house-building. He would never have attempted raising hardwood timber to the height he had built his shack midway up a pair of enormous Strangler Figs. He also did not have the wherewithal or patience to mill his own hardwood from the surrounding trees. It had taken almost twelve months to complete the main building. His lofty abode gave him generous views of the forest on all sides, with a narrow sliver of space in the canopy, affording him a spectacular view of the ocean.

Months upon months of back-breaking labour had gone into the construction of his shack, including all the furniture within; cupboards, benches, cabinets, etc. The total cost of items he had not been able to manufacture himself, like a stainless steel kitchen sink and enamelled steel vanity basin, was negligible. His upstairs dunny, (toilet), consisted of a twenty-litre paint tin with the bottom cut out to fit a large diameter PVC pipe that led through a hole in the bathroom floor, where it continued for another forty feet to the forest floor, before ending up in a large void of unknown dimensions well below the ground. He didn't think he'd be filling that hole with his waste matter in his lifetime. Another little bamboo outhouse situated adjacent to the outflow pipe, with the same type of disposal setup attached, sufficed as his downstairs toilet.

Bazza had discovered the void while drilling for water one year. The only time his 'permanently' flowing creek had ceased flowing. Rainfall in the tropics was plentiful, while capturing said rainfall required large, expensive, tanks. It wasn't even the expense of the large tanks that deterred Bazza from purchasing one. It was the hardship involved in transporting one to his isolated property. He had neither the equipment to transport it himself, were he to manufacture a decent enough roadway to get it to his shack, nor invited the idea of a delivery driver knowing his property *existed*, let alone how to get to it.

To say that Bazza was a recluse or a hermit was understating the obvious by a factor of ten. Bazza had shunned all contact with 'civilised society', many years ago. No one knew where he lived let alone his last name. His father had purchased the property way before he was even born, bequeathed to Bazza on the old man's deathbed. Bazza had been mostly estranged from his old man since about the time he decided that *society could stick it up its bum*. Sure, some smart lawyer could probably trace his name down eventually to find he had signed off on the property transfer into his name, but let them try to actually find the place on anything other than an aerial map. If they managed that near impossible task, then let them try to reach the property. It was a long property going up a steep mountainside, twisting and turning for miles before one actually came to what might pass as a road in the dry. In the wet? Forget it. A helicopter might land on the narrow strip of beach at low tide he supposed, otherwise forget that too. Could get there by the right kind of boat if you knew how to navigate the reef protecting beach access to his hideaway.

When he decided to go off-grid, he did it well. Well enough for Bazza to have to be extremely cautious with his health and well-prepared enough for the long wet season when all travel to and from his property was next to impossible. Bazza was as self-sufficient as it was possible to be. He taught himself to be highly efficient with a simple bow and arrow, which he was more than capable of manufacturing himself from available woods. Plenty of wild game to be had in the rainforest if you knew where to look, or how to lure it into range.

The ocean provided the purest abundance known to humankind, and he knew many ways to harvest that plentiful bounty. He had a tinny, an aluminium boat, to take himself onto the reef or a short way beyond anytime he wanted. He had an outboard motor that ran on bio-fuel, a concoction he made and mostly drank, himself. All his petrol motors ran on the same fuel made by his homemade still. Ninety-four percent proof, high octane 'rocket fuel', he called it. It certainly made his rear end blast away at times. All his motors had been doctored to take the fuel showing no adverse signs of wear as a result.

Naturally, no one survived in this world without some form of income to pay for such things as land rates, spare parts for all the engines he ran, basics like flour, sugar, his potatoes for the still, toothpaste and such that he didn't want to have to make himself. He returned to town once a year to stock up on all the supplies he needed which barely fit into the tray of his Ute with high caged sides. His part-time occupation saw him earning enough money to see him through and then some. Money enough saved to keep him living his frugal lifestyle for a little over five years unless another major calamity beset him. He had been wiped out around three years ago by a savage cyclone, notorious in the north. All the walls, roof, and floor of his shack had been picked up and hurled out to sea by the cyclone. Even his paint-tin dunny went flying, never to be seen again. Took him a while to find a replacement for his dunny. He was rather fond of the old one with its handmade wooden toilet seat.

Luckily, he stored all of his machinery in a man-made cave he had dug out of the side of the mountain. Everything inside the cave had made it safely through the storm. It took him many months to replace the walls and other missing necessities from his home in the tree tops but eventually, all was returned to its former state. The new aluminium screens and screws, nails, hinges for the shutters etcetera, cost him a fair chunk of his savings. Two years of solid work had seen him make up the shortfall once more.

Bazza toiled away happily most days with a variety of petrol and electric chainsaws, as well as many other electric tools which he ran from a small generator. After locating suitable fallen logs on his property, abundant after the cyclone, he would then toil hour upon hour, carving the green logs into all manner of beasties. His shack was surrounded by a menagerie of carved animals. Some he would keep, most he would sell in an art gallery in Cairns, which he supplied once a year. His work had become much sought after, and his name and reputation grew from one year to the next. He preferred highly polished, stylised indoor sculptures, but made many rough-hewn chainsaw carvings for outdoors as well.

Bazza did not see himself as being particularly talented at wood carving despite every one of his pieces selling quickly. He shied away from eager journalists wishing to write pieces about him. Shunned exhibition openings like the plague, and never accepted commissions. He carved what he liked, when he liked, *and to buggery with anyone who did not like that arrangement.* His indoor carvings occupied every available surface within the shack, stacked three deep throughout the cave, and even one or two in his outhouse. Carved wooden gargoyles sat atop each corner post of his octangular tree-house.

The clearing beneath and around his shack, he called the *Cathedral*, because of the ethereal ambiance it emanated during the quieter daylight hours, with the muted, dappled sunlight imitating the mosaic illumination cast by leadlight windows in a church. The forest floor was inches deep in the detritus of his creativity. Wood carving is all about the removal of extraneous matter to reveal the vision within. That extraneous matter consisted of tonnes of wood chips and sawdust mingling with the discarded and dead leaves shed by the surrounding trees.

Bazza revelled in the calming atmosphere of his *Cathedral*. He paid silent homage each day to the natural beauty surrounding his home, and the serenity of a tropical rainforest when it isn't inundated with the latest monsoonal deluge. At those times, all Hell breaks loose in a deafening maelstrom of falling water obliterating the senses to all other factors. To keep a dense tropical rainforest healthy, requires an average of 120 days of rainfall per year, dumping close to seven feet of rain in the old scale. Over 2000 millimetres in metric, which was basically a foreign language to

Bazza. That amount of water is massive in anyone's terms, so in the wet season, between December and March, access to or from his property was virtually impossible.

Any kind of travel through a dense jungle was hindered by constant growth of vines, saplings and undergrowth where trees have fallen to reveal patches of sunlight through the canopy. Slippery surfaces of mud and rotting leaf matter deny secure footings. Bazza normally had all his annual shopping and stocking done and dusted well before the start of December, preparing to bunker down for the big Wet and cyclone season.

It was late November and Bazza had taken care of everything to ensure he could maintain his home and lifestyle throughout the wet to come. Winter and spring had come and gone seamlessly, with very little indication of each in the sweltering temperatures of northern Australia.

The climate within the confines of his *Cathedral* was relatively constant and remarkably cooler than outside. A *semi-permanent* creek with crystal-clear waters flowing directly from his mountain backdrop cooled it like a water-cooler would a home. The breezes flowing down the mountainside atop the meandering stream wafted through his home night and day, coupled with the sea breezes soughing through the gap in the canopy in line with his shack, provided all the air-conditioning Bazza required. That, and acclimatisation, afforded him a comfortable life alone in a hideaway retreat where he was safe from interference from all but natural interlopers.

Although he would have loved to start carving after his breakfast that morning, he knew he had to crank up Betsy to make the trek up to the top road sooner rather than later. He needed to clear the path a little before the torrential rains began, and he also required some new logs. His favourite patch of ground where a massive amount of old growth timber had fallen in the wake of the last cyclone, demanded he traverse the entire length of his property to reach the top road, dividing his land at the crest of the mountain. Just over the crest on the inland side, lay the clearing he wanted to access, to cut up a fair sized length or two of logs, then haul them back to his *Cathedral*. He risked exposing the entrance to his track for a short time until the rains obscured the path once again, but knew it was a small price to pay for the bounty of fresh material to carve during the long wet.

During times of day-long rain, Bazza amassed many indoor carvings requiring detailing or finishing, accomplished either in his shack or the cave. Solar panels perched high up in the roof of the canopy, with wires leading to a massive bank of batteries provided ample current to power his LED lighting in the cave and his shack, as well as floodlighting for the *Cathedral* when required. If he needed a few extra volts to run a CD player, for instance, he used a treadle-powered bicycle, a contraption he made to give himself instantaneous power while providing some much-needed exercise. If he felt lazy, he would simply hook up his small generator.

His two stoves/cookers were fuelled by propane gas and wood respectively. Some days, his wood stores were just too damp to be effective in his combustion stove, so he would revert to the gas cooker. One or two gas bottles was all it required to keep him cooking all year long, or if he desired hot water for showering or for taking a bath in his handmade timber bath. The bath was constructed from one piece of Red Cedar, considered to have been plundered to near extinction in the north. Bazza had found a stand of truly enormous Red Cedar trees on the far western corner of his property hidden on the descending slopes of his mountain.

After the last big blow that effectively wiped out his home, he discovered two of the large trees downed by the violent winds. It was very sad for Bazza to witness the destruction of such majestic old trees, a thousand years and older most likely. The unfortunate bonanza had netted him several years' worth of ideal carving wood. Cutting the enormous trunks and branches into useable lengths was hard yakka of the highest order, taking a few days at a stretch. He would then chain several lengths to his tractor, Betsy, after winching them up to the top of the crest where he left her. He would then have to negotiate the twisting path downhill back to his home, trying very hard to keep the logs from overtaking his tractor on the way or rolling over the precipice of the narrow track.

It required nerves of steel and dogmatic patience to achieve the task without fatal injury to log, person, tractor or all three. The Red Cedar was by far the most carver-friendly wood he had found among the rainforest woods. Tulip Wood was a favourite, with magnificent grains, but seldom found of decent enough size to accommodate his carving style. Blue Quandong, by far the largest of the rainforest woods, did not carve very well and palm trees were out of the question. Wait-a-while vines, or Lawyer Cane to use their common name, was great for weaving baskets and such, but not so great when trying to navigate through virgin forest. The barbs of the vine grab hold of the clothing and hair and can prove near impossible to remove. Cutting away the clothing is regularly the best option to struggling.

Bazza climbed down the chain ladder to the *Cathedral* floor once more after meticulously cleaning his morning dishes. The smallest amount of left-over crumbs from cereals or bread would have the home overrun with ants and the like in a manner of minutes. Despite his best efforts to completely bug-proof his abode, they still managed to find ways in. He scurried about the *Cathedral* grounds and cave like a harried ant himself as he prepared the tractor for the excursion, loading up the front bucket with his largest chainsaws, oils, spare chains, spare parts, insect-proof swag and so on, taking the better half of the day. Once everything was in readiness, Bazza went to the beach for his evening wash before retiring early. He would leave at first light the following day.

Bazza's side of the mountain grew dark very early in the afternoon. Within the sheltered cocoon of the *Cathedral*, the light was sparse at the best of times, in the afternoon and evenings it became pitch-black without a skerrick of illumination, with neither stars nor the moon able to penetrate the canopy to any degree. His usual night lights came on automatically, giving a modicum of visibility should he require it. He sometimes wondered how any breeze managed to penetrate his two barriers of insect screening at all. Without them, however, he would be at the mercy of eight-legged horrors of unimaginable size, and slithery monsters of frightening strength, were they to get him within their constricting coils.

He often fell asleep on the bamboo banana-lounge situated on the veranda, sandwiched between the two sets of screens, while drinking his powerful hooch. The night grew noisy with a proliferation of insects and frogs all vying for vocal supremacy among their kind to attract the opposite sex for nocturnal, carnal, delights. Possums, flying foxes, and other nocturnal Mammalia joined in, making their presence known above the entomological and reptilian cacophony.

The *Cathedral* underwent primordial changes to transform the peaceful ambience of daytime into a veritable auditory battleground each evening. The deafening drone of countless crickets and cicadas drowned out most everything else at some point in the evening's spectacle. Grunting, squealing, feral pigs and the tumescent rumble of enormous crocodiles heralding their hold over territorial waters, mix with the general hubbub of a tropical rainforest at night, far noisier than any urban city. Then there are the nights when nothing moves or makes a sound. For no apparent reason that Bazza could ever discern, the animal kingdom shuts down, and everything is as still and silent as a graveyard.

CHAPTER TWO

Morning light entering the *Cathedral* saw Bazza wide awake, taking in the splendour of a sunrise over the ocean from his lofty look-out. He took a few precious moments to soak up the glory of nature as the first rays of sunlight brushed the horizon with shades of vivid orange, vermillion, and mauve. Registering somewhere in the back of his mind was the old adage that he should have given more consideration: "Red sky in morning, sailor take warning". The night's symphony had ebbed to a dull background hum that would soon abate. Bazza roused himself from his reverie to make final preparations for his trek. He gathered some food supplies which he packed into a plastic Esky, brewed extra coffee for his Thermos flask, and decanted a generous amount of his hooch into a plastic bottle, for medicinal purposes, to be taken internally. He fed a few handfuls of scraps and pellets to his Girls who would have to remain aloft for the next few days.

"Now, now, Girls. Don't look at me like that. If I let ya out while I'm gorn, be none-o-ya left. Brrrk, brrrk, brrrk back at ya. Do ya job and lay me some bum-nuts eh?"

He smiled as his chooks carried on about not being released to their freedom below. He set about closing all the storm shutters that may only be reached from the verandas surrounding his shack. Although he would love to have released his birds to roam the veranda freely, in order to give them more space than what was available in their sky box, he did not want to have to contend with the mess when he returned. *Dirty birds, crap everywhere if you give them the chance.*

Once the shack was battened down in readiness for his absence, he descended the chain ladder. He walked around to the opposite side of the enormous Stranglers, and reached inside a dark cavity, where the original host tree had rotted away leaving a large hollow within the healthy usurper.

A Strangler Fig starts out its life as a vine growing around a suitably sized host tree. Growing large very quickly, the vine soon encompasses the host tree within its coils until the host is no longer required by the vine. Once firmly rooted, and solid enough to stand alone, the vine succeeds in killing off the host by greedily consuming all available nutrients and water within the soil, and by preventing photosynthesis by obstructing the sunlight with its umbrella of leaves.

Bazza hauled away at the dark rope secreted within the hollow, thereby pulling the chain ladder up to the floorboard level of the shack, ensuring no visitors had easy access to his abode. Double-checking to ensure he had all the tools and equipment he required, he cranked up old Betsy, who roared to life like the old, reliable, dinosaur she was, belching her foul exhaust from the flue directly in front of him, making sure he copped a dirty lungful each and every time. He lowered the front bucket to around six inches off the ground, allowing him to semi-bulldoze his way along the path to help clear it of new growth or fallen branches. Anything larger blocking the path would have to be cut up with one of the chainsaws. If the fallen tree held any carving merit, he would note the position, to trim and retrieve the tree at a later date or the return journey. Looking around one last time to make sure he hadn't forgotten anything, Bazza nodded with satisfaction, though, he knew *there would be some damn thing he forgot; always was.*

On the way up the winding track, Bazza noted any signs of new animal tracks, or irregularities crossing his path. He hoped he would not have to empty his bucket too many times to fill subsidence holes or wash-outs. That sort of excavation generally took more time than cutting up trees fallen across the path. Once at the top, where his track connected with the top road, he would have to move aside the purposely-laid blockage camouflaging the entrance to his property. He had to remove a good hundred or more feet of obstructing trees and foliage before the road, all in the name of keeping his location a secret. It was all a little over the top, he knew, but he was damned if he was going to change his ways anytime soon.

He preferred his privacy and didn't mind his own company at all. He had never felt lonely in the ten or more years he had been there. He detested having to go back to Cairns for supplies and such. He felt depressed the moment he reached bitumen roads - a sure sign of 'civilisation'. He never stopped at the small towns in between like Mossman or Port Douglas. He ensured sort of a societal buffer zone that way, between where he lived and the people who knew him. His suppliers and an art dealer in Cairns knew him about as well as he wanted to be known, purely out of necessity. Anything more would be unwarranted and unwanted attention. He never accepted offers of a drink in the pub or someone's home while in town. Nor did he accept 'doing' lunch, *whatever that bloody-well meant.* He thought lunch was for eating, not, doing! Nope, no invitations were ever accepted or extended by Barry Ottoman while in town, or otherwise. He had his reasons for doing so, and those reasons were his business. *His business alone and if somebody didn't like that ... they could go fuck themselves.*

He kept everyone at arm's distance figuratively. He couldn't manage it literally because his art dealer, Margaret Donnelly always wanted to kiss both sides of his face while embracing him. Very awkward. He stood there like a starched fart while she went through the same bloody routine every time she saw him. She always had on powerful perfume that punched his olfactory senses a stunning blow. Conflicting scents of shampoo, soap, perfume and whatever else ladies are apt to daub on themselves, made Bazza want to retch with disgust whilst in her clutches. *Even her bloody lipstick had a scent!* It may have been the case that she used it all defensively to ward off the aromas emanating from Bazza after years in the wild. Or it may just be that Bazza was unused to strong chemical scents assailing his nostrils. Either way, he found it annoyingly confronting each year when he came to town.

He was glad to be done with town for another year. Just the thought had him sweating with anxiety and wrinkling his nose in disgust. Ahead, a few small trees had fallen across the track which he gently pushed aside with his tractor. After travelling for two hours, struggling uphill with the aging tractor, Bazza stopped for a cuppa. Cuppa hooch, that is. Coffee was for mornings only. Tea was for washing dishes in, and every other part of the day was for hooch. Otherwise, it was pure creek water. He'd brought a pallet of bottled water with him when he first arrived at the property because someone had told him about the dangers of drinking untreated creek water. *Fuck that!* It was the best tasting water he'd ever had. He emptied every single bottle of that store-bought shit and filled them to the brim with his natural stuff. He took a six- pack of it with him wherever he went.

With the tractor silent, except for the hot metal of the engine ticking as it cooled, Bazza relaxed in the tranquillity of his surroundings. A few birds chortled and a lizard or two rustled beneath the leaf litter. The purest smell of damp earth filling his nostrils, and green scenery of every hue as far as the eye could see, saw Bazza reclining with a sigh against the large back tyre of Betsy. He loved every square inch of his land, of his bit of Australia. Their family had migrated from Germany in the early sixties. Bazza was just a notion back then. His old lady had hit the roof when his old man spent most of their savings on a block of dirt in the Daintree before he was born, which they never saw in all the time they owned it. Some con-man saw them coming a mile off she would say. She was probably right too, except, once Bazza saw the block from an aerial photograph, and then finally made his way along the half-arsed excuse of a road that led to the top of the block, he knew he loved it more than anything else in his life.

Nothing could have prepared him for the first sight of his own chunk of native, virgin rainforest. The smells, the sounds, the varying greens…everything. Overwhelming, awe-inspiring, reverential. His senses went into overdrive and he revelled in every second of it. It was pure bliss the moment he emerged from his Ute at the crest of the mountain. From there he had glimpsed a view of the ocean way down below. He felt overawed by the sheer vastness of the impenetrable forest canopy all the way down to the beach. Pristine coral reefs thrived no more than a few hundred yards offshore. The formidable heat and humidity did not deter him one iota. The moment he laid eyes on his block of land he named it *Euphoria*. Bazza knew he would live there until he died. All plans for a life of seclusion began from that moment in time.

His inheritance had come at an opportune time, a time when he needed to escape the rat-race, escape the inhospitable urbanity of life among the throngs. He had come to loathe general humanity in all its guises, all its fraudulent masks. Humanity had turned on him, pushed him to reject all the mediocre values of career, family, and home. He would never again return to that form of torture. If he could no longer live in this rainforest Eden, he would simply ensure he no longer remained alive. Nothing and no one would ever convince him to leave his special place. Euphoria is what he felt surrounded by the aptly-named land. Here he could do as he pleased all year round.

Bazza broke out of his reverie to climb back onto his tractor for the hardest part of the journey. From the point he had reached, the gradient inclined alarmingly despite his best efforts to zig-zag the track up the mountain when he had initially bulldozed it. Betsy roared to life faithfully as he clunked the vintage tractor into first gear where it would likely remain for the duration of the journey to the top. Chugging along stoically like the Little Engine that Could, Betsy ate away at the steep terrain with unerring strength and pure will-power. No further obstacles interrupted the stubborn tractor or driver until reaching the deliberate blockages installed by Bazza to deter the curious. Seven hours after beginning the trek, Bazza and Betsy cleared the track to make it onto the top road at the summit.

Sun shone harshly on man and machine exposed on the mountain-top, bare of their natural rainforest canopy sunscreen. Bazza felt the full-force of the heat bearing down on him as he chugged along the open dirt road. He stopped suddenly, squinted through the bright glare at the road before him. After placing the gear in neutral and engaging the iffy handbrake, he climbed down from the tractor, searching the verges until he found a suitably sized rock to place behind the rear tyre in case the handbrake slipped like last time. He'd almost lost Betsy then. He straightened his weary body to walk forward of the tractor, inspecting the road. His examinations revealed two very widely-spaced tread patterns etched into the hard road surface.

The tracks were recent and made by something of substantial tonnage. His heavy tractor left hardly a mark compared to these tracks. They seemed too far apart to be one vehicle, yet he could not conceive of any two-wheeled cycle heavy enough to have formed the tracks. Nor could he think of two such cycles travelling in such uniformity to make equidistant tracks for any length of time. He frowned at the implications of recent activity on the upper road. His frown deepened as he noted a different set of tracks, narrower than the first in between. They were just as recent, yet not as heavy as the outer set. If Bazza had to make a guess, he would surmise that some heavy vehicle might be towing a trailer, which was absurd! Nobody in their right mind would tow anything up the treacherous road, even in the dry.

He shook his head in amazement at the thought that someone would be foolish enough to attempt something as hair-brained as towing anything in the middle of a fucking jungle! *A light weight, six by four trailer at the very most, which you could manoeuvre by hand in a pinch, but something big and heavy?* That defied explanation. Defied common sense. He was momentarily flummoxed by the revelations. He didn't want to waste the journey only to return empty-handed after moving all the obstacles to the entrance of his path. On the other hand, he didn't want to leave it exposed to possible discovery by *some nincompoop towing a fucking trailer up in the mountains*. He crouched low to examine the road carefully, going from one track to the next until he finally concluded that both sets of tracks headed in the one direction. They had not returned. The road dead-ended about ten miles ahead.

He knew some Yank owned the adjacent property. He had searched the records when the Title of Land was transferred from his father to himself. He had never seen nor heard of the owners visiting their property. In all the years he had lived here, he had never witnessed another soul on the top road other than a very rare appearance by a council grader making improvements. No tracks other than his own. Even the Forest Rangers didn't bother with this stretch. He hoped it wasn't some sawmilling mob come to rape the pristine forest illegally. The whole area was protected by law against such things, *but that didn't stop the greedy mongrels from trying*. It might explain the trailer and the heavy tracks - a truck hauling a bogey behind. He had no choice but to investigate. The road was only ten miles longer, ending at his neighbour's boundary.

With a heavy heart, Bazza began trudging along the road, determined to put an end to whatever illegal operation was underway. He sipped at his water every so often to have something to do more so than because he was thirsty. He kept an eye on the tracks that perilously straddled the narrow road. Any wider and the vehicle would have middled out on the high hump down the centre. The edges of the road dropped away sharply on either side. One false move and over you went, never to be heard from again. Deep ravines with no sight of the bottom flanked the edges. He was extremely lucky with his own property. He had found a section with a far lesser gradient down which to grade his track, otherwise, he never would have achieved it.

After a short time, Bazza came across his own track to the storm-felled Red Cedars. Nothing had entered that track. He had only done so on foot, leaving the tractor above. Anchoring his tractor to a tree on one side of the road while using his winch on the other side of the road to haul up the huge logs after he had cut and trimmed them into manageable sizes. Despite the reduced measurements, it still tested his machinery to the limit. He breathed a sigh of relief that loggers had not discovered his treasure trove of Cedar, a highly sought after wood. He continued along the road, confused about the loggers' destination. A little way ahead was the sharp bend that had almost cost him his own life on a number of occasions. He would normally have to slow down the tractor to a mere crawl to make it safely past the tight, 130 degree turn. He walked on with worry etched on his features.

Loggers could decimate a huge area in a very short period of time. While Bazza wanted to retain his anonymity at all costs, he could feel the anger rising in him as he envisioned a very public brawl. He would have no alternative but to report them to the relevant authority if he discovered any illegal activity such as logging. *How dare anyone desecrate the paradise he so loved. How dare the bludgers come to defile his sanctuary?* His thoughts tumbled over one another as he envisaged the destruction wrought by inconsiderate thieves hoping to make a quick buck. Just as he was about to let loose with an explosive curse, he stopped dead, mouth agape…

He had not been concentrating on the strange tracks as his mind wandered off. The tracks in the road had disappeared. He had to backtrack, locate where they had branched off. For the life of him, Bazza could not work out what the heck had happened. There was no way a truck towing a trailer could have turned off on the stretch of road he was traversing on foot. It was all far too steep on either side to turn off, and besides…*it was still his property*! *If they turned off onto his property he was going to…*

"Uh oh! Shit!"

Bazza ran back to the sharp bend in the road he had passed, realising what had probably transpired. He figured they had not made the bend, gone over the side for sure, with a vehicle that wide and heavy… and towing as well. The moment he neared the bend, his worst thoughts were realised. The tracks clearly indicated a steady slide from the road down the precipice on the western side of the mountain. When he reached the position where the tracks disappeared, he peered down into the gloom of the ravine far below. All he could make out was a path of destruction carved out by the vehicle as it plunged downwards. The sheer weight of the juggernaut uprooted and fractured many smaller trees. No one could have survived an accident like that. It was pure dumb luck that a fire hadn't started.

"What now Bazza? What the fuck do I do now? Nothing, that's what. They're dead. No fucking way they survived that. So, ya gonna do shit, Bazza. Nothing."

The more he argued with himself, the more he convinced himself that he had to investigate, make sure that nobody survived. If there was someone injured down there and he could have saved them, he would never forgive himself. If he could just satisfy himself that no one survived he could continue on with a clear conscience. He would not have to report the accident, and everything would return to normal. *Yeah, someone may come looking for them? So what? As long as they didn't find his track, it would be easy enough to discover what happened to the arseholes.*

Before he knew it, Bazza had returned to his tractor. He drove the tractor up to the bend where he parked, repeating the procedure of the rock beneath the back tyre. He played out the entire length of cable from the winch after anchoring the tractor with a heavy chain to a tree very close to the road. Once he rappelled down the length of the cable, he would use his climbing rope to abseil the rest of the way. He always kept a first-aid kit with him on his treks, just in case. He stuffed everything he thought he might need into a little backpack he purchased the previous year. He drank a full bottle of water before he set off, and pulled on his heavy leather gloves to protect his hands from the steel cable.

The hazardous venture down the cable took its toll on Bazza's muscles at about the half-way mark. He was still unable to discern any wreckage below in the depths of the narrow ravine. It was only once he neared the end of the cable with its large hook, from which Bazza was able to rig his climbing rope, securing it around his pelvic area and groin as a cradle, that he was finally able to relax for a short time. While he waited to regain a semblance of strength in his leaden muscles, he utilised the time to inspect the ravine. Without the glare from the sun obscuring his vision, and as his eyesight adjusted to the shadowy gloom of the rainforest, he was finally able to make out wreckage below him, caught up on the enormous trunk of a Blue Quandong.

The truck and trailer were wrapped around the trunk, hanging uncertainly on either side, aimed toward the bottom of the ravine far below. He saw then that it wasn't a truck at all, but some great Yankee thing. He'd seen the vehicles often enough during his stint in 'Afghanny', as he called it. Hummers or Humvees, or some such thing with an extra-wide chassis for stability. It seemed to have been converted into a fifth-wheeler camper set-up. *A semi-articulated camper? Why in fuck's name would anyone be stupid enough to haul something like that up this fucking mountain? Honestly?* He was too exhausted to voice his thoughts out loud, though he truly felt like shouting at the morons. The vehicle was dwarfed by the enormous tree on which it dangled precariously. Any amount of pressure on the coupling would see the two pieces come apart. That it hadn't done so already surprised him.

Bazza regained enough strength to continue rappelling downward. He didn't dare venture too close, manoeuvering himself to a better vantage point to see if there was anyone inside, as he drew nearer. He saw a man in the driver's side, slumped over the wheel. Half of his head stoved in by the immense force of the impact with the steering wheel and dashboard. Another body was barely visible in the passenger side, leaning half out the window. The amount of blood around the bodies precluded any hope of possible life. The rear compartment was vacant with one of the back doors ripped off its top hinge, hanging below the vehicle. Bazza was relieved to discover that no one had survived the accident. He could continue his quest to restock his summer wood supply with a clear conscience. He had done everything he could to satisfy his curiosity and to assuage his sense of due diligence.

Another gruelling climb up the side of the gully taxed Bazza's reserves to their limit. Reaching the lip of the road, he simply lay down for an age before he was able to resume movement. For the first time in a long, long while, he watched the beginnings of a sun*set*. A slight breeze reminded him that he should prepare his swag ready for the night. He needed a meal and a damn good slug of hooch to settle his nerves and calm his aching muscles. He moved his tractor on down the road, back to the entrance to the Red Cedar track. Setting up his swag in the middle of the road next to Betsy,

Bazza settled himself in for the night and drank insatiably from his bottle. Adrenaline spent, muscles sore and exhaustion pressing in, he succumbed to sleep in short order.

CHAPTER THREE

A troubled sleep saw Bazza rising earlier than usual. The darkness of pre-dawn was further inked by the clinging cloud covering the top of the mountain in a moist shroud. Bazza was at first, slightly disoriented, taking a while to get his bearings and to recall the events of the previous afternoon through a hooch-induced haze. He shuddered involuntarily at the thought of the dead bodies. Remembering the sight despite his reluctance to revisit the vision, he recalled how fresh the bodies appeared. There were no obvious signs of decomposition, just a cloud of flies. Deciding the accident had been very recent gave him no cause to regret the decision to leave them as he found them. He had his own concerns, and by the look of the heavily laden cloud surrounding him, the rain may start at any time. He silently cursed himself for not heeding the warning signs the previous morning.

"Red sky in morning you bloody idiot! Take the fucking warning then, Bazza. You stupid old fart!"

Precipitation in the tropics is not the kind of rain people in the cities or the country experience. When rain falls in the tropics, it thunders down in heavy sheets so dense it can buckle your knees with its weight and intensity. Trying to navigate your way through the maelstrom is next to impossible and depending on your location at the time, extremely dangerous. If he were caught on top of the mountain in a deluge, Bazza may not be able to return to his home. He would have to abandon the tractor and his equipment to the fates, while he hoofed it on foot down the steep slopes to the *Cathedral*, hoping like crazy that he didn't get washed over the side. He made the immediate decision to abandon his quest to secure more of the Red Cedar logs.

It would take him the better half of the day to return home after camouflaging the entrance to his track. Without a second thought, he packed his gear in record time and downed a quick cuppa before returning to his track's entrance. He chugged along very slowly after kicking Betsy in the guts to wake her up. Carefully manoeuvring along the road, he made his way more by feel than anything else in the lingering cloud, heavy with moisture, heralding omens of inundation.

Many hours later, Bazza was entering his beloved *Cathedral* with its carved wooden sentinels watching over his domain. He had hooked and transported the one downed tree he had spotted on his upward journey. He was not overly upset about missing his opportunity to replenish his Cedar stock. Half-way down the mountain track, the heavens opened up, releasing their load in one gigantic waterfall from the sky. He was lucky to have made it back at all. He was over the moon that he had followed his gut, insisting that he leave the top road the moment he found himself in the low clouds. He could feel the change in the weather creeping into his bones, causing his joints to swell and ache.

The torrent lasted only an hour, yet managed to ensure the track became unpassable for the next three to four months unless it was not the early onset of the Wet. In that case, the track would dry up in a week or two. Bazza was convinced the Wet had arrived early, as he had been feeling it in his bones for a few days. Luckily the area beneath his shack did not turn into a mud pool with the rain. The leaf mulch, wood chips, and sawdust kept the *Cathedral* from becoming a quagmire like the surrounds. The loamy track would be like trying to get traction on soft butter. Nothing could move on the track by foot or wheel until it dried and baked hard, however long that took.

After unhooking and man-handling the log to a suitable position for future cutting and carving, Bazza unloaded his equipment around the area according to its order of priority. While it may have seemed to an outsider that his domain was a haphazard affair, Bazza had a reason for everything he did, and everywhere he placed his equipment. He could think of nothing worse than having to locate a certain tool while he was in the carving 'zone'. He had tools and chainsaws that required placement in the cave, which he would attend to after releasing his chain ladder and lowering the Girls for a scratch and forage session. Half-way up the chain ladder, an uncanny case of the shivers ran up his spine.

Bazza turned to inspect the *Cathedral* and surrounds. While his sixth sense had sometimes alerted him to the presence of a predator, this felt different. It seemed more…ominous somehow. Scanning the area to ensure that everything was in order, he shrugged it off to continue his climb. With most of the cloud cover having dissipated, he raised all the shutters to allow the fresh air to circulate through his home, bashing on walls and doors as he went to ensure all the creepy-crawlies knew to scatter. He did not like killing animals as such, even gigantic, hairy, spiders, but that didn't mean he liked seeing them everywhere either. He raised a ruckus around his home whenever he returned after a day or more away, to scare everything back into their hiding places. Out of sight, out of mind.

"Hello, Ladies. Did ya miss ya old man? Hey? Brrk, brrrk, bgrrk."

His chooks clucked and scratched frenetically at the sight of their imprinted parent's familiar looks and voice. Bazza had raised them from chicks and they usually followed him everywhere during the day, until the moment he started a chainsaw. That would see them scatter to the four winds in a panic of flying feathers and perturbed squawks. He talked to them all day long during his normal routines, explaining what he was doing and describing his carvings to them. The moment the noise of the chainsaw stopped and they saw Bazza settle into a less bothersome activity, they would come running/flapping back to his side, begging tidbits off him, or just perching themselves on his arm, lap, or shoulder. His favourite cheeky girl would perch on his shoulder all day long sometimes; clucking away merrily.

Once the Girls were lowered to the ground where they could forage, Bazza prepared a late lunch with the three eggs he found in their cage. Three eggs from six of the Girls did not seem like many, but it was better than none. He cut up some fresh mushrooms that he cultivated within his cave, to make up a savoury omelette. Growing other vegetables was a hit and miss affair mostly, and keeping vegetables fresh was almost impossible without the facility to freeze them. He scattered potatoes around the edge of the forest where they could get some daylight and some pumpkin seeds which sprouted too readily, quickly managing to almost take over a sand dune. He made the trek to Boinga Bob's every few months to pick up some fresh vegetables from the community garden. He didn't consider visiting Boinga to be anywhere near as traumatic as his annual visits to the 'city' and even invented a signal location for either party to get a message to one another. Boinga rarely got on his nerves and looked forward to the hallucinogenic mushies, Gold Tops, Bazza grew in manure especially for him.

Hunger sated, Bazza cleaned his enamel tin plate before heading back down to complete his chores. The rain toppled a few things over and made a few puddles amid the deeper sections of wood chips. He had yet to return his chainsaws to the cave where they would be safe from future cloud bursts. Carrying two at a time in their cases, he hauled his first load over to the cave. As his eyesight adjusted to the gloom of the interior Bazza staggered back abruptly, heart thumping. He slowly backed out of the cave after dropping his saws, shaking his head in denial at what he had seen.

Bazza skimmed the area in panic, trying desperately to ascertain the path his visitor had taken to enter his domain. He shivered with dread at the possibility. The consequences of the unwanted interloper heralded a dire foreboding, a crushing despair that sought to overwhelm him. It was many moments before he gathered the courage to enter the cave once more, to confront the intruder. At the rear of the cave curled up on some hessian sacks, lay a human, in dirty, bloody, clothing. A female, bare-footed, exposed skin on arms and legs scratched to the billyo, indicating she would have bled profusely at one stage. Most of the blood seemed to have clotted in the interim. Her eyes were closed as far as he could tell beneath her bedraggled, unkempt honey-coloured hair. Her short floral dress was in veritable tatters and still retained the remnants of many Wait-a-while barbs. Her skin was an angry red with more barbs embedded in the flesh.

Bazza was temporarily confused until the answer struck him. The only explanation that could qualify was that she may be connected to the accident he came across on the top road. It was too much of a coincidence for there to be any other possibility. How she had survived that wreckage was beyond his understanding. How she found her way to his place was more confounding. He believed the only possible way it might have happened is that she came across his track's entrance while he was at the accident site. She went down while he stayed up top for the night. Somehow they had passed one another on the top road. She may have been struggling along below the roadway trying to flee from the horror of the crash, while he was chugging away up top, unable to hear her over the noise of the tractor. *Whatever the fuck happened, he was now in a quandary to end all. What the fuck was he supposed to do with her?*

The track to the top was inaccessible after the downpour. He had no way of returning her to the authorities until possibly the Dry. No way for him to contact anyone until then either, *unless he used his messaging option for Boinga?* Boinga wasn't expecting him for another month or two, so that wouldn't work. He couldn't risk taking the tinny that far again with *two* persons aboard either. He had done that once before by himself and regretted every second of the trip. *If, by any chance the sudden rain was just a false alarm? If it dried up before the real Wet started? Then? No.* If he tried to take her out in that type of scenario, he might not make it back himself. She'd need tending to before that, though. Her cuts and bruises needed antiseptic swabbing urgently before infection set in. Who knew what else was wrong with her. Internal bleeding or breakages might be possible for all he knew. He walked back out of the cave arguing back and forth with himself.

"Fuck this! What am I gonna do with her? She can't stay here that's for sure. Uh, uh, no way! What do ya mean she has ta? Fuck that mate. Nuh, can't happen, not in a million fucking years. Piss her orf is what I hafta do. Can't have a fucking sheila here. Can't have fucking anyone here. What if she gets crook? Then fucking what?"

Bazza bounced all over his secluded paradise with pure agitation and indecision, with his chooks following faithfully behind him in a line, looking up at him with curiosity and concern, while enjoying the latest game he was playing. They weren't aware of the new procedures involved in the game, what to expect at the end. Bazza staggered around shouting and mumbling to himself in ever decreasing circles until he came face to face with his line of chooks all staring at him expectantly. He smiled as he realised his foolishness brought on by their comic looks of curiosity.

He knew he had to tend to her injuries first, determine the extent of those injuries, and then play it by ear from that point. If she required hospitalisation, then he would simply have to attempt moving her. Until he knew one way or the other, it was all speculation. He raced over to the bucket of the tractor to retrieve the first-aid kit, grabbing a bottle of water and some clean rags before heading back to the cave.

He made his way quietly to her side. She was still fast asleep as far as he could tell. He began at her feet which were in terrible condition, though once the mud was cleaned away, it did not seem quite as bad. He swabbed the exposed areas with Dettol, an antiseptic solution. He used tweezers and a magnifying glass to remove splinters and barbs from all the places he could see along her bare flanks up to the hem level of her torn and filthy dress. Hesitant, confused, he decided to play it safe and begin with her exposed arms and hands, then move on to the face before deciding what to do about the rest.

Nervously, he administered to her many wounds with as much care and gentleness as he could manage. Somewhere during his ministrations, her eyes opened. It was all Bazza could do to keep from yelping when he discovered her vacant stare. He froze mid-movement, unsure of how to proceed.

"Um, sorry, Lady. Um, g'day. Can ya hear me?"

Even when he passed his hand in front of her eyes there was no movement. He felt sure it was a state of shock. He needed to examine the rest of her body but felt truly awkward about proceeding. Although he had been married at one time and knew very well what he might find beneath the clothing, he hesitated none-the-less. His marriage had ended in disaster, with dire consequences for himself. So much so, that touching a woman inappropriately after so many years caused him great distress. A war raged within him between doing nothing more or doing the right thing. Eventually he just thought, *fuck it*.

"Listen up Lady, I have ta unbutton ya dress ta take care of any other injuries, okay? Don't ya go getting upset now. I'm not trying to take advantage of ya, orright?"

Bazza slowly began unbuttoning the front of her dress as she lay on her side. Carefully peeling back the halves to expose her torso.

"Fuck Lady, ya look like ya gorn through a cheese grater. Matter-o-fact, I'll call ya Cheese until I know ya name proper eh? Yeah, listen, Cheese, I don't mean ya no harm, orright? Just gonna clean up the rest of ya cuts, love. Might need a stitch or two as well I reckon. One on ya foot and a deep gash on ya head. Ya might have a concussion even. That might be why ya aren't talking ta me? Hit ya noggin?"

Bazza worked steadily around the innumerable cuts and tears inflicted by an unprotected sojourn through an unforgiving rainforest. Bazza thought she was lucky to have made it through at all. Not uncommon for an animal to get caught in the Wait-a-while until it died. Bazza tried hard not to blatantly look at her exposed breasts, unsuccessfully, as he worked on her. Everywhere he looked he saw yet more places that required attention. He could smell that she had soiled herself as well. He was not looking forward to having to clean that bit. He could see her silken undies were all scratched, soiled, and torn, which probably meant there were more cuts needing his attention down there as well.

He was conflicted between wanting to help her and wanting to avoid touching her. Who knew what she might tell someone when it was all over? He was scared, more scared of that than he was willing to admit. He bit down hard on his bottom lip to prevent himself from simply yelling out his frustration. Diligently, he applied the first-aid to almost her entire body. Nowhere had escaped the savage elements of the hostile environment she had wandered through. He cleaned her up from head to foot. Bandages where required. Plasters where he deemed it appropriate and a few stitches at the deeper wound sites. He bathed her gently in warmed water and fragrant soap, before wrapping her up in a blanket. All the while, she looked on with a blank stare, neither helping nor resisting his manipulations.

Knowing he couldn't, and wouldn't take her to his shack, he made a temporary bed within the cave for her. The entrance door he made to the cave had not prevented Cheese from gaining access, so he made a note to improve his security at a future date. She would be relatively warm during the nights and cool during daylight hours within the cave. If he could get her moving, he may be able to persuade her to take a top and tail wash at the water's edge eventually, curtailing his need to touch her private bits. As far as he could tell without the requisite x-rays and such, she had suffered no internal damage, so required no immediate emergency hospitalisation. That was a relief to Bazza, but not an end to his worries by a long shot.

He still had to get rid of the sheila somehow. He couldn't begin to envisage an entire wet season with her hanging around like a bad smell, an annoying spanner in the works. Keeping her fed alone was a burden he didn't relish. His mind was a whirling dervish trying to compartmentalise all the conflicting scenarios presented by the intruder's presence. Every time he stumbled across a good reason to be rid of her sooner rather than later, he found a solution to the problem; meaning there was no urgency. *Clothes? No problem, she could have some of his clobber for a while. Sleeping arrangements? He could fix up one of the settees in the living room for her.* On and on it went, well into the night, while Bazza attempted to drown his woes in hooch.

CHAPTER FOUR

Bazza woke with one almighty headache. A real thumper that threatened to blow the lid off his brain. He knew it was one of those grog-induced migraines he often suffered. It would require using some of his generator power to nuke a heat pack in his microwave. Only an applied heat pack to his forehead would relieve the pain enough to allow a strong paracetamol to go to work on the headache. That, and rest. He had been lying awake for a time wrestling with the idea of whether he had imagined everything from the previous day. The more he thought about it, the stronger his brain and muscles throbbed with pain and the sooner he accepted that yesterday's events were real and not some sort of alcohol-muddled dream. He needed to check on Cheese, but had to tackle his headache first. If he neglected to get it under control, he would suffer intolerable pain for longer than necessary.

An hour later, the headache had ebbed to an acceptable throb. After ingesting some hair-o-the-dog, for medicinal relief of course, Bazza made his way to the cave, where he opened the door gently so as not to frighten the woman. When his eyes adjusted to the dim lighting provided by the LEDs, he caught sight of her sitting up with the same blank stare. Bazza settled her down again so that he could inspect her wounds, see to replacing bandages where the sores had bled through with a viscous discharge. He could find no obvious signs of infections. Any discharges were of a clear liquid, showing no hints of corruption. He gently moved her around so that he could inspect every part of her. He wondered if he could lead her to the dunny, and if he achieved that, wondered if she were capable of accomplishing anything while there.

Two minutes after depositing her within the outhouse, he heard the satisfying stream hitting the side of the metal dunny. It appeared all her bodily functions were unimpeded by the accident. Her catatonic state did not hinder her ability to at least function at a basic level. Next would be food. It was vital to get her eating in order for her to survive. Her body was working double-time to fight off the pain and possible infections of her many wounds. Her mind was in a state of chaos trying to cope with an accident where her husband

and possibly her son had both perished horribly. If she didn't replenish her nutrients, she would not last very long. Bazza gave her what he assumed would be sufficient time to finish her ablutions before opening the door. When he raised her to a standing position, he gently wiped her front bits, which he had seen his ex-wife do. She had not passed solids.

Leading the woman to a stump within the clearing, Bazza inspected her in a patch of dappled sunshine. She continued to stare ahead, despite the chickens rooting about all around them, and one even settling on her lap. Instinctively, though, her hand came to rest on the chook's back, gently stroking the shiny black feathers, back and forth. Bazza took that as a very good sign. Nature taking its course through the vagaries of trauma, installing its natural healing powers in spite of our best efforts to dismiss it. A little bit of TLC goes a longer way than all the medications and treatments in the world. There are many reasons why volunteers bring their dogs into nursing homes. The oldies get a taste of that pure affection only an animal can impart so generously, that even the most cantankerous patient can be reduced to blubbering tears at the sight and touch of a Golden Retriever or a Labrador.

Bazza dressed Cheese in a sarong and a T-Shirt. With an unfamiliar gentility, he sat her down to comb out her hair, while she continued to stroke the chook lovingly. The chook appeared to know it was being used for therapeutic purposes, remaining perfectly still. The other clucking Girls went about their business. He untangled the many knots and clumps in her hair with memories of sitting in his mum's hairdressing salon watching her going through all the motions of making women's hair look beautiful. Many a time his mother had wanted her son to learn the trade, to one day take over the business from her. Unbidden tears welled at the corners of his eyes at the thought of his cherished mum. He had not seen her in over ten years and knew well that he should never do so again. It broke his heart and he felt sure his mum had felt the same.

Bazza guessed Cheese's age to be somewhere in the mid-forties. She had definitely known a softer way of life than he. Probably had some 'work' done at some stage. Everything about her screamed money to him. Considering the rig that went over the mountainside, he assumed she and her husband had been more than well-off. She was of average height, and her curves were none too shabby. She seemed relatively fit in spite of her bedraggled appearance. He supposed it would take some time for her to come to terms with her tragic circumstances. One minute you're married with a grown son, if it was her son; next thing you know, you wake up a widow and completely alone.

"Would you mind taking your hands out of my Goddamn hair?"

"Shit, sorry. Fuck, Cheese, ya scared the crap out me. Didn't mean ta pull ya hair like that. Ya okay now huh?"

Cheese threw the chook off her lap with disgust, while examining her various cuts and contusions with growing astonishment.

"Who are you and how did I get here? Where are my clothes? Where are Jeremy and Ken?"

"That, that's a lotta questions, Cheese."

"Why do you keep calling me that? Where on God's good Earth am I? I demand you tell me where Jeremy is, immediately. Take me to him this instant or I will make sure you regret it. What…"

"Hey! Shut the fuck up wouldja? Can't keep up with all the questions. Bitta gratitude eh, Cheese? I fixed up all your cuts and stuff. Gave you somma me clothes. You're hair…and… I, I, can't take you to your husband right now, Cheese."

Bazza knew he had to be very careful how he broke the news to her. She may not recall the accident and may have blocked all the bad stuff out. If Bazza just blurted everything out she might revert back to her former catatonic condition or worse.

"Look, what's ya name, love? We'll start from there and try to get ya caught up okay?"

"I…I...don't seem to..."

"Okay, it looks like ya might have amnesia or something. Bit of a shock to the system I 'spose. So, Cheese, it is for the moment eh? Cos ya looked a bit like ya'd been through a cheese grater when I first saw ya. Ya know? All the cuts and stuff? Ya lucky I didn't call ya Parmyjarny, or Motzyrella I reckon."

"Who are you? You don't sound American, so what are you doing here?"

"Name's, Bazza, mate. Short for, Barry, Barry Ottoman. I'm an Australian. I live here."

"In America?"

"Um, nuh. You're not...in America at the moment, Cheese. You're in Australia. Doncha remember nothing? How ya got here-n-stuff?"

"You live here? Where?"

Bazza pointed skyward. Following the direction of the rough man's calloused finger, Cheese groaned as she spied the tree house. She became enthralled by the gargantuan trees in which the house was erected, almost suffering vertigo as she gazed at the overwhelming height. Bazza caught her as she staggered.

"Get your filthy hands off me you savage."

"Fuck me! Take it easy, Cheese, and they aren't filthy. Washed 'em fore I tended ta ya wounds. I know I don't look culchered and shit, but you don't hafta call me names. Bin on me own for a while. Like it that way too, so if ya don't mind, I'll ask ya ta stop getting uppity."

Cheese's nasally accented twang and her high-class airs were making Bazza believe she thought her shit didn't stink. A fact that Bazza could claim, with confidence, was perfectly untrue. He was getting annoyed but had to remember to take it easy. Patience with anyone other than his chooks was not a trait Bazza excelled at.

"Listen, Cheese, ya been in an accident and I think ya maybe hurt ya head a bit which is why ya can't think straight. At least, why ya having trouble remembering shit...I mean, stuff. Ya in Australia mate, and I got some bad news to tell ya which ya might have ta listen ta, sitting down."

"Australia? Are you sure? I cannot imagine why I would be anywhere near such an abysmal place. Where is Jeremy? He'll straighten this out, and Ken, where are they?"

"Is, Jeremy ya husband?"

"My brother, my older brother. Ken is the youngest. We were..."

"Were what? Do ya remember what ya were doing before the accident?"

"What accident?"

"Guess not. Look I'm only assuming, Cheese. Just adding up two and two here, cos I don't really know for sure okay? I came across a crash while I was up the top of the mountain yesterday...actually, the day before. When I came back home, ya showed up outta the blue and I just figured ya were part of it and somehow survived. Found ya way here. Gave me a bloody heart attack when I saw ya curled up in me cave. Were ya travelling with ya brothers, Cheese?"

"Can you take me to the crash site? I must see what happened. Maybe I will remember then."

"Sorry, Cheese no can do. The track was turned ta goop yesterdy with a big drop-o-rain. Won't get back up for a few months if it was part of the wet season."

"Are you insane? I cannot possibly remain here for months...with you!"

"If yesterdy was only a fluke and not part of the Wet; then all well and good, I may get ya out in a week or so when it dries up enough to drive on. Otherwise, forget it. Nothing else I can do."

"Don't be ridiculous. Call up the authorities and get them to send a rescue helicopter or whatever..."

"Nup, no way. No phone."

"Then email someone you imbecile."

"What's that? Not the last bit; I know that was a insult. The first bit?"

"Email?"

"Orright, forgot about that. Read about that in a science journal."

"I gather you do not have a computer, otherwise you would know about emailing. Seems I have ended up in a time warp here. Shades of *Deliverance*. Pretty soon I will hear an Australian version of *Duelling Banjos*. What about snail mail? You must surely have such a thing as that in this backwater?"

Bazza looked at her as though she were talking a foreign language.

"Ya wanna send mail by...snail?"

"Have you known nothing save for this jungle all your life? Surely you have heard of mail? Surely they have mailmen in this country?"

"Yeah, course we got posties. Not out here, though, and we certainly don't get snail...men, out here neither"

"You are being obtuse and tedious, Mr. Ottoman."

"And you, are being a bloody great pain in the arse, Cheese.

Feel free ta leave any time ya want. Don't hafta return the clothes neither. Take them and ya snooty attychude, and ya can go to buggery for all I care."

Bazza stormed off toward the beach. He knew he was being petulant, but couldn't help himself. Cheese was irritating the crap out of him. She was upsetting the status-quo he had carefully nurtured in *Euphoria*. His routines would be set on their ear if he did not get the menace out soon. He hoped with all his might that the early rain was an isolated incident. No way could he cope with this nut-case for the entire wet season. Even if the Wet had arrived, he may take her up to the top road, show her where the bloody thing went over and leave her there to fend for herself. *Bitch*!

Cheese watched him stride away doggedly with mild amusement. She was a lady used to getting her own way. That, she intuited with crystal clarity. How she had wound up in Australia escaped her beleaguered mind. Carefully, with her feet feeling the sharp edges of the wood chips, she investigated the area below the shack, looking up occasionally, casting dubious glances at the savage's abode. The man spoke like a dolt with the education of a child. She did not feel safe with him. *Had he attempted to have his way with her unconscious body already?* He had certainly removed her clothing. She would put nothing past him. She acknowledged that he had attended to her many wounds. She paid him his dues on that score. Not verbally, though. Wouldn't do to have him feeling like she was obliged somehow for his assistance.

She tried walking a little distance up the track he had referred to, only to end up unceremoniously landing on her rump. The track was pure wet clay and held no traction whatever. There was no way she was going to walk, climb or drive out of there on that excuse for a road. To her left and right appeared to be impenetrable jungle. The only other way out was the way the savage took. Out to the water, it seemed. She did not want to follow him that way. It would look to him as though she needed him and that would never do. She watched the chickens scratching around for a time before deciding to make use of what she assumed was a lavatory.

CHAPTER FIVE

Bazza started with a jolt when he heard the blood-curdling scream coming from the *Cathedral*. Half way to putting his shorts back on after a dip in the water, he hopped and stumbled his way along the path wondering what animal had wandered in that had set her off. He didn't know if he was pleased or not that the snooty bitch had woken from her spell. He preferred her all quiet and docile like, not raising a ruckus.

When he staggered into the shaded area beneath the shack, he could see neither hide nor hair of her, though he knew at once where she was when he stopped to listen. He knew there was a massive huntsman spider haunting the outhouse, and if you didn't give the door and sides a good thumping before entering, you were likely to encounter the beast in all his humongous glory. The way her scream reverberated through the *Cathedral*, he knew she was holed up in the outhouse, baled up by Goliath. He simply walked over to the outhouse made of bamboo posts and corrugated iron sheeting, where he bashed the walls and door with a heavy lump of discarded wood lying about.

"Goliath should have scampered by now, Cheese. He won't hurt ya. He's just a big, scary, hairy, son-of-a-bitch. Makes ya skin crawl ta see him, but harmless enough. He does a good job-o-keeping the insects down. Ya should see the size of them we get up here. Ya should see…"

Cheese exited the outhouse with as much dignity as her experience would allow, relieved to be out of the way of the horrific arachnid.

"Mr. Ottoman, I insist you get me out of here. I would go myself, only I don't know how. I would gladly pay your way…"

"I would love nothing more than to be rid-o-ya, but it isn't gonna happen, doncha get it? No way outta here until we have a dry spell. Can't get up the track, can't get through the bush and can't reach anywhere in the tinny. If the track dries up in a week or less, I'll get ya ta Boinga's. He'll know what to do from there. Bloody good tracker that bastard when he isn't on the mushies. Meantime, I suggest ya make the best of it, Cheese. Won't do ya much good fighting circumstance or me. I wasn't the cause-o-ya troubles, and I don't like being ordered around okay? Now call me, Bazza, wouldja please?"

"I am going to go insane if I have to stay here. Won't you take me to the accident? I need to see what happened."

"Don't know how many times I gotta say this, but nuh-uh. No way up there, and ya wouldn't wanna see it anyway, Cheese. Pretty gruesome. Ya fellas, ya brothers? They didn't make it. Sorry."

"I'll call you, Bazza if you will please stop referring to me as a milk by-product."

"Tell me ya name then? No? Any name then?" Silence. "Well, it's bloody, Cheese then. It's all I got. I warn ya, though, keep calling me, Mister-bloody-Ottoman, and you can fend for yourself against Goliath next time, and all the other greeblies around here. I live a nice quiet life here where I'm me own man and I don't appreciate ya trying ta upset me on purpose, and looking down on me, or calling me shitty names like 'imbecile'. I'm not stupid, I just don't react well ta people, specially strangers, and more specially, strange women. I'm sorry ya don't like me. I don't much like ya either, too snooty by half. And that's more-n-I said ta anyone in a lorng time. I'm going up for breaky. Come up if ya want some, or don't. Do as ya please 'cept don't touch me stuff, specially me tools."

She watched him walk over to the chain ladder where he slowly hoisted himself aloft. She witnessed him wincing once or twice along the way. She wondered idly if that tenderness were caused by her, not that it would have mattered greatly. She could hardly be held accountable for what the savage decided to do voluntarily. *Bazza, and Cheese! Ludicrous! What a ridiculous set of circumstances!* To be trapped with the Neanderthal for months sent shivers down her spine. They may end up killing one another before the track opened up. She may end up on the worse side of the coin in that conflict, though, as he appeared to possess brutish strength in that large frame of his. Hands the size of dish plates would make short work of her.

She contemplated her options as she stood alone in the warm shade. She could sense the forbidding heat at the edge of the clearing straining to spread through to the inner sanctum. She tried to feel something at the death of her brothers whom she barely accepted had lost their lives in the accident, but try as she might, she could not picture them as dead. Any feeling of grief eluded her. In her mind, her brothers were still fooling around somewhere and everything she experienced was all part of another scheme hatched by them or a very sick joke. Cheese wished she could remember the exact circumstances that brought them all the way across the world from their hometown of Portland, Oregon. *There was a plan, there always was with her brothers. Some plan involving her somehow. A trip?* It was no use, she simply couldn't dredge it up, or else didn't want to.

The smell of eggs cooking interrupted her reveries. She tested her limbs with a few stretches before deciding to chance the climb to the tree house. It at least looked habitable compared to the area beneath, or the cave. Few options left few decisions. She climbed to the house. She was pleasantly surprised by the breezy openness of the house with its 360-degree verandas, fully screened and neat as a pin. Cleaned to within an inch of its life. In the central hub was situated an octangular kitchen, through which ran the enormous trunks of the two Strangler figs, with a wooden bench top surrounding it practically all the way. One break in the bench top allowed access to the cabinetry and cooking surfaces behind. Half of the semi-octangular space beyond that on the eastern side overlooking the ocean was taken up with an open-style living area. A couple of comfortable cane lounges long enough to double as beds, low, practical coffee table between them. Low shelves making up dado walls were filled with books, DVDs, and CDs along with a fairly modern CD player. An exercise bike squatted untastefully to the side with a drive system hooked up to some mechanical doohickey.

Bazza had set a place for her on the kitchen bench on the

opposite side to where he placed himself. He was munching happily on an omelette of eggs and wonderful smelling mushrooms the size of the pan in which they were cooked. The delicious aroma permeated the house despite the effective ventilation through all the raised shutters, allowing cool breezes to waft through. She noted a large bed occupying the other, raised area, through an archway. Obviously only a single bedroom house she thought. The smell of the food forced her mind away from sleeping arrangements. She delved into the enormous plate of food eagerly.

They ate in an awkward, anxious, silence. Both parties were wary of each other, testing each other's parameters, vying for any opening to take advantage. At least, one of them entertained that ambition of advantage. Bazza just wanted everything back to the way it was without all the hassle and talk. She couldn't be here; *shouldn't,* be here. He didn't know how he was going to solve the problem. Another mouth to feed was the least of his problems. Having a woman around, demanding attention and trying to force him to her way of thinking...just not on! Bazza was exhausted before the end of the *second* day. He couldn't imagine how he would feel at the end of three to four months. Before he could wish yet again that the rain he had experienced was just a one off, a cool breeze blew in a certain tang that he knew indicated more rain.

Two hours later the skies opened up to release their load as only they can in the tropics. After a light dinner of some smoked pork much later, which Bazza had taken from the Coolgardie meat safe hanging in the breezeway on the veranda, he made up one of the cane lounges for her Highness, who still hadn't uttered a word. Not that he minded *that* in the least. He repaired to his bedroom and drew a hastily organised thin curtain across the archway shielding his bedroom for the first time in his house. He laid down on his bed chewing over the problems they faced. With the rain having set in for the season, all hopes of leaving her with the Aboriginals was out of the question. *Four looooong months!* He was glad he did not own a firearm. He felt sure he would need to kill himself in the very near future; a task near impossible to implement with his own bow and arrow.

Cheese groaned inwardly when the rain started, knowing that it was a harbinger of dire news. She understood it to mean there was to be no reprieve from the Neanderthal for the next few months while they waited out the wet season. Cheese recalled a vacation she and her brothers had tolerated with their father, in Africa, near the Congo. She remembered the rain there, a heavy, tangible weight upon a person when caught outdoors. The sheer volume of water could force you to your knees, capable of knocking the wind right out of your chest. Impossible to breathe air when you are inundated with water all about you, like trying to breathe at the bottom of a pool. Holding your hand over your mouth and nose only worked so long. She made her way to, and lay back on the cane lounge, racking her beleaguered brain to come up with a solution to her dilemma. The brain racking did not last long. They both fell asleep, exhausted from tension and frustration.

CHAPTER SIX

It rained all night, one downpour after another. Bazza woke refreshed, but with aching muscles. He had not been rope climbing since the last time he went down the mountain to his Cedar cache. That was over a year ago. Bazza waited inside his room rather than entering his kitchen to make his morning brew of rich Malanda coffee. The other product he purchased from the Tablelands was a bit of Chop-chop, illegal tobacco. It was good gear, no preservatives or additives, and without all the tax and import duties imposed by greedy governments. He rolled some Chop-chop into a paper, lay back in his comfortable bed smoking his first ciggy in almost a month.

The rain continued outside, albeit lighter than earlier. A steady drizzle, enough to fray the nerves, when a lot depended on good weather. He had no idea what to do with Cheese. She was going to drive him nuts, that's for sure. They had absolutely nothing in common, no way of finding some common ground, no subjects to talk about. Bazza didn't mind not talking. Bloody Cheese would probably do enough talking for the both of them. It was going to be one doozy of a wet season molly-coddling that one. Watching his P's and Q's, keeping his clothes on all the time. Bazza talked himself into a growing depression. The kind that came over him the moment he hit bitumen roads. *Bloody bitumen roads only meant one thing; a means to get to so-called civilisation.*

Cheese was awake the moment she smelt the first whiff of tobacco. It triggered memories of her father. She saw his face clearly in her mind, but couldn't grasp his name. Every time she came close to it, it darted back out of reach. Her father had a bushy beard all his life. She never could understand how he managed to eat his meals without the coarse hair interfering. Bazza looked a little bit like her father. Same height with the same Man of the Earth countenance, and the same long beard. Where Bazza fell far short of her father was his uncouth, uneducated, manner and speech. She barely understood a word he said, whereas her father had a deep, cultured, *basso-profundo* timbre that rumbled through his body before passing through his eager smile. She sighed as she pictured that smile that would melt her young heart whenever it was aimed at her. She loved her father unconditionally, though, there was something, some thought lurking in the back of her mind that told a lie to that memory. Some, elusive notion that all was not as it seemed in her recollections.

"Bazza, must you do that every few minutes?" she yelled across the shack.

"Watcha mean, Cheese?"

"That constant release of wind, befouling the air. Makes my toenails want to rip free and run away."

"Ya mean me ciggy?"

"Other end, Bazza, other end. The cigarette smoke is an aphrodisiac compared to the other. Don't you have to get up and make breakfast or something?"

"I'll get up when I'm bloody good-n-ready", he said, punctuating the statement with a loud fart that rattled the rafters. "Want breakfast?"

"Yes."

"Good, make it yaself. Not ya bloody butla, ya know? Kitchen is simple enough, everything there ya need. Check the Girls' cage if ya want some cackle berries."

After many moments..."Okay, I'll bite. What on earth is a cackle berry, and what girls are you referring to?"

"Bum-nuts! Eggs! Check the Girls' cage if ya want some eggs. Been off the lay a bit lately, but there might be a few."

"Definitely nothing like dad", she muttered.

"What?"

"Nothing."

Cheese decided that lying down waiting for Bazza to do anything was not going to work. He was obviously laying down the law, playing Master of the house. If she meant to make the place less of a Hell for the next four months, she had better start making nice. She could be nice if she had to be, she told herself…quite unconvincingly.

She felt a little better. Not quite so sore, but oh so itchy. Some of her wounds were healing, leaving scabs that itched intolerably. Possibly due to poisons in whatever greenery she had barged through to reach Bazza's clearing. Sooner or later she would have to quiz him about the accident. Not that she really felt up to knowing. Regardless, she had to ascertain if anything he said rang a bell. The accident may not have involved her brothers. Could've been anyone. *Not her wonderful, sweet, brothers, surely?*

Cheese set about preparing some fruit and cereal in a bowl. She rarely ate a full breakfast she thought. Which may, or may not have been true. She remembered so little of herself. Past memories of her dad and her brothers all laughing and playing together were clear in her mind. If they were real, that is. She couldn't be absolutely certain she wasn't making everything up to suit her wish of a happy family life. She couldn't shake the feeling that a big chunk of something important was missing. She had no pictures of her mother in her mind. No hint about her at all. Cheese sat at the long bench surrounding the kitchen. The morning breeze caressed her bare arms and legs, causing a pleasant chill to run down her spine.

"Bazza?"

"What now?"

"Are you going to stay mad at me forever?"

"Pissed orf at the whole bloody *thing*, not necessarily yaself. Though, ya no bloody picnic."

"Thing?"

"I don't like ya being here. Ya shouldn't be here. Someone might find out."

"God, I hope so."

"Orright for some," Bazza grumbled.

"Bazza?"

"What Cheese, what? Doncha eva shut up?"

"What is this fruit that looks like a star when you cut it?"

"Good guess. Starfruit it's called sometimes, or Five Corner Fruit. It's actually a Carambola. I made some jam out of it a while ago. A jar of it in the walk-in pantry, and heaps more in the cave. Ya like it?"

"Delicious."

"Well, that's a bloody change. You actually liking something instead of looking down ya nose at everything."

"I am sorry Bazza if I came across that way. Thank-you…for…everything. I, I'm not too good in the country, especially a foreign country. I'm a city girl, Bazza. I come from Portland, Oregon, in the United States."

"I knew ya was a Yank, I heard it in ya voice." Bazza entered the kitchen where he began to make his brew. "Ya wanna cuppa? Coffee I mean, not tea. I don't have any-o-that dishwater here."

"Coffee sounds wonderful. I, I think we got off on the wrong foot, Bazza. I'd like to start over if that's possible? I really do appreciate how you tended to my wounds. Even gave me some stitches didn't you? You did a good job and you've been very kind, Bazza. Please accept my apologies for acting the way I have. This is all very strange for me, and I have no idea who I am, or how I got here. I dread what you might tell me about that accident and yet, I feel detached from it, like it happened to someone else, not me and my brothers. Can you forgive me, Bazza?"

"Nothing ta forgive, Cheese. Ya had it rough, I'll give ya that. Not sure how anyone can come outta that orright. Ya did good to get here if that was…ya know, part-o-ya crew up there. I'm not used ta people; bin on me own a long time now. Even when I go ta town once a year, I don't talk much. Don't have much ta say. Other people usually don't have much ta say neither, at least, nothing worth listening ta." A silence ensued until the coffee was ready. "Get some-o-that-inta ya. Put hairs on ya chest that will. Sorry. A bit crass that eh? I meant ta say, it's bloody good coffee which I roast meself outta Tableland beans."

"You do a lot yourself. Is that by choice or design? Mm, yes that is divine, thank-you."

"Bitta both I reckon. Hafta do a lot on me own, cos no one else will, and do a lot meself, cos I like it done a certain way." Bazza sat down next to her, still unsure of her changeable moods, but willing to give her the benefit of doubt.

"I can see that being the case. Where exactly are we? I have no idea other than Australia, you said?"

"This here is Far North Queensland, part-o-the Daintree, which is a world heritage-listed rainforest. Tropical, gets the monsoons up here like in parts-o-Africa and India. Seen weeks of rain up here non-stop at times. Can't see ya hand in the front-o-ya face, it comes down so hard and thick. It's what makes the place so special I reckon."

"You really like being here all alone, isolated from everyone, your family?"

"Got no one other than me mum and a couple-o-brothers I don't talk ta anymore. Better for her I stay up here outta her way. I was a bittuva trouble-maker some time ago. Thought I better come up here to me old man's property, what he left me in his will, so's I could straighten meself out a bit. Got ta liking it a whole lot up here by meself. Don't get lonely with me Girls and me carvings ta talk ta."

"You're Girls being the chickens? You have names for them?"

"Yep, they're the T-girls. Up to the T's with chooks I bin naming over the years. Got Tasha, Tilby, that's the one what took ta ya like, Tabatha, Tomasina, Tish, and Totty. Topsy got took a while back. Snake got 'er."

"I noticed the carvings of course. They are very good. Do you sell them?"

"Yeah, hafta make a bit-o-money to pay the bills and buy supplies. Take 'em in once a year ta Cairns. Biggest town around these parts. A bit further up north is Cooktown. Don't like going there much. Nothing but boozers and druggos. Not that I can speak mind. Bittuva a boozer meself. Brew me own."

"Beer?"

"Nah, Rocket Fuel I call it. Made from potatas. Grow some out there near the edge along with punkins. Buy the rest from the Aboriginal camp about two hours away. Old Boinga Bob, who I was gonna take ya to if I coulda, he and I go back a long ways. If I had a mate, a best mate, it would probably be him."

"Boing…?"

"Boinga. Boinga Bob. Got his name from falling down a mountainside one time, pissed off his noggin. They reckon he made a boinking sound on his way down like a bouncing ball. Name stuck eva since. He don't drink much anymore but likes the Gold-Tops. Mushies that make him see things aren't there. Off his nut half the time. A few roos short in the top paddock if ya ask me."

The conversation dried up for a time as they enjoyed their morning brew in relative silence with only the sea breezes soughing softly through the foliage. An occasional bird call and a few insects adding their songs. Cheese was phrasing her next question carefully, weighing the pros and cons in her mind.

"Bazza, I wonder if you could tell me about the accident, please? I think I'm ready to hear about it, from your perspective at any rate."

"Ya sure? Don't want ya getting all morose or turning back inta a turnip again.'

Despite herself, Cheese burst into laughter. "Turnip?"

"Yeah, ya know, like a vegetable? Lights are on, but nobody's home kinda thing?" he asked waving a hand in front of his face.

"Well, no promises that I won't get upset. I'll certainly try not to turn into a turnip. I need to know, Bazza. As much as it might hurt, I need to know what you know. Might even help me to remember."

"Orright."

Once Bazza had explained as best he could, Cheese had tears rolling down her cheeks. She recognised her brothers in Bazza's perfect descriptions. It was like he possessed an eidetic memory when it came to describing human features, despite his limited access to the vehicle. She assumed it was because of his artistic eye in carving human faces, that he noticed everything. While her memories consisted only of their younger faces, she recognised immediately from Bazza's descriptions, the scar on Jeremy's forehead and the mole on Ken's chin. She didn't need eye colour or anything else to know it was her brothers in that wreck. She had obviously been travelling with them at that point, and somehow escaped serious injury and death by being flung from the vehicle before it left the high road. She could not begin to imagine what they were doing in this remote part of the world. Nothing in her memories enabled her to think of a single reason for them to leave Portland.

Oh, how she missed home. Growing up in Portland was every child's dream. Bliss, as far as she was concerned. A great family life doing all the Chevy Chase style corny Christmases and holidays. Skiing trips to Mt. Hood, picnics with their Labrador, Muttsy, in Washington Park, cruising all the micro-breweries when they were old enough, theatre, movies, the whole American dream family scenario. Only one thing missing, a picture of her mum in all the happiness. Only her dad playing a prominent role.

Bazza was busily tidying up the kitchen leaving everything spotless. She had to admit that despite his Neanderthal looks, he was very clean and tidy. Maybe a little on the O.C.D. side actually. He literally scrubbed every benchtop until it glowed with its rich timber hues and magnificent grains. She marvelled at the bamboo tree house that seemed very sturdy, with everything she saw having that home-made feel about it. Not only sturdy and practical, but with artistic touches everywhere, and carvings dominating every surface. The delightful aroma of highly polished wood permeated the area. Wood oils and waxes mingling with forest-fresh scents making for an olfactory festival.

Bazza had lowered his Girls to the clearing after talking to them about their neglect in providing for their supper. Cheese was amused at how gentle and loving the big man could be to his, 'dinner'. She assumed he eventually ate them, at any rate. Once their laying years came to an end, in the boiling pot they must surely go. Cheese began to think about her own hygiene. She needed to bathe, but did not relish how that might be accomplished, and felt silly for asking. She spied the magnificent wooden bathtub but saw no signs of tapware from which to fill it. No walls around the tub either, so no privacy. She did not think she was a total prude, but equally did not feel entirely comfortable being naked around a strange man despite him having witnessed her in that state already. She supposed the easiest way would be to simply go for a swim. The weather was warming up considerably and the sun would soon dry and warm her.

"Um, Bazza. I think I'll just go for a swim to clean up a little. Do you have any soap and a towel I might use?"

"Nuh."

"Nuh what? You don't have soap and a towel I can use?"

"Nuh, ya can't go for a swim. Top and tail only right at the edge and being real careful. I'll probably need ta go with ya."

"I am a very good swimmer, I will certainly not need you along thank-you…"

"Stinger season in the summer. Can't go swimming without a stinger suit and I don't have one. Could be a rogue croc out there as well. Never know, and it pays ta be super-careful."

"What about the creek then? You said there was a creek very close where I can have a quick wash?"

"If ya don't mind looking out for leeches, cassowaries, monitors and trapdoors."

"I only understood 'leeches' then. Look, Bazza, is there anything in this country that doesn't want to bite you, poison you, or eat you, including plants?"

"Ya just gotta be careful, Cheese. Ya don't know anything about it here, so I'm just looking out for ya. I don't hafta look or nothing. Ya know? If it's privacy ya need? Ya can have a tub up here if ya like, not all the time cos it takes a lot-o-work. But just this time until ya get used ta everything. Once I warm up some water for ya, I can leave and promise not ta come back up till ya done?"

"That won't be necessary. If it's alright with you, maybe later you can take me to the beach so I can have a wash then? A top and tail, as you call it? I'm not all that concerned for my privacy, Bazza. After all, you have seen me already haven't you? No, don't apologise. I understood the need."

CHAPTER SEVEN

Cheese noticed a subtle change in her outlook. Nothing specific that she could readily define, more of a gentle shift from an attitude she felt she must have possessed before the accident. She had gotten off on the wrong foot with Bazza, and she had been planning to 'make nice', for the sake of getting on, but it progressed beyond that initial notion. She had realised how snobby and cold she sounded when she first came out of her funk. Though it came out naturally, like she had been that sort of person all her life, she felt a little ashamed of her behaviour. A man, albeit a strange man, had acted kindly by helping her and she had responded with a rudeness that poured from her like beer on-tap from the micro-breweries back home.

A week had passed with Bazza in what she deemed a cordial atmosphere. Cheese had a lot to learn about life in a completely different environment from anything she had ever experienced. Everything was new and strange, even frightening a lot of the time. The more she learned, the more frightened she became. Throughout, though, Bazza had given her time to learn, showing patience and kindness. He was like the Australian equivalent of a redneck. Jokes were made galore in American society about rednecks and their laissez-faire lifestyles. She laughed along with the rest of them whenever she heard a good one, but Bazza was not a joke. She was seeing him through new eyes.

He was not a stupid man by any means. He had built a house high up in a pair of trees that withstood all but the harshest of the elements thrown at it. He was a very gifted artist producing wonderful sculptures from rare and exotic woods, or assemblages of driftwood scrounged from the beach. He was a fantastic hunter and provider, supplying all their protein requirements cooked to perfection. He was meticulously clean, though not anal as she first suspected. Not a sign of OCD or anything as worrying as that. No, he cleaned up thoroughly because he knew that ants would soon inundate his home should food scraps be left about.

Cheese began to recognise and respect the many talents the man displayed and took for granted himself. She saw him through eyes born of her fresh experiences with him, not through the conditioned eyes and reflexes of her past. Whoever she was before the accident may not have been a nice person judging by her earlier behaviour, so she consented to the idea that she may be able to renew herself and her values. She found she wanted to be a nice person and wanted to be liked in return. While her relationship with a man like Bazza was difficult for so many reasons, not the least of which being that he was something of a hermit, she found herself warming to him. His eccentricities notwithstanding, he had proven himself to be resourceful, innovative, and surprisingly intelligent. Able to converse on many subjects when he felt confident enough to do so.

Cheese recognised an opportunity to reinvent herself in an image that suited her new outlook. She genuinely suspected her alter ego had less than desirable qualities. How ingrained those previous attitudes were, she had yet to discover. She hoped she had the strength to overcome her conditioning.

Life in a rainforest was not an entirely unpleasant experience once a person came to terms with the many inherent dangers. Cheese had never been subjected to leeches and ticks before. They became an everyday occurrence of less and less concern when you knew what to look for and how to prevent infestation with practical know-how. Always wearing long socks with shorts or combination socks and long trousers, sticking the ends of those trousers into the socks, prevented most occasions of attack. She always bashed the outhouse or other structures when entering, with the large stick leaning on the outside. She never did encounter Goliath again after learning that trick.

Bazza even allowed her to venture to the nearby creek on her own occasionally, when he believed the area to be safe from marauding Cassowaries, Monitors, Feral pigs, and crocs. When he explained what all the creatures were and how they might be a danger, she began to understand the importance of constant vigilance whenever she was out of his eyesight. She understood the need to be extra mindful in the case of an emergency with no means of receiving medical treatment. When Bazza pointed out to her and made a comparison to animals she knew of in her native America, it became all too easy to imagine the perils that awaited the uninitiated. A Cassowary was essentially the same as an Ostrich and highly territorial, especially when chicks were involved. A Monitor Lizard was harder to compare to anything, but she got the gist of it. Essentially, a very large growing reptile capable of high speeds and inflicting nasty bites that become septic due to the bacteria that exists in their mouths. Crocodiles were an Alligator's big, angry cousin. While a wound from their bite might produce infection as well, the main concern was being eaten; whole. Trapdoors were basically hairy spiders that lived underground with a trap-door to their hidey-hole. Whenever prey tickled their trip-lines outside the door, they pounced with incredible speed through the door, to inflict a lethal dose of venom into the unsuspecting victim.

Bazza, was in two minds about his unwanted guest. He knew there was nothing he could do about her being there. Knew he had to do the right thing by offering her food and shelter but was upset by the disruption to his routines none-the-less. He still managed to keep up with his quota of carvings completed in the normal time-frame despite having recently offloaded his previous year's inventory. Knew he would have enough to keep his gallery owner/manager *semi*-satisfied for another year. She would always cry for more carvings and for him to accept special commissions that would attract large fees, but she would concede to his agenda in the end. It was either that or he would find somewhere else to sell his art. She understood that and protected her income source zealously.

What Bazza found worst of all, was the need to talk. It was awkward to be around someone all the time and not speak, yet he loathed speaking constantly, found it tiring having to think all the time, trying to sound like he knew what he was talking about and making it interesting enough not to send her to sleep. Cheese could talk under water with a mouth full of marbles. She could talk a glass eye to sleep he reckoned. He had spoken more in the last week than he had in the last few years and his jaw ached as a result. When the rain set in for a day or two it drove him to near distraction being cooped up with her trying to shout to be heard above the sound of the falling rain. It was like trying to talk next to a waterfall and made for a tense few days.

Bazza and Cheese had come to an arrangement where privacy needs were concerned. They worked on rotational intervals for bathing that suited each other's routines as best they could. Bazza would wake first thing every morning, put the coffee on to brew while he went down to the beach or the creek for a scrub. Cheese would remain aloft until he returned to find his coffee made and waiting for him, while he decided on their breakfast menu. They shared much of the cooking and cleaning activities equally. Bazza would leave the loft after breakfast to tend to his chores below, or begin carving, while Cheese took her turn to attend to morning ablutions and a wash in either the beach water at the very edge or the creek. Very seldom did they stumble into one another at inappropriate times.

Bazza was happiest when he was lost to the world in one of his carvings. Once immersed in the activity of creating his mostly animal sculptures, all the cares and woes of the world washed away to leave a calm tranquil centre. His carving was a therapeutic escape like no other he had ever experienced. He often found himself able to cope with all of Cheese's annoying questions and conversations after a day of efficacious carving. Naturally, carving with chainsaws and other power tools was only possible on dry days. On the other days, he was reduced to sharing their small, seemingly shrinking tree house with his less obtrusive functions like sanding, oiling, and polishing. He only read from his extensive library when he had nothing else to occupy his time, whereas Cheese would read constantly, often trying to engage him in a conversation about a particular book.

He was always self-conscious about his manner of speech and what people thought about his flagging intellect, considering his lack of formal education. Confidence in himself to converse on an even level with most people made him shy and awkward, often getting him flustered in his speech patterns. He preferred his own company, always had, and often found himself getting testy when Cheese interrupted his thoughts with constant banter. Living with someone tested out a person's character even when they were very fond of one another. Two strangers living together sometimes proved to be a time-bomb in the making.

The sound of Cheese's scream from above told him that perhaps Erik had decided to call. Bazza wondered when he would turn up and how Cheese would react when he did. He looked up in time to see Cheese clambering/falling down the chain ladder completely naked. He absently noted that her wounds were healing well, bar one on her backside that he had not seen since first administering first-aid. Sure enough, Erik slithered into view along the branch running parallel to the veranda. Cheese ran into his arms so forcefully they nearly ended up in the sawdust soup at his feet. She was shivering with fear and revulsion. Bazza was worried she may revert back to her fear induced shock.

While trying to calm her down with soothing tones and stroking her back gently, Bazza tried to avert his hands and eyes as much as possible from her exposed flesh.

"There, there, Cheese, it's only, Erik come ta visit. He won't hurt ya…much. He's jest trying to get another one-o-me me Girls. He's the one what took Topsy. He's got no poison, so won't kill ya unless he wraps ya in a big old hug. I was jest now wondering when he might show up. Sorry I didn't warn ya about him, Cheese. It's orright mate, nothing to be afraid of. Come on now, calm yaself down."

Cheese had never been so scared in all her life, except for when she first saw Goliath, and when she heard an enormous thump behind her at the creek one time, and… Oh well, she was probably scared most of the time in the strange hostile environment. It felt good to be in a man's arms where she could feel safe. She would always feel safe in her father's arms and… Well, that line of thought had some worrying gaps that required filling before she completely understood her reticence to finish the thought.

Seemed as though much of her past remained obscured with elements of suspicion attached to them. Cheese suddenly remembered her state of undress, causing her to turn bright red. She felt the flush start in her toes and quickly work its way to the top of her head. Her cheeks felt hot with the rush of blood. Her loins, however, felt a different kind of heat permeating her womanhood.

Bazza was stuck. He knew Cheese would soon remember she was naked and hugging him for dear life. She would then try to figure a way of covering her embarrassment by either becoming brusque in her manner or fleeing in a mad panic to another part of the *Cathedral* where she may find other hazards without her clothing on. He decided the only way to handle the situation effectively was to disable her from fleeing in a mad rush, so he casually picked her up as easily as if she were a child. Years of carving and manual labour had given Bazza a superb physique and immense strength in his upper body. He carried her over to the cave entrance where he always kept a spare pair of overalls and a selection of footwear.

"Go ta the footlocker in there and grab me spare overalls, Cheese. A pair of thongs in there as well, stop ya feet from picking up a splinter eh?" he said kindly while discreetly turning his back to her. He heard her quietly dressing. "Umm, don't mean ta embarrass ya, Cheese, but I gotta look at one-o-them sores on ya bum again, mate. Doesn't look too flash, and ya can't afford ta get a infection."

"*An*, infection, Bazza. Not, '*a*', infection. We are going to have to work on your diction. I see you read so I am surprised your speech is not much better than it is. Thank-you for coming to my rescue yet again. I think we need to sit down tonight so you can tell me exactly, everything I should be worried about or know about. Would you mind talking to me after dinner?" She asked exiting the cave after dressing.

"I 'spose not, Cheese, long as ya let me look at that sore as well? Or do ya want ta try it ya self? Being as where it is, ya know?"

"Bazza, I am a grown woman, and nowhere near the prude that you obviously think I am. You seem to be more embarrassed than I am by my nudity. I'm sure you have had women in your life? An intimate relationship?"

"Yeah, sure. Was married once."

That revelation struck Cheese more than she cared to admit. "Well for goodness sake, I didn't know that. Why haven't you told me this before? What happened? I assume you are no longer married?"

"Um, I uh, don't talk about it ta no one."

"Well if you want to look at my bare bottom again tonight, Bazza, I insist you talk about it then. I want to know it all, every gritty detail. Oh, that is, unless… I hope I haven't put my foot in it again, Bazza? She didn't…die, did she?"

"Nah, she's still alive, unfortunately."

"Excellent. In that case it's open slather. I want to hear all the juicy bits while you have your big hands all over my bare derrière."

"Maybe I shouldn't if ya feel squeamish about…"

"Nonsense, Bazza. Not the least. Sorry if I embarrassed you, but I think we have moved past that part of our friendship don't you think? No point in pussy-footing about one another while we are living together under a single roof. We are forced together by circumstances beyond our control, I suggest we act a little more mature and just go about business as if we were an old married couple okay? Well, without the sex part anyway. Now don't go getting all bashful on me again, Bazza. I won't attack you. Not without your knowledge anyway."

Cheese smiled a wicked smile as she walked back to the centre of the clearing. When she looked up fearfully towards the shack, Bazza touched her lightly on the arm.

"Let me go on up there and fetch him down. I'll walk him a ways off so he won't be back for a while. He *will* come back, though. It's his territory and we are smack-bang in the middle of it. The only way to be rid of him altogether is ta kill him, and I won't do that, Cheese, even if ya hate him and he scares ya. Besides, he keeps the rat population down."

Groaning. "You have rats as well?"

"Ya can jest about put a saddle on 'em and ride 'em they're that big."

"Then you leave Erik exactly where he is as long as you tell me he can't get inside?"

"Never has. Ya sure?"

"Never surer. Got any soft spots for rats, Bazza? Can I kill them if I see them?"

"Yep, ya go right ahead, we can use the protein."

Cheese wondered off to the nearest tree where she promptly vomited. After finishing, she wiped her mouth with the back of her sleeve. "Please tell me we haven't eaten that sort of 'protein', Bazza? Please tell me that wasn't… rat stew, the other night?"

"Nup. Ate all the rat a week before ya got here. Hafta kill them fellas cos they like taking me girls as well. The stew was a left-over bit-o-crocodile I marinated for a month. Smoked the rest and had it for lunch most days. He came a bit close while I was off fishing in one-o-the rivers a while back. Bloody tourist boat operators feed the buggers ta give their guests a show. Now the bloody crocs all come for a feed if they hear a boat. Sometimes they don't like that ya haven't brung them anything. Nothing scarier than seeing a twenty-foot long croc coming at ya with an appetite and a temper."

Somewhere near midday when all was still with a cloying heat invading the *Cathedral*, Bazza lifted his head, straining to hear a sound repeated. Once he was sure of the sound he rushed out of the clearing toward the beach. Arriving at the top of the beach, he peered left and right to identify the direction of the sound. Arriving breathlessly behind him, Cheese stood next to him while regaining her breath.

"Cheese, run ta the cave, just by the door on the left as ya go in, ya will see a white plastic bottle, grab that-n-the first aid kit as quick as ya can and hightail it up the beach. See them blokes there?"

Before she could answer, Bazza ran up the beach in the direction of the two people struggling in the water about twenty feet from shore. Cheese ran for the supplies Bazza asked for when she finally heard the manic screams coming from the pair of swimmers. An inflatable dinghy rested on the shore about a half a mile up the beach. When Bazza reached them they were madly waving their arms in the air, alternately clutching and grabbing at themselves. On the beach lay their discarded clothing.

"Listen to me fellas, ya hafta come in so I can help yiz. Ya gotta come in, though. No, no don't grab at it. Don't touch it with ya hands. Fellas? Can yiz hear me? Get moving fellas, NOW. Get the fuck outta there."

When Cheese returned, Bazza was still trying desperately to get the two men to return to shore. Cheese didn't understand Bazza's reluctance to go out and render assistance.

"LISTEN TO ME YA BASTARDS! GET THE FUCK OUTTA THERE!"

"Bazza, if you don't go in to help them, I will."

"Your funeral, Cheese"

"What do you mean?"

"They run inta a Box I reckon. We go out there, the same thing will happen ta us."

"How can running into a box cause that sort of pain, Bazza? That…"

"Box Jellyfish, Cheese. Worst kinda pain imaginable. The only way is ta get them ta come in so I can help 'em. C'mon ya bludgers, move ya fucking arses. I can help ya if ya come in. Ya gotta come in, though."

Cheese joined Bazza in urging them toward the beach. With her voice joining Bazza's, the flailing pair finally took notice. One man dragging the other as they made their way to the shore screaming in agony. Tearing at their arms and legs as they rolled over on the sand. Bazza was yelling just as loud for them to stop grabbing at themselves as they would only make it worse. He was unscrewing the cap off the plastic bottle that Cheese had fetched. He poured the liquid from the bottle liberally over the pair who were showing signs of developing welts all over their exposed flesh.

Gradually the thrashing became less and less as the liquid seemed to manage the worst of the stings. Bazza asked Cheese to retrieve a couple of pairs of tweezers and surgical gloves from the first-aid kit. Kneeling between the two men, Bazza went to work removing the active tentacles clinging tenaciously to the victim's flesh, delivering thousands of continuing stings, injecting lethal amounts of neurotoxins into the hapless pair. Bazza warned Cheese not to allow any of the tentacles to touch her skin. The death of the jellyfish or the release of their tentacles from the jellyfish bell, did not restrict the toxicity of the tentacles that would go on delivering their poisonous loads for a long time.

The pair worked quickly to remove the tentacles once the frantic thrashing had ceased. Bazza continued to administer the liquid to their bodies. Huge, ugly welts like acid burns blistered the pair's bodies. They whimpered and cried out regularly as more toxins entered their systems, trying to work its way to their vital organs like the heart. Bazza noticed that one of the men had most of the stings across his torso while the other had them mostly on his hands and arms. He figured one person had been swimming out while the other was behind. When the person in front swam through the Box Jellyfish and started screaming, the other went to his aid by trying to remove the long tentacles, only to feel the stings himself. It was a classic example of what not to do in such an instance.

"Bazza, what is that stuff you're pouring on them?"

"Vinegar. I know it works even if a lotta folks reckon it's not the right thing ta use no more. Doesn't stop *all* the pain, but it really helps ta knock it about, works as a neutraliser. Cheese I need ya ta dig a hole in the sand and bury these tentacles. Can't leave 'em lying about. If one-o-us steps on 'em we'll feel it as bad as these blokes."

Cheese did as Bazza asked. By the time they had finished, the two men had settled down remarkably, with only one still whimpering. Bazza and Cheese both looked upon the still man at the same time and were stunned to silence when they realised that he was no longer breathing. Bazza shook his head as Cheese was about to say something. She quickly understood his meaning. Bazza did not want to voice out loud the passing of one man while the other may yet experience the same fate. The man with the largest area of stings, obviously the one that got into trouble first, must have suffered a heart attack or other major organ failure as a result of the massive doses of venom injected into his body by one of Australia's, and perhaps the world's, deadliest stingers.

Bazza retrieved and crushed a couple of pain-relief tablets containing codeine, the strongest over-the-counter medication he could purchase, from his first-aid kit. He mixed them with some water he carried in the kit, which he gently persuaded the sole survivor to drink. Whispering instructions to Cheese, they managed to remove any remaining tentacles from the survivor, burying them afterward. While Cheese was finishing up, sitting by the man's side, Bazza repaired to the *Cathedral* to fetch the implements he would require to transport one man back to their cave, and bury the other at the high water mark, which they would have to mark clearly for identification purposes once the authorities were alerted to the accident. Bazza was beginning to worry over all the people showing up in his little corner of the world.

He returned to the beach with a makeshift stretcher that he and Cheese could drag back to the clearing with the man on top. They would come back later to bury the other one, if Cheese had the stomach to help him, that is. It was a long haul to drag the man along the soft sand to the entrance of the *Cathedral*, about half a mile from where they were. They managed to manoeuvre the man and stretcher through the narrow cave doorway, to settle him onto the cot he had made up for Cheese when she first arrived. Once they had persuaded the man to take a little more water to keep him hydrated, applied soothing antiseptic creams to the affected areas, they left him to rest fitfully. The pain killers would need to be repeated every four hours or so until he either survived or didn't. Bazza and Cheese would have to take turns watching him, tending to his wounds through the following nights. Outside the cave, they stopped to catch their breath and take toll of the situation.

"Will he make it, Bazza?"

"Dunno, maybe. He didn't get it as bad as his mate, that's for sure. He will have bloody awful scarring on his hands and arms, though, and I worry about that one across his face, near his right eye. I reckon he musta wiped his face while he still had tentacles on his hands. If he makes it through the first few days, then we hafta watch him like a hawk to make sure the infection don't kill him. I don't have any antibiotics, and those stings will come up like burns and attract infection which runs rampant in the tropics. When he wakes up termorra we hafta wipe him down with antiseptic solution, then maybe apply some Mercurochrome I reckon. Probably sting like shit, but not as bad as what he just went through."

"Who do you think they are? What would they be doing here, Bazza?"

"Dunno, getting busier than Roma Street Station around here. I think I saw the vague outline of some sort of power boat out beyond the reef. I reckon they knew enough not ta risk bringing the boat in across the reef, and took the inflatable instead. Being as it's pretty warm today now the sun's come out, they stripped down to their jocks ta go for a swim. Stupid bastards. The jellyfish spawn in the tidal estuaries at this time-o-year, then swim out after. Although a jellyfish mostly floats with the current, a Box can actually swim quite well ta get at prey in the water. Dunno what they want here, though, and I wouldn't be surprised if someone's still on the boat. Looked pretty expensive to leave alone, even out here. Anything could happen if the weather turned suddenly. Might hafta take the inflatable out at next high tide to check."

"That doesn't sound like a wise thing to do, Bazza."

"Eh? Why's that? Ya know something I don't?"

"Just a feeling."

"Women's intuition huh?"

"Something like that. It just feels odd. Two people showing up like that. I don't think they understood what you were saying, Bazza, I don't think they understand English that well."

"No crime in that, Cheese."

"It doesn't strike you as suspicious that two non-English speaking people show up on a totally isolated beach with an expensive motor launch?"

"Whatcha thinking? People smuggling? Like boat people?"

"Don't you?"

"Not bloody likely. They come over in all sorts of shit-heaps from Indonesia and that, not in expensive power boats, Cheese. Could ask you the same question, though. What were you and your brothers doing travelling in a huge, expensive rig in this remote part-o-the country?"

"Well, thank-you very much."

"Aww, Cheese I didn't mean it like that. I jest meant that we shouldn't be so quick ta judge ya know? I always like ta give folks the benefit of doubt before I make up me mind."

"Fair enough, Bazza. I understand. I still don't think it's a good idea for you to go out there to the boat tonight. Next high tide is what, around midnight? Can't you wait until the noontide tomorrow at least? It will give us time to tend to the injured man here and make sure he lasts the night?"

"You make a good point 'cept for one thing, Cheese. If they didn't have a mate on board that boat out there, it might tear loose from its anchor and get wrecked on the reef."

"Okay, but why should you risk yourself for a boat?"

"Thought ya wanted ta get out of here? Can't do it in me little tinny, but ya can get outta here in that boat. Take us right inta Cairns on that. Might hafta get *him* outta here quick smart anyway, so nothing ta stop ya getting out as well."

"I tell you what, Bazza, you have a very fine brain. Don't let anyone ever tell you otherwise you hear? I could kiss you for thinking of a way out for all of us," Cheese announced in a less than convincing tone.

CHAPTER EIGHT

Half an hour before midnight saw Bazza dragging his lightweight tinny, down to the water's edge. With the tide being almost full, it was not very far to drag the boat. Bazza explained to Cheese that he preferred the familiarity and safety of his own boat when negotiating the reef. The tide may well have been full, but that did not make navigating at night a cake-walk. He did not want to risk taking the strangers' inflatable with the high-powered outboard that he had dragged well clear of the waterline much earlier in the afternoon. Cheese was standing the first watch over the injured man. Bazza had given him some more water and another dose of painkillers, before leaving.

The dark-skinned man had deliriums in which he spoke a foreign language. While it was impossible to make out exactly what he was saying, Cheese seemed to understand more than a word or two of the language he muttered. Cheese had been spot-on with her assessment that the strangers did not comprehend their instructions that afternoon. *Pretty canny that Cheese had picked up on that so quickly; even understanding some of their lingo,* Bazza thought. He retained that little piece of information for further prognostication at a later date as he jumped into his tinny, readying his six-horse Evinrude outboard with the modifications Bazza had perfected, to take his 'brew'.

Clouds were gathering again in preparation for the next deluge to inundate the area. Even leaving the boat exposed to such heavy skies and the rough seas beyond the reef endangered the craft. By no means exposed to the open ocean, the swells grew quite large none-the-less. Another system of reefs forming part of one of the natural wonders of the world, The Great Barrier Reef, protected the waters in between it and the reef in front of Bazza's beach. He motored slowly out once the little engine sparked to life with a splutter.

Bazza could make out a night light aboard the anchored boat to guide him to its position. It was sitting just beyond the reef at a drop-off. Bazza could make out the heavy swell by the white light on its mast bobbing about like it was a floating cork. Getting through the reef would be a breeze compared to sidling up along the motor boat without scratching the crap out of the paintwork. He hoped they had a couple of fenders out from when they launched the inflatable even though it didn't require it. If there was another person on board, then there would be no problem. If it was empty, he would have to get off alongside, tie off the tinny to leave it trailing behind once on board the other vessel.

Bazza could feel the warm moisture in the air thickening as the storm front moved in. The damp air clung to his skin and soaked his clothes in the space of minutes. Using a powerful lamp attached to his head like a miner's light, Bazza manoeuvred his tinny skilfully through the narrow channel in the reef. He knew he was being overly cautious as his aluminium dinghy did not draw enough water to strike the reef at full tide, but he wasn't taking any chances. He never could figure out why people ignored their own rules or common sense to take unnecessary risks.

With the cloud cover blocking the moon and the sparkling Milky Way, Bazza had to make do with his unerring experience guiding him through safely to the other side of the reef where his ten foot tinny was soon being tossed about like a toy. He made his way quickly to the side of the forty foot luxury power launch. He whistled softly when he spied the gleaming chrome rails and polished timber decking. Mahogany doors led to the main cabin where he could just make out dim lights inside. Bazza climbed to the bow of his tinny after giving the outboard just enough revs to make it to the stern of the vessel where he could step onto the duckboard, then secure a line to one of the shiny brass cleats on the stern gunwale.

The second he had tied off and raised his head to make ready to board, he found himself staring directly down the barrel of a chrome-plated handgun. The tip of the weapon tilted up slightly, motioning Bazza up and into the vessel. A well-dressed man with a latte complexion indicated a seat at the stern where Bazza should plant himself. The man studied Bazza through shooter's yellow Ray Ban glasses, chewing on a toothpick which wobbled about his mouth like it was having a fit. The man stood approximately five foot ten, with wavy black hair that looked like it had recently been oiled. The worst part about him was his close-set eyes that drilled through Bazza like a red hot poker. Dead eyes, devoid of any normal emotions. Like the man could kill someone and chop them up while having a sandwich, a beer, and holding a phone conversation at the same time.

When Bazza opened his mouth in an attempt to converse, the man simply shook his head and made a shushing sound, placing the barrel of the weapon against his pursed lips. He was thinking so hard, that Bazza could almost hear the cogs grinding above the noise of the growing ocean swell slapping the side of the hull. The stranger motioned at Bazza, then the boat, and then indicated the shore. From which, Bazza deduced that the man wanted him to take the boat to shore, or at least past the reef. Bazza nodded uncertainly with a shrug. The spindly stranger again motioned for Bazza to move while they swapped places on the rear bench seat. Bazza entered the luxuriously outfitted saloon of polished exotic timbers with contrasting inlays, brass handles and rails, polished chrome, and beautiful tan leather upholstery.

He found most of what he was looking for despite being unfamiliar with luxury motor yachts. He located the starter ignition that kick-started the engine with the pleasant rumble of a high-performance motor capable of thoroughbred speeds. After locating and activating the electronic anchor winch, Bazza gently steered the boat in the direction of the incoming waves as the anchor was raised from its depths in the drop-off. Once the anchor was secured within the anchor pulpit at the bow, Bazza gently eased the magnificent yacht around to make a heading for the narrow channel. He poured as much forward light as the boat possessed onto their approach while nervously angling the vessel between the treacherous outcroppings he knew existed on either side, any one of which could tear a fatal hole into the fibreglass hull. The stranger, holding his weapon steadily at the back of Bazza's head did nothing to ease his tension

It was a delicate operation with a turn of almost a hundred and eighty degrees half way through, before resuming a westerly heading into the protected bay. Bazza slowed to a mere crawl, watching behind with worry etching his features for his beloved tinny. Passing through the last of the reef saw Bazza relax slightly. Without asking for permission, he guided the vessel to a spot around a hundred feet offshore where he lowered the anchor. The launch would be safe from damage by the high seas pounding the outer edge of the reef. Only uncommonly strong winds would disturb the boat while in the bay, something Bazza did not expect. After securing the boat for unoccupied anchorage, Bazza understood that he was to take the silent stranger to shore in his tinny. Bazza shrugged his acceptance and understanding of the situation with a nod of the head, feeling far calmer than he thought possible given the circumstances.

"Honey, I'm home," shouted Bazza as he entered the clearing beneath his shack, before being brutally pistol-whipped to the back of the head. Cheese came running out of the cave where she had been tending to the slumbering patient. Upon seeing Bazza being knocked to the ground, she rushed to his aid. Then she noticed the weapon gleaming in the glow of the subdued LED lighting. She clung fiercely to Bazza as he massaged a large lump forming on his head. Bleeding slightly from the impact, he winced as Cheese applied a moist rag with which she had been sponging down her patient. Cheese stubbornly refused to leave Bazza's side despite the menacing manner of the silent stranger glaring at her with murderous intentions, tinged with what might possibly be interpreted as lust.

"What does he want?"

"*Silencio!*" barked the stranger. "*Mi amigo, rápidamente.*"

"*Si, Señor.*" Answered Cheese in halting Spanish.

She urged the stranger to follow her to the entrance of the cave where she pointed out the sleeping figure on the cot. The man walked over to the other, peering under the bandages at the vicious raised welts, weeping clear liquids.

"*Que pasó?*"

"*Picaduras de medusas, muy malas Señor.*"

"*Vivira?*"

"*Quizás, si.*"

"*Mi otro amigo?*"

Cheese shook her head to indicate his other friend had not made it. Bazza looked from one to the other incredulously during the exchange with growing suspicions. Cheese explained the content of the conversation to Bazza quietly as the standing stranger showed neither frustration nor regret at the news of the lost companion. She told Bazza that the stranger had enquired about the reason for his friend's injuries and the absence of the other.

"Ya seem to know his lingo huh?"

"For some reason, I can understand every word and know how to answer, so I suppose I learned how to speak Spanish fluently at one time."

"Convenient."

"*Silencio! Hago la charla, solo contestas.*"

"Whatever, Pancho just said; tell him he can go fuck himself."

"Maybe I kill you then I fuck your little *mamacita* eh, *Gringo*?"

"Oh, so now ya can speak the English eh, ya dago bastard? Well, feel free ta kill me and do what eva ya feel like to the woman. She's a stranger ta me-n-getting stranger all the time."

The stranger raised his weapon.

"*Si lo matas todos morimos, Señor.*" Said Cheese.

"Why we die if I kill the Gringo?"

"There is no way out of here during the wet season, no way out of the bay without him as a guide, no way to survive here without him providing enough food to last three people. He has stored only enough food for one person." she explained exiting the cave.

"Is road there, is truck over there, we get out of here okay if I want. I come for...*cita*?" The man said upon spying the track in the dim lighting.

"A rendezvous, a meeting?"

"*Si*, a meeting with, *Señor* Armstrong. We go to see this man."

"Take the keys ta the car and be my guest arsehole, I'll pick ya body up off the mountainside and put it with ya fucking amigo in his sandy grave out on the beach," fumed Bazza.

The stranger raised the gun at Bazza once more, threatening to make good on his earlier threat. He peered toward the ocean knowing he would not be able to negotiate the reef by himself, then moved over to inspect the track up the slope. He tested the surface with his boot that came away muddy. He nodded his head as he came to the conclusion that he and his friend were indeed stuck for the moment, at least until his friend got better, then they could offload the pair and be on their way. "Ju know dis, *Señor* Armstrong? Where he live?"

"Nuh; and I couldn't give a shit neither."

"He live here somewhere at end of road on top de mountain?"

"Look, I told ya I don't give a shit about the bloke ya afta. Only property at the end of the road belongs ta some Yank. Owned it for years. Never seen no one there or on the road in all the time I been here. Can't bloody help ya, wouldn't if I could."

"Bazza, I don't think it will help us if you keep antagonising him like that."

"That what ya think is it, Cheese?"

"What has gotten into you, Bazza? What have I done wrong all of a sudden?"

"Ya started speaking a foreign lingo that's what. Just after ya arrived here from America, and just before this grease-ball turns up looking for some Yank dude named Armstrong. That ya surname is it? You and ya brothers 'sposed ta meet this slimo at ya property at the end of the road? All a bit coincidental isn't it, Cheese, or whatever ya name is?"

"I told the truth when I said I can't remember, Bazza. I don't know what my first or last name is and I have no idea how I got here or anything about the property at the end of the road. What is the first name of the person you are hoping to meet, *Señor*?"

"*No lo sé.*"

"He doesn't know."

"I got that, Cheese, I got that."

"*Queso?*"

"He," pointing to Bazza, "calls me, *Cheese* because we don't know my name. I seem to have suffered partial memory loss due to an accident with my brothers who both…passed away."

"*Tus hermanos tienen el dinero?*"

"*Dinero?*"

"*Si, mucho dinero.*"

"I don't know anything about money. I don't think we are the people you are looking for."

"Ju, have accident wit your brothers? Where dis crash and your brothers?"

Both Bazza and Cheese pointed up to the top of the mountain.

"Ju been to accident? Look in car?"

"Bazza saw the crash site; saw my brothers from outside the vehicle only. Bazza says it is nearly impossible to enter the vehicle without the whole lot crashing to the bottom of the mountain on the other side."

"I no leave without my monny. You take me to crash when?"

"No one is going up that mountain for at least another two months, maybe as long as three. It depends on the weather. And when it dries up, ya can get up there ya fucking self."

"We see. I theenk you like this, this, *Queso*, so I theenk you take us up the mountain when is time. Otherwise, I burn everything and kill the woman after we have *mucho* fun with her first. I theenk maybe you like these little wood things eh? I see mucho wood to burn, *Gringo*, maybe you too eh?"

"And exactly what do you think we are all going to do in the meantime, mate?"

"Where you sleep?"

Cheese and Bazza simply pointed into the air above his head. The stranger followed the direction of their fingers with his head until he was looking straight up at the underside of the shack.

"Aye, aye, aye. *Mierda!*"

He paced around the clearing debating with himself, thinking through all the problems he faced. Walking over to the cave entrance to look in on his companion, walking back to the centre where he shook his head in frustration at the pair standing before him. He stomped the ground with his boot in anger, before storming off in the direction of the track. When he returned he looked up at the shack.

"Give me your…*teléphonos movilés*, computers and every

other communications, NOW!"

"Don't have any ya, moron. Wouldn't work out here anyway. No reception. NO TELEPHONOs, wanker. Why'd ya think I haven't got help for, Cheese by now if I had any-o-that stuff? Dipshit!"

The man strode over to Bazza with fury etched into his features and murder in his eyes. He clubbed Bazza over the ear with a stunning blow that sent him sprawling.

"You call me names again I will shoot off one of your ears, then the other, then your nose…Get the picture, *gilipollas*? Deekhead?" To Cheese… "I will sleep on the boat and take the other leetle boats with me every night. I think you two will not be swimming in the water eh? You make sure my *compañero* is given the best treatment. Eef he die; you die; or worse."

After the vile man stormed off in the direction of the beach, Cheese turned her attention to Bazza who groaned while slumping to the ground. Cheese thought Bazza appeared to be quite pale, a sign that he may be concussed or worse. She walked swiftly to the cave where she retrieved the well-used first-aid kit. Supplies within the small kit were diminishing far quicker than she would have thought possible for such a small population in a remote area. She was as confused as Bazza with regard to all the strangers dropping in on his forest hideaway, which included herself. She had no recollection of her ability to speak Spanish, nor anyone by the name of Armstrong. She remembered nothing about her brothers much beyond Portland, nor anything about travelling to Australia, or the reasons for them doing so. It was a very big mystery to her, although, she agreed somewhat with Bazza that it all seemed a little too coincidental. *What were the odds that six strangers would stumble, crash, or blunder into Bazza's little world, without some connection?*

Bazza soon recovered from the shock of being beaten about the head. Bazza was a large, solid man, capable of withstanding physical abuse by nature or human. He sat up wearily, surveying the scene.

"That arsehole pissed orf?"

"Please be careful, Bazza. You shouldn't keep provoking him like that. He will end up killing you."

"Ya don't think we'll end up dead anyway once he has what he wants? Get real, Cheese Armstrong!"

"What? Why are you calling me that? I don't know what my surname is, Bazza, I'm not lying about that."

"Armstrong Enterprises is what the sign on the side of the truck read. You came from that accident unless there's a whole lotta different folk's jest traipsing all over the joint at the moment when I haven't seen another soul here for well on ten years. So, ya hafta be an Armstrong, and them blokes come ta see yaself, and ya brothers for something other than a nice little chit-chat, don't ya reckon?"

"I don't know what you're implying, Bazza, but I do not appreciate the accusation in your voice. I, I am not sure what sort of people my brothers and I were before the accident. I can only go by what I feel and know now, here, today, and I somehow believe I am not the same person I was."

"Ya come from money, that's for sure. That rig up there would be an easy half a mil, if not more. Big rig like that means ya was planning ta stay a while, in comfort. To do what, I don't know, but I reckon the money that bastard's after has ta be what ya brung him. If I had ta guess, I reckon it was for drugs, unless ya looking to be a terrorist buying guns and shit?"

"You can't possibly believe that of me, Bazza."

"I believe jest about anything at the moment unless ya can prove otherwise. I don't trust strangers, and that's what ya is, a complete stranger. Good looking for ya age I'll give ya that, nice when ya wanna be, but still, a bloody stranger and I wish ya would all jest fuck-off and leave me alone!"

Bazza rose from his prone position with all the dignity he could muster before clambering up the ladder to the shack. He gathered his bow and arrows before the intruder found them and made too much of them. He planned to stash a few useful items in a cache away from the camp. He was preparing for a few possibilities. He was not overly concerned about the intruders, as he knew he could probably swim to the boat moored off the beach anytime he wanted in the right swimming gear to prevent jellyfish stings. He could surprise and overpower the smelly dago runt with ease, then figure out what to do with him.

That was the conundrum, however; what to do with them if he did overpower them. Two more mouths to feed, and guard. He was, after-all, just one person in need of sleep occasionally. Couldn't tie them up the whole time. Couldn't really use the prick's boat to take them into the authorities without evidence of serious wrong-doing. Couldn't trust Cheese to back him. She was just as likely to be in cahoots with the bludgers. He knew he had to think of ways to stay alive while the wet season continued. Then he would have to devise a method to divide and conquer, or at least whittle down the numbers against him. Sooner or later Cheese was going get her memory back, and then she would probably revert to the person she was before. *Drug runner, gun runner…? Something?* He didn't want to be unprepared.

Bazza was glad that the man had gone off to his boat, leaving one less person with whom to share the shack. Eventually, the bloke that got stung was going be moved aloft so that they could tend to his wounds easier than climbing up and down all night. Bazza could not quite believe the year he was having. Bloody people everywhere it seemed, and everyone crashing his private party. All he really wanted was to be left alone.

All he *could* do after the messy divorce. The divorce had put paid to most of his previous plans for life. He was really only left with one option after all that, so he grasped the amazing opportunity afforded him by inheriting the property from his old man. He had enjoyed the solitude and peaceful way of life for so long that he almost cried at the intrusion, realising that it may all be lost forever.

Bazza picked up his binoculars to peer through the gap in the foliage. He observed the stranger motoring out toward his moored vessel with the inflatable Bazza had dragged to the high-water mark, towing his precious tinny behind. Anger seethed inside him, seeing someone touching his stuff without his permission, but he was secretly pleased that the fool thought he was so safe out there. Anyone with half a brain knew how to circumvent the stings of the jellyfish with the appropriate gear. Failing the use of a full stinger suit, a person could make do with a long-sleeved shirt, trousers and socks, gloves, and an old stocking over the head to keep them off the face.

When the time was right, he may use that advantage to take back his possessions and possibly scuttle the motor launch in the process to ensure that authorities were able to catch up with his unwelcome guests. Despite his natural aversion to authorities, he would not hesitate to report the mongrels for whatever nefarious activities in which they were involved. He rubbed his head where the mongrel had hit him and swore the prick would pay for it, for Bazza was a *very* patient man when it came to retribution.

He had to be patient when wood carving, knowing certain elements and procedures took more time than others. He very rarely completed one carving at a time. It was impossible to go through all the processes involved in a strict order. He was always waiting for some woods to cure before touching them, like burls for instance. A burl was essentially a cancerous growth forming on the trunk of a tree. Inside the burl, the normal wood grain of the tree species would run amok in a variety of swirls and whorls in a profusion of vibrant colours and patterns, ensuring great value for use in table tops and the like. They were often not a viable carving medium due to inconsistent grains but were highly regarded for occasional tables. It was necessary to cure the burls for several years to prevent them warping and cracking once sliced up for use.

Other woods, he would carve up green. Then have to wait for finishes to dry before proceeding. Other composites, or assemblages of driftwood, may require waiting patiently for just the right shape to float up to his shoreline before a piece could be completed. A solitary existence had provided Bazza with infinite patience and more than enough common sense to give him the upper hand in most circumstances when it came to a test of wills. He needed to see out two to four months of the wet season before his track became negotiable enough to reach the top with a vehicle like his tractor or 4WD ute. He imagined he might make it on foot sooner than that, which he secretly hoped the stranger would demand.

Bazza foresaw dozens of methods to produce the results he desired when they eventually set off. It would be up to happenstance as to which of those methods he would employ to reduce the numbers of his enemy, or reduce them to ineffectuality, to neutralise the threat. He grinned as he formulated the plan to himself. The grin faded as Cheese entered the shack. He did not envisage a good ending where she was concerned; trusted her not in the least. He had to admit that he had been warming to her, almost invited her company, albeit quiet company, to his realm. That notion had soured with the unfolding events of the night. Bazza was too exhausted to continue with the thought. Without a word, he walked past Cheese to his bedroom, only to fall onto his bed fully clothed. He was fast asleep soon after his banged up head hit the pillow.

CHAPTER NINE

Gunshots erupted amid the natural early morning cacophony.

"Ayee! Madre de dios. Es el Diablo."

Bazza and Cheese both ran to the veranda where they saw the stranger backing out of the outhouse with his weapon raised in one arm and crossing himself with the other. Bazza turned to Cheese with a grin.

"Goliath."

"Goliath", she agreed.

"It's only a harmless spider mate. Can't really hurt ya, unless ya include heart-attacks."

"He will never have the chance to hurt anyone I theenk. Lower the ladder so I can come up; and have the woman make the breakfast, pronto."

"Spit in it," Bazza suggested to Cheese after lowering the ladder.

Bazza went to the kitchen to brew his morning coffee, while Cheese checked the Girls' cage for some eggs.

"Not very many eggs again, Bazza."

"They usually don't start making cackle berries until about nine in the morning. I think ya'll find some in a basket in the pantry. I put some in there yesterday at any rate. Who knows what everyone has eaten-o-mine in the meantime."

"I don't eat your eggs unless you suggest it, Bazza. Can we please go back to the way we were? I don't want to suffer your sullen looks and responses every time I say something for the next few months. It is uncomfortable enough with our unwanted guests without us being at each other's throats surely?"

"Eat what ya want, just do as I said for him."

"She will not be doing that I theenk, *Gringo*. I weel be watching. If I see anything I don like, then I weel hurt somebody. Make the coffee, Gringo and shut up you face."

"Atsa matter you hey? Gotta no respect? Wadda ya think ya do? Itsa nica place. Ah shudduppa you face!" Bazza sang along, then hummed the old tune as the stranger scowled at him and waved the pistol about threateningly. Cheese smiled knowingly, as she had heard Bazza sing the song a few times. Bazza always managed to miss a line or two, or hit the wrong notes, wrong key, or otherwise just stuff up every song he ever tried to sing. He was hopelessly tone deaf. Cheese felt sure that his artistic talents fell short of the performing arts!

"Can you tell us your name, *Señor*, so we may know what to call you?" asked Cheese quietly.

"I am, Rafael, and *mi amigo* is Paolo. You are…*Queso*, Cheese?"

"I am afraid I do not know my actual name and, Cheese, has stuck for the time being. What do you want for breakfast, Rafael? We have eggs, cereal, or toast?"

"I weel have some eggs and beans with some chilli."

"Really? Chilli for breakfast? Bazza, do you have any chilli?"

"Got some smoked Habanero Chillies in the pantry as a sauce. Jar to the left on the middle shelf. Ya'll hafta open a can-o-baked beans for him, though. Only kinda beans I got. Take it easy on them, though, gotta last me. Love me baked beans on toast."

Bazza served up the coffee in three steaming mugs after locating an extra one from the rear of a cupboard, as they sat at the bench surrounding the kitchen. He made some toast for himself while Cheese cooked some eggs for herself and Rafael. She watched Bazza spreading some black stuff over his heavily buttered toast.

"I've been meaning to ask you, Bazza, what is that ghastly looking stuff you put on your toast?"

"Vegemite. Good tucka. Every Aussie kid grows up with the stuff. No one else likes it, though. Visitors always taste it the wrong way. The only way ta taste it proper is ta eat it on toast with lotsa butter. Can't jest eat from the jar. Tastes like shit then.

"What is it, though?"

"Um, it's a yeast extract. They brought it out years ago ta compete with another product called "Marmite", so they were gonna call it "Pawill". Get it? Ma might - Pa will? But they ended up calling it Vegemite instead. Wanna taste?"

"Sure."

Bazza offered her a small piece of toast with a smear of Vegemite. Cheese delicately tasted the morsel, expecting it to taste as vile as it looked. To her utter astonishment, she quite liked the savoury, salty flavour. To her, it reminded her of a type of seasoning she had tried at some time in her dim and distant past. She smiled at Bazza who looked upset that she had found it palatable. She nodded her head.

"Not bad at all. I think I may even have some for breakfast myself tomorrow. What's on the agenda for today, Bazza, more carving?"

"Gonna rain. No one is doing nothing today but getting bored."

"You can't be serious? It's perfect weather out there."

"Gonna come down like there's no termorra. Hope ya scuppers are free?" he asked Rafael.

"What is…scupper?"

"Drains on ya decks, makes sure all the water drains off back inta the sea. If ya scuppers are closed or blocked, ya boat will sink with the amount-o-water we're gonna get soon."

"I will send you out in this rain to check I theenk."

"No, ya won't. No telling if I come back, so it won't be me going out there ta get soaked. I'd offer ya a raincoat, but I don't have one. Good coffee eh?" asked Bazza with a smirk.

"Very soon, I theenk I weel have to kill you. I don like you, an I don truss you."

"Makes two-o-us a-migo, makes two-o-us. Ya still won't send me out ta ya boat ta check, though. Anyway, makes no difference ta me if she ends up on the bottom; if ya don't wanna go. Lotta money going ta waste, though, eh, Cisco? Ya gotta get outta here sometime eh? Don't know the roads, so ya need the boat ta make ya get-away."

Rafael stood to take aim with the weapon at Bazza's ear when a distant rumble caught his attention. On the horizon, the first of the dark clouds gathered for the predicted deluge.

"Ever seen it rain in the tropics, Miguel? I reckon ya might've. We don't measure our rainfall in inches here buddy, we measure it in feet, or metres. Reckon you seen plenty-o-that where ya come from eh? Colombia? Venezuela? Bolivia?"

Rafael inspected the opening in the canopy towards the beach for signs of the incoming weather. He looked at Bazza uncertainly, as if making up his mind whether to believe him or not, finally settling on playing it safe. He downed is coffee before rushing off down the ladder. Bazza laughed as he watched the madman hightailing down the path out to the beach, throwing himself into the inflatable, before motoring out to the boat.

"Were you fibbing about the rain, Bazza?"

"Nah, it's gonna pour real soon, but his boat's gonna be fine. Noticed the scupper drains were all opening and closing in the swell outside the reef. If he forgot ta close the main cabin door, it may get a bit damp in there, but that's about it. Stupid bastard hasn't gotta clue."

"You will get us both killed if you don't stop playing him for a fool, Bazza. I thought you were better than this pettiness."

"Jest keeping him off-balance for as long as I can. I need him ta make a few mistakes, keep him thinking all the time and wear him down. Only way we're gonna survive this. I don't play the part-o-victim well. No one comes ta my place and points guns at me, no one!"

"Do you have a plan then? Some way out of this?"

"Course I gotta plan. Not gonna take this crap lying down like a bloody pansy, but it will take a while. Gotta be patient. Nothing we can do but wait until the time is right. Ya better get down ta the cave ta make sure old-mate's still kicking. He might be able ta eat something if he's awake. We're in deep shit if he don't make it. What's his name, Polio, or something?"

"Paolo, it's Spanish for, Paul. Why did you mention those places to, Rafael? Is that where you think he's from?"

"He's from Colombia I reckon. See his face light up like a beacon when I mentioned it? He'd never be much good at poker, too easy ta spot his tells."

"What made you think he was from there?"

"Connecting dots, Cheese, connecting dots."

Fifty minutes later the heavens opened to unleash the torrent. Rafael returned moments before with a look of pure hatred twisting his normally deadpan features into a vicious snarl. He ate his cold eggs and beans in chilli sauce in silence, glowering at anything that moved. It was obvious that he wanted to vent his spleen at somebody, but knew it would be useless given the hammering din above, and around them. Bazza was casually curled up on a sofa, reading a novel. He completely ignored Rafael's return and the subsequent death stares aimed at him. He just smiled like the cat that ate the cream.

Cheese had examined her patient in the cave. He managed to eat a little buttered toast and drink a little water before taking his crushed up painkillers, then sleeping once more. His wounds showed no obvious signs of infection. Bazza told Cheese not to bind his wounds as they required fresh air to grow healing scabs, a notion she found quite repulsive. She did, however, heed his good counsel. If he made it through the following few days, it was likely he would recover, albeit with intense scarring.

The three strangers settled into a stand-offish routine of sorts during the following days of intermittent rain. Rafael continued to escape to his vessel during the night while spending his days lounging around constantly watching the mad *Gringo* and the Cheese person for signs of hatching plans or making trouble. One incident had him leaping to his feet in apprehension when he heard a loud banging sound, like gunshots. It turned out to be the woman entering the outhouse below. When she noticed him looking at her furiously, she just shrugged and told him it was for the spiders. From that moment onwards, he did exactly the same when he entered the outhouse. He had also made the acquaintance of Erik, whom he didn't mind at all. He had seen Anaconda before, so a little python like Erik, even at ten feet long, did not bother him.

Paolo was recovering well, although his hands were contracting into claws as they healed. Bazza told him he would have to splint them, or they would stay like that until they were operated on. He would select or carve perfect splints which required light dressings only to keep them in position, allowing good airflow around the healing scars. Rafael conversed with his amigo for lengthy periods as they discussed the pros and cons of their decision to remain.

From the little that Cheese overheard, she was able to relate to Bazza that the trio had spent a great deal of money to purchase the boat and supplies for the trip and that without the money they were promised, for whatever transaction they had planned, they would suffer great losses and lose face with their immediate business associates.

Rafael prowled around like an alley cat when he wasn't languishing on a lounge like a tourist aboard a luxury liner. Paolo made frequent trips around the clearing, unable to climb the ladder to the shack with his damaged hands in splints. He often went for walks on the beach where he remained frozen at the site of his mishap, shrinking inside at the memory of his best friend perishing in utter agony. Tears came freely to his eyes whenever he ventured there. His once regal, almost arrogant posture crumbled over time to be replaced by that of a stooped old man. His naturally tanned, unlined, youthful, facial features, were turning to those of a pallid old crone. His unkempt, greasy hair and poor hygiene, made him foul of temper and smell.

He was unable to take his annoyance out on the hapless pair they held 'captive', due to the care they offered and the rescue they performed. He would not be alive had they not assisted him. He may not have wanted to remain alive in his condition, but was not given the choice. Rafael would not hear of his complaining. Rafael did not much care for Paolo's good friend, Diego, as much as he. Paolo grieved for them both. Diego who died and Paolo who could not. Paolo believed he would become a cripple, would not have the use of his hands. He looked like a monster with huge red welts covering his arms, parts of his face, and torso. He looked at himself in the mirror and wondered, *what mujer would have such a monstruo as he? Would he ever feel the loving embrace of a young woman again? Would he marry, have niños?* He grew more morose as the days passed with nothing else to take his mind off his troubles.

Rafael puzzled over Paolo's depression. Didn't understand the cause of it and cared even less. He wanted his orders followed to the letter without all the tiresome stress of hearing complaints and watching his compatriot destroy himself. He mistakenly believed Paolo was made of sterner stuff. He regretted forcing his captives to care for him so assiduously. *He'd have been better off with Paolo buried alongside his friend out there in the sand*, thought Rafael bitterly. He was gruesome to look at, like an old gnarled tree, twisting with age and slowly rotting in the centre. Rafael grew more impatient each passing day, with his friend, with the constant rain, with the boredom, and with the insolence of the man called Bazza.

If the oaf had not proven his usefulness many times over, Rafael would have wiped the smug smile from his face a long time ago. When he went out into the forest to hunt, with nothing but his hunting knife, because Rafael would allow nothing else, he always returned with a kill. A pig, a big fish called a Barramundi or something else he had yet to identify. He only ever brought the latter back skinned, so Rafael never discovered what they were. Whenever he asked the Gringo, the brute only replied that they were a forest mammal full of good protein. As best as he could guess, Rafael believed they were a rabbit of some kind. Despite his loathing of the imbecile, he made a tasty stew of these forest mammals, often spiced up with the chilli sauce that Rafael enjoyed. The woman refrained from eating on those occasions, which Rafael put down to an intolerance for chilli.

The woman, Cheese, was…enigmatic. Very mysterious that she had suffered a form of amnesia from an accident. Very convenient, he believed, for a woman of her age with possible past indiscretions to be suffering such a fortuitous condition. He believed the woman to be in her mid-late forties, with 'work', having been done to limit the degradation of time on the obvious parts of the anatomy. Face: almost without question, though highly professional. Breasts: indubitably, once again, a superb job. Everything about her smelled of money and snobbery. *Puta, coño dinero*, pussy money, he called it and told her so frequently when he was feeling generous. Cunt money, when he felt aggrieved in any way. Wealth through the lure of looks and pussy to snag a person of means. She would be one to watch out for. The man, he would kill very soon. He angered Rafael in many ways, baited him to act out of character for the generally benign façade he wore. The man pushed and needled Rafael on purpose. But to what end? That, Rafael had yet to ascertain.

Rafael had no option but to wait out his time in the God-forsaken Hell, with weather much like his home. The Gringo mentioned his home. For that alone, he would have to die when the time came. He did not know how long he could take the boredom of sitting around waiting for them to have access to the mountain where his money waited. He had laid everything on the line for this venture. Outlaid vast sums, all his savings and then some, for the fastest, most comfortable boat he could purchase to bring the product to sell at an outlandish price to the Gringo, Armstrong.

It was meant to be over and done with in a matter of hours after arrival. Transfer the goods, collect the money then vamoose without anyone knowing. Back to his country to pay off his debts with enough left over to finance the next venture without borrowing funds. If he went back now, empty-handed, asking for money to make good on losses, his life would become forfeit. He would be made an example to all who would cross Don Carlos. No, returning to Colombia would be as good as signing their death warrant. He would not return without his money, and if the owners of the money were dead and he could keep the product as well…? He would wait for Hell to freeze over for that kind of opportunity, as long as he didn't allow the stupid Australian gorilla to get under his skin.

Rafael knew the rainforest well, having Venezuela to Colombia's east, Ecuador to the west, Peru and Brazil to the south. He was familiar with the Amazon rainforests, which were not so different to this. He knew the dangers that lurked within the forests and river waters penetrating the dense interior. He did not know the fauna of Australia but had seen first-hand the result of its deadly ocean-going animals. He would need the Australian to guide him and Paolo safely to the site of the wreck, then his usefulness would be at an end, along with his life.

Until that moment, Rafael would allow the *cerdo,* pig, to have his fun, to call him names that would never hurt him because he didn't actually understand most of them. He would use his upbringing in the slums of Colombia to wait patiently like the snake or the spider, for the right time to pounce on its prey.

He fervently wished he would never have to see that Goliath spider again. He had taken two shots at the dreadful beast lurking in the foul-smelling toilet, both shots missing due to his shaking hand. He felt sure his bullets would have bounced off the enormous thing had he not missed. He had seen his native Tarantulas, they were midgets compared to the colossal thing that looked as though it wanted to leap at Rafael and devour him, threatening him with non-existent, huge fangs. Once he learned the trick of banging the toilet walls first with the big stick, he relaxed a little.

Rafael had little choice other than retreating to his luxury yacht each night, as there was limited space for all of them in the tiny treehouse. He felt safer aboard the yacht anyway, with plenty of booze, and, other South American distractions, to take his mind off his worries. His decision to sleep aboard his toy served another purpose, by also preventing foolish ideas of escape by his captives using his beloved vessel. The days were infuriatingly long and tedious, watching over the pair while being mindful of all the other dangers lurking outside.

Although Rafael had experience of the jungles in his country, it never ceased to amaze him that the impenetrability of the jungle existed only within the first hundred metres or so from the edge. After that, the towering trees competed for supremacy to retain their share of the sunlight, ensuring a dense canopy was formed many metres above the ground, with little vegetation below where the sunlight was unable to penetrate. Whenever a tree fell, many young, dormant, seeds sprouted almost immediately to take advantage of the temporary access to sunlight. Otherwise, the understory of a rainforest was typically bare of most inhibiting growth. The problems for Rafael and his partner lay not in managing to make their way through the rainforest, but in making their way upward, along treacherously slippery paths.

They would never make it on foot trying to get around the mountain either. At one point or another, they would have to ascend. To the south and north he was told that big rivers made their way to the sea, impassable on foot. In the event they were to manage the ascent, it was made hazardous by creatures roaming the land. He had seen the *cerdo* caught by the Australian, knew the reputation of a feral pig, and had no wish to cross the path of a sow with young, or its angry *papá*. He had seen an example of the spiders, which he was told was not actually one of the dangerous ones. Animals, and vines that made you, 'wait a while', all sounded far too unpleasant to risk on top of slipping and sliding in the knee-deep mud.

They would wait it out. The moment the road looked accessible enough, he would force them to leave. Once he had his money, he would be rid of them both, leaving him and Paolo free to make their way back downhill at a leisurely pace, to return home rich and victorious. He would make his mark as a rich man in his country, leaving the slums behind forever. He liked the taste of the good life, boat, clothes, good booze, and all the women he could buy. He would definitely use the woman, Cheese, before he shot her. It had been a while and he needed the release. He may have to indulge before then? He could feel the weight building in his pendulous testicles. He needed to offload.

Bazza pretended to read whenever he was forced to share his abode with his unwanted guests during the day. That way he could avoid unnecessary banter while keeping a surreptitious eye on Rafael. He knew he had to tread carefully where Rafael was concerned. The man was like a coiled snake ready to strike with its venomous fangs. It would not take much to tip him over the edge. Bazza wanted him to make stupid mistakes but not have him so riled that he started unloading bullets.

He watched closely, the changing attitudes and personalities of the three strangers in his sanctuary. The twists and turns of interrelationship rivalry and attraction made for interesting viewing. Paolo had been on the outs with Rafael since he began healing. His constant whining and morbid conversations, coupled with his lack of hygiene, ensured his growing distance from the leader. Cheese had triggered a few lusty leers from Rafael, and he detected a little jealousy creeping into Paolo's demeanour. His friend had developed a real Nurse Nightingale-adoration-like affection for Cheese, while Rafael merely lusted for anything with the appropriate apparatus for sexual relief. The interplay between all of them grew edgier each day they were lumped together in close quarters, with nothing else to occupy their minds. Bazza had even cut down on his hooch to make sure he was lucid enough to catch the subtle interactions taking place around him, while he pretended to ignore it.

Bazza did not trust Cheese at all, though he assumed she favoured his companionship to that of the Colombian thugs. Something didn't add up where she was concerned and he would not let down his guard around her, nor would he allow her access to his inner thoughts. Cheese had yet to prove or disprove her loyalties. In the meantime, Bazza chose his own counsel and companionship, just as he had been doing for many years. Food would be a problem eventually, although he hoarded a lot of canned goods in the cave. Those were his emergency stores, in case another cyclone destroyed everything, stranding him within the forest for an extended period.

Trees falling across the tracks and roads were a common hazard, with larger ones requiring extensive labour to remove. Wash-outs and landslides were just as common and far more daunting to circumvent, almost impossible in some cases.

One year, without the aid of a cyclone or any other unseasonal occurrence, the top road had been washed out and impassable for nearly six months before the District Council repaired the damage. Bazza had to risk using his tiny dinghy to travel down to the Daintree River, where he bummed a lift at the barge crossing into the nearest township, Mossman, to get some urgent supplies. To maintain his independence, he purchased a cheap, non-roadworthy vehicle which he piled high with provisions for the return journey. He abandoned the vehicle at the river where he transferred the contents to his tinny in several trips down the river to the mouth, where he transported the loads up the coast to his hideaway. It was a laborious and dangerous process he hoped never to have to repeat. He would never think of using the tinny to take Cheese out of there after that experience. It was hazardous enough in good weather with only one person aboard, let alone during foul weather with two.

Bazza was nearing sixty years old as far as he knew. He rarely kept track of the years any longer. His days of intense labour were numbered. He knew he had to get some savings together to see him through his retirement years when his carving days were over, or when his creations were no longer popular.

The menace of the strangers in his camp threatened to shorten his time-span upon the planet, something he hoped to avoid for a good while. Bazza wasn't afraid of dying, just the method of his passing. One past incident in his life had him treasuring his remaining moments above ground. He didn't want to shorten that time unnaturally, and he especially didn't want some South American arsehole dictating the length of his time on the planet. Bazza knew that he, and possibly Cheese, would be in dire straits once he guided them up the mountain. If in fact, the rig he saw piled against the tree half way down the other side of the mountain contained the money they sought, his captors would no longer have a use for him. He knew he would have to implement his plans before then. He just had to find the right time and circumstances.

Cheese had no idea what was going through Bazza's mind. He confided in her less and less. Not that she ever felt as though she had his complete trust. It was just that she felt she had made some headway to befriending him. As the days passed, the tension in the camp grew exponentially. Paolo's depression sought to bring everybody down, while Rafael silently seethed like a lit fuse waiting to blow. Bazza maintained it, keeping the fuse lit with continual taunts and insults. Rafael was as angry at Paolo, as he was with Bazza. On top of that, he kept leering at Cheese in a lustful manner which made her fearful. They were sitting on a powder keg while the rain battered their location and their senses. Something would have to give in order for there to be peace.

She almost screamed in frustration when a break in the weather had Bazza suggesting he take Paolo for a fishing trip out to the reef. They needed some supplies of fish to vary their diets. Fresh fish offered many vitamins and minerals essential for the body. Excess fish could be smoked or dried, to last for a much longer period. Bazza had been using methods taught to him by the Aboriginals in Boinga Bob's camp. While it was a fantastic idea to separate the two strangers who were getting on each other's nerves, it meant that Cheese would be left alone at the camp with Rafael. A thought she could not bear, knowing he would be tempted to try something without Bazza there to protect her. She volunteered to accompany the men, despite her distaste for fishing. She had no recollections of fishing that she was aware of, but she had seen and smelled the fish that Bazza brought home from his rare expeditions. That was enough to raise her gall but a far better proposition than being left alone with Rafael.

Rafael had reservations about the idea. While it seemed an ideal opportunity to be rid of Paolo for a short time, he didn't trust the Australian, thought he might be hatching a plan. Paolo had one hand free from splints, so Rafael gave him a spare firearm, with strict instructions to be very watchful of the pair. The first sign of danger he ordered Paolo to shoot the man first. The woman would be easier to control after that.

Paolo was glad for the distraction, yet he worried about being on the water again. He feared the stingers more than anything in his life. He could never again endure pain such as that, no matter what. At least he would have the woman on board to keep him company. He had an infatuation for the older woman that went beyond the Florence Nightingale syndrome. She was the one thing keeping his spirits lifted beyond certain despair. He would have liked the opportunity to be alone with her again in the cave, while she nursed him tenderly once more. His hands and arms were on the mend, with only one hand remaining in a splint. His other had lost only minor mobility after its release from the splint. It was tight and ached, but Paolo no longer felt like a cripple.

"Hey, Poncho, any special requests?"

Rafael quickly fired a shot between Bazza's feet into the sand on the beach. "A bit of respect, Gringo, and make sure you all return."

"Respect is a two-way street, Gomez. My name is, Bazza, not, Gringo. If ya can remember that, maybe I'll start remembering better meself, eh? Do ya want some fish or not? No skin off my nose if we don't go. I can eat baked beans till the cows come home."

"Keep away from our boat with your leetle tin thing, and get out of here while I am in good mood."

"Hafta be back fore two-thirty. Rain will come down again then I reckon."

Rafael looked up at the clear sky with a doubtful expression.

"Half past two; down she'll come; count on it. Feel it in me bones."

Bazza started up the outboard after filling the attached tank with his special brew. Paolo was seated at the bow, with Cheese evening the load on the middle seat, while Bazza remained at the stern, steering the tinny out toward the reef. "Hey, Polio, if we don't get lucky on the reef, we might try the mouth of the Bloomfield River, okay?"

Paolo, not understanding him clearly over the roar of the noisy little outboard, nodded absently. His mind was occupied with a crippling fear of the water. He strained to watch for signs of the deadly stingers that nearly cost him his life. Little did he know that many other dangers awaited him if Bazza was successful. Bazza believed that the wet would end sooner than expected. By his intuitive feel, the group had maybe a month longer, if that. It meant that Bazza's plans needed to be brought forward if he and Cheese were to survive their predicament. One or two spells of clear, sunny days would dry up the slopes enough to attempt an ascent on foot, which Bazza believed Rafael would demand in lieu of the track becoming accessible to vehicular traffic.

Bazza would anchor on the reef for only a short time before feigning bad luck. He knew of several places on the reef where fish were scarce. He wanted to get to the Bloomfield where he had a chance of implementing stage one of his plan. Regardless of Rafael's threats, he had to try to separate this pair of antagonists before Paolo regained his sense of purpose and reaffirmed his loyalties to his travelling companion. His well-being was making a come-back since the removal of the splint on one hand. Bazza saw the exchange between Rafael and Paolo with the weapon being secreted, unsuccessfully, to Paolo's waistband under his shirt. It would take some play-acting on his part to accomplish what he had in mind, and he fervently hoped Cheese would play along if she cottoned on to the deception.

"Fishing's stuffed here I reckon. Must be all the fresh water from the rain. Reckon we better try our luck in the river, eh?" asked Bazza an hour after dropping anchor.

Paolo looked around him at the tranquil waters on the inner edge of the reef. The crystal clear waters revealed nothing evident swimming underneath the boat. Bazza had caught nothing in the time they were anchored, although he was unaware that Bazza surreptitiously removed the bait from his handline's hook before it entered the water. He acceded to Bazza's request without fully understanding the man's thick Australian accent. Paolo's understanding of English was rudimentary at best. Cheese had to translate most of the time when he looked to her for an explanation.

Once he understood the request, he nodded his head with a shrug of indifference. He was glad to be doing something other than sitting around in the gloom beneath the dark canopy of the forest.

Enjoying the hot sunshine on his face, he removed his shirt. His arms showed the angry red welts of his encounter with the notorious Box Jellyfish. The weals were similar to acid burns following the sinewy trails left by the long thin tentacles. Bazza was not sure of the man's wisdom in exposing the fresh wounds to the harsh tropical sun. A sunburn on top of his healing wounds would be very unpleasant to endure, however, it would not compare with what Bazza had in store.

Bazza motored the tinny toward the mouth of the river where he turned inland. Bazza rigged a handline with a lure, which he released slowly behind the stern of the boat, set to an inner tube springer line. The rubber inner tube springer would take the brunt of an attack by a large predatory fish, hopefully, a decent sized Barramundi. He unwrapped a large smelly bait from a hessian bag he had been keeping wet. The leftover carcass of a large Trevally he had caught on another expedition had the appropriate ripeness to suit his purposes.

"Hey, Pablo, got a good job for ya mate. Do ya hand and arm good to get it in the water and have some exercise. Jest want ya ta hold the bait in the water like chum, to attract a nice big fish ta me lure okay? Gotta get down inta the water at the front-o-the boat to make sure the scent goes down onto the lure."

Once Cheese translated, Paolo reluctantly agreed, taking the smelly bait off Bazza with a wrinkled nose. Cheese gave Bazza a look of concern that attracted a very subtle shake of his head. Bazza told Cheese to relate to Paolo, that he had to swish the bait around a bit to activate and spread the smell, along the boat's wake. Paolo seemed oblivious to any secret communications between the pair while enjoying the coolness of the water on his hand, and the wind in his face as he turned forward.

Bazza shot a hand out to calm Cheese when she spied a shape on the muddy banks of the river she recognised. A shape that slithered into the water once the tinny had passed. Several similar sights accompanied their passing as they motored along steadily. Paolo, in the bow of the boat, had closed his eyes in a semi-dream state as he enjoyed the relaxing spray of the water around him while the tinny chopped through the small river swells. Although the rubber springer announced loudly that a fish had accepted the lure, Bazza ignored the signal, keeping a close eye on the riverbanks for a familiar resident, a real denizen of the Daintree.

When the monster finally struck, as Bazza knew it would, it was a destructive force that took all of Bazza's know-how to prevent the small boat from capsizing. It struck, lightning quick for a creature of over a ton and twice the length of the ten-foot dinghy. The mighty reptilian monster seized the arm of the hapless human holding an enticing bait in its immense jaws, smashing together with more power than a hydraulic hoist, crushing bone like brittle twigs. Bazza casually leaned across Cheese to take hold of Paolo's flailing left arm, to oppose the pull from the leviathan engaged in a death-roll with the right arm, being twisted and pulled inexorably away from its socket. Cheese was screaming hysterically while Paolo thrashed about in epileptic-like convulsions of horror and agony, his life-blood gushing away through the gaping cavity in his upper torso where his arm was once attached.

Bazza deftly steered the boat away from the roiling juggernaut only inches below the surface of the water. The giant crocodile, known to locals and tourist operators as the largest of its kind to inhabit the area, is fed regularly by the tourist boats operating during the dry, cooler, winter months. Bazza utilised that knowledge in the hope that he could lure the enormous beast to lunge at Paolo's exposed arm holding the bait. The smell of the rotting fish carcass would have been too tempting for the croc to resist during the leaner wet months when very few tourist boats operated. He had to time it to perfection and ensure the croc did not take the entire body under. He needed a live body, or a corpse to return to Rafael, with Cheese as a witness, to shake suspicion from him.

Whether Paolo survived or not, he was now out of action for the duration, no longer a threat or a hindrance to his plans. Rafael would be pissed off but unlikely to enact retribution without clear knowledge that Bazza had a hand in the 'unfortunate' accident. He would warn Cheese to remain silent about the bait. It would be a good test of Cheese's loyalties to see if she complied with his request. With only one of the enemy to contend with, the odds were gathering in Bazza's favour to survive the ordeal. If Paolo died, almost a certainty, Rafael may move into the shack with them. It would be an inconvenience, but no more.

Bazza directed Cheese into caring for the injured man once the boat was out of danger and she had calmed down. Applying a tourniquet was out of the question, so Bazza used a small butane torch he carried with him to effect minor repairs and maintenance on his tinny, to cauterise the cavity before the man bled to death. He was already too far gone to do more than whimper plaintively despite the intense pain. Having nothing more than the smelly hessian sack to stuff into the hole, Bazza removed his clean shirt to further convince Rafael of his sincerity in helping the man. Cheese used strips of her own borrowed shirt to secure the wadding to the site of the wound, by wrapping it around Paolo's torso and around the neck.

Cheese was visibly shaken, trembling with fear and revulsion. She shied away from Bazza each time he drew near. Bazza allowed her some personal space and time to come to terms with everything. Her decision time was approaching. He would soon know where he stood with her, one way or the other. He pulled in his catch of Barramundi, still hooked to the end of his trolling line. The presence of a decent fish should further demonstrate Bazza's intentions, he thought. Dispatching the fish swiftly by piercing its head with a large knife, Bazza proceeded to fillet the fish deftly on a cutting board that he placed on the centre seat while steering the boat with his hip.

She watched on in dreaded fascination at the cold, calm manner displayed by the man she had once thought to be a mere oaf. That he showed signs of intelligence at times, did not come as a surprise. That he displayed traits of cold-blooded, pre-meditated, acts of callous butchery, left her stunned. If his intentions were to scare her shitless, he had succeeded admirably. If his thoughts were to win her over by way of stealth and treachery, he was much mistaken. The brevity of her memory notwithstanding, she was hard-pressed to recall a more brutal act in fiction or fact. What made it worse, was the calm, collected demeanour of the man as he attended to dressing the fish so nonchalantly.

His final act, before they arrived back at their stretch of beach, left her speechless. Bazza purposely inflicted wounds with a sharp awl, to both his arms, before wrapping them in strips of cloth left over from Cheese's shirt. Bazza made himself appear as though he had been injured by the crocodile while helping the victim, in turn, becoming a victim himself. Cheese wrapped her arms around her bare torso, chilled more by the callous premeditation than from the cooling breeze as clouds blotted out the sun. In stunned silence, she watched as Bazza slid back to the rear of the boat daubing spots of blood across his face and chest while he restarted the boat. Bazza stared at Cheese, defying her to reveal what she knew. With his jaw set firmly, and his eyes revealing depths she didn't know existed, he continued to challenge her silently.

As they neared the shoreline, Rafael was waiting for them. Cheese began yelling before they beached the boat, for Rafael to run and get the first-aid kit. Rafael stalked to the boat with murder in his eyes when he saw Paolo's pale body awash with blood. He began to withdraw the pistol.

"No, Rafael, no. It was not our fault. It was a crocodile. *Un cocodrilo.* You must get the first-aid kit if…"

"Sorry, mate. I tried ta warn him about putting his arm in the water, but he said it soothed the wounds. I, I'm sorry. Nothing I could do."

"Later, Bazza, we need…"

"Nah, Cheese. It's too late. He's gorn."

The three of them stood there witnessing the death of a man as he breathed his last. Loss of blood and the immense traumatic shock had taken its toll on his depleted reserves. Cheese gasped as she realised she was holding a dead man's hand. Repulsed by death, by the deeds she had witnessed, by everything occurring to her tormented brain, she exited the boat and ran from the scene back to the shack. Rafael stood in uncertainty, studying the evidence of the dead man, his obvious injuries, the attempts to administer aid, and finally, the condition of Bazza, who looked worse for wear.

"*Un cocdrilo?*"

"Yeah, big, big, coco…thingo. Crocodile, mate. Massive fucker with jaws this big." Bazza gesticulated with arms out wide.

Rafael watched in silence as Bazza cleaned the boat, removed the body to the top of the beach where he stopped to await orders. Rafael nodded slightly to give Bazza the go ahead to bury the body of his friend. After crossing himself, Rafael retreated to the shack, to allow Bazza to finish. When Rafael re-entered the *Cathedral* he saw Cheese donning a new shirt of Bazza's up in the shack. He admired her curves as she reached high to pull on the cotton T-shirt. Felt his groin agitating at the smallest glimpse of her bare breasts before they were covered once again. He considered the notion of implementing his plans for the woman while the Australian was occupied. Just as he made up his mind, he noticed that the ladder to the shack had been raised.

"Perra de mierda!" he spat as he skulked about the clearing attempting to come to terms with the change in circumstances. Without Paolo's assistance, his situation took a turn for the worse, far worse when he considered the weapon he had given his friend, a weapon that he did not seem to possess upon his return. If the Gringo had secured the weapon, he showed no obvious signs. *The firearm may have fallen overboard in the struggle with 'un cocodrilo'* he considered. His situation was becoming untenable, and he had to make a decision soon regarding his future. Rafael seriously considered leaving Australia and the cursed jungle called the Daintree. Nothing but calamity had occurred since his arrival. He felt his temper rising uncontrollably.

"Señora, eef you do not lower the ladder now, I will shoot your fucking teets off!

"Really, Rafael, there is no need for hostility. I am not at fault for your friend's accident and neither is, Bazza. If your friend had simply heeded, Bazza's warning, he would still be alive," answered Cheese from the veranda.

She lowered the ladder dutifully to allow Rafael to climb into the shack. Once aloft, he back-handed Cheese viciously, causing her to fall to the floor gasping.

"I don truss you. Don truss you or the focking, Gringo. You say anything more, I keel you. Now make somthing to eat!"

Rafael stomped off to the veranda just as the skies opened up at exactly 2:30 pm. Cheese gathered herself from the floor to walk to the kitchen where she began to prepare an omelette with cheese, onions and chilli sauce the way she knew he liked. Her cheek stung where he hit her. It would leave a mark that Bazza was sure to notice. It could mean trouble.

Bazza returned an hour later, dripping wet from the downpour that continued. Long after the rain stopped, the trees would continue to drip as if the rain had never finished. For the time being, the deluge continued, blotting out all other sound. Bazza went straight to his bedroom where he dried off before changing into dry clothes. When he emerged, he noticed the tension in the shack and immediately suspected something. Approaching the kitchen, he saw the mark on Cheese's cheek and eye, which was beginning to swell. He hid the knowledge beneath a couldn't-care-less attitude.

Bazza stepped into the kitchen where he readied himself a late lunch with some cheese he had made from long-life milk. It was not his best attempt at making cheese from the pitiful product but it would do. He assumed that Rafael would take to sleeping in the hut with the advent of his missing partner. The Columbian would not trust Bazza and Cheese to remain obediently within the confines of the area whilst he remained aboard his boat. The dynamics would change and the tension would grow. Bazza knew he had to tread carefully from here on. Witnessing the results of Rafael losing his temper with Cheese meant the runt had become unravelled by the loss of his friend.

The next part of Bazza's plan had to be discussed with Cheese. Her defence of him at the beach confirmed at least, that she was on his side for the time being. He would confide part of his plan to her when he was able to steal a moment with them both away from their captor, probably at night. Her approval was desirable, as her future might depend on the outcome. He did not want to risk getting her offside with presumptuous activities affecting them both. He did not look forward to approaching the delicate scenario with her.

Cheese watched carefully as Bazza stepped around her politely in the kitchen as he prepared his meal. She tried to keep her face averted to dissuade his inspection but knew it was to no avail. Bazza was perhaps the most observant person she had ever met. Nothing escaped his attention. She finished with Rafael's late lunch, serving it to him on a tray out on the veranda, returning to the kitchen bench where she sat to eat her own meal, without chilli sauce. She needed her space after everything that happened. Cheese was still coming to terms with the brutality displayed by a man she thought to be kinder and gentler than the behaviour he exhibited on the river and afterward. She watched as he stood before her eating from a carved wooden platter in the shape of a fish.

"Thank-you, Cheese."

Cheese did not at first understand why Bazza had thanked her loudly enough for Rafael to hear over the din of the rain. She recognised that he was play-acting for Rafael's sake, but could not discern his purpose. She then became aware that he had indicated the glass of cordial she had poured them both automatically. She nodded her head in appreciation, though she gave him a questioning look. When Rafael paid them no attention, Bazza leaned forward conspiratorially…

"I need ta speak ta ya about the next stage of me plan. I think the mongrel is gonna ta stay up here at night now. If ya wanna be safe, and so's we can talk privately, I want ya ta announce that ya will be sleeping in me bed from now on. Don't do it straight away or he'll be suspicious." Bazza noticed the look of concern clouding Cheese's features. "Don't fret mate, I don't got designs on ya or nothing. I'll leave ya more alone than he will if ya sleep out here."

Cheese nodded eventually. She understood there were things to discuss that could not be overheard, and little chance of that happening with Rafael's constant presence in the shack, or around them on the ground during the day. She did not relish sleeping in the sitting area with Rafael sleeping on the opposite settee, with only a coffee table separating them. While she did not look forward to sharing a bed with Bazza, she believed it to be the lesser of two evils. She did not condone Bazza's actions on the river. The taking of someone's life, directly or indirectly, made her nauseous. To think she had a hand in the deception, made her want to curl up in a foetal ball for a week.

Bazza had shown a side of himself she had not foreseen, and neither liked nor appreciated. She believed that other methods of arbitration were possible to reach a compromise with the two strangers. That a solution to all their needs lay in calm discussion using common sense and logic. She did not understand why men had to resort to violence each time they were confronted with difficulties. *No wonder the world was in such a mess with men ruling it for so long.*

She was unable to visualise a female president in her lifetime. Had never remembered seeing a female in the race. She supposed it might be possible someday. *Hell, it may even come to a black man running for the Whitehouse someday?* Distraught by the day's trauma, she yawned loudly, pushing aside her plate of half-eaten eggs. Without saying a word, she vacated her position to walk calmly into Bazza's bedroom where she lay down and closed her eyes.

Bazza was a little surprised by her actions, intending for her to make an audible announcement so that Rafael would not be suspicious. After a moment's reflection, he decided her strategy was sound, of not making a show of something requiring nothing more than blending together to become an 'item' for all intents and purposes. He nodded his head in approval. He busied himself with the dishes, washing away everything fastidiously, including Rafael's plate. After everything was in order, and the rain continuing to fall in sheets, Bazza made his way to the bedroom also, where he gently laid next to Cheese. With every intention of having a discussion with Cheese, he promptly fell asleep.

CHAPTER TEN

Cheese woke before midnight with a hand clamped firmly over her mouth. It took a moment before she saw Bazza motioning to her in the dark to remain quiet. Once he perceived the nod of her head through his hands, he relaxed his grip.

"Sorry, Cheese", he whispered. "I wanted ta make sure ya didn't cry out or nothing. The mongrel is asleep in the sitting room, using ya old bed. I knew he would give up going ta the boat, which gives me the chance I was hoping for. Not tonight, cos that's too soon, but in a coupla night's time, I wanna go scuttle his boat?" Seeing Cheese shake her head, he couldn't be sure if she didn't understand his meaning, or disagreed with his plan. "Sink it, I wanna sink it. I wanted ta check with ya first, cos it might be a while longer before I can get ya outta here without it. If we can't use the roads, the only other way is by boat, and me own boat's too small for that. Whatta ya reckon?"

"It's a bad idea. I think we need the boat as a last resort to get out of here."

"Thought ya might say that. Look, it's gonna stop raining soon, I can feel it. When it dries up enough, he's gonna make us walk outta here, up ta the crash site I reckon. He doesn't care about having ta get a car up there like we do, he jest wants ta get up there ta get some money outta the wreck. After that, we're dog meat if he still has the boat. No way will he let us live once he has the dosh."

"What if you just moved the boat somewhere he can't find it?"

"Take me half the night or more to do that. If he wakes up and I'm not here…" He left the thought hanging. "What about if we grind up some pain killer in his coffee or cordial?"

"If we can do that we might as well tie him up and take over?"

"Yeah, you're right. And he usually watches us like a hawk when we prepare anything for him. I could get away for an hour or two, but no longer. He's pretty bloody canny that bastard. If anything happens ta me, yiz is fair game, Cheese."

"Can't you just clonk him on the head while he's asleep?"

"Cheese, it was bad enough what I done today. I purposely lured a bloke to his death when I knew there was crocs about. I know ya don't think it, Cheese, but I am not a cold-blooded killa. Got that bloke's pistol he had in his trousers, and I got me bow and arras. Coulda done that anytime, mate. It jest, it jest… I can't do that ta another person without me being in the army. Not right. A croc did what had ta be done, but I damn near fainted when it happened. Don't ask me ta kill no one cold, please?"

"You have no idea how relieved I am to hear that Bazza. I feared you'd gone off the reservation this afternoon. I was so scared that you were capable of such a thing, that I was worried what you would do next. So you don't plan to kill him then? What do you plan to do?"

"Best ya don't know it all, mate. That way it'll come as a surprise ta ya as well so's ya won't give it away. Got a coupla ideas in the noggin, depending on what happens. Be nice if we could have the coppers get him somehow. Anyway, scuttle the boat?"

"If you think you have to, Bazza. I'll trust your decision."

"I hafta make it look like it got loose in the night and ran onta the reef. If I take it out ta the reef and sink her, leave a few bits floating about and on the shore, he should get sucked in, unless he wants to dive in and check her out. With the stingers out there, I don't think he'll be such a mug, though. Need the rain as a cover for me to slip out. So whenever it rains next, I'm outta here okay?"

"If he wakes up, we're as good as dead you know?"

"Maybe, but he won't knock us orf till he's got the dosh. Open slather then, though."

Bazza and Cheese lay awake listening to the softening rain, neither able to return to sleep immediately. Cheese snuggled closer to Bazza, laying her head against his chest. Bazza responded by placing a protective arm around her shoulders. They lay like that till the early light woke the pair the next day. Rafael was standing in the doorway with a nasty sneer on his face.

"*Puta!* You sleep with me tonight."

"No. No, I won't. Do what you will, kill me if you like, but I will never sleep with you. If you try to take me forcefully you will have to tie me up thereafter or kill me, because if you don't, I will eventually cut off your cock and balls, if you have any."

"Jeez, remind me ta stay on yiz good side will ya, Cheese?"

Rafael stormed from the room cursing in Spanish all the way to the bottom of the ladder. Two slugs tore through the floor near where Bazza and Cheese lay. Evidently, Rafael was in no mood for being rejected. Bazza and Cheese decided to play it very cool for the rest of that day. Bazza also decided to delay his plans for a while to allow the lunatic to simmer down a tad. They were playing with fire and one false move would see them scorched.

"Bazza, while we are up here out of earshot, I have something I want you to explain. You have mentioned in some sort of vague way that it was wrong for me to be here, meaning my presence as a woman? Last night I more or less invited intimacy from you that you ignored, even spurned? I gather you are not attracted to me? Or is there some other reason? I wanted to know the nitty-gritty of your marriage once, but you seemed very reluctant to discuss it. Is it something to do with that?"

Sighing heavily, he raised himself to a seated position on the side of the bed with his back to Cheese. "I 'spose I hafta talk about it huh?" Bazza asked the question without requiring an answer. "Yeah, it's ta do with me marriage. Ya not hard on the eyes. Seen worse for damn sure. I, I had a bad marriage, mate. Two young people that married for no good reason and it all went ta shit real quick. She turned nasty, real nasty when I caught her having it off with someone."

"Do you mean she was having an affair, Bazza? I don't always follow your Australian idioms."

"Yeah, yeah, having an affair. Having it off with someone means just that. I caught 'em, in our bed, and I was fair-dinkum pissed orf. Felt like killing 'em, Cheese, I really did. Couldn't do it, but I was really angry. Anyway, couple weeks later she set me up like. Staged a scene for a hidden camera without sound. Lured me inta the bedroom to make it up ta me, coming on all sexy like and everything. Had on real skimpy undies and a cammysole, frilly stuff, like I only seen in magazines. I couldn't understand what come over her, Cheese. She was acting all animalistic, grunting and urging me ta be rough. Ordering me ta grab her hair and tear orf her undies. Wanting me to be brutal with her and asking me ta, ya know, take her from behind?"

"Why did you go along? You must have suspected her surely?"

"Well yeah, I didn't trust her an inch, but I was getting carried along, getting pretty bloody worked up by that stage. She had a damn sexy body, and knew how to work it. I was getting beyond self-control, worked up into a right sexual state. I had ta have her then and there like there was no termorra. And no termorra was exactly what I got. When they showed that film in court, I was done like a dinna. I was fucked two ways from Sundy, Cheese, and the jury ate it all up. Her weeping tears and crying marital rape and shit; sexy night gone wrong with me setting up the camera ta get off on. Cost four years of me life, Cheese and I swore off all people, specially women, from the moment I got out."

"How long ago was all that?"

"Got out over ten years ago, never touched a woman, or been close ta one since. I get real nervous in a crowd, specially when women are around. I get so's I can't talk for shit when I'm near a bloody woman, and I don't have any idea what do with one anymore anyways. Sorry if I come across wrong. I like ya more-n-most I reckon, but I can't get close ta no one anymore. I was scared stiff all night jest holding ya. Can't kill anyone either, otherwise, the cops'll have me. Lock me up again for sure, and throw away the key. I can't get inta that kinda trouble again and don't try ta make me, Cheese."

"I was never happier than when you told me you couldn't Bazza. I was worried about the sort of person you were when I saw how you orchestrated everything yesterday. That took some cold-hearted planning. I thought maybe I was wrong in my estimation of you, but what you admitted to me last night told me I was wrong. I don't know what sort of a person I was before the accident Bazza, not a very nice one judging by the way I first treated you. I don't want to return to that person's way of life, whatever it was, and I'm so glad you are not the cold-hearted person I thought you might have been. I am truly sorry for your experiences and promise one thing to you. I will not do or say anything to anyone to get you into trouble with the police."

"Ya wouldn't hafta do much ta get me in trouble. I do wanna try and solve our situation without killing that bastard and getting meself inta more strife. Try ta hurt him a little, see if I can get him ta piss orf maybe; without him hurting us. It'll take the right set-o-circumstances and an awful lotta luck."

A week of sunshine passed quickly, with Rafael showing signs of impatience, scuttling Bazza's plans rather than the Colombian's boat. The track, in constant shadow from the rainforest canopy, remained an impassable bog. Rafael's temper grew with each day he saw Bazza and Cheese sleeping and staying together every spare moment. The intense heat, coupled with the endless boredom made Rafael impossible to deal with. His growing lust for Cheese, extenuated by his inability to have his way with her, saw tensions rising to boiling point. Bazza backed off considerably with his goading behaviour. His taunts had placed him in a position of persona-non-grata *before* he began sharing a bed with Cheese. Afterward, it was a case of one step wrong and all Hell would break loose. Bazza planned carefully for the time when Rafael would force them to take him to the crash site.

In Bazza's mind, he planned out the approximate route they would have to take when taking into account the unusable track. The best option was to follow the creek at the rear of the *Cathedral* as far as possible until the terrain became too overgrown, or blocked by boulders, to pass. The trouble with creek beds was the break in the overhead canopy that allowed prodigious undergrowth along the length of its banks. For the most part, the *easiest* thoroughfare was in the creek itself. Navigating the banks was fraught with hardship and often impossible. Unfortunately, the enormous volcanic boulders, some as large as houses, occupying the creek halfway up the steep slope precluded the possibility of utilising the creek bed farther upstream.

The steepness of the slope made any ascent through the forest a gamble at the best of times. During the wet season, it became the stuff of nightmares. Falling trees were common due to the inordinate amount of growth festooning each and every branch in their upper reaches. Staghorn ferns growing as large as bovines and weighing close to the same, bond to most tree trunks of appropriate size and strength. Combined with a profusion of other fernery, exotic orchids and bromeliads, clinging tenaciously to the branches, collecting moisture in their foliage, made for very top-heavy trees. Landslides, also, were an ever-present concern.

Feral and native animals populated the forests in large numbers, making safety a prime factor. Then there were the pervasive dangers of the pesky flora with which to contend. Bazza believed the best method to reach the top road was by way of a deep ravine, giving maximum height to the trees therein, thereby allowing them their best chance of walking in sections devoid of undergrowth. He did not relish the idea of hacking a pathway through endless miles of fronds, vines, and saplings in the more exposed areas.

Direction was not an enormous problem, as ensuring a constant path upward would see them cut across the top road eventually. Reaching the site of the wreckage, assuming it had not broken either the tree or the connection holding trailer and vehicle together onto the tree, was another problem entirely and not one he was confident to deal with. If the wreckage had disengaged and plunged to the bottom of the ravine on the opposite side of the mountain, he did not believe they had the reserves or could carry enough provisions to ensure their survival, after reaching it. Always providing they were able to do so safely.

They could carry enough food and water with them to last a few days at most considering the hostile terrain. Should the need arise to be fleet of foot, in the case of a rampaging feral pig for instance, then travelling light was essential. Basic first-aid supplies were crucial in dealing with the minor cuts and abrasions the forest was sure to impart. Salt for the leeches, salves for the insect bites, lotions and potions for this that and the other, all necessary for navigating the wilds of Australia's northern climes according to the dictates of Bazza's immense experience.

Rafael prowled the *Cathedral* like a caged animal, growling audibly at the slightest lapse by his captives. He needed to be under way, to get his hands on the money owed him before his unofficial banker sent out a collection team to redeem the funds borrowed. If that happened and he was caught without the funds, the consequences would include the loss of several body parts. Body parts Rafael deemed indispensable to his future way of life, specifically, the body parts between his legs. A finger or two would present a surmountable problem. Losing his manhood and being made to possibly eat them, did not rank high on Rafael's wish list. He made the mistake of informing the *Padrino*, the Godfather, Don Carlos, about his destination, including a detailed map. All of which, Don Carlos had cleverly insisted upon before any funds were released to his trust.

Don Carlos had infinite resources at his disposal. Sending a few henchmen as debt collectors across the ocean in one of his many smuggling vessels would not tax his coffers in the slightest. Rafael knew that his benefactor would simply make arrangements to profit from such an expedition, using the opportunity to wrest away from Rafael his contacts, or ensure a load of contraband found its way into a new country. Whatever the Don did would assume a profitability. The man had a Midas touch for illegal revenue and ill-gotten gains as well as from his legitimate enterprises. His reach extended to all continents and his reputation drew great respect from the ignoble of society. Anyone would be a fool to cross swords with such a man, and to that man, it would seem that Rafael had deliberately done so. To him, it would appear very clear that Rafael had absconded to Australia with his money, where it would be assumed the young man hoped to live out his years in relative luxury while enjoying his spoils. Don Carlos would believe, after the months that passed without word from Rafael, that he had been betrayed by his wife's cousin.

Don Carlos' wife, Lucia, had asked that Rafael be fronted the money for the new venture, thinking it a feather in her cap when her cousin's plan succeeded. Unbeknownst to Rafael, his pretty cousin now resided in the bellies of piranha, and other such inhabitants of the Amazon River. Don Carlos had given every one of his lieutenant's and their minions free access to her, to be used in every way imaginable, when he finally concluded that he had been duped. His wrath was legendary among the locals who had suffered his tyranny for many years. His sadistic acts of reprisal for conceived indiscretions, real or not, became folklore tales with which to frighten the old and young alike. His tales of atrocity exceeded urban myth to become the nightmares of reality.

It is said, and believed, that his unusual walking cane was carved from the thigh bone of an extraordinarily tall man who had the misfortune of crossing the Don during his teenage years. That man wheels about the outskirts of Villavicencio on a plywood board with castors. He has no tongue, no eyes, and no legs. Don Carlos is said to keep several local drunkards in a constant state of inebriation, with standard orders to release their bladders only upon the crippled beggar. Rumour has it that one of those drunkards disobeyed that directive by urinating in his pants while unconscious in a side alley one evening. The drunkard woke several days later bursting to unload his bladder once more, only to discover nine-tenths of his penis had been removed and the opening cauterised and stapled. His arms had bloody, burnt, stumps where his hands had once existed. Incoherent entreaties of assistance from him to the local townsfolk fell on deaf ears. He died a horrible, excruciating, death.

Rafael, recalling well the legends and mistruths surrounding the Don, also knew that the *facts* were far worse than any fiction regarding the man. He knew his days were numbered and that Don Carlos would be drawing up plans to solve the problem of his wife's cousin with meticulous, evil, genius. He had to get to the money before Don Carlos' lieutenants arrived. Marcos and Chico were the left and right hand of Don Carlos for as long as anybody remembered. Without a doubt, they would serve the same position for *El Diablo* at the end of their mortal service to the *Padrino*. Rafael was certain he had only a short time before the Colombian Godfather's henchmen arrived on Australian shores with clear instructions to end Rafael's life in the cruellest way possible, after securing the money owed to him.

No amount of explanation would serve his purposes once they arrived if he did not have the money on hand. Excuses would be ignored, and entreaties for mercy would be met with the cruellest indifference. Rafael seethed with annoyance and impatience born of an ingrained fear. Not only would he suffer the fate of the damned, his entire family would be treated to the same. His friends and friends of friends would also be given the opportunity to taste the wrath of a demon. He had gone onto the track several times to gauge its use in accommodating a vehicle but saw no signs of traction evident. Rafael was in a fevered panic, desperate to escape the fate Don Carlos had in store.

Everything had fallen apart from the moment he and his companions arrived. First; they landed on the wrong part of the coastline thanks to faulty navigation equipment, intending to make landfall a few kilometres to the north. Then, they were unable to find a way through the reef until high tide, around noon that day. He sent his two companions with the inflatable dinghy to make their way along the beach to their intended landing site, or until they made contact with their buyer, Armstrong. Instead, the fools decided to go swimming, which cost one of them his life and the other, a painful reminder of their stupidity until he too perished. Rafael had heard the pitiful screams from where he was anchored. Through powerful binoculars, he witnessed their demise at the hands of the big man who would not enter the water to help them. He swore he would get his revenge on the coward at the first opportunity. He did not fully understand what occurred but knew the cowardice of the man was responsible for their pain and suffering, a debt he would return with interest. Then the cursed rains changed everything.

If they had been able to go directly to the top road to find the Armstrong property, Paolo would not have gone on the fatal fishing trip. The rain made any movement by foot or vehicle either too dangerous or impossible. That was until the rain stopped over a week ago. Rafael knew that vehicular access might still be problematic, while a trek on foot might be possible. He ordered Bazza and Cheese to join him.

"De rain has stopped, no?" he asked Bazza.

"Maybe; for now. I think it will rain again before the wet season is finally over, but how much rain we get and when…?"

"I theenk maybe ju lie to me. I theenk de rain is *terminado, si*? Tomorrow; we go. No funny business, no tricks. If ju make problem; I make beeger problem for ju!

CHAPTER ELEVEN

"What exactly are you going to do, Bazza?" asked Cheese as they lay in bed the following morning before first light crept in.

Forest sounds of the Daintree were abating gradually from their nightly orchestrations. Between the frogs and the crickets playing their mating tunes at decibels close to human intolerance levels, Bazza and Cheese found very little time to engage in nightly discourse without waking Rafael. Bazza considered the question thoughtfully.

"I have a coupla options depending on how we go and what I might see. Nothing concrete and I wouldn't want ta give ya too much of a head's up in case ya gave it away. Dunno about ya acting skills yet. This bugger's not a total idiot, so I gotta play it safe."

"Very well. I suppose I deserve that."

"Nothing ta do with ya, mate. Dunno enough meself yet."

"Promise me you won't take too many risks? I wouldn't like to see you hurt or worse, and I don't like my chances if you are out of commission."

"Not ta worry, she be Jake, mate."

"What?"

"Means, it'll be orright."

With daylight trickling through the canopy, the trio saw to the business of packing for their trek. Bazza estimated that they would require a minimum of two days to reach the road, another day, taking their time, to reach the wreck site down the other side, and another two-day return journey. They had to ensure enough food and spare clothes for at least five to six days, and enough first-aid items to deal with most eventualities barring major emergencies. Bazza made sure to supply himself and Cheese with full cover clothing, and thick socks to combat most of the insects and plant life. He gave Rafael and Cheese a machete each for when they may have to hack through dense patches. Rafael quickly took hold of those sharp instruments, saying he would pass them out only if they became necessary. Bazza just shrugged. If the fool wanted to add the extra weight to his backpack, that was his business.

Bazza fashioned a pair of jungle boots for Cheese out of tough canvas sports shoes with the toes stuffed full of rags to take up the room unoccupied by her small feet. A pair of makeshift gaiters running up her calves with her long trousers tucked in, to guard against leeches and ants getting under the trouser legs. Bazza had a pair of army surplus jungle lace-up boots that reached his mid-calf. Another pair he offered Rafael, only to have them thrown back in his face. Rafael would brook no argument to the way he dressed in jeans and t-shirt. Bazza and Cheese just shrugged when they heard his derogatory comments at their style of dress.

After a hearty breakfast, the trio made their way out of the clearing in the direction of the creek at the foot of the mountain. The sweat had already gathered in their underarms after the short walk. Rafael seemed to smirk at the other pair who were showing signs of struggling with the heat, while he was comfortable in his T-shirt. When they reached the creek, Bazza and Cheese took a moment to splash water over their heads and soak their long-sleeve workwear shirts. Bazza then led the troop along the creek bed upstream. The breezes flowing down the mountain on the cool waters of the creek acted like natural air-conditioning, cooling them down for the next stage of their journey.

Bazza became serious in his vigilance the moment they were clear of his normal stomping grounds. Checking every path that ended at the creek bank, investigating the various tracks and obvious animal paths to gauge the frequency of their use. Rafael fumed each time Bazza ordered them to remain in the creek bed while he investigated what seemed to be nothing. The day heated up considerably, demonstrating true tropical forest heat and humidity at its worst. Water intake was vital for hydration in the moisture-sucking atmosphere, as was the upkeep of precious salts leaking out through sweat. Rafael was soon soaked in his clinging cotton t-shirt, while Bazza and Cheese remained relatively sweat free with singlets absorbing the moisture and vents in their shirts catching the slightest breezes to cool their bodies.

When they had been walking for over three hours, the last hour overland due to inaccessible reaches of the creek, Bazza called a halt, to rest and eat by the creek side once they had returned. Passing out canteens and rations, he noticed Rafael removing his Cuban-heeled cowboy boots and socks to place his feet in the stream. When he saw Cheese about to do the same, he surreptitiously shook his head when he was sure she was paying attention, to warn her against it. Understanding the signal, but not the reason, she acquiesced with a questioning look. Both he and Cheese sat on a boulder at the side to eat their lunch, while Rafael oohed and ahhed at the luxury of cooling his feet. It was one of those rare moments in a rain forest when not a sound could be heard except the gentle susurration of the water cascading over the rocks, until they heard a yelp from Rafael who finally discovered the reason the other two had not opted to remove their footwear; leeches! He snatched at the things with disgust and horror marring his features.

Bazza watched on with hidden amusement as the Colombian struggled to rip the slimy leeches from his feet and ankles. Little did he know that ripping them free was possibly the worst method of removal. Leeches have in their systems a natural anti-coagulant that allows the blood to flow freely from their victims into their mouths. When they attach themselves and bite into the flesh, they employ a mild anaesthetic that allows them to pierce the flesh without the host's knowledge, they then inject the anti-coagulant to get as much blood as quickly as possible into their bodies before they drop off by themselves, fully engorged. However, if they are ripped off prematurely, the anti-coagulant remains in the host, causing excessive bleeding. Bazza found the best way of removing the leeches was simply to apply salt liberally over their bodies which they absorb immediately bringing about their immediate release and demise.

Bazza knew that Rafael would end up continuing to bleed for a time afterward, and possibly even miss a few leeches further up his leg, beneath his jeans. The incident would not cause serious harm but may slow him enough to make more errors in judgement. Bazza needed Rafael to succumb to his own arrogance, to lure him into a potentially hazardous mistake. A few leeches causing blood-soaked socks and boots was a good start. Cheese sighed with relief when she saw Rafael struggle with the loathsome creatures. She was very pleased that Bazza had stopped her from making the same mistake. Even so, she checked herself thoroughly before moving off.

A half hour later saw Bazza standing still in the middle of the creek with a raised hand to motion his followers to a silent stop. They watched as Bazza cocked his head from side to side to judge the distance and direction of whatever caught his attention. Cheese strained her ears to catch the sound, hearing nothing but the creek. Bazza stood still for nearly five minutes while Rafael grew ever-more impatient. Finally, he could take it no longer and simply stormed past Bazza to take point. After walking for a short time, Rafael turned to find his troop remaining behind. He was about to bark a command when he heard a faint rustling in the leaves ahead of him. With a loud squeal from the mother sow, the farrow of pigs burst through the foliage by the creek to demonstrate their discontent at the human trespassers.

When Rafael turned to run backward, he hobbled unsteadily through the stony creek back to where Bazza and Cheese had climbed onto large boulders a little way off. He joined them quickly, narrowly missing being gored by the tusks of the boar leading his family. The family of pigs, including many youngsters, was raising all Hell trying to reach the trio stranded on the rock. Feral pigs, of plague numbers in North Queensland, were ferociously protective of each other and their territories, eating almost anything, killing livestock and plundering crops with wanton destruction.

"You heard them didn't you?" asked Cheese as she observed Bazza casually sitting down upon their rock to wait out the milling pigs.

"Nah, smelled 'em. Stinky bastards they are. Smell 'em a mile orf if they're upwind. Didn't know which way they were heading but I saw a slight path off ta the side there, which is where I figured they would come from. They probably would've if they hadn't seen bug-a-lugs there, tromping away up the creek like a typical tourist."

"Why ju no tell me about de pigs, *Gringo*?"

"Look, Gomez. You wanna survive in this forest ya gotta do what I do and say, and fuck-all else, got it? Do what I do! If ya wanna do ya own thing, then don't blame me if ya get hurt. Now, empty ya boots, put some new socks on, and let's go."

"Empty boot? Water?"

"No, blood, Sanchez, blood."

When Rafael removed his boots to reveal his blood-soaked socks, he nearly fainted. Even Bazza was surprised at the amount of blood he poured from his boots, albeit diluted by creek water. Cheese turned her head away to avoid retching at the sight. Rafael eschewed his boots for more practical Nike runners and new thick socks. Bazza applied plasters to the wounds, finding two more leeches higher up the calf, which he removed using the salt method. Rafael scowled at Bazza in a manner that left little doubt as to its meaning. Bazza knew he had to rein in his behaviour, knew he could have done much more to warn the ignorant bastard about everything. He had to play the game very carefully, never fully giving Rafael the opportunity to see how he was being manipulated. By the same token, he needed Rafael's obedience to a certain degree in order to manoeuvre him into an act that would free Cheese and himself of the evil bastard's menacing presence.

"Ju are trying to keel me no?"

Cheese and Bazza froze when they registered the statement. Bazza knew Rafael was no idiot, but he didn't think he would have it all figured so quickly. Bazza reached into his waistband beneath his shirt to remove the weapon Rafael had given Paolo before their fishing trip. He casually handed it to Rafael butt first.

"Coulda done that any time I reckon. I don't kill people mate. I'm just a woodcarver who wants ta go back ta living his life in peace and quiet. Sooner I get ya ta that wreck up there, sooner ya can leave. If ya don't believe me, shoot me now and get it over with. Good luck with surviving on ya own and getting ya boat past the reef,

Gonzalez."

Rafael wondered what had happened to the gun he gave his friend. He assumed it had been lost overboard when the *cocodrilo* had attacked. That the Australian had it all the time and did not use it, told him much about the Gringo coward. He would see to the *cobarde* soon enough. What the Gringo said about the reef reminded him to leave him alive until they returned. He would have to suffer the *pinchazo* until that time. His original plan to kill him on top of the mountain was not a good one. Rafael did not want to end up trapped on the inland side of the reef waiting for Don Carlos' men to catch him. The thought of what awaited him if he should fail to deliver payment to the *Padrino* threw him into a chilled sweat.

Eventually, the pigs grew disinterested in the hapless trio perched out of reach, and continued downhill along the semi-concealed trail. Bazza was the first to dismount the volcanic boulder that afforded them safety. He knew full well the damage a mature boar could inflict upon fragile humans. He had seen one of Boinga Bob's grandsons mauled pitifully by a beast half the size of the one they faced moments ago. The local Aboriginals considered it a rite of passage amongst their tribe's youth to kill a feral pig using only traditional weapons. Unfortunately, there was no backup of modern firepower once the hunt went awry, rendering the unlucky victim of one such hunt, permanently disabled.

Once the group assembled their scattered belongings shaken free during their escape, they continued along the shallow creek bed. Rafael relinquishing the lead to the experienced bushman. They were silent for more than an hour of slow trekking into the deep ravine. The creek they were following climbed steeply at the bottom of the ravine, with several small waterfalls along its course. Very soon they would be forced to leave the relatively open space of the creek to bypass farther, unscaleable waterfalls. Once they entered the gloom at the bottom of the ravine, Bazza paused to take in the magnificence of the ethereal realm into which they entered. Towering Foxtail Palms and rainforest hardwoods competed with one another for supremacy to capture the most sunlight far above their heads. In the lofty canopy blocking nearly all the direct sun, they observed birds flying about freely, feeding on the fruits and seeds available only in the upper reaches.

"No wonder the ancients worshipped trees. I'd sooner worship this magnificent display-o-nature than some fairy tale invented by people ta control the populace of the time", whispered Bazza in a state of awe.

"Rather deep thinking there, Bazza?" said Cheese.

"Dunno about that. Listen, there's a clearing a little way uphill where we should stop for the night. We'll camp in the middle of a bunch-o-palms, which I will surround with some Wait-a-while vines to keep us safe from pests during the night, sorta like a corral of thornbush like they do in Africa."

"Why we no go longer?"

"Ya got eyes that can see in the dark, Esteban? The moment the sun goes down behind this big mountain here, it's gonna get dark quicker-n-shit down a dunny pipe. Ya wanna keep going? See ya." Bazza gave Rafael an infuriating little wave.

Cheese ignored the exchange to start walking to the clearing she imagined she saw up the slope and to the left. No sooner had she taken a dozen steps, when she found herself completely disorientated. Looking behind her revealed no other person. Looking every which way told her nothing about where the two men had vanished to. In a near panic, she walked back in the direction she believed she had travelled, only to be stopped short by Bazza's voice above and to the right of her position.

"Watch yaself, Cheese, easy ta get turned around and lost in here. One tree looks like another and only up and down ta go by when the sun's gorn. Send a bloke mad in here if he don't know shit from clay."

Cheese was floored by the possibility of getting lost in only a few seconds. Bazza was right; one gigantic tree looked exactly like another with no hope of knowing directions other than up and down the slope. Yet, she did not understand the slope's directions either.

They were in a deep-sided ravine which meant that up, on three sides, could mean almost any direction. Once they left the creek, it was almost impossible to determine their course to her mind. Cheese quickly moved to join the two men moving slowly against the steep sides of the ravine. Bazza halted when he found the group of palms he was searching for. The vines remained in place from the last time he sought shelter there. It required only one or more strands to reinforce the clearing to make it safe.

Safe, was actually a euphemism. They were not technically safe at all. The temporary enclosure gave them more of a notion of safety than actual protection should wildlife investigate in earnest. At the most, it would be a slight deterrent for a mildly curious piglet. It would have no effect on slithering snakes, creeping spiders, rampaging boars or a miffed cassowary. To keep them off the ground, Bazza slung makeshift hammocks between the trees to accommodate their light-weight sleeping bags. Nails were driven into the tree trunks where branches were not available. Night descended with its customary abruptness in the middle of a rainforest on the eastern slopes of a large mountain.

Even when their eyes became accustomed to the darkness, seeing a hand in front of your face was next to impossible when true nightfall descended. Bazza strung up a night light to bathe them all in its insect repelling, dull, yellow ambiance. He had once made the mistake of using a normal low wattage clear bulb in his night light. When it attracted every insect and predator within a mile radius, descending on his forlorn shape within his hammock in plague numbers, he learned his lesson. The rechargeable, battery-operated light, emitted only a glimmer with which to make out the immediate surroundings, to belay disorientation when waking during the night. Bazza advised the others to have a bite to eat and attend to their nightly ablutions before creeping into their sleeping bags. He showed them how to zip themselves in using the netting around their heads to prevent most intrusions.

Cheese immediately felt a primordial fear disturbing her mindset that refused to budge despite her bravest attempts. Rafael muttered to himself as he relieved his bladder loudly onto a tree within their enclosure.

"Thanks for that, Hernandez. Nothing like the smell of piss all night ta make ya feel right at home. Wanna shit in me hammock as well?"

"Shut your focking mouth, *Gringo*, before I shut it for you."

"Charming! Remind me ta introduce ya ta me mum one day."

"If you don shut up, I keel your *madre* too."

"I wonder if you can both please shut up so a girl can get some sleep around here. I imagine we are in for a tough hike tomorrow and I need some rest."

The night exploded with sound as though on a timer. Insects, frogs, and other animals heralding the nightly mating rituals, the intensity of which can leave a person stunned. All hope of sleep in the mêlée seemed impossible, yet all fell asleep within moments. For Cheese, wrapping herself tightly in the sleeping blanket, like a butterfly chrysalis, instigated the false child-like notion that what she couldn't see, couldn't hurt her.

Two hours later when the night sounds had abated, thunder broke in the distance. Bazza recognised the sound immediately through his light sleep. He quickly removed two waterproof ponchos from his backpack, covering Cheese and himself. He only had the two and knew the Colombian would be royally pissed off when the rain started. Bazza hoped the storm would bypass their immediate area, but knew better. Within the hour the rain started far above in the canopy. The rainwater slowly filtered through the dense cover of leaves to reproduce the rainfall beneath. The air grew cool with breezes managing to find their way into the forest. Bazza remained alert for any irregular sounds that heralded danger. Creaking boughs and trees rubbing against one another within the ravine accompanied the splattering noise of the heavy raindrops falling from the tree-tops.

He noted furtive rustling sounds within the leaf litter a few yards off. He assumed it was either a brush turkey or a Cassowary, foraging for food. A Cassowary could be a worry if it had chicks, but only if the humans emerged from their cocoons. Bazza drifted off with his senses on full alert. Rafael cursed silently at the realisation that rain was falling yet again. Worse than the misery it brought, was the fact that the rain may prevent them reaching the top road. If he found that was the case he would make the other two pay for his frustration in the morning. His balls were way overdue for release, and he had run out of all patience for the big sack of shit constantly goading and tricking him. He looked forward to exacting his revenge on the idiot. The fool hadn't the sense to bring along wet-weather gear. Rafael would teach him a few lessons about preparation.

Sleep overcame them when the rain departed. The night turned silent, with only the breeze whispering through the leaves far above them. The air filled with the musty, dank, aromas of rotting vegetation accompanying the recent rainfall. Nocturnal insects, reptiles, and mammals went about their nightly tasks in complete harmony with the forest. Bazza smiled contentedly within his drowsing slumber, secure in the familiar environment. Flying foxes winged silently through the forest in search of edible fruits supplied in abundance by nature, to have their seeds distributed throughout the forest in the guano.

The rainforest around them woke before sunlight began to penetrate the canopy. Creatures of all varieties could be heard either creeping away to sleep off the daylight hours or emerge from their dens to forage. Bazza watched as a very large Carpet Snake slithered through their enclosure on its way to a morning meal of rodents or frogs. He marvelled at the dizzying arrays of scaly patterns repeating themselves along its fifteen-foot length, mesmerised by its smooth passage and silence in the leaf litter beneath them. Not long after, he caught sight, the briefest glimpse, of a Trapdoor Spider, exploding from its hole to snare a passing insect that tripped one of its silken alarm strands. To Bazza's practised eye, he managed to see the creature clearly, where most would not have noticed a thing. Bazza idly wondered if the spider could come into play, being situated directly beneath the Colombian's hammock. He dismissed the thought just as quickly, knowing that a Trapdoor seldom emerged for anything as large as a mammal or human. It would be a very unlucky person to get bitten by a Trapdoor Spider.

He ruminated on all the possible outcomes of their escapade. A truly hard climb awaited them. Made more arduous by the recent rains. The steepness of the slope ahead once they left the relative ease of ascending along the stream, played heavily on his mind. They had to make the top road by nightfall, as there was nowhere to set up another camp on the imminent slopes. They had no choice but to reach their destination by that time. Bazza wondered if the Colombian would be in a foul mood once he discovered that he and Cheese endured the rain in relative comfort under their ponchos.

Bazza knew that he was testing the tenuous limits as far as the Colombian was concerned. He felt the changes in the man's moods like he felt changes in weather. His mood barometer clearly indicated a frozen change in the wiry man. While the forest awoke languidly in the dim light, Bazza eased himself from his hammock as quietly as the snake he had witnessed. Still fully clothed and dry, he donned his backpack and slipped through the enclosure of vines with their vicious thorns. He made his way quietly from the camp, returning to the creek, now running rapidly once more from the night rain.

Moving as swiftly as possible on the slippery, moss-covered boulders strewn through the creek bed, Bazza made his way up the steep slope to a point where the creek could no longer be followed. It was as far as Bazza had ever ventured along the deep ravine. A waterfall, the first of many, presented an impassable obstacle. The water ran through a volcanic shelf with a hole in its centre, eroded over the millennia. Underneath the shelf, a shallow cave offered shelter and safety for a traveller. Inside the cave, glow worms lit up the ceiling like a starry night. Bazza inspected the cave to make sure it remained exactly as he had discovered it years before. If the chance came that he and Cheese could escape from the Colombian, they may make use of the concealment. The sound of the water gushing through the hole in the ceiling into the deep clear pool below obscured all other sounds.

After his satisfactory inspection of the cave, Bazza made his way back along the creek for a time, then up the left-hand side of the steep ravine by way of a grappling hook cast ahead to latch onto the high buttressed roots of the forest trees. Rainforest soil is nutrient deficient at depth. Trees have adapted to the conditions by producing a high buttressed root systems, over fifteen feet high in many cases, spread over a large surface area to gather the most nutrients possible in the surface layers. Those roots, branching out in all directions from the massive tree trunks, allowed Bazza to gain purchase with his grappling hook when the root ran parallel to the slope. Once he clambered to one tree, he would make for the next and so on.

After an hour of searching for a possible route to the top road with suitable rest stops between, Bazza made his way back to camp as quickly as possible. The heat and humidity of a tropical summer's day was building by the time he returned, drenched in sweat from his physical exertions. He stood a little ways off the camp to change into dry clothing. Cheese observed surreptitiously from within the folds of her hammock, as Bazza stripped off his army surplus fatigues. She was amazed at the pronounced musculature of his torso and thick arms. She gazed with unashamed interest at his surprisingly hairless buttocks, when considering his hirsute features above. Bazza represented the largest man she had ever seen naked or otherwise in her limited recollections. Rafael was almost feminine in comparison to the burly Australian.

Cheese felt a warmth pervading her senses, an inner glow and a radiant heat emanating from her womanhood. Her heart gave a flutter when Bazza turned toward her revealing a continuation to his large proportions from the front. While his hairlessness extended to his chest, his pubic region was a mass of black curls with a smattering of the ubiquitous grey ones, visible even at a distance. Only once he was fully dressed, did Cheese show signs of waking from her cocoon. Bazza approached the enclosure, carefully removing the obstructing vines to allow her a free passage from within. Rafael began to stir uncomfortably. Bazza prepared a little fire from whatever dry wood he was able to salvage to make a brew, while they had a breakfast of canned spam and homemade pickle sandwiches. The bread Bazza had made in his camp oven was getting a little stale, but sufficed. Bazza brewed the coffee in the typical rough bushman fashion by placing the grounds directly into the billy of boiling water. A simple sieve placed above their mugs would filter most of the coarse grounds when the strong liquid was poured through.

Bazza watched with silent satisfaction as the Colombian struggled to extricate himself from the wet sleeping bag, to stand before the weak fire in an attempt to get dry.

"Ya better take ya clobber orf mate. Get all kindsa rashes in this stink if ya don't have dry clobber, specially on ya feet."

"I don't have no spare. You give me spare?"

"Nup, me only other set is as wet as yours from sweat."

"Why from sweat? Thinking of escape?"

"I coulda escaped anytime I wanted ta, Santiago. Nah, I had to scout ahead to find a way up the bloody mountainside, and it's hard yakka from here on I gotta tell ya. May as well keep ya wet clobber on actually, gonna get wet soon anyway I 'spose. *I*, wouldn't though."

Cheese regarded the interplay with only mild interest as she sat down to enjoy her coffee and breakfast. Rafael decided to follow Bazza's advice, by stripping down to his leopard print jocks, which brought a smile of derision to Bazza's lips.

"Better orf without undies in here, Rodrigo. Ya'll get a terrible groin rash if ya wear 'em. Rubs like buggery. Better ta air ya sausage and sprouts if ya don't want jungle rot."

Rafael looked about uncomfortably in the presence of a woman and a strange man. He finally conceded to the sensible advice he had been given to strip himself entirely while holding a hand tentatively to his groin to cover himself. He was clearly embarrassed to be undressed, exposing his surprisingly fair skin. In contrast, Bazza had the bronzed appearance of an Adonis. He grew annoyed when he heard Bazza chuckling.

"Som thing fonny caveman?"

"Bloody little akchally."

Cheese coughed as she swallowed a sip of coffee at the wrong moment, sending waves of tension through the little man. He sensed he was being made a fool of and had difficulty finding an appropriate response whilst naked. Steam rose from his wet clothes hung up on twigs poking from the moist soil next to the fire. Bazza attended to packing up the temporary camp while the Colombian stewed in silence. He smiled a huge smile as he passed Cheese, which almost set her off laughing. She had to fight to restrain her mirth.

After an hour, Rafael's clothes were nowhere near dry but would have to suffice, and the camp was packed back into the respective backpacks. Bazza made sure the fire was fully out by dousing it with two canteens of water before burying the remains in damp forest soil created from decades of rotting vegetation.

"We'll go back ta the creek where we'll fill our canteens again. From there, we go up ta jest before the waterfall, then orf up the side. Gets bloody tough from there, so keep ya water up ta yiz. Don't go dehydrating or nothing. Salt tablets in ya kit. Have one with every second drink. Don't have no fancy-shmantzy energy drinks here, so watch yaselves."

They marched off in single file with Rafael bringing up the rear, grumbling about everything he had to endure. He regretted every moment after he had approached his cousin to get Don Carlos on board for a loan to finance the crazy venture. He would have been far better off if he had just asked his cousin to get him into Don Carlos' cadre, the inner circle of trusted employees. He questioned his stupidity, his need to be rich quickly. He was a condemned man the moment the loan repayment had become overdue - over a month ago. He was a walking dead man. His plan to retrieve the money with which to fulfil his debt to the *Padrino* was fatally flawed. His best chance was to secure the money and then flee. Cover his tracks and go somewhere he could not be found. He knew he could never return to his beloved Colombia, to his family. His mother would suffer the most; for far too long if he knew Don Carlos. His family was as good as dead, or wishing they were.

Trudging up the swollen creek proved strenuous. Worse by far were the boggy, steep banks on either side where they would have to battle the undergrowth. Bazza kept them going for an hour before calling a rest stop some way before the waterfall and cave. He wanted to keep the Colombian from seeing the cave in the event he and Cheese needed to take refuge there after staging the 'accident' he had planned. In a small clearing he spied earlier, he walked his followers to the rest area. From a thermos of coffee he had prepared from the morning brew, he poured three small cups and handed out packed sandwiches of pickled pork. Pickling his kills of feral pigs proved to be a very efficient way of keeping meat far longer than by other methods.

Rafael slumped to the ground in a heap, exhausted by the morning's exertions, spent from the worry and turmoil of his panicked mind. He would love nothing more than to kill the two aggravating nuisances and be on his way to another country, but knew he needed money to achieve that goal, knew he needed the Gringo to get him to the loot. The bitch, the *puta*, he needed only for entertainment purposes once the Gringo was out of the way. He would enjoy the activity with the older lady. He would enjoy her pain as he used her in ways a lady would not consider normal. His lust for her grew with every moment along the trail as he watched her ample behind jouncing before him. He pictured her naked body beneath and above him so clearly that he found it hard to contain his anatomical reactions.

Cheese felt the tension in the air between them thicken to near palpability. She observed carefully the interplay between Bazza and Rafael, the looks directed her way from Rafael whenever she turned to peer backward on the trek. She knew she would not be safe without Bazza. She felt the heat and humidity in the cloying atmosphere sucking the moisture from her body, sapping her of vital minerals and salts, depleting her reserves. She wondered where the journey would end and how many would finish. She was not scared, so much as exhausted and confused. Parts of her former life drifted in and out of reach as she walked. Nothing forming a static picture, nothing concrete. Just vague perceptions and odd feelings randomly creeping into her consciousness.

Bazza observed the Colombian with increasing interest. He perceived the little man to be close to a minor breaking point. How the runt reacted once he breached that point was anyone's guess. Bazza assumed it would not bode well for him and Cheese. If it came to a one on one with the wiry man, Bazza had no illusions that he would fare the better of the two. The weapons the man carried made all the difference, and Bazza had no wish to tackle an armed opponent. He swirled all the possibilities about in his mind like a barman mixing a cocktail. One possibility kept rising to the surface of the heady mixture. Before he could commit to the scheme, he weighed all the pros and cons he could think of as he quietly sipped his coffee.

He sorely missed a nip or two or ten, of his hooch. He had not partaken the entire time he had been at the mercy of the Colombian. He imagined that the bastard would be very hard to control if Bazza had revealed his 'cellar' of hooch. It was not safe to introduce alcohol as potent as his mix to the cauldron of volatile personalities. Bazza shrugged as he thought about the relaxing time he might be enjoying were he alone once more.

"You been this way this morning?" asked Rafael

"Yep. Had ta scout a way for us ta continue. Saves time if I do it meself."

"Where we go now?"

"Well, we got our work cut out for us now. We gotta go uphill that way", said Bazza pointing roughly south-west. "Ran a rope out already from one point to another as far as I could go ta save some time. I know there is a bit of level ground about an hour away. Saw it from the top once. We should be able ta travel along that for a while. If I'm right, I reckon that level trail will zig-zag upwards at a much gentler gradient, all the way ta the top. Get us there be afternoon I reckon. If ya don't slip orf that is. If ya do; ya fucked."

"You would like that very much no? For, Rafael to be…fucked?"

"No hiding the pleasure for me there, eh? Yeah, it would solve a few problems for us if ya went for a little trip down the mountainside, so watch ya step. If ya thinking I might be tempted ta give ya a little nudge to help ya on ya way, think again, Manuel. I'm not the killing kind like yiz are, which I proved by helping ya mates."

"One; perhaps. *Not* both. Ju did nothing but wait on the shore while my friends were in trouble."

"That how ya saw it happening, huh? Seen those welts on ya mate? If I went out, I woulda copped that meself. Woulda done them two no good if that happened. Both woulda died and me as well possibly. Stopped Cheese from going in, otherwise she'da been cactus making it four down. Nuh, say what ya want, we did the right thing in that circumstance. All the life-saving manuals I read say the same thing. Check 'em out yaself if ya don't believe me. Got plenty of 'em back at the shack. Had ta learn a lotta that shit when I set up on me own."

"I weel read your books when we return. If not as you say…"

"Yeah, yeah, yeah. I die. I get it, Pepe. Getting real old that threatening shit. Might goad me inta giving ya that nudge after all if ya don't shut up with all that crap. Time ta get moving. Ya want that money ya keep talking about, or ya wanna have it out now between us?"

Bazza did not wait for an answer as he rose to his full height, towering over the little man. Before Rafael could say anything, Bazza stalked off to show Cheese how to use the guide rope to proceed up the steep slope. Bazza paid no attention what-so-ever to the seething Rafael, struggling to his feet behind him. Bazza knew he had lit a fuse, but refused to kowtow to the little worm. Death was not the worst thing that could befall a man, only final, so Bazza went about his business casually ignoring the runt.

The threesome set off using the rope Bazza had secured between the trees earlier, rising up the near vertical slope of the ravine. Progress was very slow with many rest breaks to massage sore hands and to catch their breath. The time ebbed slowly by as the heat of the day rose to exhausting temperatures. Not a breath of wind existed in the natural sauna, not a sign of a break in either the canopy overhead or the monotonous terrain. Once they reached the end of Bazza's rope, the going slowed up considerably as they waited for Bazza to grapple the next tree. The steepness of the slope was merciless on their legs, straining to keep them standing almost parallel to the gradient.

Tree after tree they tackled, making use of the enormous buttressed roots over which to throw the grappling hook, and then hauling themselves up the rope until they reached the tree. There, they would have to either walk around the high roots or scale them in order to access the next tree. Sweat escaped every pore, leaving them soaked and reeking of sour body odour. Cheese groaned loudly as she heaved her abused body up and over the roots, unable to control the quivering muscles in her legs.

Just as they were nearing a point of complete exhaustion, unable to proceed, Bazza announced the last travail before they would reach the relative convenience of the quasi-trail. Once upon the semi-flat surface of the trail leading to their right, they all collapsed in a breathless heap. In the far distance along the trail, Bazza observed a break in the forest gloom, possibly caused by the advent of a fallen tree. Depending on the length of time the tree had been on the forest floor, would determine its usefulness to Bazza. He hoped the tree had fallen a year or more ago. It would not take long for the undergrowth to start sprouting new growth in search of its share of sunshine, competing with other flora in the ever-present urgency for dominance before the canopy closed off once again.

None of the other small clearings Bazza had spied along their path had yielded the right conditions to set his plan in motion. He feared he was running out of time and options. Within a few hours, they were poised to reach the top road. Bazza did not like their chance of survival much past the point where the Colombian believed his captives were no longer of any use. He knew his survival depended on his ability to delay the discovery of the wreck site as long as possible. If the Colombian was unaware of their proximity to the road, Bazza may be able to string him along for a time in the hope of finding a suitable location for his plan.

Rafael grew excited at the possibility that they may be reaching the top road soon. He could not be rid of the Australian soon enough. He knew he risked his boat trying to navigate the reef himself, but could stand the man no longer. Each moment he spent with the oaf ate away at Rafael's resolve. He couldn't bear it, and his need for sex outweighed his good judgement. Until his muscles regained strength from their leaden state, however, he could do nothing. He swore inwardly as his impatience demanded action over prudence. He sighed in frustration as he lay upon the path winded and wounded from exhaustion.

Bazza quenched his thirst with a mouthful of water from his canteen. He used the precious liquid sparingly, knowing a refill was out of the question until they returned to the creek several days later. He rightly assumed that the stupid Colombian would not be so wise with his water rations. He had schooled Cheese quietly in the need to preserve her water. She would follow his instructions dutifully, having experienced Bazza's bush-sense first hand on many occasions. Bazza eyed the path they would take with relief, knowing that they would not have to expend as much energy on the remainder of their trek. Although still an acute incline, it was nowhere near as steep or dangerous as the preceding climb.

Bazza steeled himself for the necessary danger about to befall them if his plans failed, or indeed, even if they succeeded. What he admitted to Cheese held true. He was not a person to casually do harm unto others. What his ex-wife did to him deserved retribution, but he did not ever consider that path. As it was, he was known to local police for his past and avoided all contact with them or trouble that might draw unwanted attention to himself. He would not back himself in any courtroom against accusations of wrong-doing. One word from the law and he would be back inside in a heartbeat. He balked at the risk of harming someone without sufficient, provable cause. He would sooner die than face prison again.

A shadow passing over the forest reminded Bazza of their need to move on or be caught by nightfall. He raised himself wearily from the damp, mulchy soil, to don his backpack once more. Behind him, he could hear Cheese grunting with the effort to struggle into her own backpack. Rafael made no sound as he gained a second wind with the end of their travels in sight, metaphorically speaking. He moved past Bazza in a brisk fashion to take point. Bazza simply shrugged and moved on behind Cheese.

Five minutes later, the clearing Bazza spied earlier came into prominent view along their path. An enormous, old-growth tree had succumbed to its shallow footing to careen into several others on its downward path of destruction. The resulting large break in the overhead canopy gave dozens of ferns, palms and native saplings their chance to be free of dormancy, test their mettle against competitors all vying for height in the limited amount of time that sunlight was available. Many other types of vegetation took advantage of the opening to grow in the clearing only long enough to flower and send future generations of seeds throughout the forest, before being overtaken by the hardier residents and giants of the forest.

Rafael almost ran to the clearing, to be free of the pervasive rainforest causing him a sense of claustrophobia. He paid no attention to Bazza's warning to be careful or to slow down before he injured himself. He would do as he pleased with no apparent signs of danger present. He entered the clearing with pure joy suffusing his features, leaning back to soak up the welcome rays of sun, already beginning their westerly heading beyond the mountain. Bazza deliberately hung back to allow the foolish man to go about whatever he wished, warning Cheese to slow down. They walked on side-by-side, neither uttering a word.

Rafael used the time waiting for the other two to catch up, by walking like a tight-rope walker along the fallen behemoth. He was giddy with pleasure at being free of the cloying forest. The tree had naturally fallen downhill, making the ascent up the trunk a slippery affair. Rafael nearly lost his footing a couple of times before the mossy section of the tree trunk eventually proved too slippery. Rafael teetered to one side wind-milling his arms frantically to stay on top of the felled tree. Before he could fall off, he managed to grasp a sapling growing next to the giant. The sapling was barely a year old and not able to withstand Rafael's weight.

Above Rafael's head nestled precariously in the upper branches of the young sapling, was a nest of leaves glued together by silken threads. As he was overbalancing, Rafael lost grip of the thin trunk of the sapling, attempting to find purchase on another branch higher up, or another sapling nearby, inadvertently clutching on to the nest of leaves instead. The nest tore along its bottom half as Rafael's hand grasped it, exposing the insides and its inhabitants to the hostile environment beyond. Enraged by the fatal disturbance to their home and kin, the inhabitants of the nest, falling freely upon Rafael's head, made their feelings known.

At first, Rafael was befuddled by the falling debris as he descended by the side of the log in an undignified heap. Once at the bottom, however, he began to feel the repercussions of his clumsy act. Thousands of insects vented their spleen at Rafael for his rude interruption to their tranquillity. Grasping unprotected flesh in their mandibles they broke the surface of the vulnerable epidermis. Once a break was achieved, they would arch their abdomens, almost unnaturally overhead, to aim their rear ends at the site of the break, whereupon they would squirt an acidic fluid into the exposed flesh causing a mild sting, made exponentially worse by the sheer number of insects all acting in the same defensive manner. Rafael screamed in confusion, overwhelmed by the multitudes of ants crawling all over him, especially his face, inflicting innumerable stings.

Bazza and Cheese came running the last few yards to assist the stricken man flailing blindly to be free of the insects. Rafael had no way of knowing that Green Ants were not capable of inflicting grievous harm unless he suffered an allergic reaction. For all he knew, they were as lethal as the jellyfish that took his friend. Bazza tried as hard as he could to calm him down, assuring him that they were only ants and that he was in no danger of dying in the short term. Soon, Bazza and Cheese were also covered in the stinging ants. Bazza hauled the writhing body of Rafael roughly over the log and back to the trail. There he went about methodically removing the ants with a swish broken from a nearby tree.

Rafael eventually calmed down enough to assist the pair, who then turned their attentions onto themselves. It took many minutes for most of the invaders to be dissuaded from further attack. They sat on the track picking at themselves whenever they felt yet another sting on some part of their bodies. Rafael's face and exposed neck had taken the brunt of the onslaught while Bazza and Cheese had only their hands to worry about. Rafael sat up with misery etched on his features, and anger screaming inside. He watched Bazza roll back the sleeves of his shirt to reveal several ants clinging tenaciously to the flesh of his forearms. He observed with distaste how Bazza bit the abdomens off a few to eat. Bazza then brushed off the remainder before setting off in search of something.

Rafael saw him walk to a particular tree with large leaves. Grasping one in his big hands, Bazza sat on the trunk of the fallen tree massaging the underside of the leaf onto his forearm, where the ants had attacked. Rafael watched with growing incredulity as a smile of relief appeared on Bazza's face. Rafael wasted no time in getting to his feet to rush to the tree where Bazza had picked the leaf.

Cheese moved quickly as well to follow suit. As she

approached Bazza's position she felt a vice-like grip on her wrist. She looked questioningly at Bazza who appeared dazed and pale. He would not release Cheese, who struggled to be free of the painful grip. Bazza gave her a pleading stare, stopping her in her tracks. He gave Cheese a very subtle shake of the head to indicate that she should not copy his actions.

Ahead of Cheese, Rafael reached the same spindly sapling from which Bazza had selected the leaf. He quickly tore off two leaves that he turned upside down before applying them to his face and neck. He was about to administer the same treatment to his hands when he began to feel a terrible pain, a burning, stinging agony that threatened to eat his face away like acid. The more he touched the affected areas, the more it hurt. The more it hurt, the more areas became affected by the touch of his hands acting to relieve the pain. Rafael's first instinct, was water, to stop the burning sensation. His panicked state brooked no argument from his false notions, sending the man streaking back along the path, past Bazza and Cheese, in an attempt to reach the stream at the bottom of the mountain, screaming pathetically.

Cheese almost reached out to stop Rafael as he passed the pair in his manic sprint to find relief in the waters of the creek but was held back once more by Bazza's fierce grip. Rafael tore past them. His mind knew only one thing, and his body obeyed. He raced back down the path in a blind panic.

"I, I don't understand. What happened? He only used the same leaves you…Bazza?"

Bazza had paled considerably.

"Go fetch the backpacks, Cheese, hurry."

Cheese ran back to the trail where they had dumped the packs to run to Rafael's aid. She raced back to Bazza's side.

"What, Bazza, what is it?"

"Inside the first-aid kit, yiz'll find a roll of sticking plaster. Cut off a heap of strips and stick the ends on ya arm. Stop looking at me like that, Cheese, hurry the fuck up wouldja?"

"What is it, Bazza, what happened? I thought you knew about everything that could harm you in the forest? How…oh!"

"Now, put a pair of gloves on. One strip at a time, work your way methodically up me arm. Press one strip of plaster on me arm, rip it orf and throw it away. Get another one, keep going. Never use the same one twice. Don't let the strips touch ya bare skin. For fuck's sake hurry up mate it hurts like a bitch. Yeah, that's it, then do me hand when ya finished with me forearm."

"So you deliberately hurt yourself to lure him into doing that? I saw your face, you looked so relieved when you put that leaf on your arm?"

"Shoulda been-n-actor eh, Cheese? Fuck, I'm gonna feel that for the next six months."

"I have some water in my canteen…"

"Worse thing for it. Whatcha doing is the only thing ta do. That fuckwit is probably headed back down ta the creek to try ta relieve himself. Gonna make it worse by an order-o-ten."

"So what is it Bazza, I didn't see any sap leaking out or anything?"

"Stinging tree. Bloody forest is fulla them. Mainly in clearings and along streams where there is more light, though. Millions of tiny hairs with stinging barbs underneath the leaf. Painful bloody things they are, that keep on giving ya pain day after bloody day for months and even years. Every time I go ta have a bath or wash me hands, I'm gonna feel all that pain over again. That poor bastard is in for pure Hell if he survives the rush downhill, which I bloody doubt. When he throws himself in the creek, he'll wish he was dead. It may well send him round the twist if he does make it."

"Round the twist?"

"Bonkers, nuts. It might send him loopy-loo, Cheese."

"Abigail. Abby."

"Come again?"

"I remembered my name just then. It's, Abigail, Abigail Armstrong."

"No shit?"

"No shit, Bazza."

"Well, fuck me dead. Ya still, Cheese ta me, though, orright? Ya looked like ya been through a cheese grater when I first saw ya, so, Cheese it is."

"Fine, Bazza, now keep still. This will take a while."

As Cheese methodically stripped the tenacious leaves' hairs from Bazza's arms, along with many of his own, they were able to monitor the path of the Columbian's mad plunge down the mountain side by the piercing sound of his pitiful screams continuing until he was far below.

CHAPTER TWELVE

Bazza and Cheese continued on their trek up to the top road in a companionable, casual atmosphere.

"Why exactly, are we continuing up to the road?"

"Ya family is up there, Cheese, ya need ta say goodbye at least and get what ya can from the wreck that might be yiz. Might be important for later, like ya passport and shit."

"I don't know how comfortable I feel about seeing my brothers like that. I don't want to fall to pieces on you."

"Natural ta grieve. Worse for ya if ya don't. Remember anything else?"

"Bits and pieces only. It comes in fits and starts like a broken film at the cinema. Small fragments of clarity and larger segments of a blank screen while the projectionist repairs the film. I remember when I was a child with my father and brothers. I can't seem to focus on my mother somehow. Perhaps she wasn't around long enough for me to remember, I don't know. That bit is really fuzzy. I know my name at least, though I don't mind your nickname for me, Bazza. I don't think I ever had one besides, Abby."

"Dunno if I can call ya anything else anyway, mate. Kinda got used ta calling ya that."

"Do you think he could have survived?"

"Dunno, don't care."

"Thought you said you felt bad about hurting someone?"

"Yeah, well, that wasn't a 'someone', Cheese. That was

something vomitus that got coughed up by a pestilent rat, or got shot out the arse end of a diarrhoeic Wombat. Never seen such a poor example of humanity, bar me ex-missus. Rotten. Rotten to the core that mongrel bastard was, and I couldn't care less if it lives or dies. I actually hope it suffered something chronic. Serves the fuckwit right, pardon me bad language."

"I have heard much worse I think. Bazza, I have a feeling, and it gets stronger all the time, that I was probably a real piece of work before the accident. If my brothers and I were going to meet with Rafael and his crew, it could only have been for illegal reasons. I am truly scared about what we may find out. Can we just go back, return to what we had before that lot turned up?"

"More at stake here, Cheese. Ya need ta get things in order, legal-wise, before ya become a fugitive of the law for outstaying ya welcome or something. Ya gonna need some dough ta help ya with everything, maybe get yaself back ta that Portland place ya talked about? Oregano?"

"Oregon, Bazza. Oregano, is an Italian herb."

"Oh, right. Use that in me sghetti. Make a pretty mean sghetti, Cheese, with heaps-o-garlic and stuff."

"How's your arm?"

"Gotta stop reminding me about that. Hurts like a real bitch and isn't gonna get no better any time soon. Ya did good ta get the worst of it orf, but it won't stop hurting for a bloody lorng time. Can't imagine that all over me face; like ta kill meself sooner-n-put up with that sort-o-pain."

They reached the top road before nightfall. Being on the top of the mountain without a canopy above them, meant they would have longer afternoon daylight hours than in the depth of the forest. They decided to use the time they had left to locate the site where the truck ran off the road. Once there, after some basic instructions for the following morning and a bite to eat, they laid their sleeping bags atop their ponchos just off the boggy road, under a panoply of stars accompanied by a three-quarter moon.

The top road was an offshoot from the main road between Cow Bay and Cooktown. While the road was randomly maintained by the local council as a means of reaching the unofficial Aboriginal camp located sou-west of Bazza's property, it was rarely used and left in a poor state during the wet season. It would only be re-graded when the road was baked dry. Some years there would be no maintenance at all. The road at the sharp bend where the fifth-wheeler had toppled over the edge, was little more than a goat track.

Bazza believed they had seen the last of the monsoonal rains for the year. While they would still experience the occasional spots of rain throughout the remainder of the year, they should expect no more of the spectacular inundations. The road and his track would be accessible by vehicular traffic within a week, more or less. He would then have to take Cheese into the authorities in Cairns, or he could drop her off in Mossman he supposed. He mulled over the various outcomes of their expedition to the wreckage the following morning. Christmas and New Year had come and gone with the fantastic indifference it generated in Bazza every year. They were nearing, or just past his birthday in February to the best of his knowledge.

How far over sixty years old he was, Bazza couldn't remember unless he worked it out from his year of birth, and even then it required knowledge of the present year to calculate the difference. Bazza did not really care enough to be bothered. What gnawed away at the barriers he built around himself, were the invasive memories of his shared moments alone with Cheese. As much as he hated to admit it, he liked her. Liked her more than he ever thought possible. He had grown very used to his ways and was never lonely he thought, until he found out how much he missed the company of a woman. Something he hadn't thought of in a very long time.

He was under the impression that Cheese might have fancied him at one stage, but put that down to him being the only man available at the time. The same could be said of *him* if truth be told, Cheese being the only female within cooee of his joint. When you are the only port in a storm, there are many takers who leave their fussiness behind upon entering the calm waters. He couldn't be sure how Cheese felt about him and was not even certain of how deep his own feelings ran. Despite every barrier he maintained, she found a way over, around, or through them. She was easy on the eye. He had not lied when he told her that. She had some age on her…and curves. She was no slim Jane, that's for sure. Bazza wasn't exactly a prime example of manhood himself, and so felt unqualified to pass any sort of judgement in that regard. He argued that it was too late for him to change his ways. Too late to take on board the burden of a relationship with a broken woman.

Cheese became a sort of thorn that worked its way beneath his skin, an irritation he found impossible to remove, became a part of him almost, it had remained there that long. While he outwardly detested the notion of having a stranger share his private Shangri-La in the wilderness of the Daintree rainforest, inwardly, if he allowed it, he was yearning for like-minded companionship again. He enjoyed sitting by another person in companionable silence as they both pursued individual activities. Admittedly, she pestered the crap out of him while he was trying to concentrate on a book or a carving, but even that became less bothersome over time. He could only guess about her actual background which she claimed to have forgotten. As there were no physical indications of trauma-induced amnesia, he had only her word for her condition.

If he developed some sort of workable relationship with Cheese, he wondered what would happen, when or if, she finally regained her full memories. *Would she revert to the arrogant bitch he had first come across? Would she even want to know him anymore?* Too many questions without enough guarantees for Bazza's liking. Too many imponderables. *A man could send himself mad thinking about everything that may or may not come to be.* Bazza was a man who liked to take things as they happened, one step at a time. The first thing on the agenda was to have a look at the wreck tomorrow, *if,* it was still hung up on the trunk of the enormous tree. If it had slipped or broken free, to be resting on the forest floor on the other side, they might be stymied. He didn't fancy a long trek to the bottom of the mountain on the western side.

Morning came earlier on the top of the mountain, heralding another hot day of summer in the tropics. At six o'clock, the temperature was already nudging thirty degrees Celsius. The day was only going to get hotter and muggier. Bazza rose early to reignite the small campfire from the glowing embers of the fire he had built the previous evening. Placing his trusty billy on the edge of the fire, boiling up his favourite brew, was a pleasure he always enjoyed when away from his shack. Cheese murmured when the aromatic scent hit her nostrils.

"Mmm, don't know what you put in my water last night Bazza, but I had the best sleep."

"Why wouldja think I…"

"It was just an expression, Bazza, not an accusation. You shouldn't take everything so literally. I promised you, I wouldn't hurt you and it's a promise I intend to keep. Oh, would you look at that magnificent sunrise over the ocean. What a view, Bazza. Breathtaking. I… I am…lost for words."

"That'll be the day."

Cheese slapped him playfully. "Bazza! That's a terrible thing to say. I, I…guess I don't really stop talking do I?"

"Nuh. Talk under water with a mouth fulla marbles I reckon. Have a cuppa."

"Ahhh, a cup-o-joe sounds wonderful."

"Cuppa what?"

"Joe. Cup-o-joe. It's an American saying I believe, which someone from my youth once told me, comes from a shortening of the term, "cup of jamoke, a combination of Java and mocha, where the best coffee came from around the 1930s. It was a term first recorded by an officer in the military. Fancy me remembering *that*."

"Cuppa Joe eh? Used ta know a fella name-o-Joe. Be pretty chuffed ta have a coffee named after him. Name ya poison, Cheese."

"How about a couple of Vegemite…sangers, is that what you call them?"

"Bewdy. Yeah, sangers is right. Ya getting the lingo down pat eh?"

Bazza passed her two Vegemite sandwiches wrapped in clear cling wrap. They both stood watching the view and sipping their coffee while munching contentedly on their 'sangers'. Bazza stole a sideways glance at Cheese, admiring her elegant profile in the morning light thinking; *a man could get used ta waking up ta that*. Gazing into the depths of her sapphire-blue eyes when she turned to him, Bazza felt the first stirrings of an emotion he felt sure he had conquered many years ago. He fought hard to push that emotion back down into the abyss where it belonged, before abruptly breaking the mood of the moment.

All business, Bazza packed up their meagre camp and doused the fire. Cheese immediately became aware of a change in his movements and character. She wondered if her proximity had caused it. She wondered if she might be breaking through at last. She had been aware of his observations of her, felt his eyes upon her as surely as if he was touching her. She felt a thrill in her she may never have experienced before and longed for. Bazza elicited a softness and a caring in her she found inexplicably comforting. She found herself wanting nothing more than to share simple pleasures like eating a Vegemite sanger with him in the morning while watching the sunrise. She yearned desperately to be near him as often, and for as long, as possible.

For possibly the first time in her life, at least to her abbreviated memory, she found herself longing for a man. To be with *him* in more ways than a momentary sharing of the flesh could provide. She knew instinctively that the feeling was alien to her, that it was the first occasion for her. Cheese suspected she had a life filled with men before she came to Australia, men who would do her bidding. Though Bazza was not a handsome man, nor even a man of means, he possessed character traits that inexorably propelled her to him. His physique was pure masculinity, with strong body aromas matching that brawn. She did not find it unpleasant after a time, in fact, it had a strange allure that set her senses tingling. She found it difficult to admit the realisation. She felt more than a little confused by it. She could, however, not deny it. She was falling in love.

"C'mon, Cheese move ya arse, daylight's wasting, and we got a shitload ta do."

Then again, maybe she was overplaying it.

Bazza grasped the coil of rope, the end of which he had anchored to a tree trunk on the eastern side of the mountain, tossing it over the precipice on the western side. He had given her a crash course in abseiling the previous evening. They would be descending on the same rope, as Bazza could travel with only so much rope and equipment. He rigged them up to the rope with all the professional equipment to safely abseil to the wreck. He checked earlier with his binoculars, to make sure the vehicle remained hung up on the tree where he had first discovered it.

While it was possible and preferable for him to make it down the steep embankment on his own, he recognised that he had to take Cheese with him. It may well be her last chance to say goodbye. He hoped she was prepared for the grizzly sight. He knew he wasn't. Over the side he clambered, with Cheese following close behind. The temperature dropped noticeably the moment they entered the gloom. The rich forest earth sent its heady aromas wafting over the pair as they cautiously descended.

To Bazza, it appeared that the vehicle had not moved since he saw it last, when in fact, it had. The trailer had shifted considerably lower, pulling the towing vehicle with it, so that the Hummer was almost horizontal, teetering against the gargantuan trunk emerging from the forest floor. How the connection to the trailer held, was anybody's guess. As the pair drew nearer, he decided it would not be possible for one of them to *enter* the vehicle if they saw anything worth retrieving. He informed Cheese of his observations as they drew abreast of it. Slumped in the two front seats, were the bodies of her brothers, Jeremy and Ken.

Cheese did not react at the overwhelming stench or the sight of the bodies subjected to the elements and rainforest inhabitants during the wet season. She remained stoic in her resolve to pay her respects and salvage what she could from the experience. The rear, passenger door, had come away from its top hinge, dangling precariously beneath the vehicle. Through the opening afforded by the broken door, Cheese spied a large leather carrying bag. She began to get excited at the prospect of finding evidence of her past life in the bag, moving to unclip herself from the rope. Bazza quickly intervened to point out the inherent dangers before she had an opportunity to meet with certain calamity.

Bazza manoeuvred the rope bearing both their weight to gain a clear line of sight to within the vehicle. From his pack, much lighter with all unnecessary items removed, he retrieved the small grappling hook he had used on their journey up the mountainside. After several tense moments missing the handles of the bag with the hook, both vehicle and tree groaned disconcertingly. Bazza finally managed to pull the hook under one of the handles.

No sooner had the bag left the opening when the shift in weight was enough to cause a reaction. The vehicle began its inexorable slide over the trunk as gravity finally gained the upper hand. With no more than a creak and squeal, the rig slid free of the tree to plunge trailer first into the depths below. Within seconds they heard the crash of the rig as it hit the bottom without hindrance from further obstacles. The forest swallowed the sound of the smashing, twisting metal like a blanket had been thrown over it. A dull thud was all that accompanied the metal juggernaut upon reaching its final destination.

Climbing with the bag in his hand proved bothersome, so Bazza transferred the bag to his back, being thankful for the large handles allowing him to fit the bag over his depleted backpack. Bazza and Cheese continued their ascent without any further ado. He suspended the rope and grappling hook from a belt loop in his army surplus BDU trousers. The climb was arduous for their fatigued limbs, having exerted themselves for two days to reach the top. They were thankful for a downhill excursion when the time came to leave, although the remaining trek would be far from easy.

They lay panting for long moments once they reached the top road. Neither able to move much due to muscles like jelly. The black leather bag lay between them, untouched after Bazza unloaded the extra burden. While he was physically stronger than Cheese and ultimately more acclimatised and suited to the rugged lifestyle, he never-the-less felt drained by the exertions. He was, after all, no longer a young man. The years were catching up. His chest ached where his heart laboured to regain equilibrium. He swore again to quit his casual smoking, something he had promised himself a dozen times or more over the years

It was nearing midday on the third day since departing the shack. Bazza did not think they had the stamina to begin their descent immediately. He would not make the same trek down the mountainside following the route of their ascent, preferring to risk the boggy track down to the shack. If it seemed solid enough in the morning, they would use that path which would see them return to the shack in one day's hard travel instead of staying one more night in the forest. He could see that Cheese was almost spent and he fared little better. He had only avoided the track in the first place to lure the Colombian into some sort of trap. Had they used the track originally, as well they may have, for Bazza suspected it to be solid enough to hold them, he would not have found any opportunity to be rid of their adversary.

Gathering themselves slowly, they made their way back to where Bazza's track intersected the top road. He had cleared a small site where he often parked his tractor. It was there they would camp for the night. He would build a small fire to cook some hot food instead of dining on sandwiches. Bazza knew of a turkey mound nearby, where he would place a few snares.

On the top of the mountain, the air cooled quickly toward the afternoon. Bazza had set his snares around the turkey mound in the hope of catching a scrub turkey. The male Australian Brush Turkey will make and maintain a mound of leaf litter from ten to fifteen feet across and about three feet high, which he builds to attract a female. The mound needs to be close to thirty-three degrees Celsius at its heart to attract one or more females with which to mate and lay eggs in the mound. The male will spend most of his daylight hours scratching around to keep his mound at just the right temperature, measured by tasting the mound every so often. By placing a few snares at strategic intervals around and near the mound, Bazza felt confident he would snare the colourful character for their dinner the following evening.

Cheese took the time during Bazza's absence to study the contents of the black leather bag. Inside she found several items of interest including her passport and those of her deceased brothers'. Some papers and deeds filled in many of the blanks for her. She was delighted to find what appeared to be some of her own clothing, until it turned out to be nothing more than negligee. After emptying the bag, she removed the obvious false bottom to reveal stacks of Australian currency in denominations of fifties and hundreds. Without counting, she estimated the amount to be close to a quarter of a million dollars. Bazza whistled when he saw all the cash laid out in front of her.

"Looks like ya might be worth knowing, Cheese", Bazza remarked upon his return.

"I imagine this is what, Rafael was after. What he was going to exchange it for is still unknown and not made clearer by anything in here. I did find my passport, though, and some very interesting paperwork. Seems we, that is, I, own the property adjacent to your's. We are officially neighbours according to what I have here. From what I can make out through dates and such, is that my father purchased the property with his Australian wife about ten years ago. I have no recollection of my mother and I am almost certain that I was born in America, so it obviously means that he took a second wife."

"Where is she? If she's still alive, the land should belong ta her."

"Died some six years ago according to the death certificate and her will leaving everything to my father. It appears as though Dad was planning to move us all to Australia recently as we have all our immigration papers up to date that gives us all permanent residency. Dad's death certificate dates to six months ago with his will leaving the property to us, his sole heirs. Looks like we were all set to make the move a month or so before that, when his passing delayed things. I assume my brothers and I were making good his arrangements to live here permanently after he died. I, I can't remember any of it Bazza, not a single thing. I feel so, so, much like a traitor to my family for not remembering."

"Probably explains the big rig. Ya brothers got that thing made up in the States and had it shipped over I reckon. Yiz was probably thinking-o-living in it while yiz built something on the land. Still doesn't tell us what the money was for. If ya had all that cash, what would ya want more for?"

"I couldn't begin to guess, Bazza…" Cheese whispered as tears formed in the corners of her eyes.

"Ya know, ya bin pretty brave till now. Reckon it's about time ya let it go eh? Get it outta ya system?"

Bazza didn't wait for an answer, going to sit by her to offer a comforting arm around her shoulder. Cheese lay her head against his chest and wept for her shame at not remembering, at the loss of forgotten parents, and the loneliness she felt. It was good to let go of pent up emotions causing her distress. It felt good to be in a man's arms who wanted nothing in return. It was also very confusing trying to come to terms with all the known and unknown information in her head. She released the tensions in unabashed tears that flowed freely down her cheeks. Her sobs clashing with her aching ribs from the extreme exercise of the previous days.

Gradually, her sobs subsided and the tears dried. She sat there with Bazza, enveloped in his arms, feeling a tenderness overtaking her senses, a certain joy suffusing her being like nothing she had ever felt. She knew with pure certainty that she was in love, despite never recalling the feeling or knowing if she had ever experienced such emotions. She felt light-headed with the knowledge, warm in the heart and clear in the mind. She lifted her head to peer at the big man. She gazed into his deep, dark brown eyes, beseeching him to understand how she felt, begging him to know how to respond.

He did. Their lips met. Tenderly at first, barely touching. Surprising Cheese that such a large man could know such gentleness. Gradually, passion overcame the pair as caution withdrew; making love feverishly, but expertly, like two people who have known each other an eternity. Reacting to each other's needs and wants in perfect symmetry and harmony, oblivious to the world around them, all thoughts of dinner, danger, or worry, diffused like the sun over the western horizon. Night crept over the mountain, covering the couple like a comforting blanket.

CHAPTER THIRTEEN

When Bazza and Cheese re-entered his beloved *Cathedral* the following day, they breathed a sigh of relief in unison at the familiar sight. Before they could relax, Bazza stiffened abruptly, sniffing the air. Bazza searched about him but saw nothing obvious out of place. The ladder for the shack had been raised before they left and the girls were merrily clucking away in their cage aloft. Bazza sniffed again certain he detected a foreign fragrance mingling with a familiar one.

"Cheese, I want ya ta go up ta the shack and make like a happy little homemaker, like ya bin living here for ages. Sing, hum, clean or cook something. Go along with whateva I tell ya okay?"

"I…what is it, Bazza?"

"Dunno yet, jest do like I ask please, mate? Will ya?"

"A happy little homemaker I'll be if that's what you want. You sure about that?"

"No time for that now, mate. Ya gotta get up there, and make like we just got back from a regular trip, orright?"

Bazza checked the entire area of the *Cathedral*, including the cave. Nothing appeared out of place, yet something had the hairs on the back of his neck standing on end.

"Bazza?" Cheese called over the veranda railing of the shack once she ascended. "It's not…him…is it?"

"Don't think so, but shush. No more talking now. Go about ya 'daily routines', mate."

Bazza made his way along the path to the beach. Once clear of the forest, the scent became clearer. The familiar scent, was the remains of a fire on the beach. A blackened circle within a sandy depression, had been recently established no more than ten feet from where he stood at the top of the beach. The foreign fragrance, was a lingering wisp of cologne. It was barely a trace, but undeniable to Bazza's keen sense of smell. He surveyed the beach left and right as far as he could see. Nothing. Out in the bay, the Colombian's vessel remained at anchor. The inflatable dinghy and his tinny remained high and dry where he had placed them when the Colombian decided to abandon sleeping aboard his vessel.

Bazza saw no signs of the fire's owner, nor did he see any other craft within the bay or beyond the reef. Whether the fire had been lit by the Colombian, he could still not bring himself to say the person's name, he could not know. He didn't believe so for no other reason than the faintest aroma of cologne which he knew was not worn by the man they knew. In the time they were all together in the shack, he had never detected a similar scent.

Whoever had visited the bay had departed. How long the visitor/s stayed away, he had no way of knowing. That they would return, was a sure thing he would bet on. That it had something more to do with Colombia and money was also a no-brainer. He felt very relieved that he and Cheese decided to hide the money and the bag a mile up the winding track before they continued on their homeward journey. At the side of the track was another circle of tall palms that Bazza likened to a circle of mushrooms, even calling it, "The Fairy Circle"; in the centre of which, they buried the bag and the contents, except Cheese's underclothing.

"False alarm Cheese, ya can stop play acting now," yelled Bazza as he re-entered the *Cathedral*, then made his way aloft.

"What was it?" asked Cheese the moment he climbed up to the shack, entering the kitchen area.

"Dunno, more-o-the same I 'spose. Think we had company while we were away, and I'm pretty sure it wasn't the mongrel. Didn't smell right."

"Didn't…smell right? You can't be serious?

"Keen sense-o-smell. Had it all me life, but sorta cultivated it back in Afghanny and while living alone out here. Come in handy more-n-once I kid ya not."

"All right, I'll bite then. What did you smell?"

"Someone lit a fire on the beach, recent as four, maybe five hours ago. Bottom of the fire was still warm, and…"

"And…?"

"You're gonna think I'm nuts."

"I already think that," she admitted with a smile. "So, you may as well tell me."

"Cologne or aftershave. Jest a real tiny whiff, lingering, like on the air, or maybe on the sand, or something. Maybe it rubbed on some driftwood, I dunno, but it's there, Cheese, no mistaking it."

"It could have been, Rafael. You believed he might have made it. He could have come back here couldn't he?"

"Coulda been the mongrel, but I don't think so. Too…orderly and unfamiliar. We been sleeping near the bastard and I recognise his stink, just like I do yours."

"Well, thank-you very much."

"We all gotta distinct smell, Cheese, even ladies; specially ladies sometimes. I don't mean nothing bad by it, mate. Once I get me nose on someone, I can pick up their scent on the wind real quick. Nothing special about it, jest practice I reckon."

Bazza knew he was being tactless and that if he wasn't careful he would ruin what they had. They hadn't said a word about their interlude. When Bazza woke, he simply extricated himself from Cheese's languid form within the sleeping bag, to prepare the brew for their breakfast. Afterward, they packed up silently, each privately pondering the night's events. They worked their way down the track, the descent being considerably easier, burying the bag at the fairy circle, before making their way into the *Cathedral*. Bazza was not a child to be embarrassed or awkward about his actions but neither was he confident about his feelings or their reciprocation. He had never had a one-night-stand before and didn't particularly cherish the idea of their intimacy being relegated to that category.

Cheese felt content within herself, knowing her feelings and her body. She had connected instantly with Bazza, forming a seamless union of the flesh, unequalled in her memory. She knew instinctively that she and Bazza would endure in their relationship. While she believed a discussion of sorts was on the cards, she felt it was not as essential as it may have been had they been younger. With maturity came a confidence in one's self and others to the point where a need to immediately know each other's mind was not an issue. She was happy to wait for a quiet moment when they would broach the subject casually. Foremost in her mind, was the possibility of yet another interloper. She felt sorry for Bazza having to deal with more interruptions to his hermitic lifestyle.

Cheese was terrified at the prospect that Rafael may still be alive and possibly stalking them. She had no real way of knowing the effects of the Stinging Tree or its repercussions. The way Bazza described it to her, she could not imagine herself surviving such an occurrence. Bazza had handled his personal encounter with aplomb, but she could see him wince often when he did not mask it as well as he thought. He had been very careful not to allow his affected arm or hand to be anywhere near her exposed flesh during their lovemaking, which proved problematic and comical at times. Later in the evening, she had watched in fascination as Bazza applied melted wax from a burning candle to cover the afflicted area. He then tore away the cooled wax along with his hair and what he hoped would be more of the microscopic plant hairs.

"I reckon we'll find out soon enough who our visitors were. Got some sorta idea what type they might be as well."

"Care to elucidate?"

"Pretty simple really - it'll be someone higher up the food chain than the mongrel, in whatever enterprise he was involved in."

"And you deduce this how?"

"Well, just connecting the dots again, Cheese. That weedy little fart was acting real nervous and worried last coupla weeks. He probably has ta answer ta someone higher up. When everything went south on him; wrong landing site, dead delivery boys, no money and a whole lotta wet coming down, he knew he was in deep shit. His boss wasn't jest gonna give him whatever it was for sale after probably bankrolling the venture, then wait for eva for payment. Nuh, it'll turn out ta be the squirt's boss for sure, or his calling card anyway."

"Calling card?"

"Someone ta rough him up a bit, or worse. Make him know that the boss isn't happy."

"Those are a lot of assumptions based on what, a hint of a smell?"

"I hope ya get ta prove me wrong, Cheese, I really do. Don't wanna be right on this one, but I reckon I will be."

"What do you plan to do?"

"Keep an eye out, is about it. Unless ya wanna make a run for it?"

"Can we get a vehicle up the track?"

"Not yet."

"Where would we 'run' to then?"

"Hide out for a while till things settle, till they all get the f… get off my property. Might even go ta Boinga Bob's. His mob'll look after us for a bit. Don't eat his cooking, though. Laces everything with Magic Mushies. Off his nut mosta the time."

"What about his boat, Bazza? Could we use that to get out of here for a while? You said we could use it to get to...Cairns?"

"Yeah, Cairns. I been thinking about that. We both agree that the mongrel wasn't high up the ladder right? At least, if he was branching out on his own, he had a backer, or he was on someone's payroll?"

"I got the feeling he was independent but had a backer. From what I heard of his conversations with, Paolo, he was troubled about owing money."

"Right. So, connecting the dots from what we know, his boss, his backer, or some calling-card henchmen came looking for him. Stayed long enough to light a fire, real casual-like, on the beach while they waited. Probably gave this whole area the once over without leaving a trace to arouse suspicion. I reckon they waited just so long before going up the coast a bit ta where the prick was supposed ta have landed."

"What makes you think they knew the right location where Rafael was supposed to have made landfall?"

"If they knew enough ta come ta Australia in the first place, then it stands ta reason he gave 'em coordinates. They went there first and backtracked till they spied his boat, or vice-versa. Either way, they'll be back because his boat is here. Ya reckon they'd go away and give him the opportunity ta make a run for it in his boat while they're gorn?"

"What are you suggesting?"

"Only one way ta make sure he doesn't scarper while they're gorn; booby trap it."

"No?"

"Figure it logically. They came, they saw his boat. They leave again looking for him when he doesn't show up. How do they stop him escaping while they're orf looking for him? They may even have left someone on the boat. Thought of that? If they did, that bloke will already have reported sighting me on the beach. Coulda been Mr. Eau de Co-log-nee himself on the boat while he sent his minions ta search up the coast? Mighta smelled *him* on that boat."

"Your sense of smell is really that good?"

"Bloody oath! Saved me bacon a few times, the old schnozzle has.

"Oh, Bazza, I don't mind admitting, I'm scared. It would appear to all intents and purposes that my brothers and I were definitely their customers for whatever it was we were looking to purchase. I am so, so, sorry for bringing men like that into your life. Perhaps you should send me on my way?"

"Wouldn't make much difference now. They're coming back and I'll be in the thick of it again whether I like it or not. Ya know eff-all anyway with ya memory gorn, so ya might be better orf play-acting like me missus or something. They don't know ya from a bar-o-soap, so ya got no cause ta be scared...more-n-usual."

"After last night, the thought of being your...missus doesn't sound too bad to me."

"Aww, ya had ta bring that up huh?"

"You feel uncomfortable talking about it?"

"Only coz I know it'll come out all wrong if I do. I don't talk well ta people, Cheese. Get all...unconfident."

"You've been talking to me all this time and have sounded like a very intelligent person capable of holding his own in anyone's company. You have made brilliant deductions and assumptions that have kept us alive. Devised plans based on countless scenarios. You have a deep-grained knowledge of this forest and her perils. I very much doubt that you would not make yourself understood to me if we were to broach the subject of having had sex last night. Brilliant, tender, loving sex under the stars. I concede that I thought you were a bit of an oaf when I first saw you, but I know better, far better now, Bazza."

"I jest feel awkward talking about stuff like that, specially coz-o-what I been through. Ya know?"

"We are two consenting adults, Bazza. There is nothing anyone can do about that."

"Until something goes wrong. I know women can turn, and turn real bad when they're in a fix. Not saying ya would do the same, but I gotta be real careful. Fact is; ya haven't thought it through and neither have I. What are ya gonna ta do *here,* Cheese? And *I'm* not going anywhere else. It will come ta nothing; us. Shouldn't-o-done it. I feel bad for letting me dick get the better-o-me…again."

"Well, I don't regret what happened and neither should you. I wasn't expecting a marriage proposal you know? I hoped we could just let nature take its course. See where it takes us. We aren't spring chickens anymore, Bazza, and I doubt there will be many more opportunities for us both. I don't know if I could live here, but…"

"Shhhh." Bazza cocked his head to listen. He turned to the direction of the break in the canopy affording him a bird's-eye view to the ocean. A large, luxury, ocean-going vessel appeared beyond the reef approaching from the north. "Holy Dooley! This bloke's got some dosh. That bewdy must be over a hundred foot I reckon. Looks like the decision's been taken away from us. They left someone on the mongrel's boat and that someone radioed in the sighting of me on the beach. The ship can't have been too far away ta get here that quick. Musta been on its way back already."

"What are we going to do?"

"Can't run now. We're not prepared and it's getting late. I say we act like a twosome when they come in. We say we saw the runt and tell them what happened to the other two…sort of. Then tell him we showed the runt the way and he took orf on his own?"

"What if they don't believe us?"

"No reason not ta. Unless the runt's been communicating with 'em, I don't see how they could figure anything else. Try not ta say too much. With that Yankee accent, they might get suspicious. If they cotton on jest make out ya from Canada or something."

"How long before they get here?"

"Take 'em a while ta get through the reef, even at high tide. Then they speak ta the person on the boat, then they come here. They'll know it wasn't the runt on the beach, coz I gotta long beard and he didn't look like he could grow one in a million years. Doubt they'll come in till morning. Look, Cheese, they came here ta get back what's theirs. They already got the runt's boat and whatever was on it. They might figure ta find that arsehole and give him what for, but I doubt they're gonna go traipsing about looking for the payment. I don't think *we* figure in it at all if we can convince 'em we don't know where the runt is."

"I hope your right."

"So do I, mate. So do I. Meantime, how about some dinner eh? Starving!"

CHAPTER FOURTEEN

Early the following morning, Bazza saw two men approaching the beach in another inflatable dinghy; one with a centre console. Bazza could tell from the postures of the two men that one held a superior position to the other. Bazza assumed that a third person remained aboard the ship anchored beyond the reef. The head honcho was reclining casually in the rear of the inflatable while his employee attended the centre console.

Bazza could just detect the faintest whiff of cologne wafting in on the morning breeze. *The head honcho must bathe in the shit*, thought Bazza. He watched as they neared the beach. The employee making sure the inflatable was side on to the beach to allow his boss to step onto sand without getting his boots wet. The head honcho stunk of money from head to toe, arrogance, and authority oozing from his exfoliated pores. He was stereotypical of a Colombian drug lord, at least to Bazza's mind. Dressed in a suit that would have cost more than Bazza made in a year of selling his carvings, complete with Panama hat and Cuban-heeled snakeskin boots. His greased-back coiffure ending in a pony-tail of jet-black hair. All he needed was the proverbial gold tooth to finish off the tableau.

The employee looked like a billboard advertisement for steroid abuse. A cotton shirt two sizes too small stretched at the seams over the enormously muscled physique. Bazza guessed the man's biceps to equal the girth of his own thighs. The man had no neck to speak of. He was not a very tall man and looked like the human version of a battle tank. Bazza would not back himself in a fight with the man.

The two men walked to the top of the beach once the goon had secured the inflatable with an anchor. There, they assessed the area with calculated interest, determining the risk, if any, in proceeding upon private property. Both men automatically touched secreted weapons in response to threat assessment. Emboldened by firepower, they began the march up the sandy path to Bazza's *Cathedral*.

Bazza studied the men from his lofty perch as they entered the *Cathedral*, clearly familiar with the layout from their previous exploration.

"Help ya, mate?" Bazza inquired of the startled pair below him.

"We are looking for someone, a friend of ours", said the smarmy one with a voice that dripped venom with every word.

"On private property?"

"We were not aware that this was private property."

"Ya own it do ya?"

"I, I don't understand?"

"Simple enough question. Do ya own this property?"

"Of course not."

"Then ya know ya trespassing. Didn't ask me permission ta enter. Didn't announce yaself. Jest marched straight in like ya own the joint. Coulda shot ya for that ya know?" said Bazza with a smirk, watching the startled reaction from the pair below. "If I had a gun that is."

"Forgive me, *Señor*. My name is, Don Carlos Montoya and this is my associate, Marcos. I did not mean to trespass, sir, we are looking for my good friend, Rafael Dominguez. That is his boat out there in the bay. He came here with two other men?"

"Usually go looking for ya 'good' mates, with weapons?"

"Excuse me?"

"Don't try ta bullshit me, mate. Marcos, there has one tucked into the back of his duds, and yours is under ya suit jacket in one-o-them fancy holster thingies. Blind Freddy could see 'em."

"You are very observant, *Señor*….?"

"Bazza. Ya can call me, Bazza, and this is me missus, Cheese."

"I am pleased to meet you, Mr. Bazza. Can we come up to talk to you?"

"Talking now aren't we?"

"I am getting a sore neck, Mr. Bazza. Please, we only want to know if you have seen or made contact with our friend."

"Probably dead by now I reckon."

"Who?"

"All of them."

"You know this?"

"Two of 'em, yeah. I know for a fact, two of 'em are gorn. The other skinny runt ya after should be dead by now, but I can't say for certain, no. Come on up if ya want, but ya can leave all ya weapons including those pig-stickers, on the ground there."

"Pig-stickers?"

"Knives, bucko, knives. Bad enough ya come barging onta me property unannounced. Having all that weaponry on yiz makes me real suspicious and nervous, it does."

Cheese shot Bazza a look of concern. She had followed the conversation from inside the shack. When Bazza turned to indicate that she should lower the ladder, she was immediately alarmed. Bazza just shrugged to indicate that he did not see an alternative. The two strangers were just as likely to shoot them from the ground. Up in the treehouse, they were sitting ducks. She backed away slowly as the two men entered the shack.

"Well in the interests-o-better relations, name ya poison fellas? Bit-o-home-made hooch, or coffee?"

"A little early for anything stronger than coffee, Mr. Bazza."

"Jest, Bazza, okay? None-o-that formal shit around here, Don."

"Then, Carlos will do for me."

"Thought ya said ya name was, Don?"

"Don Carlos Montoya. Don, is an honorific title."

"Ya got good English there, mate."

"I went to a very good school in England as a child, and finished my schooling in America; Harvard."

"No shit?"

"No. What about you, Bazza, what did you major in?"

"School-o-hard knocks mainly. I don't have no fancy education. If ya trying ta make me feel small coz-o-it, forget it. Don't give a fuck for fancy schooling and all the bullshit they fill ya head with. Trying ta tell me ya got that tub out there with a degree in business, or economics? Unless ya hit it big on the stock market, ya had Buckley's chance-o-that."

Carlos eyed Bazza steadily with a steely glint. He knew the big man was making spurious observations about his enterprises. *The man had big cohones that was for sure.* He needed information from the man and was not confident of trying to force the information out of him. The woman, on the other hand, presented either leverage or another means of extrapolating the truth.

"I did imply something derogatory and I apologise, Bazza. I have been told that I can be quite the snob sometimes, and I hope you can forgive my impertinence? I would like to accept your offer of coffee."

"Cheese, make us a cuppa wouldja love?"

"Now, Bazza. You suggested that you knew the fates of some or all of the men I mentioned?"

"Yeah. One bloke, name-o-Diego I think, copped it just after they got here. Got done in by a stinger called a Box Jellyfish."

"I have heard of these killer jellyfish here in Australia. You have another called an Irukandji? Kills by injecting a toxin that takes some time to take effect on the major organs."

"Yeah, worse than a Box I reckon, coz ya don't know about it till ya dead. Bloody little ya can do about it as well. Ya know ya shit, that's for sure."

"Rafael and…Paolo? I think that was the name, Marcos?"

"*Si, Paolo*", Marcos replied.

"Wow, it talks too huh? Thought he was mute there for a bit." Marcos scowled at that. "That one, Polio, he got stung too trying ta help his mate, Diego, but he survived. Cheese here nursed him back ta health. He was real morose after that and eventually got took by a monster crocodile when we went fishing. Ya mate, the other one held us here at gun point while the rain season stopped him from getting ta the top road. Got us ta guide him ta the top on foot. Last I saw-o-him, he was high-tailing it down the mountain side after the silly bastard wiped his face with a Stinging Tree leaf. Took off like a shot screaming like a sheila all the way. Fuck knows where he is now, and I don't give a rat's arse."

"Hence your warm welcome for us?"

"Ya could say I was getting pretty pissed orf by then, yeah. No strangers here in ten years on me own and suddenly it's fucking raining people from other parts-o-the world. I dunno what they were after, he never said, and I didn't care."

"Surely you were curious, Bazza? Rafael must have told you something?"

"Nuh. Not a thing. He told me he needed ta get ta the top road quick as, and that's it. I tried ta take him up there when the rain stopped, but he wouldn't listen ta me about all the dangers we got here. Went orf in front-o-me, all huffy like, coz I was too slow for him and he got himself in a mess. Haven't seen him since. Cheese and I got back yesterdy, jest after the two-o-ya been here and had a good look around me property."

"We touched nothing, how could you know we were here?"

"Smell ya a mile away. Whadda ya do, have a bath in that fancy co-log-nee?"

Carlos' hairline moved back and his jaw clenched in anger. He was unused to insults. Seeing Marcos attempt to move, he stayed the man with a head shake. A tic in Carlos' cheek was the only indication of continued annoyance, as he accepted the coffee served to him by Cheese.

"Thank-you. This smells like excellent coffee. South American?"

"Orstralian, from the Tablelands, south west-o-here." Explained Bazza as he turned to point in the direction he had mentioned. While Bazza and Cheese were looking away, Carlos quickly swapped coffee cups with Bazza.

"Bazza, I understand that you were ill-treated by my friend and for that, I apologise. He is an uncivilised man of very low education and standards. I will deal with him when I find him. If Rafael was trying to reach this top road you spoke of, it was there he would be meeting someone for his business dealings. You say you are unaware of the nature of this business and that you do not care to know. I am very happy to hear this. I would like to offer you a business proposition."

"Not interested." Said Bazza with a knowing smirk, having witnessed the coffee cup exchange in a mirror on the wall.

"You haven't heard what I am offering yet. I am a very generous man to my friends."

"You're here hunting your 'friend' with guns and muscle. That sort of generosity I can live without."

"I have other means of persuasion when dealing with people whom I find less than friendly."

"I get the feeling ya threatening me, Mister. Ya don't have lasting relationships do ya?"

"Nonsense. No threats, simply friendly advice. Now, I wish to get to the top road as well. What do you need to take me and Marcos up there?"

"I don't take advice from anyone, much less someone I jest met. I'm not ya friend and never likely ta be. If ya get the idea that musclehead here can take me, think again. He might be bulked up on 'roids, but I got real strength from physical work and a bit-o-height advantage. Now, I don't need nothing from ya that I don't already have. I already took one fool up ta the road and he fucked up bad. I don't wanna take any more idiots up there."

"You should not be trying to make me angry, Bazza. I am not a man to be fooled with. I have only a little bit of patience and that is being used up very quickly. There is nothing to stop me from using my weapons once I am on the ground."

"If ya make it that far? Gotta ask yaself what I mighta told Cheese to lace ya coffee with given that I knew ya was up ta no good."

The silence that lay between the combatants was as tangible and ominous as a coiled viper. Carlos weighing up the possibilities that he may have been poisoned, and Bazza wondering if Carlos would call his bluff. Bazza brazenly sipped his coffee with a mischievous grin. Carlos broke out in laughter when witnessing Bazza do so.

"Very good, Bazza. You had me believing it for a moment. You even had me believing you did not see me switch the coffee cups when you were not looking. I have misjudged you and I think the others did too. With your knowledge of the forest, I can see how they could easily be led into a trap by you. I will not make the same mistake. I will make you an offer to take me to the top road. If you reject my offer I will find another way and no hard feelings. As a gesture of good will, I am going to leave you the boat in the bay either way. It is a very handsome boat, an expensive boat, paid for with my money. I give it to you on top of a sum that you name to take me to the top road."

"Ya know what I want more-n-anything?"

"Tell me, and if it's in my power, it's yours."

"I jest wanna be left the fuck alone, to live my life in peace and quiet like I have been for the last ten years. I'll make a deal with ya, though. Come back termorra, and the track'll probably be dry enough ta drive on I reckon. I'll give ya me car keys and ya can drive yaself up ta the road. No need ta worry about me luring ya into no traps or anything. I don't *need* anything, but if ya say the boat's mine, I'll take it if ya damage me car, or scarper with it. Good enough?"

"I will take that deal, Bazza. I will see you in the morning bright and early. I will swap keys with you. My boat for your car? I guarantee you that you will be way ahead in the deal."

"I also want ya ta leave the hardware behind when ya return. I see or smell guns, knives, anything like that, the deal's orf. And I *will* smell 'em."

"Very well. I promise we will leave all weapons behind. I sincerely hope you will reciprocate?"

"No guns, jest a bow and arras for hunting, a few skinning knives. None of which will be here in the morning, give ya me word on that."

"Excelente. Marcos, vamanose."

Bazza and Cheese observed the pair making their departure, after retrieving their weapons, right up to the boat in the bay where they remained. Bazza then flew into a repeat of the activity that saw them prepare for their journey on foot to the top road days before. Cheese followed suit silently, helping where she could, trying hard not to disrupt Bazza's concentration. She understood what Bazza had in mind, feeling the overwhelming urge to run, herself.

Bazza scooped canned consumables and other items into a backpack, enough to last them a week or more by Cheese's estimation. Spare clothes, ponchos, candles, torches, and spare batteries were packed away with consummate skill. Bazza poured laying mash into a trickle-feeder for his girls to feed on while they were gone. A hanging water container of the same design should see them well-watered for a lengthy period. Cheese watched with amusement as Bazza clucked to them, imagining that he was understood. Cheese admired the affection he showed the birds and giggled when the chooks cocked their heads to 'listen' to their friend and imprinted surrogate parent.

They ate a hasty, but full breakfast, before gathering themselves. Bazza's hand and forearm still troubled him from his encounter with the Stinging Tree, wincing occasionally whenever anything touched the affected area. Cheese had to continually remind herself to avoid those areas when making contact with him. She felt her chest swelling with pride as she watched the big man go about keeping them safe with methodical precision.

"You're not new to any of this are you, Bazza? You've had training?"

"I was a soldier in Afghanny. Saw lotsa shit there and damn glad when I got outta there, and the army. Not proud of any-o-that, Cheese. You wanna know why I can't kill? Coz-o-that. Saw too much of it, did too much of it. Changed me inside. For the better, I reckon. Me ex didn't think so, though. Thought I was a bit of a pussy after that."

"I don't think that. I think you are a stronger man than you were back then. Not wanting to kill is not a failing, Bazza, it's an admirable trait. I wonder that you are not more mixed up by what you must have experienced over there."

"Who's ta say I'm not? I am a hermit living in the dangerous jungles of North Queensland, flirting with certain death from various quarters every single day. Sometimes I think I exchanged one war for another."

"What are we going to do?"

"I gotta get ya outta here, Cheese, fore they figure out who ya are. Still don't believe we can take a car up the track, so I reckon we gotta walk out, up ta the high road and maybe get ya ta, Boinga Bob's. I'll drop ya off there and backtrack to where I can lead those bozos on a bittuva wild goose…"

Bazza was alerted by a familiar sound. He looked out through the canopy to see the inflatable taking off from the Rafael's boat.

"Fuck-me-dead! These arseholes play for keeps. I reckon all they did out there is what we just did. They packed for an extended journey on foot. They're coming back ta kill us."

"How can you possibly know that? Why would they? They can't make it on their own."

"I think they beg ta differ. They don't even care that we can see 'em from here. Nah, that arrogant prick believes they can make it on their own and I'll bet the goon talked him into it. All bluster and bravado; 'roid rage taking hold-o-the mutt. I could see it in his eyes, he wants a crack at me. We gotta get outta here, mate."

"Where to?"

"Dunno yet. Seeing them blokes coming already kinda changes me plans." He turned to his chooks. "Bye girls, see ya soon eh?"

Without checking to see if she was following, Bazza set off down the ladder. After Cheese descended, he hauled the ladder up again via the hidden rope. A quick glance around him told him that there was little else he could do to protect his property or belongings. Without ceremony, the pair wandered off in the same direction they had taken on their previous trek.

"You can't be thinking about using the same tricks on those two?"

"No plans at all at the moment. Jest getting outta here. Follow the creek again as far as possible, then we'll see."

"You really believe, Carlos would harm us?"

"After that last mongrel threatened us and hit me, I don't doubt for a second that the boss-man will do everything in his power, and worse, to get what he wants. Just wish I knew what he wanted. Can't be that bit-o-money in ya bag, Cheese. Not enough there ta get him excited. What, coupla hundred thousand maybe?"

She mulled it over while following. The natural length of his stride had her hurrying behind him, leaving her breathless within moments.

"Slow down please, Bazza, I can't keep this pace up. I am as confused as you about that bit. If you look at the boats these guys are motoring around in, the sum of money in the bag seems a paltry amount to be going to this much trouble for."

"Only one has a boat, Cheese. The other has a ship, not a boat."

"What's the difference?"

"A smart man once told me, that a *boat,* is something ya get inta, when a *ship,* is sinking."

Bazza kept up the gruelling pace to be as far away as possible when the pair arrived. Distance was the only means of securing safety for Cheese and himself. The atmosphere beneath the canopy steamed up as the temperatures outside soared. Cheese and Bazza were soon bathed in sweat as they made their way up the shallow creek bed.

Sound was reduced to the ethereal silence when the heat stifled normal activity within the rainforest. The strength-sapping humidity took its toll on the pair as they struggled forward. Bazza believed that the men following them would be unprepared for pursuit in the rainforest, but possibly immune to the extreme heat and humidity. Bazza surmised that if they were from Colombia or parts thereof, they would experience similar climates to that of Northern Australia. They might even be acclimatised to jungle conditions if they had experience of the renowned Amazonian jungles penetrating parts of Colombia's borders to the south.

Bazza counted on the fact that they were probably incapable of tracking them. Keeping to the shallow creek bed for several miles negated the need to camouflage their tracks. That would only be required once they left the creek, something Bazza did not plan on too soon. It would take some intrinsic bush skill or dumb luck to enable the pair to catch up to Cheese and Bazza. He had no idea how determined or resilient the pair would be in their pursuit. Bazza huffed loudly as he struggled to keep the pace he had set for them. Only when he was totally out of breath, heaving heavily, with Cheese trailing way behind, did he stop for a break.

Bazza sat on an exposed boulder without leaving the creek bed. He waited until his breathing slowed before taking a swig from his canteen. When Cheese finally managed to catch up with him, she collapsed onto the rock beside Bazza, clutching her side where she was experiencing pain.

"Ya probably got a stitch, mate. Ya need ta have a drink and grab one-o-them salt tablets. Might pay us ta sit in the stream and cool down for a bit before we take orf again. I'll take it a bit slower here on. I think we got ahead of 'em enough."

Cheese couldn't say anything through the deep breaths and the pain wracking her side. She gulped great mouthfuls of water from her canteen, which soon emptied.

"No option but ta fill it from the creek, mate. Hope ya gut can stand it. Lotsa Giardia hereabouts."

"What, what…the fuck is Giardia now?"

Bazza raised his eyebrows. "You swore."

"I can swear. I'm old enough, and know how, Bazza. Now tell me. What is this new threat?"

"In the water generally. It's caused by a parasite distributed by way of faecal matter in food and water. Causes nasty gut problems that last for ages. Shit through the eye of a needle at twenty paces ya could. Cramps something chronic."

"Just full of good news aren't you?"

"Mosquitos can be a problem here too. Dengue Fever and Ross River Virus. Ya don't want that shit, so ya need ta put on ya repellent at night, mate."

"Repellent?"

"Mud. Only thing that works against 'em if ya outta the shack."

"Terrific! I'll be looking like a native in no time, and smelling like one sooner I expect. Why do you stay here, Bazza? What's wrong with running water, sanitation, and going a few streets away for necessities? You don't even have to live in a capital city to get those things."

"Wouldn't have all this, that's why. Silence - no bloody people jabbering away at ya night and day, no cars or sirens, no fucking telephones and rude people talking on 'em next ta ya. They live on the fuckers, specially kids. I hate it all, wouldn't live there anymore if ya paid me. That's why it wouldn't work 'tween us, Cheese. I'm not going back ta the city and ya won't be able ta hack it out here with me. No future, mate."

"I wasn't being literal, Bazza. I was having a bitch and a moan because I am totally exhausted. I have had more exercise in the last week than I imagine I've had in the previous year. I look like something the cat dragged in and I smell worse. I have been threatened with guns and bodily harm, not to mention rape. I have lost a lot of weight unintentionally by wandering through this endless bloody jungle and I haven't had a decent steak and fries or salad in I don't know how long. I've been more scared than I could possibly imagine and it isn't getting any easier, but I can cope with it, Bazza. I am learning to be harder and more resilient each day. I can see the beauty in this place and I am very fond of you, so don't give up on me and stop trying so hard to push me away. Now before you say another negative word about us or me, I'm going to slip into this water and just die for a while okay?"

"Chips."

"I beg your pardon?"

"Not fries. They're chips here. Not those skinny little fuckers ya have over there. Good solid chunks-o-potato deep fried till a golden, crispy brown, and usually served with beer-battered fish or…well, jest about everything actually. Chips-n-roast, chips-n-sauce, chips-n…"

"I get the picture, now shut-up please? You're making me hungry. I just want to cool down in here for a bit."

He joined her in the cool water. The air was clammy without the slightest breath of wind to take the edge off the relentless heat. Cheese moaned with pleasure as she immersed herself beneath the shallow, crystal-clear, rippling water. With the last of the monsoonal rains having abated, the rivers and creeks were reduced to a normal flow rather than the torrents rushing down to meet the ocean or join other rivers.

Bazza relaxed as he joined Cheese in the water, allowing his tensions to drift away on the flow. He closed his eyes to meditate with his head below the water for as long as his breath allowed. Cheese watched him in fascination after searching herself for leeches when she emerged, which soon turned to concern the longer he remained under. After two minutes she was nearing panic and began nudging him with her foot. When he did not respond she launched herself at him, lifting his upper torso from the water by reefing at his shirt. He came to the surface with a grin on his face that infuriated Cheese.

"What is wrong with you? Are you trying to check out and leave me with those two?"

"Whatcha talking about, Cheese? Hold me breath lot longer-n-that. As a kid I used ta be able ta swim under water for the length of an Olympic-sized swimming pool. Even thought about having a crack at that longest free dive thing. Saw a movie about that once and wanted ta have a go eva since. I reckon that'd be the duck's nuts diving way down inta the deep, dark, silent, ocean."

"Yes, well give a girl some warning about your super-human abilities in future would you? You scared the life out of me. I swear I've aged a dozen years since meeting you. I don't think I can take much more of all this." Cheese sat back on her haunches. "You got me thinking before, Bazza, about what exactly, Carlos and the others were after. You were right, it doesn't make much sense that they would get all het up about what must be a minor sum of money to them. I've been racking my brains trying to remember something about it all. Why my brothers and I came here? Do you think it was drugs? Carlos sure fits the bill, doesn't he?"

"That was my first thought, Cheese, but I can't see it now. Not only does it not make sense when looking at ya brothers-n-you, it don't make sense when I think-o-the amount of money in that bag. Something screwy is going on, that's for sure. Ya already look like ya come from money, Cheese, and not jest pussy-money either like the mongrel said. I reckon ya come from money with ya old man. I reckon ya knew money all along and maybe married inta it as well."

"What makes you think I'm married?"

"Didn't say that. Reckon ya *were* once, but not anymore, otherwise, ya woulda been here with ya hubby as well, not jest ya brothers."

"Connecting dots?"

"Trying ta. That rig up there is probably about half a mill on its own. Getting it over here, and yaselves, woulda cost a pretty penny as well. So what would ya buy drugs for? Nah, something else going on here. Boss man wouldn't come here in his fancy *ship* for a paltry coupla hundred grand. Never did get ta have a squizz in the twerp's boat. Mighta found something ta explain it. Nothing else ya found in that bag? It had a false bottom, did ya look under the real bottom?"

"The bottom board was attached to the bag, Bazza. I didn't think to look further than the money. It was flat, what could it possibly hold?"

"Dunno. Whaddya call them computer disc things?"

"CD Roms? Are we talking spy stuff now?"

"Bit far-fetched I know. Clutching at straws coz I can't figure it out. We better get moving. I don't think they can track us through the forest, but I still want ta get as far away as poss… Shit!"

"What is it?"

"Smell that? It's bloody Enrique and his puppet. How the fuck…?" After a moment's thought Bazza said, "Cheese, strip naked, everything off including ya shoes and socks."

"If you wanted to see me naked again…"

"Not the time, Cheese. Strip now and fucking hurry. Only put on ya second pair-o-shoes for the moment and then we gotta run like fuck."

Bazza and Cheese quickly stripped off all their clothing, donning only a spare pair of shoes before heading off once more. Bazza ran as far away from the discarded clothing as possible with Cheese barely able to maintain a passable pace some fifty feet behind. When Bazza judged his distance sufficient, he leaped out of the creek to begin trekking at a ninety-degree angle to the creek. Once he and Cheese had run through the forest for approximately five minutes, Bazza ordered Cheese to rest while he removed his backpack to reverse the journey on his own.

By backtracking to the creek where they emerged moments ago, Bazza was able to carefully disguise their movements from the creek all the way to where Cheese sat, exhausted and miserable.

"Cheese, open ya backpack and take everything out. Check every single item we took with us. Then do exactly the same ta mine. I hafta go off that way a bit ta see if they know which way we went. Because the creek does a dog-leg before leading to the spot where we ditched our gear, I can cut across to the other side of the bend through the forest ta see if they are still following the creek after us."

"I don't understand. What am I looking for, Bazza?"

"Tracking device. Thought it was all too easy. He knew we were gonna ta take orf and he made sure he could follow us. Once he finds our clothes, if the device is with them, we might be right for a while. If it's still here, we're in deep shit. Check everything really carefully. I'm hoping like crazy it was on the clothes we were wearing. Hurry, I'll be back as soon as I can."

Bazza rushed off to intercept their pursuers before they reached the bend. By cutting across land he had every reason to believe he would reach his destination before them. What he would do once there other than observing their forward progress was anybody's guess. Bazza thought at the very least he may satisfy himself that he was correct in his assumption that they had planted a tracking device on them at some point. He would be able to witness them following some sort of electronic hand-held device if that were the case. If not; he would be stymied for an explanation.

With the consummate ease of man well-versed in the art of

travelling through a dizzying terrain of identical trees to reach a predetermined destination, Bazza made his way unerringly to the reconnoitring point. The scent of the perfumed man hung heavily in the air, increasing in intensity the closer he came to the creek. Before Bazza reached the creek, he hunched down to get out of sight of anyone walking upstream. He found a place from which to observe the creek without being visible.

Bazza did not have long to wait before he saw the two men approaching the bend in the creek at a quick trot, with muscle-man in the lead holding an electronic transponder in front of him. Both men wore backpacks containing provisions and whatever else they deemed important. When they came to the bend they slowed. Marcos held the device out in front of him, pointing directly in Bazza's direction, while his eyes were following the line of the creek off to their right. The pair discussed the situation when the head honcho caught up with the beast. They debated their theories back and forth. Marcos was inclined to leave the creek and take the overland route, while Carlos was undecided. In the end, Carlos won, seeing the two men continue along the creek as before with Marcos in front setting an energy-sapping pace.

The creek bed, where not slippery with moss and algae-covered rocks, was soft sand. Bazza was surprised at how fast the pair were able to travel considering the difficulties. Their only slight advantage over the pair was Bazza's ability to move quicker in the forest. Bazza quickly decided on a strategy he had used to great effect during his training days in the army. He reversed his direction to head back to Cheese. Time was of the essence, and he and Cheese were running out of that precious commodity at an alarming rate. He ran hard and fast for many moments before breaking into the small clearing where he left Cheese.

"Forget it, leave everything behind, we don't have time. We're going back. Follow me and keep up Cheese."

Bewildered, Cheese numbly tossed aside the backpack she had been holding to run after Bazza in her ill-fitting, borrowed sand shoes. Two naked bodies running pell-mell through the forest, slipping, sliding, and falling. They were completely at the mercy of the elements and their pursuers. Bazza bounded ahead of Cheese, bullying his way through any undergrowth they encountered. He was being torn and scratched brutally by the forest. Cheese did not fare much better in his wake.

They only stopped for a breath when they came to the point in the creek where he had observed their pursuers having the debate over which way to proceed. They entered the creek once more to head back toward the shack. Bazza stopped suddenly. Training his head around in all directions to grasp the elusive sound. A barely audible, alien sound in the rainforest. Bazza was so attuned to all the sounds of the forest that anything other than natural forest sounds stood out clearly in his auditory memory. He was confused by the sound if what he assumed were true. More than likely it was the receiving unit used in tracking them making the sound. If that was true, then their pursuers sounded as if they were getting closer as opposed to gaining distance.

"Cheese, I dunno what's going on but it sounds like those fuckers are coming back. Won't take 'em long ta get here either. I have an idea, but it's bloody risky seeing as I can't be certain-o-something. I want ya to go back the way we jest come. Back ta the backpacks. Get there and stay there. Can ya find ya way?"

"What is it? How come they're coming back?"

"Coffee. No time ta explain, Cheese, I gotta run like fuck ta get 'em off ya track. Can ya get back ta the packs and our clothes?"

Cheese nodded uncertainly. She hugged herself to stifle a shiver despite the cloying heat making breathing difficult.

"Good girl. Now get going. I'm gonna try ta get back ta ya tonight but might take longer. Ya stay put and get dressed okay? If ya can manage ya hammock fine, if not, roll yaself up in ya poncho and keep as still as ya can all night. Go!"

Bazza watched Cheese clamber awkwardly out of the creek. He suppressed a sigh at seeing her well-rounded, perfect derrière, healed to astounding perfection, jouncing away into the forest.

"Ya *are,* a looker, Cheese, a damn fine looker."

Bazza raced off in the opposite direction. He aimed to loop around in front of his trackers again, making them get out of the creek to follow. His plan was to make the waterfall with the cave by nightfall. By going overland it would slow his trackers down considerably. He needed to run as fast and far as possible. He needed to prove his theory but to do so, required a line of sight. He did not trust proximity again. If his pursuers reached the discarded clothing in the creek, they would be aware that their targets had figured something out. They would only follow in a straight line from then on, knowing that following the creek would no longer necessarily lead them to their targets.

Bazza raced into the gloom of the forest leaving a clear trail behind. Blood from various scratches and footprints would confirm to his trackers that they were dead on his heels. He didn't know if he could keep running like a madman for much longer. He no longer had his canteen and was not in the creek to grab a mouthful of water on the hop. He was sweating profusely, draining his body of essential elements. He hoped to maintain his loping run for an hour, needing to reach the cave. A semblance of a plan was fermenting in his brain.

By late afternoon, with the sun dropping over the western side of the mountain, the forest plummeted abruptly into semi-darkness. Bazza knew he was nearing the falls because he could hear them clearly. His pursuers were only a few minutes behind him. He had to slow his pace considerably so as not to take a tumble on a tree root or exposed rock. Any form of injury would spell his immediate capture and probably his demise. He heard the duo several times during his dash through the forest. Marcos, the brute, was clearly revelling in the pursuit like a hound on the scent. Thankfully, he heard both voices at times, meaning neither man was chasing Cheese. They were content to follow him alone.

Bazza slipped into the cave as he crept up the creek. The water began to chill him despite the heat trapped in the forest. Bazza swam to the deepest part of the cave pool, directly beneath the waterfall passing through the hole in the roof of the cavern. The cavern itself was dimly lit with thousands of tiny pinpricks of light emanating from the glow worms. Bazza waited, treading water, trying desperately to achieve a bowel movement. He had never had to attempt something like it before in such circumstances and found it near impossible to do so on command with all the tension he felt. The longer he took, the more he risked being discovered by his trackers. He saw the first signs of them as they shone a torch back and forth in front of the cave's entrance. Bazza descended to the bottom of the pool as he saw them enter the cave.

Beneath the water, a muted roar and darkness enveloped him. He began to relax. Meditated as the probing torch beam shone overhead in sweeping arcs. He played back in his mind the events of the encounter with the strangers in his shack. When the coffee was served by Cheese, he had turned away for a moment to point in the direction of the tablelands, where his regular coffee was grown. In a mirror on the wall, unbeknownst to Carlos, Bazza observed the man switching coffee cups with him. Bazza thought Carlos had switched cups because Carlos believed it might have been spiked with something, when in fact, it was Carlos who spiked his own cup with a tracking device, which he then swapped for Bazza's. That moment when Bazza believed he had Carlos thinking that he had spiked the coffee, was pure play-acting on the man's part. Bazza began to suspect he had *swallowed* a bloody transmitter soon after he detected the pair reversing direction in the creek to follow *him*, instead of the clothing.

Bazza relaxed further into his meditative state to gain the precious moments he required unseen beneath the surface of the water. He believed that the transponder held by the pair indicated direction only, not distance. If it indicated a distance they would know he was under water a mere ten feet or so from their position at the edge of the pool. They had to assume that Bazza was somewhere on the opposite side of the pool hiding in the recesses of the cave. The only way they could reach the other side was to wade across the pool. Bazza believed the pair would wait him out, maybe even fire a few shots randomly to flush him out.

He had been underwater for over a minute. He knew he could stay a little longer, but he would have to surface soon. They might not see his head immediately once he surfaced for air, especially as he would rise directly under the waterfall, but it was not a chance he wanted to take. He concentrated hard on the task, only to find it a futile exercise. There was only one method he knew that would enable him to produce a bowel movement - anal insertion and manipulation underwater to mimic an enema. He had done it a few times as a child when sitting for long moments on the dunny with nothing occurring. Through a combination of inserting his finger into his anus and manipulating the rectum at the edges, he was able to induce an action. With distaste, he mimicked his childhood memories, while the icy water chilled him to the bone. All the heat of exertion had escaped his body, leaving him shivering, desperately yearning for warmth, and severely impeding his capacity to remain under water.

His lungs were struggling with the lack of oxygen, screaming at him to surface. His entire body shook with the onset of hypothermia. Bazza resisted the impulse to surrender, to break through the surface to breathe in a lungful of sweet fresh air. Every muscle and fibre warred with his brain to surface. His resistance grew weaker. If he did not surface soon, his instinctual reaction would be to open his mouth, to take a lungful of air no matter where he was. His hand moved quicker to force himself into an unnatural ablution, totally out of his daily routine. Just as he felt himself start to fade into unconsciousness, he felt his bowel reacting to the stimulus.

Seconds later, the resulting faeces moved downstream quickly, caught in the fast moving flow. Bazza, unable to hold on any longer, rose to the surface beneath the heavy cascade of water. Shielding his mouth from the spray all about him, he gulped in a life-saving breath of air. He stayed hidden beneath the spray for as long as he dared, filling his lungs with oxygen. He was unable to detect any movement within the cave through the curtain of water surrounding him. He knew he would have to emerge from the water soon, in order to prevent hypothermia. While water in the tropics did not reach temperatures anywhere near that of colder climates, pure mountain water, descending into a pool within a cave was more than adequate to cause death by hypothermia, if exposed long enough.

Bazza eased himself from under the waterfall. Once in the clear, he discerned no movement or light from the banks. Slowly, his eyes adjusted to the darkness within the cave, allowing the glint from the glow-worms to illuminate the scene. He was alone. His pursuers were following his floating faecal matter with their transponder for the moment. He hoped his turd would not get stuck in an eddy or get caught up too soon on an obstruction. He needed a little time before they cottoned onto the fact that they were no longer following a human being. He desperately required some time to get back to Cheese and his clothes to get warm.

Bazza slithered from the pool on his belly to make sure that he produced no visible profile from the exterior. Crawling through the bat guano, insect detritus, and mud on the cavern floor, he reached the opening where he surveyed the creek and surrounds carefully for signs of his pursuers. Satisfied that he was alone, he gratefully raised himself to begin his trek back to Cheese and the warmth he required so desperately. Bazza strained his ears and nose for any signs of pursuit. He knew he had gained only a small amount of time until they became aware of the ruse.

Bazza had only recently read about ingestible micro-transmitters in the science magazines he enjoyed. He falsely believed they were not readily available to the public, being mainly for military or medical use. He knew then, that his adversaries had formidable resources at their disposal. Bazza pondered the possibility that they may also have thermal imaging equipment and night-vision goggles, a combination of which would see him and Cheese discovered in no time. Bazza knew that their lives depended upon evasion at all costs. He had no idea what the boffins were after, or what the truth behind their circumstances may be, but he suspected that far more was in play than previously assumed.

When he reached Cheese, she immediately clasped him to her, wrapping herself around him to provide warmth to his chilled body, then balked at the smell of his mud-covered skin. They huddled as silently as his chattering teeth allowed, ensconced beneath her waterproof poncho. Cheese rapidly rubbed him over to create the friction necessary for immediate warmth. She did not bother asking any questions, knowing that silence was paramount and that Bazza was probably incapable of speech in his present state. They remained glued together for over an hour before Bazza eventually stirred.

"Cheese, we can't stay here. I reckon they got some hi-tech equipment that will bring 'em right here fore we know it. Let me get some clobber on, then we'll scram, okay?" He whispered.

"Right now, I'm so scared I'll do anything you say. Just let me help you and don't run off and leave me again please?"

"Jest trying ta protect ya. These bastards are fair-dinkum scary and bloody well-prepared. I need ya ta start thinking again, mate. See if ya can dredge up a memory or two will ya? We need ta know what all these blokes are after. I'm missing something here, something important, and if I don't figure it out soon, we are gonna get killed."

"What's the plan?"

"Going back ta the bag up the track. We missed something, something they believe is worth killing for. If we know what it is we might have something ta bargain with. If we don't find it, we're fucked!"

"Can you find your way there in the dark, Bazza?"

"Dunno; soon find out. Just hope I fooled them two long enough for us ta get outta here. We hafta take it real easy walking around in here at night, Cheese. Not only ta stop from making a lot of noise, but ta avoid accidents. I'm still as cold as a penguin's penis here, but I'll hafta live with it. Get warm enough once we get going. I'm gonna tie ya ta me waist with a bit-o-rope, mate. Otherwise, ya'll lose me. Here stick that end around ya."

"A new twist on the old ball and chain eh?"

"Ya lost me there, mate?"

"Never mind."

Bazza and Cheese stopped talking as they took off in the approximate direction of the track. Bazza was aiming at intersecting the track about a quarter of the way up the mountain if he could manage that in the dark. The rainforest allows next to no light to penetrate the canopy, making it blacker than black below. Bazza could not allow the use of torches he brought along for fear of being seen. A torch light would stand out from far away, making them easy targets to follow. Only when Bazza believed they were far enough from their hunters, would he dare use the torches, sparingly, with a hand covering most of the lens. Until that time, they made their way stealthily across the forest floor staying as low to the ground as possible.

Bazza told Cheese of his suspicions about the hi-tech equipment the Columbians might have. The information chilled Cheese more than the night breeze wafting down the mountain. Each time they heard a noise like leaves rustling or movement on the forest floor, they had to stop long moments to determine the nature of the noise. Cheese followed blindly behind Bazza on the end of her short lead, bumping into his back on numerous occasions. She grew frustrated at being totally blind within the hostile environment. She grew more afraid each time they paused, imagining their antagonists attacking them from out of the darkness with cold ferocity.

Around midnight, after stumbling about blindly for so long that Cheese began to wonder if Bazza knew his way at all, he finally turned his torch on and kept his hand off the lens. Cheese welcomed the light like a long-lost friend, breathing a big sigh of relief. Her relief was not long-lived, however, as Bazza quickly moved off again, shining the torch in front, leaving Cheese in the relative darkness behind him once more. Although Bazza had good light to see by, he moved cautiously none-the-less. One wrong step on the steepening grade could see them injure themselves seriously. One slip from either of them would send the other tumbling after.

An hour later saw Bazza setting foot on his track. He paused long enough to cause Cheese to question him.

"Which way to the bag, Bazza, up or down?"

"Trying ta get me bearings, ta recognise something. Bloody hard in the dark, everything looks so different. I think we need ta go down a fraction till we hit the log that I moved. That's where we cut off the track ta the fairy circle."

"Where do you think the other two are?"

"If I was 'em, I'da gorn back ta the boat or me shack. They woulda searched an hour or two then gave up I reckon. Not gonna do much good in the dark. They'll be bloody pissed orf that I cottoned onto-'em. Pretty fucking sneaky it was too."

"So, what was it? If it wasn't on our clothes, where was it? They never touched me or you in the shack did they?"

"Ingestible emitter. I caught that mongrel swapping coffee cups with me. Saw him in the mirror when he thought I wasn't watching. I thought he was just being clever, thinking I had spiked *his* coffee. He musta put it in his own cup then swapped with mine. I knew they had medical capsules that ya could swallow, but I didn't know they had anything so advanced and obviously available in the right circles."

"How on Earth did you get it out?"

"Ya don't wanna know. Believe me, ya don't wanna know. I, don't wanna know, but I'm stuck with it up here", said Bazza pointing to his head.

He led off down the track for a short ways, before reversing his direction to move upward instead. He ignored Cheese, who giggled behind him in the dark. They walked in silence for another ten minutes before Bazza veered off the track, to shortly arrive at the circle of palms where they had hidden the bag. Bazza decided that trying to find anything in the bag at night was a risk. Besides possibly missing something vital, the light would be a beacon for many miles in every direction. If the Colombians had not given up the chase, deciding to linger within the vicinity of the shack, they might happen to see a flash of light in the pure velvet darkness.

He pressed Cheese close as they lay upon the ground to nap for a short time. Neither Bazza nor Cheese had been able to have a drink or fill their canteens in a long while. The awkward trek had left them weak and thirsty with only the coffee in their thermos to assuage their thirst. Bazza had to rethink their plan of action based on what they found or did not find the following morning. Meanwhile, his eyelids drooped the moment he lay next to Cheese, who wrapped her arms around the big man in a warm embrace.

Bazza could not remember the last time he felt such solace in a woman's embrace. The very thought of such a thing mere months ago would have sent him into an anxious panic. It was a condition bordering on a phobia with Bazza from the time he broke up with his ex-wife. It was an alien feeling to have a female in such proximity without Bazza feeling nauseous with terror. His ex-wife left scars that he believed would never mend. That he felt them healing at long last surprised him, confronted him, and consoled him all at the same time.

CHAPTER FIFTEEN

Bazza woke suddenly, alert, anxious. Something had

strummed his sensors like prey tripping a Trapdoor's silken alarms. He worked the sleep from his eyes, his senses trained onto the forest with seasoned acuity. His nose perceived nothing of significance, his eyes distinguished nothing out of the ordinary, yet the hairs on the back of his neck presaged impending danger. Without broadcasting his suspicions he continued his furtive glances about him as he gently woke Cheese from her catatonic slumber.

Whispering as softly as possible without appearing to do so, Bazza informed Cheese to act as though they were unaware of the immediate danger. Bazza could not explain who or what exactly caused the alarms to ring in his head, or from which direction danger may emerge. He did not want to retrieve the bag from its hiding place until he was positive they were alone. The nagging irritation persisted. Bazza decided the best way to play it was to simply stop, open a can of baked beans and have a cuppa from the thermos. Acting as casual as possible, he and Cheese sat down to their meagre breakfast.

The forest was unusually silent in Bazza's opinion. It had a foreboding quality to it. It was not the natural quiet that eased from night cacophony to daytime ethereality. It was a tense stillness that invaded his senses as surely as the chill entered his body in the pool the previous evening. The heat began to make its presence known, though it was not the heat that caused a droplet of sweat to make its way slowly from Bazza's eyebrow to his chin. The clammy intensity increased exponentially with every passing moment.

When the shot rang out, it startled the entire forest into frightened sounds of retreat, in the air and on the ground. Cheese, who had instinctively ducked to the ground, began to raise her head when no further sounds persisted. She watched as Bazza toppled to the ground like a felled tree. The side of his face was covered in blood where his ear had been sliced by the projectile. Before Cheese was able to render assistance, an eerie, slurping voice called out.

"Don moofch."

Cheese could not make out the direction of the wet, syrupy

voice. She stayed flat to the ground, keeping an eye on Bazza for signs of life. While she could easily identify the split in his ear, she was unable to determine if the bullet had damaged anything else. She silently prayed that the bullet had not entered Bazza's skull. She wept for him, and herself, believing Carlos or Marcos had managed to track them despite all their subterfuge. She was wholly unprepared for the nightmare that emerged from the forest.

Walking unsteadily toward her was the stuff of horror movies without the need for props or make-up. A hideous face devoid of the epidermis, revealing the raw, weeping, bleeding, muscle and flesh beneath. A grotesque parody of the human form found in most medical practitioner's offices for demonstrating underlying facial tissue and muscles. It moved forward in an ungainly lope like one of the undead in a zombie movie, with one glaring exception. The eyes burned with a fierce intensity that threatened to destroy anything in its path. Clothing of torn and tattered rags, as if in preparation for a Halloween party, added to the movie-like impression.

When it arrived at their position it stood at the edge, piercing Cheese with a menacing, unblinking stare. It appeared that its eyelids were glued open by blood and weeping matter congealing in the folds between lid and brow. It gave Cheese the impression of what the eyes of a deer might look like when caught in the headlights of a vehicle at night. She shivered involuntarily at the thought of being consumed by some horrible creature from her worst movie experience. What it said next did not dissipate her fears in that regard.

"Foo, bak binch."

Cheese blinked in confusion. She did not understand what it wanted. It gripped a hand weapon firmly, a highly polished weapon, while pointing to something near her.

"Bak binch, bak binch", it slurped and smacked with a drooling relish.

"Oh, baked beans right? You want some baked beans? I hope."

The thing nodded vigorously flicking fluid over her. Cheese slowly sat upright, retrieving a second can of baked beans from Bazza's backpack. Bazza lay prone, only his heaving chest indicating life. Cheese was able to see a nasty graze along his scalp where the bullet passed before slicing the ear. To Cheese's amateur mind, it appeared as if the shooter had been shooting from a raised position, possibly from a tree, reasonably close to their position, to enable an accurate shot from a handgun, or inaccurate if the shot was meant to enter the skull. Cheese opened the can which she offered to the thing standing before her. It snatched the proffered can with an urgency born of need. She watched in disgust as it discarded the spoon to eat greedily with filthy, blood encrusted hands.

Cheese barely contained her impulse to retch while watching it gorging on the baked beans with sickening slurping sounds. Baked beans and tomato sauce dribbled from the corners of its mouth, adding to the festering ooze adorning its face. It was only when Cheese noticed the footwear, Nike runners, that she finally realised what, or rather, who, it was. Rafael, sans facial skin, abruptly threw away the empty can demanding more of the same. Cheese complied to the request with resigned equanimity. She knew that both she and Bazza were in mortal danger. One false move would see Rafael lose control, shooting one or both of them without hesitation.

He was obviously deranged as a result of the 'accident'. She could not begin to understand the torment he had been through and how it resulted in the ghoulish presence before her. Nothing her mind could conjure explained the evil thing that morphed from the man she once knew as Rafael. His wide-eyed stare had a crazed, maniacal, malevolence to it. His ragged appearance with open wounds and abrasions covering his body told of a wild, panicked run through the rainforest, reminiscent of the misadventures she must have experienced during the flight that brought her to Bazza's shack.

As Rafael slurped loudly on his baked beans, Cheese could see him clearly plotting a course of action for his captives. She harboured no delusions of a happy outcome for her and Bazza. Her brain raced rapidly through dozens of scenarios in a vain attempt to find anything that might save them. Bazza groaned, causing Rafael to nearly choke on the contents of his full mouth, causing his eyes to widen further if that were possible. Rafael threw away the second empty can, pointing his weapon squarely at Bazza's forehead, shaking with excitement at the thought of being rid of his enemy.

Cheese helped Bazza to a sitting position when he came fully awake. He neither baulked at the sight of the nightmarish vision standing over him with a gun nor showed the slightest hint of surprise. Bazza simply nodded his head in resignation that the foul thing before him was the reincarnation of the Colombian mongrel who owned a face when last they saw him.

"Use bark did ya?" When Rafael did not respond…"Ya know, bark from a tree ta rub orf the stinging hairs? Only it took the skin away as well huh? Shouldn't-o-rub so hard, mate. Do yaself irreparable damage that way. Garn, get it over with ya mongrel. Shoot me dead and fuck orf back ta ya own part-o-the world ya dago prick. I've fucking had ya ta me eyeballs ya piece a shit."

Rafael inched forward with his finger straining on the trigger of the weapon, grimacing with a rictus-like delight to finally kill the Gringo. Nervously, the finger tightened on the trigger till only a touch was required to release the pin into the bullet's base to release the powder charge, sending the lead projectile into and through Bazza's head. Cheese and Bazza held their breath as they waited for the inevitable. Sweat beaded on Bazza's brow despite feigned nonchalance.

All three heads swivelled in unison when they heard the sound coming from the bottom of the track. Bazza recognised the sound of his four-wheel-drive vehicle slowly grinding through the gears on its upward journey. Cheese and Rafael looked confused. Rafael, whose mind was seriously damaged by the events of the previous days, could not fathom why a vehicle would be making its way up the mountain towards them. He only knew fear. Fear of discovery by the authorities, or worse, by his boss. His unblinking eyes almost shed a tear of frustration at not being able to kill the Gringo. With a wild roar of anger, he flung his tormented body into flight away from the perceived danger. Bazza and Cheese watched in astonishment as he disappeared into the gloom.

"That'll be them other fuckers. Heard the shot probably. Found me Ute keys and are having a go at getting up the mountain ta find us and whatever it is they're looking for. Can't believe the tenacity-o-these pricks. Ya thoughta anything?"

"No. Let me look at that cut and your ear, Bazza."

"Nah, no time, mate. We gotta get the bag. Make like a tree and leave."

"Very funny. Your warped sense of humour is going to get us both killed one of these days, *mate*."

Bazza and Cheese dug furiously to unearth the bag from its hiding place, while the vehicle drew unerringly closer, belching diesel fumes into the humid air. Bazza knew that the vehicle would draw level with their position in only a few moments. While they could not be seen directly from the track, the path leading to their clearing was well-marked. Obviously, the earlier gunshot had brought the others motoring quickly to the sound. Bazza and Cheese had to get out of there fast.

Once the bag was recovered, a headlong rush into the forest ensued. Bazza made sure to run off in a different direction to the mongrel. He did not fancy running into that freak again anytime soon. Bazza was still somewhat groggy and light-headed from his near death experience but managed to keep up a healthy pace, leaving Cheese behind in his wake. Bazza angled their flight to take a long loop to connect up with another tributary of the creek that ran by the rear of his shack. They would follow that until they reached the southern end of the beach.

Behind them, they could hear the loud whine as the Ute increased its revs to redline level while it made its way up the steep grade.

The Colombians were not being kind to Bazza's four cylinder Ute, punishing the machine by maxing out the revs instead of idling up the track at a modest pace, allowing the diesel's low gear torque to eat away at the gradient like the proverbial tortoise. Bazza knew that his Ute might not survive the treatment dished out by the ignorant pair in charge. Everything occurring since running across Cheese was either dangerous, costly, or both. He did not know how he would manage once the ordeal was over, if he survived. Who knew what the men had done to his home while he and Cheese were gone. The only thing he could rule out was that they might have set fire to everything. He would have smelled that long ago.

Cheese stumbled along behind Bazza who set a punishing pace. After half an hour of a gruelling, energy-sapping, sprint through the disorienting forest, Bazza emerged through a patch of dense undergrowth, into a stream of crystal-clear water meandering casually in its path downhill to join another river, before finally heading out to the ocean. Bazza collapsed headlong into the cool, refreshing water. Cheese was unsure if Bazza had deliberately brought them to the site of a deep pool, or if he simply stumbled upon it. Either way, she was glad simply to fall into the water head-first.

Neither moved for moments as their chests ached from the exertion of their dash. The invigorating water rejuvenated their fatigued limbs and muscles. Both gulped water from their hands as they replenished their dehydrated bodies. Cheese felt deliriously happy to be floating in the quiet pool after the terrifying run. She honestly believed that she and Bazza were living on borrowed time, knowing that they should both have perished at the fairy circle. They had escaped death too many times for there to be any chances remaining.

She didn't know what Bazza had in mind, but she was willing to argue with whatever he thought of next. His track record to date left much to be desired and her faith in his logic waned. She was bone-tired of the tension, of the fear, of the exhaustion, and most of all, the rainforest. She yearned to be anywhere else but in the rainforest. She felt an overwhelming claustrophobia under the canopy. She had to escape into the open, to be free of the cloying atmosphere threatening to collapse on her. Never could she remember a time when she felt so much anxiety about a location. She eyed the bag that Bazza had flung off at the last moment before plunging into the water.

What evil resided in that bag, she wondered. *What could*

possibly have driven her and her brothers to the ends of the world, followed by such inhuman filth? She felt a horrible, undeniable guilt at having exposed Bazza, an innocent bystander, to all the evil she had brought with her. Where it would all end was anyone's guess, but she was determined to create some distance between her and Bazza. His temperament was transgressing into impulsive gestures that would see him dead unless she dissociated herself from him. He was a good man, too good to be involved in such a mess. Her selfish needs had brought him nothing but misery and pain. It was time she stood up for herself, left Bazza alone to live his life as it should be.

"I can hear them cogs grinding away up there, Cheese. Need some real good lubricating they do. Watcha thinking?"

"I think it's time, Bazza."

"Time for what, mate?"

"I think we need to split up…for good."

"Wow, sick-o-me company already?"

"You know it's not like that."

"I know damn-well that ya said ya wouldn't do something? Promised it. Now ya breaking that promise!"

"Bazza, no, I meant…"

"Save it! Been there, done that. Garn, orf ya go then."

Bazza stormed off after collecting his backpack, leaving Cheese with unvoiced protests locked in her open mouth. Lost for words, she wrenched herself away from her stasis by gathering herself, the bag, and her own backpack, to run after the fleeing figure. Her oversized and soaked army fatigues, as well as Bazza's cast-off sand shoes slowed her progress considerably, but she managed to finally catch up to him at the beach.

"Now just you hold on one cotton-picking minute, Mr. Barry Ottoman! Turn around and look at me you son-of-a-bitch. I was talking about splitting up for *your* safety, to stop exposing *you* to whatever it is I've brought to your doorstep."

"Good intentions huh? Splitting up means splitting up, Cheese, no matter what language ya speak, and last time I heard, ya English was fine. Ya think I'm gonna be any safer if ya get going by yaself? Ya dreaming ya silly bitch. I'm fucked no matter what ya do. Them bastards aren't gonna let bygones be bygones with me, whether they catch up with ya or not. Don't be such a drongo."

"I, I…just thought… We haven't been doing so well together, maybe you would be better off without me?"

"Alive aren't ya? I was willing ta stick it out. I haven't given up. The only thing I haven't done which I coulda, was kill the fuckers. I was a trained soldier, more trained than most in all sorts-o-shit. Hand-to-hand combat, firearms, me bow and arra, all sorts-o-ways-o-killing, but I won't do it. I'll keep running 'em around in bloody circles till they drop dead or give up. Don't even know what they're after yet. If I knew that I might have a better idea of what ta do. Until then, I run like fuck."

"I'm sorry Bazza. You've been very, very good to me. More than I deserve, that's for sure. I wasn't thinking clearly I suppose, and yes, the best intentions hurt just as much as the worst. I feel so guilty about everything that's happened to you. I was only hoping to make it easier. I can see that was stupid of me. You're right, they won't stop with just me now. They have the type of personality that would hunt you down out of spite alone, or for fun in Marcos' case. Please forgive me Bazza? I have strong feelings for you despite what you believe. I did think you were running out of options, though, and I just thought you might have a better chance on your own."

"I could do a Hell of a lot better on me own, but I made the choice to stick with ya, and I don't make them sorta decisions lightly. I'm bloody loyal and dependable to a fault. No one ever had a better friend than me if I decided ta accept someone's friendship."

A weighty silence hung between the pair as they stood at the top of the beach in the brilliant sunshine. Cheese felt lousy. Her suggestion had sounded to Bazza exactly like someone wanting to break up a relationship. When she replayed it in her head she saw the hurt she caused, the one thing she promised she would not do. Cheese knew that her best chance of survival was to stick with Bazza. Unfortunately, that wasn't *his* best option.

"We need to search this bag, don't we? We need to find something to make sense of all this."

"Not here, though. Too exposed."

"Back at your shack?"

"Nah, not safe there. Only one place I can think of at the moment."

Without saying another word, Bazza began walking northwards. Cheese followed.

"I thought you said it wouldn't be safe back at the shack?"

"Wouldn't be", said Bazza continuing to walk ahead.

"But, isn't this the direction to your shack?"

"Yep."

"Bazza?"

"Yeah?"

"Friends?"

"I'm letting ya follow me aren't I?"

 "I guess I deserve that."

"That-n-more."

She followed him a couple of miles back along the beach to the point where the path from the shack emerged onto the dunes. He told her to wait at his dinghy for him, while he crept back to the *Cathedral*. Cheese searched the bay and the ocean beyond the reef for the ocean-going vessel that had brought Carlos and his men to their shores. Before she could think further, she rewound her thought to realise she thought of the area as belonging to her and Bazza. It surprised her that she felt such a strong connection. She had not consciously thought beyond the present circumstances. She did not think she could ever realise a connection to such an inhospitable region of the world.

Out in the bay floated the boat in which Rafael had arrived. Beyond the reef, the other vessel belonging to Carlos lay at anchor. A magnificent specimen of some 120 feet of opulent luxury and sleek lines. Even from a great distance, the ship appeared like some grand, bejewelled, dame, languidly lounging on a li-lo upon the calm waters. She could not fathom the reason a man of such obvious wealth would have in chasing her down. The money in the bag was a pittance to a man who owned such a glorious vessel. Before she thought more on the matter, Bazza appeared from the path carrying a fuel container.

He loped over to his dinghy. He pulled back the covering tarpaulin, to expose the fuel tank and outboard motor. With practised dexterity, he quickly transferred the contents of the container into the fuel tank on the dinghy after taking a quick swig for himself. He pumped the fuel through the hose to the outboard via the black rubber bulb on the fuel line. He then hauled the dinghy around to face the water. Pushing hard from the rear, he quickly began pushing the lightweight dinghy down the beach effortlessly. Once in the water, he ran back to the top of the beach to retrieve the backpacks and the bag. He ushered Cheese into the bow of the dinghy to balance out the load while he started up the reliable outboard. Within moments they were boarding Rafael's vessel.

He hesitated before entering the cabin, remembering the last encounter that saw him staring down the barrel of a gun. What they saw in the cabin surprised and shocked them. It was like a bomb had detonated aboard tearing everything apart except for the hull's exterior. All the furniture and timberwork lay in splinters. Deck linings and hull inner linings chopped to shreds with a fire axe. The contents of all bottles, cupboards, and drawers strewn about the wreckage of floorboards.

"Bloody generous-o-the bastard ta give me a boat after he smashed it ta smithereens. Not worth a cracker now. Lucky it actually still floats."

"Do you think they found what they were looking for?"

"Doubt it. They probably wouldn't be looking for us so hard if they'd found it. They must reckon either that we have it, or that other bozo."

"I think you're right about one thing, Bazza, whatever it is they're looking for, it has nothing to do with the money in this bag or drugs. What could it be?"

"Only two things drives men ta such extremes - wealth or power. If it's wealth, it's the sorta wealth that can change the economy of a small country. Power, ta change the *leadership* of a small country. Dictatorial power, greed, and religion; the three things that fucked the world. Or maybe they are jest all the same fucking thing."

"Pretty pessimistic outlook."

"Tell me I'm wrong."

"What now?"

"I think it's time we took that bag apart. Dump the stuff over here where we have a bit of flooring left."

Cheese upended the bag onto the deck, spilling the bundled money and underwear onto the only remaining intact deck section. Bazza kept a lookout while Cheese went through every item meticulously looking for split seams in clothing, hidden slips of paper within the bundles of money, and turning the bag itself inside out. After a few moments, Cheese sat back on the floor, stymied.

"Nothing, Bazza, absolutely nothing!"

Nothing was said as he weighed all the evidence. Everything pointed to an exchange of some sort between Cheese, her family, and the mongrel. The mongrel was after the money. Of that he was certain. It was all the twerp kept on about the entire time they were stuck together. His boss wanted something else entirely. It stood to reason that Cheese and her brothers were looking to buy something off the little Colombian and his cohorts. Something he had in his possession was worth around two hundred thousand bucks. Whatever it was for sale, was either purchased or…stolen, from the boss. Something so precious, that nothing would deter the boss from his quest to retrieve it.

Assuming the boss found it, it begged the purpose behind their continued pursuit. Even if the boss didn't find it, it didn't explain why he thought Bazza or Cheese might have something to do with it. They weren't in cahoots with the runt, and the boss had to know that. They told him they were being held against their will. They explained how everything happened and the boss had no idea that Cheese was in any way connected with the original transaction to exchange money for whatever was being sold.

Bazza looked carefully at the contents of the bag Cheese had emptied on the deck. A small pile of her undies, indicated that the bag had belonged to her originally. A stack of money, not enough to cause such a hullabaloo by any stretch of the imagination. The bag itself holding nothing else. The false…bottom!

"Cheese, that false bottom. We haven't taken the leather cover off ta see if there is anything hidden there. Take that knife from the sink and carefully slice it open along one edge."

Cheese did as she was asked without any enthusiasm. She held no hopes of a surprise awaiting them in the ordinary board separating the clothes in the bag from the money when they first found the bag. She gently sliced open the stitched seam joining the leather pocket together containing what Cheese believed would reveal nothing but stiff cardboard, or a thin piece of hardboard. What she pulled out from the open pocket was neither.

Bazza inspected the thin, laminated object, possibly old parchment. Cheese and Bazza sat staring at the object for some time with mixed feelings about their discovery.

"Can you make anything out, Cheese?"

"It's some sort of map."

"No shit? I'm talking about the writing, know what language that is?"

"It seems to have a Spanish flavour to it, but nothing that I recognise. Maybe it's Portuguese?"

"It's bloody old that's for sure. Has a really odd colour and texture ta it, like no sort-o-paper I've ever seen. Odd sorta shape too huh?"

"Could be old parchment. That would have discoloured over time. Probably why they laminated it."

"What about leather? They used leather back then, didn't they? Thin kid leather or something like that eh? Only, what's that thing there, at the edge?"

"Hard to say. It is very, very old and was probably very brittle. I cannot imagine why my brothers and I would have such a thing and what it could be for. Obviously, some sort of coastline, see anything familiar?"

"Why would I see anything familiar?"

"Well, think about it. We, my brothers and I, came here with a map of some sort outlining a coast. Has to be something to do with *this* stretch of coast don't you think? Otherwise, we wouldn't be here, surely?"

"Yeah orright, didn't think-o-that. Still doesn't look like anything around here, though. If that map is as old as I think it is, might not be very accurate anyway. Wasn't supposed ta be any explorers in Australia before Chooky and Tasman, though. My history's not much chop. Never did take ta that old shit in school."

"Chooky?"

"Captain Cook, the bloody old chook, sailed around Australia…?"

"I'm putting that down to having to be an Australian to know that, Bazza. Who's Tasman?"

"Some Duchy that found Tasmania and called it Van Diemen's Land, after some council member of the Dutch East India Company, I think. Like I said, my history knowledge is kinda limited."

"So nothing about Spanish or Portuguese?"

"Ya testing me here, but I think I remember some theory about the Portuguese being here before anyone else, but it was never proven, and I doubt the English tried too hard once they claimed it as their own, know what I mean?"

"I think old Spanish and old Portuguese were very similar. If I had to hazard a guess, I would say that this was in written in old Spanish, Old Castilian, or it was sometimes called, Medieval Spanish. It is very faded and it doesn't look like I would imagine old ink looking after centuries. It's almost like….oh, my…"

"What?"

"Yuck! Oh, Bazza, if that is what I think it is, I don't want to think about it, or look at it."

"Can't be that bad. It's laminated and it's bloody old. Tell me what you think."

"Doesn't it look like a tattoo to you? That, that thing you pointed out, isn't that a…nipple? Oh, I think I am going to be sick."

Cheese rushed out of the cabin to hang her head over the rail. Though nothing came out, she felt wretched all the same. Bazza remained in the cabin, examining the map with renewed interest.

"I think ya nailed it, Cheese. It does look like a nipple, a bloke's nipple I 'spose. Definitely see it now, but… hey, that's why it doesn't make any sense, or look right. Where's the other nipple? It's only half a torso, half a map. We got mostly the mainland here and a bit-o-coastline. The missing bit must have some more details of the coastline and ocean on it."

"So, if this part of the map was ours, then maybe we were looking to buy the other half? Yuck, I don't want this one or the other half thank-you very much. What on Earth could the map lead to for it to be worth all this trouble and money?" Said Cheese upon her return to the cabin.

"Something as simple as treasure? A bloody treasure map eh me hearties?" Bazza remarked, mimicking a pirate voice.

"It would have to be a whole lot of treasure to warrant bloodshed and theft and my family travelling all over the world. This part of the planet is not known for its treasures as far as I know, let alone pirates with really bad accents." said Cheese with a smile. "Australia was largely undiscovered while all the piracy and…oh dear! I just remembered something, Bazza. My father. I remember my father was never around much while I was growing up because he was always off looking for stuff. He was a navy diver when he was young, coming across an old wreck where he found his first gold coin. That led him on one wild goose chase after another all over the globe. Crap, he was a treasure hunter. A treasure-hunting dreamer."

"Anything else?"

"Yes, unfortunately. My mother left him while we were quite young. She couldn't put up with being poor any longer and took off while he was gone. She left us with his sister, Aunty Sarah. That's why I could not picture my mom no matter how hard I tried. She wasn't around long enough. Left when I was only three. I remember enjoying my father's company so much when he was at home, then he would get a sniff of information and off he would go again."

"Don't remember anything about this stuff, or what it has ta do with Australia?"

"No. I keep getting a few snippets at a time, leaving huge gaps in between. I…I do recall something, though. A story he used to tell me, a bedtime story. It had to do with treasure, but I don't remember specifics. He had plenty of tales, but that one especially, he would recite to me often. It, it's just there at the edge, Bazza, but I can't quite... No, it's no use. I can't seem to force it. Sorry."

"So, ya old man was a treasure hunter and somewhere along the line he finds out about this piece of a treasure map. Maybe he knows which part-o-the world it's leading ta, maybe he doesn't. He, coincidentally, marries an Australian sheila, which allows him ta purchase the block down the end of the road, next ta mine. Pretty cold if that's what he done. Then, he somehow finds a connection or a lead ta the other half once he has this half in his possession. Just when yiz is all set ta come over, he carks it. Ya brothers musta been in on it all if they carried through with the plans ta get here and take over the transaction. Yaself as well probably."

"Oh, it all sounds terribly heartless but I'm having trouble disputing your theory. I recall that my father would do almost *anything* to get his hands on anything treasure-related. He was obsessed with it. Our home was always full of maps, charts, and research books. He devoured historical books and had a brilliant memory for facts. He could literally recite the entire manifests of sunken cargo ships from memory. He lived and breathed treasure from the moment he found that first doubloon. Drove my mother to drink with it."

"Ya old man then makes some sorta connection with the mongrel to make a deal ta get the other half-o-the map maybe? The mongrel seemed ta make out it was supplied ta him, like contractual or something. Coulda been lying about that I s'pose. His boss either went along with the venture only ta see if it would lead ta the other half, or he didn't know about it. He musta loaned the idiot some money, though. That makes sense. He fronted the money for this boat and his trip ta Australia, ostensibly ta set up a connection for future transactions, only the mongrel had his own agenda."

"So Rafael knew about Carlos' map somehow and made arrangements on his own to sell it to my brothers? Meanwhile, Carlos believed that Rafael was making inroads to another lucrative outlet on his behalf, possibly for drugs?"

"It's a theory. Dunno that it holds up, though. Too many unexplained gaps. That little monkey sure was high on something most mornings. Maybe it was just his own gear."

"It's all conjecture at this point, but at least we know more than before. I still think it's disgusting that we have human skin here, tattooed human skin. We can't even translate the few words on it without some internet access, even then it's doubtful we'll be able to translate it accurately. You sure you don't recognise anything on there Bazza?"

"Impossible ta know for sure without seeing the rest of it. Take any small section and blow it up like this, could be any-bloody-where. Hard ta make out the bit we got as well. Faded ta buggery and can't read nothing ta give me a heading. Nah, couldn't even make a guess. Wish we could just give it ta the boss man and be done with it, but it wouldn't solve our problem. He must know about something bloody special, ta go ta all the trouble he has. Bringing his monster ship here and all. Nothing but trouble in this. Dunno why ya woulda had any part-o-it Cheese if ya say ya hated what it did ta ya old man and ya family."

"Like I said, I think I was a different person then. Maybe my brothers convinced me of the possibilities, or I really became as besotted at the prospect of treasure as them and my father. I hope I never revert to that person Bazza. I'm slowly gathering memories of my past and in every one I collect, I see a piece of me I would rather not see. I lose a little more respect with every fragment of the past that I regain. Come on, let me have a look at that graze on your cheek and your torn ear."

After attending to his wounds, they drifted into a troubled silence, each lost in their own thoughts. Bazza did not foresee a good ending and Cheese wondered if she could overcome her obvious past predilections to transform herself. She failed to mention to Bazza that she had also regained fragments of memory regarding her marriage, which, as Rafael, and later Bazza, had assumed, amounted to 'pussy money'. She loathed that term since Rafael first mentioned it, secretly cursing him for twigging to the fact and placing an objectionable name to it. That she was deserving of the distasteful moniker, brooked no argument. Knowing she once thought she was able to gain anything by simply spreading her legs, filled her with disgust.

Bazza considered all the ramifications of their discovery, tossing them about in his mind like a professional juggler. Altering the order and rhythm in an effort to make the individual elements form a cohesive pattern. Pieces of the puzzle remained a mystery. The treasure, if in fact, it was a treasure, would have to be substantial to create the amount of interest and urgency displayed by the players in this drama. That the boss man was involved in many aspects of illicit trade went without saying, though, there was not a single shred of evidence to suggest it apart from weapons.

Illegal entry into the country and personal weapons aside, Bazza saw no first-hand evidence of banned substances or major weaponry. There did not appear to be any signs of a sex trade or human smuggling. He considered the possibility of going to the authorities with the information they had, but it didn't seem much to go on. Just a lot of conjecture and assumptions. He didn't fancy calling in the cops unless he had something more substantial to report with evidence to back it up. He had more reason to fear the cops for himself and Cheese's involvement in a number of deaths.

He settled himself into a comfortable sitting position on the plush lounge arrangement, albeit in tatters, as the sun began to sink over the mountain. Cheese joined him, settling under his large arm, sidling up to him in companionable silence. They listened to the gentle waves lapping against the hull of the vessel while they shared a can of baked beans. As the light gradually dimmed, their eyelids grew heavy and their limbs became leaden from the extreme physical exertion and tension they had endured. Against their will, they drifted into a deep slumber.

CHAPTER SIXTEEN

"Buenos días Señor", said Don Carlos Montoya to the startled pair aboard Rafael's boat. "I hope you slept well my friends? It has been a privilege and a challenge getting to know you, Mr. Bazza. I respect you for your great courage, your wisdom, and your resourcefulness. You managed to outsmart the great, Don Carlos Montoya the Third. Not an easy feat I assure you, but you are not in my league, *Señor*. I am here, with you and the…woman. She is not your wife according to the passports. You thought I wanted the money? Very handy, but hardly worth my time and patience. I am not so cheap as that. Do you have it?"

"I have a lot-o-fucking things. Like a treehouse, a property I can call me own, a car-n-tractor…"

"If you want to be funny with me, *Señor*, I will start by placing a very funny bullet in you and then your friend here if you are still amusing. Marcos is more than happy to provide such a comical solution to my waning patience. I want the other half, and I want it *rápidemente*. When I have the two halves, we will know where we must go, and you will tell me where that is."

"Ya may as well kill us both then, coz I have no fucking idea what ya talking about. Half-o-what? Ya want half me land, me house, what? Ya already swapped me car for this piece-o-shit boat ya wrecked. Nice going, arsehole. Stuff up the motor as well?"

"You were never going anywhere in this vessel of course. I could not let you leave our company so soon. What do you think, Marcos, do we believe that he is ignorant of our quest?"

When Marcos made to answer, he was silenced with a shake of the head by Carlos. "No, Marcos, you must never answer a rhetorical question. I am willing to give these persons a chance to explain everything before I decide on an answer to my question. Put your gun away for now. I don't think our guests will continue to be funny. They will not be rude anymore either. Bazza, I admire your ingenuity and your…spunk? True, admirable, Australian traits. *True Blue* eh? Yes, I admire greatly the Australian spirit, the famed spirit of the ANZACS. A force to be reckoned with on a global standard. I will promise not to threaten you anymore if you will promise not to insult me? We will then have a little discussion to determine the depth of your combined knowledge. Firstly…" peering at her passport. "Abigail Armstrong, is that your name, or not?"

"You know it is. I didn't for a while. I was involved in an accident and could not remember anything for a long time. I found my way to, Bazza's place and he kindly helped. I still don't remember anything about the crash or why we were here."

"We?"

"My brothers. They died in the crash."

"It was your brothers with whom my man, Rafael, was going to meet?"

"We, Bazza and I, assumed so but didn't know for sure.

"Rafael informed me that he was on his way to Australia to meet with a man named, Armstrong to open negotiations between us. I furnished him with some funds with which to accomplish the task. My wife, Lucia made a fine argument for her cousin. What the pair did not know, was that I knew they had stolen something from me. Something I treasured more that my dearly departed wife and her thieving cousin could ever appreciate. The artefact has been in my family for many generations, handed down from one head of the family to the next.

"I used the information of the theft to my advantage once I found out about it. You see, I was always going to find out about it. The two fools did not know that I visited the artefact every week on the same day at the same time. A sort of a way for me to pay homage to my ancestors. I truly hoped that I would be the one to finally unite the artefact with its other half. Knowing that Rafael had stolen it with hopes to sell it, led me to believe, that perhaps, the idiot might actually lead me to something my family has sought all their lives. Even a moron might get lucky once in his life, so I allowed Rafael to abscond with my precious artefact in its hermetically sealed container. That brings us to why *I* am here. Now kindly explain *your* involvement without leaving anything out. You first, Mr. Bazza."

Bazza related the entire story once more, exactly how it occurred without embellishments, up to the point of retrieving the bag. From then on the account became mostly fictitious, ending with them fleeing Rafael, to when they boarded the boat. Cheese repeated everything, corroborating all that Bazza had told Carlos, adding only a few minor details that gave no evidence they knew of the existence of any kind of map or artefact.

"I can only say, Mr. Montoya that whatever I knew before the accident, is mostly lost to me at the moment. I remember things like my father's face and events of my childhood, but nothing from my adult years. I would dearly love to have my memory back. If you know of a way to bring it back, I will gladly share all that those memories bring back with them."

"I believe a lot of what you both say, you mix the truth with the lies very well. I know that you must have been back to the accident site because you have all this money here and that bag?"

"I found the bag on the side of the road the day I was on the top road before I returned to my shack and found Cheese. I kept its existence hidden from her while I determined her purpose on my property. I did not trust her and the convenience of her memory loss at all. I only told her about it a month ago," Bazza lied.

"All that money and you were not tempted to use it? You do not strike me as a very rich man, surely you could have used that kind of *dinero*?"

"Couldn't care less for money and the kind of filth it breeds. I have everything I want back at me shack. Unless ya…?"

"*Don Carlos* has touched nothing. Everything is where it was when you left so suddenly. Why would you do so? I gave no indication that you were in any danger?"

"Don't trust ya, never will. Ya gave every indication that ya would do whatever was necessary ta have ya way. I may not have known who ya were, but I knew ya type. I knew we had ta make a run for it. I *didn't* know ya had the sort of technology ta put a tracking device inta me coffee. I had no idea then, what ya were after and I still don't have a clue. I just want ta be left alone, and ta protect what's mine."

"I am curious how you would know about the tracking device, *Señor*, it is a very new development and mostly secret."

"Elimination."

"Meaning?"

"Got rid-o-everything on us including our clobber-n-ya still come after us. Only one possibility left, and that was the coffee. Pretty slick."

"I think, you are not all what you seem, *Señor*. I misjudged you, several times, and I will not make that mistake again. Now, I will ask only one more time, where is it?"

"Ya can ask as often as ya like, won't change the answer. Care ta enlighten us what all the fuss is about, senior?"

"*Señor*, not *senior*. I am much younger than you old man."

Carlos ruminated on all that he had heard, separating the wheat from the chaff as best he could. The wheat, being the truth, was liberally contaminated by the bothersome lies; the chaff. Carlos understood the need for certain information to be kept from him just as a lawyer knew that his clients withheld certain damaging information in order to gain the cleanest defence. Whether that retained knowledge consisted of the information he required, was a matter for deliberate consideration. Bazza and the woman knew their lives depended on telling a certain amount of truth. They would not be foolish enough to risk their lives cheaply. Carlos thought about the reason he had travelled around the globe, whether to divulge the truth of his lifelong quest.

The family's quest for as long as their lineage in Colombia. The artefact had been the driving purpose behind their family's relentless pursuit of power and wealth. Carlos had heard the tale from his father on his fifteenth birthday. The birthright and legacy that would pass into his care on the deathbed of his father. His father related the tale numerous times to his son, until Carlos knew every detail by memory, and could recite it verbatim every time his father asked him to repeat it over the ensuing years. The one thing their family lacked, was the extreme power, and legitimate respect known only to the mega-rich of the world. He, Carlos, would see the fulfilment of that legacy in his lifetime, to enact the changes it would bring about. To see him and his family on a throne of their own making as a veritable king of his country.

Carlos would become the royalty of Colombia through such wealth as few minor countries have seen. The kind of wealth, that would see his beloved country come into the prominence it deserved. His shady past would vanish in the blink of an eye to make him a hero, honoured in the annals of history's rewritten texts. A new kingdom would emerge from the downtrodden reputation of a drug empire, garnered over many decades. The heady heights to which Carlos aspired could not be measured by mere peasants. His family's secret traversed the centuries intact through their generations to end up with him, as the patriarch to a legacy that would see him encapsulate the new kingdom of Montoya. A fitting name for the birth of a new nation, ruled by a benevolent ruler, Carlos the First.

Carlos remembered the *list* vividly as explained to him by his loving *papá*, Escobar Montoya the second of his name, taken from the first Escobar Alejandro Montoya, from whom the lineage was born. The list, *the manifiesto,* of the fabled treasures, the contents of which were known only by his family.

When the Spanish king, Charles I, abdicated his crown in

1526 to his son Phillip II, he knew that Spain was in trouble. At the time, there were also many other threats to the Spanish empire and her colonies, among them; French privateers plundering their shipping. Around the 1540s, flotillas of treasure ships were established to employ safety in numbers against the pirates. The '*flotas*' as they were called, were used to distribute European goods to the colonies as ballast, to then return to Spain with the haul of silver and gold mined from the colonies. Charles I, who still held great influence with his son the reigning monarch in 1555, organised a special *flota*, leaving from the colonies with many years' worth of minerals held in abeyance while the pirates rampaged, to cement the continued wealth of his beloved country, and the successful reign of his son.

Also in 1555, a French privateer by the name of Jacques de Sores was reputed to have sacked Havana. Very little else was historically documented about the French Huguenot pirate nicknamed "*L'Ange Exterminateur*", The Exterminating Angel. It was believed that he attacked Cuba in the hope of finding Spain's stores of silver and gold, but found little of any use. His spies had neglected to inform him that several years' worth of mine production had left port several days earlier in a large *flota*. Frustrated by the lack of plunder to be found, the pirate swore to make good the promise to his men by planning an audacious attack on the flota. By commandeering a Spanish vessel left at port for repairs, Jacques devised a brilliant strategy.

Reports of the attack were sketchy at best, except for one account. The account of Jacques de Sores' young Spanish-born cabin boy, secured by the attack on Cuba, used for a variety of purposes by the notorious pirate. The young boy soon earned the great affection and trust of the swarthy pirate and was thereby entrusted with the greatest secret the young man was ever likely to know.

Unlike "normal" attacks on Spanish fleets that were soon quelled by sheer numbers, Jacques de Sores *joined* the fleet under the cover of darkness flying friendly flags on the mast of the acquired ship. When the fleet put into a sheltered cove to wait out a particularly vicious squall, the canny pirate ordered his men to commandeer the fleet during the early hours of the morning. All but two of the *flota's* ships were scuttled with all life on board lost to the briny, after transferring the contents of all their cargo holds to the two remaining vessels and that of the pirate's; said to be the largest cargo that ever sailed. Jacques made good on his promise of wealth to his crew. By modern standards, the cargo of silver alone was said to be in the billions of dollars, without the addition of the plentiful gold and precious gems.

Having murdered all who sailed in the *flota*, officially, nothing was ever recorded of the attack, or afterward. Rumours fell far short of the facts, and only the barest few of those managed to circulate within the pirate community. Fleeing the cove left the pirates at the mercy of the continuing storm that threatened to escalate. Many months later, with crews starved and close to death, the three vessels, near to sinking and in grave disrepair, at the mercy of the tides and prevailing winds, broached land for the first time. It was a strange land, totally unfamiliar to all who crewed the ships. Jacques, sensing the hostility and possible mutiny of the crew in the presence of a vast fortune, decided to cache his treasure before anything transpired. Maintaining all control of muskets and sabres, he set the men to work on hiding the massive cargo in a hidden location costing many lives in the process.

Close to land, an exposed reef at extreme low tides, revealed a grotto, leading to a long cave, which led to a large cavern that Jacques estimated to be on the mainland. Should the sailors carrying the goods to the cavern suffer any kind of delay, they were quickly drowned by the incoming tide. Extreme low tides did not last long, forcing Jacques to work his men until they dropped, transporting every single ingot, coin, and gem to the cavern, losing half of his crew in the process. Most of the rest were put to the sword the moment the labours were completed.

A bare skeleton crew of ten men, loyal to the captain, were allowed to remain alive to sail the single remaining ship back to France. Only the cabin boy survived the journey. A Spanish ship found the boy clinging to the upturned wreckage of a skiff. That boy, Escobar Alejandro Montoya I, settled into life in a part of the Spanish colonies that was to become Colombia.

On the chest of Escobar, was tattooed the location of the fabled treasure by a fine artisan of the trade. The canny Frenchman also ensured his own crew were incapable of reading the lettering, though most were illiterate anyway, by having him tattooed in

Spanish rather than French. Made to endure the process of being tattooed for endless, torturous hours, day after day, Escobar swore to seek his revenge on the villainous Jacques. Watching the pirate being eaten by sharks after Escobar sliced off one of his hands holding onto the overturned skiff, gave Escobar the satisfaction he desired.

No one, save Escobar, ever knew the full story or the location of the treasure. Even Escobar had no idea to which coastline his tattoo referred, despite years of research, always with vague questions and partial references.

On his deathbed, Escobar gave specific instructions to his two children, Santiago and Felicia. Both children would inherit a half of the precious map after it had been carefully removed from his body and preserved in the way of the Egyptians. Escobar had sourced artisans capable of performing the task, ensuring the map was cut in such a way that it was impossible to verify the location without both halves. He forced his children to swear the secret to their graves, telling only their first-born son in each lineage, the tale of their legacy and to gain their promise that they would spend their lives in pursuit of a treasure that would change the world and their family's destiny.

Santiago Miguel Montoya, Escobar's first-born son remained in Colombia, while Felicia's family eventually ended up in North America, where the two family lines became separated after time. Many generations of Montoya men had attempted to reunite the families. The Civil war in America meant the loss of many birth records. Carlos believed that the other family line had been a member of the South's aristocracy with a severe reputation for mistreating their plantation slaves before the war. From the little he could find out, it was determined that the family had been wiped out along with all records of their existence and their estate destroyed. No sign of the other half of the treasure map was found or heard of since.

Carlos' reputation for brutality, centring on his obsession with the legacy to become the irrefutable leader of a new nation by way of purchase, suited his inflated ego tremendously. His illegal activities brought himself and his family comfort and a modicum of perceived power, but not the ultimate goal to which Carlos aspired. Though a well-educated man showing outward signs of indentured culture from a long lineage, he was a man of few principles and little regard for human life where his family was not concerned.

Carlos was nothing if not thorough. The moment Rafael had mentioned the name Armstrong as his contact in Australia, coupled with the theft of his beloved artefact, Carlos began a line of inquiry into the Armstrong name. Finding several references to a man by the name of Trent Armstrong, a former US navy diver who made several discoveries as a treasure hunter, piqued Carlos' interest immediately. Trent Armstrong had a relentless urge to find 'the big one', it was reported. So obsessed was he that he eventually became estranged from his wife, leaving his children in the care of others, for long periods. Much remained the same from what Carlos could tell until something occurred that had the man changing his style dramatically, by marrying an Australian woman.

A simple title search revealed a parcel of land he purchased under his wife's maiden name of, Estavore. Without a single piece of evidence, Carlos believed intuitively that the Estavore line came from the family in southern America. Someone had escaped the carnage to settle into a new country where their name meant little. He was certain that Trent had discovered, by accident or design, the other half of the map that must have travelled with the Estavore family to their new home. Possibly the only innocuous artefact that they were permitted to bring into the country. With nothing more to go on, Carlos decided to allow Rafael to lead him to his destiny, to reunite the two halves of the family, and more importantly, the map.

Carlos did not believe in coincidences. There had to be a specific reason that a treasure hunter from America suddenly decides to marry some Australian woman with a decidedly Spanish-flavoured name. That union then leads to a connection between them and Rafael's cousin Lucia, which in turn results in the theft of his beloved map. There could be only one reason for the theft of the map - to reunite it with its mate, to sell Carlos' half to the owner of the other half. Carlos would follow that lead to the ends of the earth.

The loss of his wife, Lucia, was of little concern to Carlos, who used her as a vessel to birth him a son and nothing more. A wet-nurse was employed and then a qualified nanny served to ensure that Lucia had little contact with or influence over the boy, Escobar Carlos Alejandro Montoya III. He had used and abused the mother until she betrayed him, then there was no longer a reason to keep her alive. He could still hear her screams as she was taken time and time again by all the menfolk in his employ. He laughed at the sweet music of her pitiful pleas. Day after day until the voice could no longer be heard. His son was unaware of his mother's passing and cared less.

Carlos viewed the pair before him with disdain, knowing he had to play nice with the pair to attain what rightfully belonged to him. He would enjoy their demise once he had what he came for. Another nagging thought interrupted his dalliance with dark memories. He wondered whether it was possible that the map indicated the Australian coast. He did not think that the American, Trent Armstrong would purchase land without a reason; a very good reason. If it turned out that the treasure had been secreted somewhere along the Australian coastline, then he may have further need of the big man, and maybe the woman too.

"I believe that you are not being *entirely* honest with me. I detect certain discrepancies, possibly missing information. It is important for you to do this, you believe, to preserve your lives. It is what I would do also, so I cannot blame you. I can tell that you know what I am after. That means you know the whereabouts of the item. If you truly do not know the location of the item I seek, then I really have no further use for either of you, except for maybe a little sport."

"Thought ya said ya would stop threatening us?"

"If you showed me respect. You have failed in that regard by lying to me."

"According, only ta yaself. I have no idea what the fuck ya talking about. If Cheese ever did, she doesn't know now. Just coz ya don't believe us doesn't make ya right. How do we know if we saw what ya after if ya won't tell us what it is?"

"Ahhh, which comes first eh? I think there is no answer to the question of the chicken and the egg. Maybe a man of religion would say that God came first and all else after? The money, what was that for?"

"We thought it had ta do with drugs, seeing as ya mate and yaself fit the bill of ya typical drug baron and his goon from South America. That suit ya wore the first time I saw ya probably cost more-n-me car."

Carlos rose with a sudden burst of uncontrolled rage burning inside. He was sorely tempted to retrieve his firearm in order to shoot the insolent swine, Bazza, in both kneecaps. Calming himself, he gradually returned to a sitting position. He had to restrain Marcos as well who had withdrawn his weapon, pleading with his eyes to be let loose on the big man.

"I will let that one go just this once. I am not a common drug runner or 'baron', as you put it. My business interests are quite legitimate, and I have aspirations to redeem the reputation of my beloved country from that of a drug haven. Certainly, much money has been made from the trade in the past and continues today. *I,* am a respectable businessman and I have dealings all over the world."

"Which is why ya here, probably without anyone knowing, with guns, threats, and demands huh? Sure, ya just a businessman. I'm jest the Queen-o-the Nile too. I know bullshit when I hear it mate, and I smell plenty of it right now. Whatever ya are, it isn't legitimate, or not entirely anyway."

"Very well, Marcos, shoot the woman."

"Yeah, do that ya moron and ya'll never see the other half-o-ya map."

Carlos put up a staying hand just before Marcos was able to make good the command by his boss. "So, I was right, you do know more than you told me."

"Yeah, and ya told us less than ya woulda, had ya been legit.

We saw the map…thing. I guess it was a map? Old writing on it and a …nipple?"

"Where is it? Tell me now. You have no idea of the map's importance to my country."

"And to the man in possession of the full map no doubt?"

"I will ask just once more. Where is it?"

"The monkey's got it. Took orf with it just before ya got up the track with me Ute. Took it orf us at gunpoint, then hightailed it the second we told him it was probably his boss coming up the track looking for us all."

"Rafael is still alive?"

"Sorta. Not much left-o-his face and brains."

"What do you mean?"

"Told ya how he wiped his face with the wrong kinda leaf? Looks like he used rough bark or something ta scratch the sting away, only, every time he touched his face with his hands or the same bit-o-bark, he would have put more stinging hairs onto his face. Sent him around the twist I reckon. Coupla Roos short in the top paddock if ya know what I mean?"

"He took the map? What was it in, what sort of condition was the map in?"

"Looked like it had been preserved. Real delicate without that I reckon. Barely readable; if ya knew the lingo that is. It was in the bag there. Cheese and I were trying ta work it out, make sense of the thing, when the runt showed up foaming at the mouth, slobbering and looking real ghoulish. That's when he shot me. He grabbed it and ran for it when we heard the Ute coming up the track."

"If you are lying to me…"

"The map, whatever it is, means nothing ta us. We have no reason ta lie about it anymore. Search the boat if ya don't believe us. Look, I don't care about the bloody thing, I didn't even see it for long before the prick showed up waving his gun around. Not the bloody first time he did that either."

"We will find, Rafael and deal with him. Meanwhile, I would like you to be my guest aboard the *Madonna,* named after my blessed mother and the virgin. I would like to show you my portion of the map to see if you recognise anything, please?"

"Not sure how much of ya so-called hospitality I can take, but s'pose I do have a look at ya map? Then what?"

"I will be most grateful, Mr. Bazza."

"Yeah, I saw how grateful ya were when we swapped our assets. We taking this tub out ta ya floating palace?"

"I will see to the repair of your boat and a very generous reward if you are able to indicate a location from the map. We will take our inflatable if you do not mind?"

"Sugar in the tank, or rigged ta explode?"

"You have a bad habit of wishing to provoke me, Mr. Bazza. I suggest you…"

"And you have a bad habit of underestimating us, Mr. Head-Honcho. If I'm wrong, why aren't we taking this boat instead of the bloody inflatable ta get past the reef? Half way ta low tide by the look of it, and ya want ta frig around in a blow-up boat around very sharp obstructions. Seems ta me like ya gotta worry about *this* boat if ya willing ta take ya chances in the other!"

"Suffice it to say that I have disabled the vessel to ensure it remained within sight. Are you able to navigate the other boat out of the bay safely?"

"Maybe."

Before they left the main cabin, Bazza cast a glance at the overhead map compartment, wondering whether Carlos would twig to the fact that he had hidden the map in plain sight. Bazza had secreted the flat, innocuous map among the many other charts after inspecting it the previous evening. He enjoyed the fact that the Colombian had been within arm's reach of the map the entire time aboard the wrecked vessel.

While Bazza underplayed his ability to get them through the reef, he remained cautious. Carlos and Marcos sat on the rear seat with Bazza at the centre console steering the vessel delicately through the perilous outcroppings of the reef, poking above the waterline. Cheese remained in the bow with a worried expression. Bazza knew that Carlos' 'invitation', was merely a euphemism for the *command* to accompany him to his yacht. He had no idea how to play out the scene to a satisfactory conclusion. He saw no happy endings for Cheese and himself. Carlos' indignations aside, he knew the man for what he was, a cold-hearted, money-grabbing, power-hungry, individual who would stop at nothing to attain his goals.

Bazza whistled softly as they neared the yacht. "That's some tub ya got there", he shouted above the roar of the outboard motor.

"She is magnificent no? An Ocean Alexander 120. One hundred and twenty-one feet in length, with twin MTU 12 volt 2000 diesels, capable of cruising at 16 knots. Brand new, no expense spared. Five staterooms and four cabin crew quarters. It is a state of the art ship that practically runs itself without the need for a large crew. Myself and my two men sailed her here from the Gold Coast."

"You bought it here?" asked Bazza.

"Seattle, USA. Commissioned her to be built to my specifications, then sailed here. Last minute modifications and repairs from her shakedown voyage completed before I picked her up."

"How much she set ya back?"

"About a million dollars American per foot."

"So, ya not short of a quid. What's this all about, if not money?"

"Destiny. The chance for my family to realise their destiny and to change the world."

"Hmm, I think Hitler said something similar. Or was it Stalin? Some megalomaniac anyway. Everyone always believes they have a better system for the people, which only ends up being a better system for themselves. The general population usually end up as slaves to a new master in any dictatorship."

"You wish to engage in a debate, Mr. Bazza?"

"Well now, Mr. Head-Honcho, I don't think I could win that there debate. No one was ever able ta convince a tyrant of anything. Their egos are just too big ta take on anything that might go against their way-o-thinking. I'm just a dumb old Aussie. Wouldn't know shit from clay, or me arse from me elbow, about anything."

"I do not believe your simpleton act for a moment my friend, not a single moment."

"Then you know damn well that I am not, nor ever will be, ya friend. I am very choosy when it comes ta mates."

"Then you and I are not as dissimilar as you would think. I too, choose my friends very carefully. I choose my enemies even more assiduously."

"Ya make enemies, ya don't choose 'em."

There we part company. I definitely choose whom I will make a friend or an enemy. It is a calculation based on current circumstances. Whether there is an advantage to be gained or not."

"That has nothing ta do with friendship. A mate, a real mate, will stick by ya through thick-n-thin without any thought-o-gain. Get killed for ya if he had ta. If ya have ta pay for ya mates, then watch out if ya ever in need. They'll let ya down in the blink of an eye. See how many people actually stay with ya if ya stop paying 'em."

Aboard the *Madonna,* Chico greeted Carlos with a look of concern over their 'guests'. Bazza and Cheese gasped in awe at the opulence of the luxury yacht. Hanging from the rear davits of the *Madonna* was a fishing/diving vessel easily costing more than all of Bazza's assets combined. Inside the main cabin of the tri-level motor yacht, was a bedazzling display of wealth beyond anything Bazza had ever witnessed. The gleaming brass and chrome, the exquisite white leather furnishings, the artwork and timber panelling, left them breathless. Bazza felt downright out of place amid such sophistication. He was afraid to touch anything or sit down for fear of breaking something costing thousands of dollars. He knew little of art but swore he saw an original Picasso hanging in a glass cabinet. Hermetically sealed no doubt.

"Jeez, I hate ta see ya slumming it like this mate. Must be hard ta take?"

"Chico, have the map brought up here, please. Have a seat on the lounge if you would, Mr. Bazza. I would like to get down to business. I retrieved my half of the map from Rafael's boat where he stowed it while entering the country illegally. In a cavity between the outer hull and the inner wall, in his cabin. Very clumsy. Any official would have found the artefact immediately had he been boarded and searched. Not that anything would have come of it. It holds no intrinsic value, other than being an ancient document."

"I reckon the authorities mighta had pause when they discovered the substrate don't ya think?"

"Ah, so you recognise the material used? That would be my ancestor, Escobar Montoya I, or should I say, half of my ancestor? You see, here is the other half. Marcos, see that he has a magnifying glass and anything else he requires, while I attend to some business. Order anything you like to eat or drink. Marcos is a great bartender and Chico is a magnificent Spanish cook."

Chico placed Carlos' piece of the map on the low coffee table in front of Bazza. Carlos exited the cabin to go below to his stateroom. Marcos titled his head at Bazza to enquire about his beverage preference. Bazza and Cheese opted for coffee in light of their missing breakfast. Chico went to work in the galley below to fix everyone a breakfast of omelettes, Spanish style. Bazza turned the map in the only direction that made sense to him. That being; the torso upright. The map; the owner's right side, was mostly ocean, while the other portion he had studied the previous evening had been predominantly the mainland. He then understood how the map might be considered to be part of the Australian coastline if toward the upper chest area represented north. It was a highly detailed representation of a small portion of coastline. The cartographer would have sailed up and down the coast numerous times to create the exact details of coves, inlets, and river mouths with such precision.
Bazza had an inkling as to the location the map detailed when he combined what he saw before him with his memories of the other half. He could not be certain, however. The map had been drawn centuries ago on human flesh with body ink. Much of the detail was badly faded, and the language meant nothing. Luckily, the map was under glare-proof glass, allowing him to see the map clearly under the harsh neon lights of the main cabin. Bazza picked up the magnifying glass to study the map in all its minute detail, committing it all to memory as he would if studying a picture of a carving subject. Another problem that the map presented, was the passage of time itself that may have altered the coastline in the intervening years.
Bazza could not make anything of the writing and was

uncertain of everything else. He might apply several possible lengths of coastline to the map without being correct. He felt sure that the Colombian would have passed the image through a computer with programmed algorithms to recognise similar patterns to modern charts. How Bazza could hope to recognise it if modern technology failed, was beyond his understanding, yet…there was definitely something gnawing away at his subconscious. He could not be sure if it was on the map in front of him, on the other map back at the boat they left, or a combination of both. He could feel a migraine building, which would see him useless in a few hours if he did not rest, eat and get some pain killers.

"I need some pain medication, coupla paracetamol will do. I didn't bring any," Bazza asked no one in particular.

Marcos rose to fetch some as Chico returned with a sumptuous breakfast feast of eggs and vegetables, buttered toast, fresh fruit, and superb smelling coffee. Bazza and Cheese dived into the repast with gusto, having eaten only a share of baked beans the previous evening. Marcos returned with a couple of capsules, which he handed to Bazza with a sneer. Bazza made a show of swallowing the medication with a mouthful of coffee.

Carlos joined them in short order. Marcos and Chico were ordered below to have their breakfast in the galley. Carlos ate silently, staring at Bazza and Cheese, impatient for them to finish. He desperately hoped that the Australian might have some information about the map. He did not give in to the temptation of rushing the man to answer. He had waited all his life for the moment to arrive. A small wait to get breakfast out of the way would not tax him.

"Ya know what the writing is all about?" asked Bazza eventually, wiping away the crumbs from his mouth with a starched napkin.

"I have had it translated from the old Spanish. It gives some descriptions of the coastline and the reef and a little about the moon and tides. I have run the map through every modern recognition program available, to no avail. I believe the directions are a sighting, for lining up on the location once you are close. Standard navigational techniques back then. Line up a course between a headland and a mountain say, to gain a heading with which to arrive at a third point, the location."

"Can ya give me those translations ta help me, or do I have ta guess?"

"They will be of no use to you until we are in the approximate area. Nothing in the translations will help define the part of the coast it pertains to."

"How the fuck could ya know that? Give me a coupla landmarks and I might know what I'm looking at."

"I know because I have had every expert on ancient maps, every modern cartographer, and every other person of significance on this planet working on different aspects of this map for all my life. Everyone agrees, that only when near the coastline indicated will any of the landmarks make any sense. They are far too general to be a guide to the location. There are millions of locations which fit the general descriptions given. If you can get us near, I will give you the all the translations."

"Tell me that ya definitely know that it's part of an Australian coastline at least?"

"I cannot tell you that with any confidence. I am making many guesses along with an excessive amount of research. Something led the Armstrong family here, to purchase land here, to immigrate. Something led them to contact my wife's cousin, Rafael, with a deal. It is too much of a coincidence not be about the map. Rafael stole the map from me with the help of his cousin, to sell to the Armstrongs, who had access to the other half. This we now know because you have admitted to seeing it. If we assume that the woman's father was not a total madman, we must deduce that the Australian coastline comes into play. A further assumption from the information indicates that the land her father purchased may well be near the coastline indicated by the map."

"Lotta assumptions there. I have ta agree with ya way-o-thinking, though. Stands ta reason."

"Do you have any ideas at all? Can you get us close with what you see, or do we have to have the other half?"

"What was that ya said about the moon and stuff?"

"As close as we can determine because of the ancient language and the severe fading obscuring the text, it says the exact location may only be reached at a time of extreme low tides."

"That may have been true then, when they did not have access ta diving gear. Might not be true these days?"

"Exactly. I am not paying much attention to the difficulty implied, only to the notion of an exposed reef at extreme low tides."

"Of course, this map was charted a long time ago. Things change. Reefs disappear, grow somewhere new, sea floor moves, landmarks change, everything!"

"Which is exactly why I am not bothering to tell you the translations. They are practically useless. Say, for instance, a fire had gone through the mainland at the time. A marker heading indicating a large boulder on a mountainside, may not be visible once the forest regrows around it. An earthquake may have dislodged it, any number of things can occur over the course of the centuries. We estimate the date of the map to be around the end of the 1500s or very early 1600s. My ancestor settled in Colombia around 1610 as far as we can tell."

Bazza studied the map once more with Carlos and Cheese looking on. He turned the map every which way, asking Carlos for several Australian charts to compare it with. Carlos had a fine set of charts from all parts of the globe aboard his ship. It seemed that he had spent a large portion of his life afloat on several generations of ships in search of the location. Bazza concentrated on one particular section. Once he had studied it long enough and compared the two maps several times, it seemed to all, Marcos and Chico had joined them by then, that Bazza had made a decision.

"About five or six years ago, I went on a fishing trip to a small reef I stumbled upon. Couldn't tell ya if it was on a map or not. Probably just marked as part-o-The Great Barrier Reef. Changes all the time, so no way ta be certain. I got me anchor wedged good-n-tight, in among the bombies. In about twenty foot-o-water it was, but I couldn't just cut the anchor orf. I had ta have a go at getting it loose. I dived down, just with me snorkelling gear. Near blew me eardrum out I can tell ya. Didn't know about blowing-n-holding me nose at the time. Still don't hear too well from that."

"The point?"

"Yeah orright. I managed ta get me anchor orf the reef, and as I was drifting with the strong current down there, I came past a grotto. Couldn't stay long enough ta explore or nothing as I was busting for air. That grotto looked big and deep, though, from the little I saw, and it might be sorta around an area looking like the map indicates. I pretty much planted the location in me head ta have another look with some scuba gear at a later date. It's the only clue I got, and I may be way orf base. Dunno if I can even remember exactly where it is anymore. Ya got diving gear on board?"

"Naturally. I have been hunting for this all my life and I am prepared for any eventuality, including rebreather units for extended dives."

"Well, I can try-n-find the spot again for ya, and see if it's right or not. If not, I got no other clues, nothing."

"Marcos and Chico are experienced captains with all certificates necessary to sail this ship. Tell them where you want to go. We set sail in one hour. Marcos, listen to what he says, place us in the general area he wants to go, then let him have the wheel, while you stand by. Chico, see to the preparations," commanded Carlos as he went below.

"Psst, what are you doing, Bazza? We can't just give them what they want. Do you even know where you're going?" Asked Cheese when they had a moment alone, while the Colombians prepared to set sail.

"What else can we do? I'm outta ideas, mate. Didn't figure on them finding us in the dago's boat. He probably had a motion sensor alarm installed to alert him the moment anyone boarded the bloody boat. Either that or Chicky-boy there saw us from this ship. Maybe, if we give him what he wants he'll be in a better mood? Dunno if I can find the spot again anyway, so it might all come ta nothing."

"He'll be plenty pissed if you don't find it. I hope you know what you're doing, Bazza. Somehow, I think our lives depend on it. No pressure", she said with a shrug and a smile.

Bazza did not bother to answer her as Carlos re-entered the main saloon. No one spoke as Carlos oversaw the preparations with satisfaction. Bazza detected a fanatical gleam in the Colombian's eyes. He recognised it for what it was; greed. The pursuit of wealth. Treasure hunters were all lured by the same scent. Purists would have everyone believe it was the hunt, rather than the prize, or the attached worth, that drew them to its lure. Bazza saw nothing of that purity in the Colombian's eyes. He saw nothing human at all in the Colombian's eyes. He saw a deep malevolence, which he often encountered and associated with the ingrained hatred and contempt in the Mujahedeen of Afghanistan for anyone foreign. He had witnessed first-hand the treatment meted out to his countrymen at the hands of the murderous bastards. The Colombian had a vile depth to his personality that Bazza observed in his eyes, causing him to shiver.

Bazza removed himself from the Colombian's vicinity, to stand near Marcos, who began to haul in the anchor. Bazza was glad the large ship had been anchored past the reef on the sandy bottom. A large anchor like the *Madonna's* could do untold damage to a reef as it was being hauled in over the brittle coral. Bazza pointed out a northerly direction to Marcos, who manoeuvred the large ship expertly to follow the Australian's lead. Bazza began to look about in all directions landward, trying to gain a bearing with which to navigate.

Bazza recalled the landmarks he had noted when he committed the site of the grotto's discovery to his memory many years ago in his little dinghy. It was only a mile or so offshore. Of that he was certain. He did not possess sophisticated fish-finding equipment at the time to simply plot in the coordinates for future retrieval. Actually, he still had nothing more sophisticated than memory to go by, having never purchased any modern technology in that regard. Indicating minor course deviations to Marcos while Carlos remained seated with Cheese nearby, Chico busied himself aft, preparing the vessel on the rear davits. Bazza watched with growing interest, all the gear being retrieved from below. He had a little experience with scuba gear, but everything was on a far more sophisticated level than anything he had seen.

"Hey, what the heck are those bloody great things?" Bazza asked.

"They are rebreather units, used for extensive dives," Carlos replied.

"Just how far inta that grotto ya thinking-o-going?"

"As far as we need to."

"I hope ya don't mean me, in that, 'we'.

"You and the woman will be joining us."

"Fuck you! I'm not going inta that bloody grotto. I got no real scuba experience, and I couldn't give a rat's arse for no fucking treasure, mate."

"You cannot possibly expect me to leave you two alone on

board, can you? I am not so foolish to do something like that. You will both be accompanying, Marcos and myself on our investigations, should you find it for us. End of discussion. Go about your business with, Marcos. I do hope you are being straight with me? I would not be very pleased to find out you are taking us on a wild goose chase?"

"Didn't make any promises that I could either find it again or that it has anything ta do with ya map. Try, is what I said, and try, is what I'll do. And if ya think I'm the sorta bloke who would leave people below the water while I took orf, it goes ta show how little ya know about me. I don't think like yiz at all. Most people wouldn't."

"I did not become the man that I am by trusting people. 'Most people', do not attain the level of success I have attained, so they have few qualms about trusting others. You are trying my patience with this idealistic drivel. Keep your indignity and morals for the peasants. I am beyond such trivial nonsense."

"Spoken like a true dictator. I can see it now, 'Montoya the Monster' quells the rebellion with a shower of benign lead. Seig fucking hail."

Carlos nodded to Marcos who swung a vicious elbow into Bazza's face, smashing his nose. Cheese screamed before launching herself at Carlos, who casually threw her to the floor. He placed a boot on her neck with enough pressure to stop her struggles.

"Allow me to make something perfectly clear to you both. As you have surmised, I have a dark history. I have done many things to ensure my family's survival in a dog-eat-dog world. I will not hesitate to engage any method at my disposal to reach my goals. I have been more than patient with you two. I have shown you far more hospitality than I would a fellow countryman who displeased me. It is clear that my kindness has been mistaken for weakness. Let me assure you that no such weakness exists. If either of you fails to act cordially in future, I will demonstrate my darker side with great satisfaction. Do we understand each other?"

Cheese managed to nod her head despite the great weight pressing down on her exposed neck. Bazza merely grunted, holding his nose on the bloodied floor.

"Mop up the mess you made on my floor before I make your girlfriend lick it up. Never insult me again, or you will be very, very sorry. That is not a threat, by the way. I do not make threats. I make promises that I can keep. Marcos, if he says or does anything more to annoy me, shoot him in the leg or the arm. If you miss and kill him, I will feed you to the sharks, piece by piece while you are still alive."

Bazza mopped up himself, and the floor as best he could with a rag he kept in his trousers. His ear still hurt from the bullet that grazed his cheek, but his nose throbbed like nobody's business. At the first opportunity, he would have to reset it. He wondered how long he could last underwater with a blocked and broken nose. He had tested the man's mettle and found the limits. It was a lesson learned and the information was well-received. He kept his silence from then on, praying for an opportunity to return the favour. He knew then, that he would have to resort to breaking his vow. That he would be forced to take care of them all to ensure their survival.
Cheese attended to Bazza's nose as best she could, worry etched on her features. Bazza detected something else in her demeanour that gave him cause for concern. Carlos sat back in the comfortable leather lounge with a look of satisfaction, certain that he had regained control of the situation. He thrived on the amount of fear and control he could wield over other mortals. It was a soothing salve to his insatiable needs. Marcos spoke to Carlos in Spanish. Bazza did not understand, but Cheese was able to comprehend the exchange. She inspected Bazza carefully. Chico re-entered the room to check on the commotion.

"You *idiota*. How do you think he will be able to help us if you drug him?"

"It should have taken effect by now, *Padrino*. I don't think it is working."

"You didn't *think* at all, and you never should. You two do nothing unless I tell you, understand? I don't have time to waste waiting for the pig to have a little sleep. Do we have anything to counter the effects, an upper or something? *Cocaína*?"

"Got everything Boss."

"Chico, get me something to make sure he does not go off to sleep."

"Don't bother, Esperanza, I didn't take the pills he gave me. I knew he was up to something", said Bazza with a nasal splatter.

"Bah! Incompetent fools. Always this buffoon tricks you, and still you underestimate him. How long before we get there you bloody Australian bastard?"

"Maybe another ten minutes or so ta get ta the spot I remember. Could take anywhere from hours ta weeks ta find the grotto again, if, it's there."

"You get us close and leave finding the grotto to me and my equipment. I will find it in a very short time without getting my feet wet."

"Sonar?"

"Not just sonar. Multi-beam scanners, magnetometers. The very best underwater detection system money can buy. It will tell me everything about the ocean floor within a ten-mile radius of the ship in brilliant, true-life, 3-D pictures. I even have a 3-D printer if I want a model to be made. Nothing will be left to chance on this expedition. Nothing will stop me from realising my destiny. If I need more, I can shoot a seismic charge into the ocean floor to get a better and deeper reading. Did the other half of the map indicate how far into the cave we must travel? We have only the location of the entrance and an undisclosed distance to the cavern with my half."

"I only saw it briefly, but I got the feeling it was something like a mile or more. Don't see how anyone back then coulda used it ta stash a treasure."

"The entrance was said to have been exposed at extreme tides."

"The grotto I'm talking about is maybe twenty feet down. Don't know that it would be exposed at low tides?"

"You said yourself that coastlines change over time. Reefs are born and die over the centuries. Oceans rise and fall with climate changes. Islands are raised from the seabed all the time. It is quite possible that the entrance submerged. Ocean subsidence, tectonic plate movement, can all result in mammoth changes. The map originates from a pre-recorded time in Australia's history. It may well be the first map of, and the first discovery of, Australia."

"If that's true, then it belongs in a museum. It would be a vital part of our history."

"That will never become a reality. I will not be sharing my treasure with the Australian government by way of duties and taxes at some monstrous level. I could not even be sure they would recognise my claim. No, it is mine. My legacy. Paid for by the blood of my ancestor. No one else will see one cent of what rightfully belongs to me and my family."

"Yeah, I seen ya generosity."

"I made a promise of compensation for the boat. Take me to my inheritance and I will be more than generous."

Bazza muttered something under his breath so as not to be heard. His nose hurt too much to want to be hit again in the same place. He knew he was skating on thin ice again and the closer they came to the site, the antsier the Colombian became. An annoying rat-a-tat came from the man's boots on the polished timber deck. Cheese had returned to the lounge where the Colombian sat, saying little, and avoiding all eye contact with anyone. Marcos concentrated on his task, while Chico busied himself readying the diving boat.

Bazza silently contemplated the actions he would be forced to take at some point, reneging on his promise to himself. His opportunities would be limited, and his skill level would have to equal that of many years prior. He was uncertain if he was up to the task. Cheese presented complications to the equation. He felt duty-bound to protect her no matter her origins, or her state of mind. Once Bazza committed himself to a person, physically or emotionally, that bond was set in stone. Like Excalibur, it would take a fantastic occurrence for that loyalty to be removed.

Cheese felt a sliver of fear work its way down into the marrow of the bone. The second she felt her life slipping away under Carlos' boot, all her memories came flooding back in a tidal wave that threatened to pummel her senses into oblivion. Her emotions were travelling on a roller-coaster at perilous speeds while her past deeds came back to torment her. She felt lower than it was possible for a human being to feel. She remembered with crystal clarity, the tale her father recited to her at bedtime. The tale of the treasure to make kings of paupers in all its gruesome details, including the harrowing account of the tattooed boy. She knew they were facing death if they proceeded. She knew she could not possibly survive the events to follow. Knew what awaited them at the hands of the monster connected with the treasure named; "*El Tesoro del Diablo*", The Devil's treasure. The Devil was the boy who cut off the hand of his captain to keep the treasure for himself.

Her father had heard whispers of the fabled treasure for all his treasure hunting years. Barely a half word or a fraction of a rumour escaped the sealed lips of everyone in the dominion of the seekers. Her father came across a valuable piece of information dating back to the American Civil War. The sacking of a South American plantation homestead where all members of the owner's family were butchered by their slaves, bar one. Through painstaking research and investigations, her father discovered the rescue of one female member of the household who held a special place in the heart of the family cook. The Negress slave hid with the girl and an odd artefact that meant the world to the poor child, in a coal cellar, until the house had been ransacked and burned to the ground.

The pair escaped to the north where they adopted one another and continued to live together until the old lady finally passed away from a sudden heart attack. The young lady gave birth to a son many years later, relating to him a story on his fifteenth birthday that he would remember all his days. The boy, Emilio Estavore, eventually made it to Australia with his family, where his great-granddaughter, married a man by the name of Trent Armstrong. Having no child of her own to whom she could pass down the story of their legacy, Señora Valentina Estavore-Armstrong revealed the story to her husband, who had known of the connection all along.

Cheese's father married into the Estavore family for the purpose of attaining information or…the map. Cheese determined that her father must have known about the map, or at least, heard rumours of it before committing to the marriage. She felt a deep humiliation and great shame for the deceit carried out by one of her name. A great weight descended upon her drooped shoulders as she took on responsibility for the insidious acts of her father, her brothers, and herself. Cheese, in her defence, only became aware of the whole scheme after the death of her father, when her brothers explained their plan. That fact did nothing to alleviate the pain, nor the responsibility she felt.

A sudden revelation caused Cheese a sharp intake of breath. Carlos quickly turned to her with annoyance. He was lost in his own thoughts and had no wish to be disturbed from the pleasures of his daydreams. Cheese became unaccountably sad at the thought that she and Carlos were *related* by marriage! Her father married into the Estavore family, who descended from the original Montoya family to immigrate to the United States. Only after their father remarried, did he have the final pieces of the story which he then related to his sons, then by proxy to her.

She felt ill. She sensed a malodourous canker forming deep within her core that would be near impossible to excise. The tumorous growth began its inexorable spread to all living tissue within her curvaceous frame, leaving her with a deep melancholia.

She was no longer afraid of the dive. She had been well-trained for diving by her father. The reason for her intense fear was the regained knowledge of her past. She was deathly afraid of reverting to the person she once was. She desperately wanted to be rid of her prior personality, wanted to be rid of those memories that bathed her in this detestable glow.

Cheese's whole life before she met Bazza had been spent in the pursuit of wealth; an addiction inherited from her father. She chose a man to marry, based purely on his financial standing. *"Pussy money!"* She cursed silently. Cheese was stunned by the depths of her depravity and cunning in procuring a lifestyle of excess. She was guilty of prostituting herself to attain her desires. The cancer grew exponentially with each memory purloined from the abyss. Cheese felt an overwhelming urge to fling herself from a tall building. She might climb to the top deck where she could hurl herself overboard, but knew it would not bring about her demise. She was an excellent swimmer and diver, able to hold her breath for as long as three minutes underwater. In her youth, she had stayed under longer, but a lifestyle of parties and alcohol had reduced that capacity. She slowly resigned herself to her fate, accepting that she would be incapable of the epic changes required of her to become a person of honour and integrity

"I need ta get up ta the top deck ta find the spot. Can't do it from in here" Bazza said.

"Marcos, go with him. You know my orders."

Marcos nodded solemnly as the pair exited the main saloon for the top tier. Marcos would be able to steer the ship from above while Bazza used the advantage of height to pinpoint his position from his vague recollections. Chico had completed his preparations of the diving boat, taking station at the inner wheel while Marcos made his way topside. Carlos had not moved from his place on the lounge. He studied the old map before him with a sinister grin distorting his features, and with cold, dead eyes, a faraway stare delivering him into the past.

CHAPTER SEVENTEEN

Bazza held his index finger and his middle finger in a 'V', one hand-span distance from his chin, to line up the two points on land until they were exactly at the tips of his fingers. Manoeuvring endlessly to the position had tried everyone's patience to the extreme. Bazza would not allow Carlos to use his bag of tricks until Bazza had satisfied himself that he was as close as possible to his original bearings about a mile off the coast on the edge of a reef with a steep drop-off.

"Orright, that's about as close as I can get ya ta the spot I remember. If it's not the spot, I can't help ya. I'm lined up with a depression in the crest of my mountain and the mouth of a river." Said Bazza upon re-entering the cabin.

"You must have had some salt in your veins at one point in your ancestry because those are almost the same words the map makes reference to. You may have inadvertently stumbled across the entrance to the cache without being aware of its significance. Why did you make a note of the position?"

"Always wanted to do a bit-o-exploring in an underwater cave. Never got there, though. Getting a bit long in the tooth for that sort-o-caper nowadays."

"How is your knowledge of underwater geology? Any idea why there would be a long cave in this area? Long enough to catch the unwary of the time with an incoming tide?"

"Ya mean, folks going in far enough ta get caught by an incoming tide? That's gotta be a long bloody cave ta do that."

"Not really. If an extremely low tide reveals the opening to the cave, the stand-still of the tides lasts only a half hour or so before the new tide takes over. If we assume that the tide does not empty the cave entirely, leaving it to stay in water about ankle to knee-deep, then people enter the cave at first opportunity, giving them how long, before the cave fills? An hour, maybe less? I imagine the incoming tide at extreme levels would surge in very quickly to fill the cave. Anyone caught inside the cave would perish were they not near the entrance."

"Yeah, orright, I can see that. Only thing I could think of ta make a cave long like that would be a lava tube. Plenty-o-those on the mainland. Never heard-o-one under the sea."

"Very good. That is exactly what I believe. When it first formed, it may well have started on the mainland, which then flowed into the ocean quickly cooling the exterior while the lava continued to flow within. It is a fascinating concept. Tunnelling by nature, performed at many levels above the capacity of man. You have seen the other half of the map, what is the length of the cave in your estimation?"

"Couldn't say. Didn't get long enough ta know what I was looking at. Can ya gizmos find the entrance?"

"We will know soon enough. Marcos will be plotting the sea floor as we speak. We should be getting real time images on my laptop in moments", Carlos answered while retrieving his laptop computer from a desk to the side of the saloon. "I have instant access to all on-board functions through this interface."

Carlos watched the small computer screen, anxiously waiting for his moment of triumph. The satisfied leer forming on his face explained the story to the onlookers. It was clear that the modern equipment had quickly identified the approach to the underwater cave. Carlos' brow creased with concern.

"According to this, that cave is over a mile long. No wonder men drowned while stashing the cargo. I do not understand how they achieved such a thing in those times. It can only have been done over several years while waiting for the right tides. The cargo weighed approximately 2700 tons, with three galleons carrying 900 tons each, according to my memory of the manifest. Over fifty thousand ingots of silver alone, each weighing as much as a hundred pounds or 1200 troy ounces. Gold, silver eight-reale coins (pieces of eight), and jewels made up the rest of the cargo. One silver ingot retrieved from the *Atocha* from 1622, sold at auction in 1987 for $42,000 American dollars. Do you see now why this find is so important to my country? Billions of dollars waiting to be claimed in my family's name for the future of Colombia."

"Hope ya don't think Cheese-n-me can help ya haul that outta there?"

"You will be required for the scouting mission to locate the prize only. After it is found, arrangements will be made to extract the goods. Your services will be at an end. I am in a good mood, do not pursue this line of questioning. Do well by me and I will do well by you. I will offer you nothing more than that."

"How the heck do ya expect two novice divers ta swim that far under water?"

"I'm a fully qualified and ticketed diver up to a hundred metres with over a thousand hours logged," replied Cheese in a flat tone, leaving Bazza confounded.

"I am well aware of your expertise Mrs. Abigail Armstrong-Abernathy. Your father and brothers were all of a very high calibre when it came to diving according to all the information I was able to gather about you."

"Fuck me dead," muttered Bazza. "Change that ta one novice diver then. How the fuck am I going ta adjust for pressure with a broken schnozz?"

"I have diving helmets to allow for communication underwater, so stop wasting my time with your inane concerns. They are of no interest to me. If your nose bothers you, perhaps you should learn some manners?"

"Yeah, ya got me, or should I say ya hired help got me? If ya wanna try me one-on-one sometime, I'd be happy ta oblige."

"Still trying to test me? I would have thought even you might have learned by now that my patience is extremely limited. I have trained in all forms of unarmed combat, and would be happy to teach you another lesson at a more appropriate time? You will be diving with us regardless of your experience, and if you should fail to survive the dive, it will be one less problem to deal with and one less expense when I no longer have to see to the repairs of your boat."

Bazza knew full well that the carrot being dangled in front of his face was a false sign of the prick's generosity. He was being taken for a fool, with the promise of riches and reward, when Bazza knew what awaited him and Cheese once the prize was discovered. He had to play his cards right to manage their survival. While Bazza feared the consequences of his actions, were they to be discovered, he was left with little choice and secretly warmed to the prospect of the imminent challenge. Three armed and very dangerous men against one lethal male combatant and one female of curious origins and abilities. Bazza tossed the possibilities around in his head for a time.

Marcos manoeuvred the diving boat, fully laden with all the necessary gear, suspended on the rear davits, to hang over the stern ready for release. Carlos entered the diving vessel to take charge while Marcos operated the controls to lower the boat into the calm water. Chico had taken station on the top tier steering platform of the *Madonna* to keep a lofty view of the proceedings, keeping them on station at their point of arrival. Bazza and Cheese remained on board while Carlos manoeuvred the dive boat alongside the *Madonna* once released from the pulleys.

"Marcos, tell Chico to lower the anchor."

"Now just a Goddamn minute! I'm no fucking Greenie by any stretch-o-the imagination, but I'll be fucked if I'm gonna let ya drag a bloddy-great anchor and chain all over a pristine coral reef. Ya could easily fuck up years-o-delicate architecture under there and possibly damage the reef to the point-o-extinction with a beast like the *Madonna* hauling her junk all over the bottom. Ya can't do it,

Carlos, I'm begging ya. It's a heritage-listed natural wonder-o-the world for millions ta see and enjoy as long as we look after it."

"Very passionate, Bazza. Glad you finally learned how to say my name. Very well. I applaud your conservation ethics for this magnificent display of nature. Marcos can you line us up on the spot again and plot the coordinates into the Sat Nav for Chico?"

"If ya let me, I'll run up and line it up for ya and give Chico me own references as a visual back-up once he's plotted the pozzy. Then he can run out ta sea a bit and wait away from the reef, even drop the anchor?"

"I suppose you want us to run a light pick for the diving boat as well? Without a chain?"

"That'd be grouse mate. I know it's a bittuva hassle but I really do feel protective of Australia's greatest treasure."

Marcos, come on board and do as he asks. Mrs. Abernathy? Care to join us?"

"I prefer, Cheese if you don't mind. I've become very attached to Bazza's name for me."

"As you wish. Okay, everybody, *rapidez*. I want to be in the water soon to make use of the available daylight left to us even though it will be dark enough once we enter the cave. Marcos, make sure we have plenty of lights as a back up to the helmet lights. We will use the scooter's lights as long as we are mobile, to conserve battery power to the helmets. Unless there are obstacles, like a cave-in, we should reach the end in less than an hour."

Marcos and Cheese boarded the diving boat resting against the fenders hanging over the side of the *Madonna*. Bazza made his way aloft to relate his positioning instructions to Chico. On his way, Bazza watched carefully to ensure the top deck, nearest the wheel, would not be clearly visible from below. As he approached the top, Chico was at the wheel monitoring their position carefully.

Chico was expecting to hear from either Marcos or Carlos and so, was unprepared for the sight of the Australian as he approached. Bazza positioned himself on Chico's left after informing him that he was going to give him the visual clues with which to position the vessel, so as to plot the coordinates into the equipment.

Bazza used his right arm at full stretch to point to the mainland where the crest of his mountain was visible. Explaining to Chico how he needed to line up the ship between the depression on the crest and another marker to the right, Bazza began a sweep of his right arm in a wide arc to indicate the marker. Chico did not realise until the last second how fast the sweep of Bazza's arm was travelling until the hard edge of Bazza's right palm connected with Chico's larynx, crushing the delicate cartilage, cutting off all air instantly. Had Chico not panicked, he may have been able to withdraw his weapon to shoot, however, all he could do was clutch at his damaged throat in a vain attempt to breathe. Bazza held Chico in position so that the man would not fall backward and possibly over the railing, revealing his ploy. Once the life had ebbed from the inert body, Bazza secured him to the wheel by lacing his flaccid arms through the spokes to make it appear as though he were still in control of the vessel, then securing him with the radio cord. If either of the other Colombians decided to pay Chico a visit before they cast off, he could be assured of his demise.

Bazza raced down the ladder as quickly as he could before boarding the diving boat. He had set the course of the *Madonna* to head slowly on a known heading. Without delay, Carlos ordered them to steer away from the *Madonna* while he instructed Marcos to be ready with the light pick once Carlos had positioned the boat directly above the opening of the grotto. The diving boat's navigation equipment was equal to that on the *Madonna*. Carlos ensured that all relevant information had been transferred to the boat's computer. Bazza chanced a glance back to the *Madonna*, sighing inwardly when it looked to all intents and purposes like Chico was standing at the wheel, guiding the ship out past the reef. Bazza hoped like crazy that Carlos would have no need to communicate with Chico, either while aboard the diving boat, or during the dive. It was a chance he had to take in order to even the odds a little.

Carlos guided the dive boat to the coordinates expertly, then ordered Marcos to cast off the anchor. Carlos started gearing up in a dive suit the moment the boat was secured, not wanting to waste a precious second to delay the discovery of his destiny. He was bursting with anticipation and a sense of adventure, never once casting a glance or a thought to Chico or the *Madonna*. Marcos assisted his boss with the bulky rebreather units, the best that money could buy - military grade. At best, a diver utilised only about ten percent of the oxygen supplied by normal scuba gear. A rebreather unit recirculated the unused oxygen and filtered the carbon dioxide build up within the system, allowing the diver many extended hours under the water.

With the assistance of motorised scooters propelling them underwater, they would make the very most of modern equipment for their exploration. Once the location of the treasure was discovered, plans would be implemented to recover the vast haul. Carlos would leave nothing to chance, having purchased a submarine with which to evade authorities while transporting the precious cargo. Carlos estimated ten round trips with the submarine to remove the bullion from its resting place to his home. The vintage Russian submarine was only capable of holding a few hundred tons of cargo per trip. The old diesel boat required surfacing several times along its journey to charge its batteries and vent exhaust fumes. If too much weight were forced upon the old girl, she would find surfacing near impossible.

Carlos tested the diving communication equipment once everyone had donned their gear. Getting all clear signals from everyone in their immediate party, they fell backward over the side of the boat. With Carlos in the lead following a navigation aid attached to his wrist, he motioned everyone down. He had placed the boat above the shallow reef. Angling seaward, Carlos led the foursome over the edge of the reef where it dropped off dramatically, into the deep blue water. Bazza kept a watchful eye out for the predators he knew to populate the deeper areas of the reef where the cooler currents provided a plethora of prey. White Pointers, Bronze Whalers and many other varieties of shark were commonplace near Australian reefs. Bazza had seen his fair share of monsters, including enormous Hammerheads in great numbers, all along the edges of the Great Barrier Reef. He was not comfortable trespassing in their home.

The sea scooters were the very latest in high-tech equipment, delivering them speeds of up to 10klm/hr, however, running them at a top speed reduced battery efficiency, so a cruising speed of 4-5klm/hr was recommended. Carlos had chosen the slimmest, most lightweight model available to the professional diver, delivering the most power to weight ratio. Though he was very capable of diving great distances without the aid of a scooter, he knew that speed was of the essence. They may well have to abandon the contraptions if a cave-in restricted their access. A crash course in their simple operation saw everyone adjusting easily to their use.

Carlos levelled off at the 30-foot mark, traversing the edge of the reef to find the entrance to the cave clearly indicated on his wrist device. The cave was situated in a narrow ravine dividing the reef, leading landward. Both sides of the ravine were heavily encrusted in sharp, coral outcroppings. Carlos motored cautiously between the menacing walls until he could make out a dark opening in the distance. Huge Potato Cod, easily six or seven foot in length drifted idly by, curious about their visitors. Their cavernous mouths were easily capable of swallowing a human head whole. While the rest of the human bodies, encumbered with the bulky breathing apparatus may not fit, the fish could effortlessly decapitate any of the divers.

Fortunately, humans were not on the Cods' menu for the day. All about them in the clear depths, loomed the various shapes and sounds of a healthy reef in full swing. Parrot Fish and Wrasse gnawing at the coral, and the currents swishing between the bombies made for a surprising cacophony to the uninitiated when diving the first time. The soothing sounds and bright colours never ceased to fascinate Bazza, who had long ago been introduced to the wonders of diving on the reef. Many years ago, Bazza had given over every spare moment of his time to his passion for fishing. Until it became necessary for him to retrieve an expensive lure one day in favour of breaking it off. Once he snorkelled down to the release the lure's hold on the coral, he became entranced with his surroundings. So enamoured of the ethereal beauty did he become, that Bazza spent more time under the water than above it from that moment. He no longer fished for pure pleasure after that.

He found it hard to keep his eyes from wandering to the

dizzying array of colours and movement surrounding them. The profusion of brilliant hues from enormous clams and schooling fish sought to distract him from his purpose. Although he knew he must keep his wits about him and concentrate on the tasks at hand, it did not prevent him from admiring the vast beauty that surrounded him. Cheese also found it difficult to avoid being distracted by the life and colour about her. Although vastly experienced at diving, it did not mean she had lost her fascination with the underwater world of reefs and wrecks. It buoyed her emotions to the point where she momentarily lost the all-pervasive melancholia that descended upon her with the return of her memories.

Carlos, in the lead, navigated the ravine carefully, with Marcos bringing up the rear of the quartet. As the gap in the coral at the end of the ravine emerged, he slowed his pace considerably. It appeared to him that a certain amount of destruction was inevitable in order to gain sufficient passage to the opening, overgrown with coral during the intervening years underwater. Carlos hoped that the bothersome Australian would not object too vociferously to the suggestion. Carlos ordered Marcos to the point position to clear the opening with the tools at his disposal.

Bazza watched in growing horror at the mutilation of the coral impeding their access into the cave. He knew he couldn't deter the maniac from his mission, so didn't waste his breath on objections. The amount of destruction wrought by the Colombian did not begin to compare with what might have occurred by anchoring the *Madonna* above. The anchor chain attached to the colossus that was the *Madonna*, would have caused untold, permanent destruction to the reef, decimating a hundred-foot circular swathe of ancient coral growth. Foolish fisherman and divers alike caused irreparable damage to large sections of the reef in just such a manner each day. Tourist operators knew to anchor well away from reefs or at permanently anchored pontoons while on dive tours, whereas visitors hiring private vessels were ignorant of the catastrophe caused by their careless anchoring. Often releasing their human wastes and garbage into the fragile ecosystems as well, causing contamination and wildlife hazards.

Marcos cleared a large enough opening with a pinch bar, to permit the bulk of a person wearing the rebreather units and a sea scooter to enter the grotto in relative safety. Carlos was the first to turn on his lights before slowly edging his way into the dark maw, only to backpedal frantically immediately after, followed by a highly agitated, enormous, Moray Eel. Once clear of the entrance, the eel slid past the divers to seek refuge elsewhere. Carlos turned livid upon hearing laughter from Bazza and Cheese. Without a word, he turned to the cave once more, where he powered through the entrance pell-mell in a flurry of bubbles. The others gradually followed at a more sedate pace.

Inside the cave was a stark contrast to the picturesque seascape outside. Only a little way past the entrance saw an end to the coral, unable to survive without the sunshine. While there were certain soft corals present, they lacked the brilliant colours of their exterior cousins. All plant and animal life diminished considerably the further they proceeded. In moments, nothing remained visible outside the sea scooters' light beams.

"Settle in, conserve your energy for what will probably be a long swim people. Marcos, stay in the rear and keep a close eye on our friends. Wouldn't want them getting into any trouble now, would we? I will warn you if I come across anything blocking our path."

"Yes, boss."

Bazza could only just make out the sides of the cave at the periphery of Carlos' scooter beams. It seemed wider than it was. Maybe ten feet across and perhaps five feet in height. He pitied the poor saps trudging down the tunnel all those years ago, stooped to avoid the ceiling, lugging tons of ingots along after them. The only transportation method of which he could conceive, consisted of a floating platform made of wood, bearing the treasure, being hauled along the cave by the sailors. Small wonder people died. It was only when he spied regular markings on the cave walls and the odd piece of ancient, preserved lumber, that he changed his mind about the method. Bazza surmised that a series of gantries had been built by their ship's carpenter along the entire stretch of the cave, along which would be attached many pulleys with which to haul the enormous load from the ship to the end. That assumption caused a spark of interest in Bazza that he stored away in the back of his mind.

Bazza wondered idly what method the Colombian would employ to remove the treasure. It wasn't long before they came across their first reminder of the inherent dangers associated with the eerie tomb. A human skeleton, semi-submerged in the silty, sandy bottom, lay bathed in a pool of light from the scooter. Carlos supposed that all of the deceased pirates had been stripped clean by creatures of the deep, despite the length of the cave. Blind sea creatures inhabited the deepest depths of the darkest ocean, so it stood to reason that creatures would survive in the farthest reaches of the cave. He moved forward in silence, secretly overjoyed at the discovery, the first sign that he was truly on the right path. He almost hyperventilated with the sheer excitement coursing through his system. He had to consciously relax his breathing in order to conserve precious air.

Time sped by in total silence, broken regularly by the sound of their own breathing. Only the occasional ghostly white shrimp or luminescent jellyfish altered the lifeless monotony of the tunnel. Bazza felt a hopeless claustrophobia in the confined darkness with only the light from the sea scooters penetrating the eternal inky gloom. He wondered what monsters might lurk in the dark, icy, realms.

Cheese allowed few thoughts of exterior circumstances to interfere with her interior turmoil once clear of the colourful distractions. Her self-loathing aimed lethal barbs at her attempts to emerge from the abyss of her thoughts. Her emotional distress denounced all efforts to attach worth to her persona. She was unable to ascend from the depths of depression to take any further notice of her surroundings, or to care for her well-being. She succumbed to the notion that she was not deserving of redemption. She felt desolate at the thought of losing Bazza's respect, and more importantly, his love.

She had come to realise that her affection for Bazza had grown into something far stronger. She knew that her love was reciprocated. That thought depressed her further still. When Bazza heard the full story of her past, he was unlikely to remain in love with her. If she could no longer like herself, she felt sure no one else could either. The spiral of condemnation and depression sent her to the extreme limits of her emotions, pushing the boundaries into uncharted territories that suggested institutionalisation. The mind can be its own worst enemy at times, and she recognised the slippery slope she navigated.

Carlos powered along at a pace that did not suit the conditions. The light from his sea scooter barely extended to a distance of ten to twelve feet in the eerie gloom. Decades of silt layers ascended in clouds behind him as he motored above the bottom of the cave. He was eager to be the first person to lay eyes on his family's fortune. As he closed in on the prize, Carlos could sense the years of pursuit and worry fall away to join the disturbed silt. The many dollars spent in the hunt for his legacy would soon be justified a million-fold if the lists were true. Thousands of silver and gold ingots waiting for centuries beneath the surface for Escobar's ancestor to discover and retrieve.

So lost in his reveries was Carlos, that he did not register the blockage before him until it was almost too late. The sudden stop of the electric motor did not, however, cease all forward momentum, as it collided heavily against the barrier, with Carlos unable to prevent the collision. Bazza narrowly missed piling into Carlos at the last second by angling toward the side, with Cheese smashing her sea scooter directly into Carlos' back, unable to make out anything through the silt clouds disturbed by the two scooters in front of her. Marcos, some distance behind, managed to avoid the pile-up in time, waiting for the silt to settle before making his way forward.

Bazza wasted no time while Carlos was temporarily out of action and they were hidden from Marcos behind a screen of disturbed silt. He grabbed Cheese by the wrist with a fierce grip, zig-zagging around the chicane of debris littering the tunnel floor after activating his helmet's light. Within seconds they came to a fuller blockage halting their progress. They would have to abandon the scooters in order to squeeze through the opening at the side of the collapsed tunnel. Shards of light from above penetrated the darkness momentarily as they squirmed through the narrow opening.

He had to man-handle Cheese all the way, fighting a seeming reluctance from her to escape the clutches of the Colombians. He had to drag her along after him into the clearing on the other side of the cave-in. Once through he motioned for

Cheese to haul arse, shoving her off to continue along the tunnel. Once he was sure she had understood the message, he returned to the aperture in the blockage. Above the aperture, a large boulder extended from the wall at a precarious angle. A few smaller stones wedged in underneath the boulder was all that prevented it from collapsing into the tunnel to block the opening entirely. Retrieving a knife he had taken from Chico, secreted under his wetsuit, Bazza began to prize away the smaller stones. He managed to wiggle only one free before he saw the lights from the Colombians' helmets shining through the hole. They were almost upon him when the second stone came free, releasing the behemoth above to come crashing to the tunnel floor in a cloud of silt.

Bazza felt the projectile lancing through the tiny hole remaining in the blockage, by its passage through the water beside his arm. Too small for human passage, yet large enough to permit a hand holding a spear gun to reach through. He saw the spear gun reversing its course, ostensibly to be reloaded. Unable to remain longer to inspect the success or failure of his ruse, Bazza quickly turned toward the darkness once more, to join up with Cheese.

"Cheese, if you can hear me, I managed ta delay the bastards, but I don't know for how long, so get a bloody move on and don't wait for me."

"What's the point Bazza? We have nowhere to go and you've only succeeded in getting him pissed."

"*Pissed off*, Cheese. I got him *pissed off*, not *pissed*. In Australia, getting someone pissed, means getting them drunk."

"You really think now is the time to be giving me lessons in Australian idioms?"

"I would listen to her if I was you, Mr. Ottoman. I am 'pissed *off*', more than you can imagine. You have nowhere to go and you have just signed your death warrants."

"Aw, we were doomed anyway fuck-knuckle. I just chose to arrange my own battle ground instead of yours. Might find a few other ways ta stop ya yet, so fuck you, arsehole."

Cheese and Bazza could hear every word Carlos spoke to Marcos as he ordered him about to get the obstacle out of the way. It was off-putting to hear their voices at such a perceived proximity while they attempted to put as much distance between them as possible. Then they heard an instruction that sent shivers up their spines. Carlos had plans to blow up the obstruction with explosives. Bazza knew the shock waves from an underwater explosion could harm them significantly without any form of protection, while the Colombians had the chicane of debris preceding the blockage to obviate the effects of the blast. *Their* only way to remain moderately safe was to gain as much distance in as short a time as possible.

He forced his muscular legs into prompt action, accelerating down the tunnel toward the fleeing figure of Cheese in the distance, barely visible in the light of his helmet. She was a strong swimmer, but nowhere near as strong as Bazza when he set his mind to a course of action. Using every advantage of arm strength and leg power. Bazza caught up with, and passed Cheese soon after. He angled his helmet light back and forth illuminating the sides of the tunnel as he swam.

Several moments later he found what he was looking for; a niche at the side where a small cave-in had a occurred, giving them a modicum of a shield against the incoming shockwave. Bazza signalled Cheese to get closest to the wall, allowing him to use his bulk to help protect her. She was about to argue with Bazza when he shushed her with a finger to his faceplate while shaking his head. He managed to make her understand that the others would be able to hear them.

He did not want to give away the fact that they might survive the blast. He wanted every advantage available to them, and getting their kidnappers to act overconfidently could assist them in a small way. Before they could settle in for the wait, they heard the fantastically muted explosion in the distance. Bazza braced them both for the expected wave to hit them. Little did they know that the explosion would cause more than simply removing the blockage, it would cause a large portion of the tunnel between them and the Colombians to collapse, magnifying the intensity of the wave surging in their direction.

When the wave hit, it took them both with such force that it sent them hurtling end-over-end down the tunnel. Bazza managed to wrap his large frame around Cheese as much as possible, making them a large ball bouncing around on the bottom and off the sides of the tunnel. For what seemed an eternity, they tumbled along in the tumultuous water, unable to make out anything in the cloudy darkness. Bazza was protecting Cheese's breathing unit as much as he could while they seemed to strike every available surface, time and again. One advantage of the frenetic ride down the tunnel was the distance they gained from their adversaries. The disadvantage was, of course, the possibility of life-threatening damage to their breathing equipment.

Gradually the tidal wave decreased to allow them a hint of control, but not before being bludgeoned by the many objects caught up in the swell. One of the objects, Bazza caught after being struck painfully in his mid-section, turned out to be a small gold ingot. Bazza eventually saw it clearly enough to identify it. As the swirling maelstrom began to settle, he noticed the bars strewn haphazardly about the tunnel floor, just before he thumped lightly into a wall, signifying the end of the tunnel. Unbeknownst to the pair, the tunnel floor had gradually angled upward bringing them higher.

While they survived the explosion reasonably unscathed, sporting only minor bruises, Bazza struggled when he realised he was no longer able to breathe air from his damaged unit. He rose to the surface of the pool within a large cavern. Cheese, observing his struggles, tried to prevent him from what she assumed he might do. He warded off her attempts to stop him from removing his mask.

"No Bazza, you mustn't..."

Too late. He had removed his helmet, thereby exposing himself to the possibility of toxic air within the cavern. She watched tearfully as he wriggled free of the encumbering equipment. She attempted to give him some of her air, knowing they could survive for a time using the buddy breathing system, but he batted her hand away. As she regained her composure, she was stunned to see him before her with an idiotic grin on his face. She felt like slapping him for trying to make light of his circumstances at his time of death, until she realised he was breathing. When she shot him a questioning glance, he nodded his affirmation. She followed suit by removing her helmet cautiously. The air tasted slightly stale, but not harmful.

Cheese had assumed that the tunnel to the cavern had been submerged so long that it was not possible for fresh air to enter. She did not even consider that air could have traversed the length of the tunnel even when exposed at low tides. People had been reported to have died while exploring lava tubes on land due to air toxicity. Oxygen tanks were necessary when exploring the long caves.

"How could you possibly have known the air would be breathable?"

"Take a look around ya. Ya think them bozos back then got all the way here dragging heavy cargo, then back in one go? Before the tide turned? Nah, they had a crew in here all the time hauling away on a conveyor line rigged up along the tunnel, with other crews on the ships loading and hauling the empties back. Had ta be air in here. I saw some signs of construction as we were swimming along that got me thinking about it. Nothing else made any sense."

Cheese looked about the large cavern for the first time. A large flat area off to their right was completely covered with layers upon layers of silver ingots, rotten chests exposing their precious contents where the wood had disintegrated, and yet more bullion. Gold and silver, dulled by the years of accumulated dust filtering in with the fresh air from above. Cheese peered upward to where a straight shaft shot clear through to open air. The entire find was a huge anti-climax to her. She was expecting the gleam of the precious metals to bedazzle her, lift her spirits to another realm like it would have for her father. Instead, she felt underwhelmed by the dull display of fantastic wealth before her. She peered upward once more.

"Volcanic vent I reckon. I'll bet we are somewhere near the bottom of our mountain on ya old man's block-o-land. Bet that's why he bought it. He musta figured out enough ta know it was thereabouts."

"Bazza, all that is well and good, but what are we going to do? We can't just stay here and wait for those...men to reach us."

"Yeah, I know. Betta get ya clobber orf, mate. Gonna get too hot in here ta wear the suits. We hafta hoof it from here."

"What are you talking about? Hoof it? You mean walk? Walk where?"

"Back home of course. Get in the Ute, drive the fuck away from here and tell the coppers everything."

"Did you hit your head or something, Bazza? How are we going to just walk out of here? You certainly can't mean going up there? Even if we were able to get all the way up there, neither you nor I would fit"

"Fuck no! I mean following the cave all the way back till we get to my creek."

"You've lost me. *Your* creek?"

"No time ta explain, mate. Gotta get going *now*."

Bazza had already started stripping down to his undies, the only thing he wore beneath the wetsuit. Cheese followed his example. Wearing only their briefs and rubber booties, they took off toward the rear of the cave with their torches lighting the way. They did not know how close the Colombians were behind them and did not wait to find out. A narrow path led away from the main chamber in a general westerly direction.

"How could you possibly know about this path?"

"Saw it on ya map. Didn't know what it was at the time, but figured it out after seeing the other half."

"You remembered what you saw? What, have you got a photographic memory or something?"

"I'm a wood carver, Cheese, I study diagrams and pictures of me subjects before committing them ta memory, so I don't have ta keep referring ta them while I carve. It saves a lot-o-time if ya remember 'em."

"How far do we have to go?"

"That was a bit hard ta tell. The map didn't actually show anything more than a few yards. I don't think them blokes back then actually had the resources ta explore much of it. Probably couldn't go far with only candle light."

"Then how do you figure there is a way out?"

"Connecting the dots again Cheese. I found one-o-them silver pieces-o-eight embedded in a lump of old wood once, in a pool below a waterfall. Never found anything else and never did think ta look anywhere other than following the creek up the bloody mountain."

"So...?"

"Struck me while I was trying ta elude those clowns when they were tracking me, that the cave beneath the waterfall might have an opening underwater that leads ta somewhere. I thought I might go back there and try it once we were rid-o-the Colombians. After seeing both halves-o-the map, and finding the cave and the path, I sorta added two and two together. Once I saw them silver coins over there, I figured that coin I found could only have come from here."

"Just because a *coin* made it to your pool doesn't mean a human being can. Big chance you're taking there."

"Better than staying here ta cop it from those two pieces-o-shit."

"Can't argue with that big fella. Lead on."

Half an hour later, with the sides of the path closing in on them and their torches beginning to dull, Cheese began to lose confidence in the big fella's plan. Bazza found that they had more space at a lower level, prompting him to begin crawling on all fours. They both found the going hard on their exposed knees. The air became hot and humid within the confined space, causing sweat to run freely from their pores. Cheese found the building moisture uncomfortable, stopping often to wipe away the excess. Without a supply of drinking water, they both felt the symptoms of dehydration beginning to wear them down. Bazza continued to lead the way with Cheese close behind. He had asked her to turn her torch off. They would make do with one at a time to extend their time with light. Neither wanted to be stuck in a cramped cave without a light; a nightmare not worth contemplating.

Bazza did not feel overly confident about his hypothesis, or about their ability to reach the pool beneath the waterfall, the longer they travelled. He knew what waited behind them, though, and that kept him moving. One troubling observation made him feel nauseous. Their air supply was gradually thinning, or turning stale. He couldn't be sure which. They had travelled a fair distance from the small vent supplying breathable air to the cavern with the treasure. Unless they reached a point where new air came in from the direction they were travelling, they would not make it.

Bazza knew that Carlos would not waste valuable time in pursuit once he reached the cavern accommodating his treasure. He would begin to make plans for retrieving the bounty immediately. He and Marcos would probably return to the dive boat to call in the hired help. Returning to the cavern was not an option even if it were safe to do so, because both he and Cheese would not be able to return through the tunnel to the ocean with only one rebreather unit, always assuming the Colombians had left it there. Remaining in the cavern with its bountiful air supply was a useless proposition, because eventually the Colombians would return with a lot of help and hired muscle.

The moment Bazza believed their situation could not get

much worse, his hand descended into freezing water, while his head, painfully, found the end to the path. He was unable to lift his head more than a few inches, unable to move about or turn within the confined space. He tested the space below the water with his torch to ascertain the geography as best he could. His breathing was laboured as he spoke.

"Cheese, I got good news, bad news, and worst news."

"What's the worst news?"

"The cave sort-o-ends up here and we hafta swim underwater for I dunno how far and probably die."

"Swell. And the bad news?"

"We stay where we are and slowly asphyxiate."

"So we die on the move, or we die staying still?"

"Something like that. I could maybe go first and if I don't make it, ya can go back ta the cave and wait for the mongrels?"

"Not going to happen. Not enough light to make it back anyway. We made how many twists and turns during our trek? A dozen, maybe more? No, let's just go forward and take our chances. What's the good news?"

"Plenty-o-water ta drink. Tastes bloody terrific. Okay, but before ya go, ya gotta lie still for a few moments ta relax and control ya breathing. Ya won't get a proper lung full-o-air unless ya do that. Who knows how far we gotta travel underwater eh? So, I'm gonna just lie here and meditate a bit. Ya gotta do the same when ya slither up here."

During the unearthly silence..."Bazza?"

"Um, meditating here, Cheese. Ya know, before the whole swimming-ta-me-death-underwater-thing?"

"Yes, sorry. I just needed to tell you something very important. Bazza, I remember everything now."

"Yeah, figured that when you mentioned the bit about being an expert diver."

"Can you just turn off your torch a while. I don't want you to waste the batteries while I'm telling you this."

"Jeez, this can't wait?"

"No! It has to be now...in case. In case...you know, we don't make it."

"Gotta give us a chance, eh? Don't give up on me, buddy."

"Bazza, shut-up would you please? This is not about being a defeatist. I just have something I need to say in case the worst happens. I remember everything about my life now and your original assumption about me was one hundred percent correct. I come from pussy money. I literally spread my legs to bag a rich husband for whom I had no feelings. I have been a first-rate bitch my entire life. Everything was fine until my husband threw himself from a fortieth storey window when the stock market crashed. I lost everything. House, car, jewellery, husband... Shit! See? I didn't even list my husband first, that's how low I am."

"Not 'am', Cheese, *were*. Ya *were* that person. I don't believe for a second ya still are that same woman. I don't fall in love with them kinda women, mate. I don't take chances for that kinda..."

"Whoa! Back up a minute, buster. What did you say? You don't what...?"

"Fall in love for that kinda woman, the kind ya think ya still are. If I thought ya were that, I'd never-o-done nothing for ya, or with ya."

"Could you say that first bit again please, Bazza?"

"I reckon I love ya, Cheese...Abby. Couldn't imagine being without ya no more. Ya kinda grew on me, and just kept on doing it. I didn't want ta say nothing coz, I didn't think ya felt the same. Abby? Aww, I gone and made ya cry now, coz I opened me big gob and stepped right in eh?"

"You couldn't be more wrong, Barry Ottoman. I am in *love* with a man for the first time in my life. In love with a big old softy from Australia. I don't deserve your love, though, and that's why I'm crying. Now stop calling me, Abby. My name is, Cheese. We have to get out of here and I am expecting you to pull off a miracle that I believe only you can do. Bazza? Bazza?"

Bazza had slipped away silently beneath the frigid water. His heart ached for the woman he left behind, fearful that they would not survive their ordeal. He used his torch in short bursts to conserve the flagging power in the batteries. Every momentary flash of light gave him a mental picture of the next ten feet. Luckily there were no underwater obstacles that he was aware of, with plenty of depth. Despite his meditation before taking his last breath, he was unable to fill his lungs to full capacity. He estimated that he might have only two and a half minutes of swimming in him. If he didn't surface by then he would perish.

He cruised along at an easy pace. His air was used slower at a cruising speed, where his muscles were not using up excessive amounts of oxygen. Slowly, Bazza felt the onset of that time where his lungs simply wanted more oxygen and his instincts told him to open his mouth. He had to force his mouth closed and his body forward, past the point of pain, past the point of conscious thought, forcing his body to continue even though his only wish, was to curl up in a ball and float into oblivion. Time suspended while all sound and sight receded, leaving him to kick his legs along beyond his will. His mouth half opened, but he managed to force out the water.

When Bazza broke the surface of the water just as his torch blinked out, he half-choked on a mixture of air and water entering his mouth. Unable to expel the water completely, he continued to choke as he tried desperately to fill his lungs. Coughing and spluttering while his lungs protested at the intrusion of liquid into their domain, he finally managed to control his breathing. He thumped his torch a few times to no avail. He was groping around in the darkness completely disoriented. The roof of the cave was mere inches above his head, but the air was clean and fresh. He was able to feel the coolness on his cheek to detect the direction he must follow.

Cheese burst from the water beside him, gasping in panic. Bazza tried to calm her while she went through the same coughing spasms. He held her in his massive arms as she slowly regained her regular breathing. Before long, Bazza became aware of a tickling sensation on his bare legs and torso. Using Cheese's torch, he directed the light underwater. Tiny bubbles accompanying a minor venting of fresh water from the bottom indicated the presence of an underground spring. If Bazza's assumptions about the direction they were headed were correct, it explained the consistency of water in the creek behind his shack, despite no water flowing from the waterfall in times of severe dry. Unless they missed more than a couple of seasons of wet, which had occurred only once during his occupation of the land, the water in his creek continued to be provided by the natural spring rather than the accumulation of water above the falls in a catchment area fed by gravity.

Cheese searched Bazza's eyes for signs of regret, or disillusionment. She felt vulnerable about revealing her true feelings, and an overwhelming joy at the news she was loved. Although Bazza and she had made wondrous love together, she felt that love had not originated from the act...for once. It was an enlightening notion. Normally, confessions of love for her after sex were met with banality and boredom, like it was exactly as it should be, an expected outcome for a well-executed ploy. She did feel a little guilty about her first thoughts after meeting Bazza when coming out of her catatonia. She had reacted immediately from her conditioned reflexes, attempting to gain her will with the subterfuge of sexual manipulation.

What she saw in Bazza's eyes and in her heart was totally foreign to her preconditioned notions. She saw a tenderness and deep concern for her well-being in his eyes. In her heart, she felt an aching need to be with him, near him, at one with him. There, in the darkness of the cave, treading water, with only her torch light illuminating their faces, they peered lovingly into one another's eyes with an unabashed fondness for each other, cradled in each other's arms. They did not want to break the moment, did not want the magic to end. Strength flowed through their bodies, buoyed by the confidence of shared love. Bazza smiled like a man with a winning poker hand, and Cheese smiled in return. He kissed her gently, lovingly, passionately. Cheese wrapped her legs around him, causing them both to sink beneath the surface.

"I think we better get going, love", suggested Bazza as they resurfaced. "Gonna get too bloody cold soon if we don't get outta here. While I could think of a coupla ways ta get warm, it wouldn't last all that long."

"Absolutely right. I think the next time we make love, I want it to be in our bed."

"*Our*, bed eh?"

"You bet."

"By the way, did I ever tell you how sexy ya are - specially when ya only wearing knickers?"

"You can tell me later big boy. I am getting cold now."

"I can tell. Poke someone's eye out with one-o-them."

Bazza narrowly escaped the clout aimed at his head as he waded away quickly. Once their eyes adjusted to the darkness after turning off her torch, they became aware of the glow worms on the ceiling of the cave. Like stars in the heavens, the little pinpricks of light guided them along the underground stream. At times, the stream became very shallow, making them crawl along, barely scraping through the narrowing waterway, coating them with cold, slimy mud, rank with bat guano. The foul stench in places where the water level dropped away to leave only the putrid mud, threatened to make them empty the contents of their delicate stomachs. Breathing in short, sharp bursts, was all they could do to keep from throwing up.

On and on they crawled, swam and nudged their way along the endless waterway. Once they were again in a pool of deeper water, they managed to wash away the worst of the acrid uniform they had donned during their journey. The air about them immediately smelled cleaner for the effort. Olfactory senses restored, they continued forward. Before either of them became aware of the change, a minute amount of light altered the visibility around them from an inky blackness to subtle hues of grey and black.

Then, from the gloom came a shard of dim daylight, piercing the grey with a glimmer of hope. Bazza and Cheese hurried their pace without conscious thought, each wanting to escape the misery of their confinement. Quicker and quicker they paddled, eventually coming to a narrow space between the surface of the water and the roof of the cave. Ducking into the water to pass through the opening, they were overwhelmed once they surfaced, with the roar of the waterfall within the cavern. Bazza remained under the cascade of water until he felt every last vestige of the foul mud was cleansed from his body. He removed his undies to wash them out thoroughly. Cheese followed his example happily, laughing with relief, never happier to be alive. Unable to contain their need any longer, the two bodies were drawn to one another inexorably until they were entwined in the act of love-making, free from their restrictive surrounds, and deliriously happy to have escaped.

Cheese leaned back in Bazza's arms sighing with delight as he entered her, causing her muscles to spasm immediately in an orgasmic celebration, joined soon after, by the gushing flow of Bazza's intimate warmth. Their bodies remained entwined as they made their way to shallower water, where Bazza was able to stand. They huddled together for warmth and comfort after the harrowing experience of near death, after all the events of the previous months, after confirming their bond with an act of love. Gradually, silently, they dressed in their meagre clothing to leave the grotto for the open air where the humidity would soon replace water droplets with sweat. Neither Bazza nor Cheese could complain about the heat as their body temperature rose to normal once more. On a positive note, Bazza was surprised and delighted at the absence of leeches. He believed the foul-smelling mud may have acted as a repellent for the loathsome creatures. He made a mental note to test that theory at some point.

CHAPTER EIGHTEEN

While the atmosphere outside the cave was far warmer than inside, the available light was fading fast. Ignorant of the passage of time while spelunking, they were greeted with the remnants of daylight fading quickly as night descended. In a short while, Bazza and Cheese found themselves barely capable of groping their way along the creek bed. Neither starlight nor moonlight of sufficient quantities made its way through the dense canopy to allow safe navigation. Eventually, Bazza called a halt to their blind travels in order to avoid serious injury. He led his companion to the side of the creek where they huddled together within the comforting folds of the buttressed roots of a forest giant. Exhausted to within a whisker of total depletion, they fell asleep instantly.

Bazza woke to the sounds of the forest he had grown to love, as the morning light intruded upon it's nightly competitor. Dappled sunshine wove its way through the multi-layered, leafy, blanket far above them, casting fluttering shadows of wind driven leaves about them like ghostly moths escaping the dangers of daylight. Skinks and other reptiles wriggled their way among the leaf litter on the forest floor in search of breakfast. Frogs burrowed beneath the detritus of the forest to seek shelter from the predators and heat. Bird song filled the empty morning air with a sweet orchestration, all seemingly in perfect synchronisation, to produce a natural overture with which to start the day

Cheese slowly stirred within Bazza's embrace. He watched as she came awake, fascinated by the small interplay of conscious and subconscious thoughts while the mind evolved from dreams to reality. Her big blue eyes opened suddenly when she finally became aware of their circumstances and immediately softened upon seeing his welcoming smile. He bent down slowly to impart a gentle kiss upon her waiting lips.

"I could get used ta waking up beside ya."

"Hmm, not sure if I could get used to waking up in our current situation, but definitely nice to be waking up with my man. How are you feeling? I haven't had a chance to inspect all your wounds for a while. Your ear?"

"Yeah, hurting some. Bit worried about all that gunk we waded through infecting it. Who knows what sorta microbes and bacteria are thriving in all that. Funny, though. I can't feel the effects of the stinging tree anymore. What about yaself, any damage?"

"I'd be more worried about what lifeforms may lurk in that beard of yours. Me? Sore muscles, a few bruises and scratches, nothing much. We were lucky. I don't think we're going to be as lucky in future. Not entirely sure how we survived in the first place. You say you found a piece-of-eight in that pool under the waterfall? You deduced from that flimsy bit of evidence that human beings could make it there well?"

"Didn't see that we had a lot-o-choice than ta try. Didn't fancy getting harpooned by that mongrel once he showed up at the treasure cave. To hope that they didn't survive the explosion woulda been asking too much I reckon. So, I don't think we're safe yet. If they were able ta go back ta their dive boat, they'll be on their way ta me shack for sure. If they didn't, they will be following us ta the pool under the waterfall, if they aren't there already.

"Wait a minute. If they could make it back to their dive boat, why would they bother coming back to your shack? They would just go back to the *Madonna* to make arrangements for loading the treasure. Even if they wanted to get even with you or me, Carlos would not give pursuit of us precedence over fulfilling his, 'destiny'."

"Um... yeah, if, the *Madonna* had the capacity to assist him."

"Bazza? Why would the *Madonna* not have the capacity to assist him?"

"By my reckoning, it will have ended up on a particular section of the reef it was aiming for before we left."

"With a fully-qualified captain at her helm who would have easily avoided such a calamity with all the modern technology aboard?"

"If that captain had been capable of making the course corrections ta avoid the reef."

"If? Chico looked perfectly capable of reading the instruments to avoid collisions with obstacles when we left? Why would you... Oh, I see."

"Couldn't let them mongrels get back ta the ship, and had ta cut down the opposition numbers against us a bit."

"Permanently?"

"The ship mighta survived."

"But not the captain?"

Bazza shook his head, hoping that Cheese would not judge him too harshly.

"It's about time."

"Huh?"

"Look, Bazza, while I applaud your ethics and all, I did think it was time. You were more than capable of ending this venture yourself without resorting to these elaborate plans involving animals, the forest, and God knows what else. I understood your reluctance but, seriously Bazza? You were acting in self-defence after all. We could have avoided a lot of this."

"The army taught me lotsa ways-o-killing Cheese, and I gave 'em their money's worth. I got involved in special training, which meant they could recall me anytime they wanted. I had ta make out that I didn't have it in me anymore ta avoid 'em recalling me. Then after I went ta jail, I had ta avoid ways-o-getting put back there. I couldn't just, *deal*, with those mongrels at first. When the odds were too heavily stacked against us, I had ta act, but I didn't like it, and I'm really worried about what'll happen now. When I took care-o-Chico it couldn't be construed as self-defence. The bloody cops have ta get involved now and that could spell the end-o-me and me life here."

"Bazza, don't get me wrong. I am very grateful that you are not the barbarian I thought you were, but I did begin to wonder what sort of man you were turning into to allow people to push us around. I am glad to find that you have limits to your patience. I did not like our chances when we were so heavily outnumbered."

"Yeah well, I still don't like our chances just sitting here talking. Those mongrels are coming and we gotta be ready for 'em. So let's get going."

"Aren't you forgetting our other little roving problem? He does have a gun remember, and is extremely dangerous now?"

"Probably taken care of by now. No time ta explain. Gotta get home and get some clothes on ya before I lose me willpower again."

"Whatever happened to thinking I was artificial? You know, 'had some work done'?"

"Um, did I voice that at some time? Ya musta misheard me or something."

Cheese began to move off down the creek. "No, you mentioned it once or twice actually. Just for your edification, though, I'll have you know that I have not at any time been 'under the knife', or been injected with anything to enhance parts of my face. I am all natural thank-you very much. Yes, I led a privileged life at one time, but that all fell apart when my 'rich' husband took a swan dive from a skyscraper window. I think an Australian might have described my situation after that as 'not having a pot to piss in'."

"I think maybe me body showed ya what I think-o-ya Cheese. If ya say it's all natural, then I take ya word for it, and would probably have liked ya either way. I'm looking forward ta hearing ya full story at last. It's all come back has it?"

"Unfortunately."

Neither spoke for a time as they made their way toward Bazza's shack. Around them, the forest grew quiet as the exterior heat shimmered through to the interior in increasing waves of humidity. Sweat soon drenched their exhausted bodies as they laboured along the stony creek bed, concentrating on keeping their balance on the slippery rocks. Bazza stopped suddenly, cautioning Cheese to remain quiet. With a look of pure dread for what may happen next, she looked to where he was pointing. Puzzled, she gave him a questioning look. Bazza pointed lower, toward a pool of water a few feet in front of them.

As she concentrated on the area ahead of them, she began to notice movement in the water, just below, and occasionally breaking the surface of the pool. A little creature with frenetic movements dived, dipped, and paddled about the pool with great dexterity. Bazza whispered the name of the creature softly into her ear. She had never seen a Platypus before, either in a zoo or in the wild. A fascinating oddity, occurring nowhere else in the world. She knew very little about it despite acquiring an extensive knowledge of aquatic animals and fish. She did know they were a very shy, mostly nocturnal, egg-laying mammal. While the water was crystal clear, it moved so quickly and often, that they failed to get a good enough sighting to appreciate the beautiful little creature.

Bazza motioned them onward, wanting to be clear of the area as soon as possible. His hackles were rising the longer they remained in relative proximity to the cave. He needed to get back to the shack where they could get some clothes on and plan for possible eventualities. He did not think either of the Colombians had expired as a result of the underwater detonation they had set off. The shaped charge was directed towards Cheese and himself, who copped the worst of the resulting shockwave and mini tsunami.

Cheese pondered the earlier conversation they'd had, puzzling over the ramifications of his words. 'Probably taken care of ', is what Bazza had said in answer to her questions about Rafael. She ruminated on the possible meaning of the ambiguous statement. She could not identify any moment in her memory where Bazza had the resources or time to have, 'taken care of ', anything. Tramping around in the middle of the forest wearing next to nothing while that crazed creep was on the loose unnerved her more than she was willing to admit. She shivered at the thought of his lustful leers whenever she was in his presence. She knew without a doubt that her fate would have been sealed were it not for Bazza.

The closer they came to the shack, the more worried Bazza became. Two thoughts troubled him. The first; being that the head honcho had lied to him regarding the state of his property once they left, and the other; was the niggling notion that the Colombians may have overtaken the sleeping couple during the night. He would not have put it past them to have kept up a murderous pace despite their undeniable exhaustion. Bazza had placed himself and Cheese a little way from the creek between high roots, making them impossible to see unless they were literally stumbled upon. The Colombians no doubt had spare torches that enabled them to navigate the cave and the creek, while he and Cheese had lost all battery power, making their way in the dark towards the end.

Bazza did not believe he would have woken if they passed their position during the night. He had slept soundly, albeit uncomfortably, waking with a crick in his neck to add to his other woes. His nose felt swollen and his long beard, still smelled of the obnoxious guano infused mud. He swore he would smell that vile sludge until the day he died. It was in their hair, their ears, eyes, and noses, even after washing themselves as thoroughly as possible. He smelled it emanating from the pores of his skin as perspiration. He could not imagine how he must have smelled to Cheese while they kissed and made love. He knew he tasted the sludge in her mouth; so it stood to reason that she experienced the same. That thought embarrassed him. He tried to rid himself of those thoughts as he concentrated on the possibility of the Colombians being in front of them.

All caution escaped him once he neared the Cathedral, witnessing first-hand the devastating result of the Colombians' treachery. Every last one of his carvings, hacked to pieces, lay strewn about the forest floor among the sawdust and mulch. While his shack appeared intact, Bazza slumped to his knees in utter despair at the sight of his ruined art. A year's worth of labour, of back-breaking hardship to haul the wood, carve and finish it...all gone, never to be repaired or repeated. In all Bazza's years of war and loss and prison, he had never felt such inconsolable grief as he felt at that moment. Unbidden tears ran freely from his unbelieving eyes. The Colombians knew exactly how to hurt him, the way to touch him like nothing else would. He had poured his heart and his soul into his creations, breathing life into the inanimate logs. He had literally given blood, sweat, and tears for his art.

Cheese wept in empathy for Bazza as he kneeled upon the earth, feeling depleted over the loss of creations that held his essence. The sap that oozed from the carving's wounds was his own blood seeping slowly onto the forest floor. Cheese did not attempt to either comfort Bazza or urge him to action. She knew he must be allowed time to absorb the shock and despair of the intentional attack. Cheese wandered over to the enormous Strangler Figs that supported the tree house. She carefully released the ladder. Slowly made her way upwards to the house in order to change and find something for them to eat. She did not think Bazza would be hungry but knew he must eat something.

Bazza roused himself eventually, making his way to the base of the Strangler Figs. He made his way up the ladder where he joined Cheese at the kitchen. Fresh coffee awaited him, which he slurped eagerly.

"I am so very, very, sorry, Bazza."

"Thanks, mate. The bastard knew how ta get ta me. Sorry, ya had ta see me blubbering out there. Can't remember the last time I did that."

"If you hadn't I might have clobbered you. I can only imagine how heartbreaking it is. I have seen how much of yourself you invest into those beautiful works of art. Is there any hope of resurrecting any of them?"

"Nah, they're fucked. Wouldn't do it anyway. I hate patching up busted carvings. Tried it once or twice and they never felt the same anymore, like they were somehow disconnected from the original intent. Can't explain it any other way. Once they get a blemish, I just don't wanna bring 'em back anymore."

"How will you manage without your income for the year?"

"Not good. Not good at all. Oh, I don't mean I'll lose everything. I'll have ta work hard for a year or two ta make up for it, maybe even have ta take on a commission or two. I just..."

"I understand. Part of you has been destroyed along with them hasn't it? It's going to take some time for that part of you to heal?"

"Yeah, yeah, that's it Cheese. Ya hit the nail on the head there. I'm not much good with words, so I probably can't explain properly most-o-the time."

"Your expression is your woodcarving, Bazza. You do your explaining as well as anybody through that medium. I don't think you do all that badly with words, though. Here get some eggs into you. Have you said hello to the girls yet? They must have missed you while we were away. Listen to them clucking away over there."

Bazza walked out to the veranda where he schmoozed with his Girls for a short time before making his way back to the kitchen where he ate his breakfast with gusto, asking for more.

"See, you still have your silly Girls, plus one in your life, old man."

"Watch the 'old' bit will ya? Spring chicken ya self are ya?"

"Hardly. What now, Bazza? It's not over yet is it?"

"Nup. I reckon it's time, Cheese. High time we got outta here. After we've finished eating, we gotta start getting some gear together and leave. Up here, we're just sitting ducks for those bastards with their guns. Gotta get this fight outta here so our house don't get fucked up as well."

"Do you mean that?"

"Huh?"

"*Our* house? I like the sound of that, but can you really feel like that about this little piece of paradise you built for yourself?"

"Paradise? Thought ya hated it here?"

"Anywhere with you would be paradise, Bazza. I love you."

"Yeah?"

"Yeah."

"Our house it is then, or wherever we make our home after all this is over. Answer me one thing, though? I can understand the bastard getting back at me through me carvings, but what's he got against me dunny? Why'd he have ta knock the bloody dunny over?"

Bazza and Cheese came up with the answer at the same time.

"Goliath!"

"Ya bloody rippa mate. Bloody Goliath went on the attack, so should we. Time ta finish all this."

With a look of steely determination in his eyes and a firm set to the jaw, Bazza went about organising supplies. Gathering what they needed from the shack, they departed for the foreshore. Bazza explained their need to scuttle the boat out in the bay to cut off any escape route. Unable to spot any sign of the Colombians or their dive boat, Bazza set off with the remaining inflatable from Rafael's boat, towing his dinghy. He would scuttle both boats once safely aboard his dinghy. Once back on shore with Cheese, witnessing the remains of the luxury motor launch disappearing beneath the strengthening waves, gave Bazza pause to search the skies. The usually calm bay had chopped up considerably with a building wind and a darkening sky. In the distance, Bazza observed a troubling sight that left him feeling uneasy.

Bazza recognised the signs. He remembered with grave acuity the last time he had seen a similar vista on the horizon. The roiling sky had heralded a natural fury unleashed upon the land with devastating results. It had decimated the area, and with it, his home.

"Bugger!"

"What?"

"We're in for it. Cyclone coming. Bad one by the looks and feel. Feel that wind picking up? Feel that change in air pressure? Don't get that unless it's heading inland. I gotta pull me dinghy right inta the bush and lash her down before she flies away. Gotta tie down everything at the shack as well. Pull down all the shutters and hope like shit it don't hit here with full force. Last one wiped me and everyone else out, including most-o-the banana growers between here-n-Innisfail. Cost-o-bananas skyrocketed. Hurry, mate."

"How long before it hits?" Cheese asked as they hurried back along the path.

"*If*, it hits, probably a while yet. Problem is, we get the edge of it anyway and that will be here in no time. Winds can build ta hundred miles an hour at the edge of a bad one, double that near the centre if she comes ashore. Either way, we're in for a blow."

Once the dinghy was safely lashed upside down to a fallen tree trunk, Cheese and Bazza made their way back to the shack. It took the pair a considerable length of time to secure everything on the ground around the shack before they had to think about climbing the ladder to begin closing off the shack. The wind had increased noticeably during their period of activity on the ground. Threatening clouds darkened the area beneath the already dim canopy to near night conditions. The wind whistled through the trees. The eerie, haunting, sound like the notes from a pan pipe, were deep and melodious.

Hustling up the ladder, Cheese felt an ominous foreboding that sent a chill up her spine. What may have been her natural woman's intuition was pinging away with great rapidity. It almost caused her to let go of the ladder rungs in order to prevent her ascent to the shack. Bazza happily collided with her backside as he climbed past her legs. Halting only momentarily, Cheese continued her climb after feeling her backside nudged by Bazza. She tried to force the gloomy thoughts from her brain as she neared the top of the ladder.

She found herself staring directly into the waiting barrel of a hand-gun. The breath caught in her throat, constricting with fear. The immediate halt on the ladder caused Bazza to collide with her once again. Before he could admonish her for stopping once more, he caught sight of the reason for her delay. Standing on the deck of his shack, was Marcos waving a gun at them both to get up the ladder and into the shack. For Bazza, he was reliving his moments boarding Rafael's boat. For Cheese, it was a totally horrifying, new experience, which left her mouth dry and her heart racing.

Marcos' grin turned into a sinister sneer when Bazza arrived on the deck. Before Bazza had the chance to say anything he was greeted with a roundhouse smash to the face from Marcos' huge paw that left him reeling. Lounging on the sofa, Carlos' loud, superficial laugh revealed the ugly truth of his personality. Bazza barely recovered when another blow sent him sprawling to the deck. Cheese quickly knelt by his side, only to be hauled away and thrown on the sofa next to Carlos who eyed her lustily. Marcos continued his assault on Bazza with vicious kicks to the midriff. Finally, Carlos waved his hand to signal an end to the hostilities.

"You two think you are very clever, eh? Finding the way out

of the cave? Well, you are not the only ones who can find their way out of a tight spot. The explosion worked a little better than we expected, forcing us to follow your path after reaching the cave. I am surprised you both made the underwater swim. That was a long time underwater with only one breath. Fortunately, Marcos and I had emergency oxygen canisters, so we didn't need to hold our breath. Little ones, holding about five minutes' worth only; more than enough to complete the swim. Thought you could get away huh? Not in this or any other lifetime, bitch."

Carlos leaned over and slapped Cheese hard across the face. With his pinkie ring turned inward, it left a stinging gash across her cheek. Blood slowly oozed from the open sore, which she was too stunned to notice. Marcos dragged a semi-conscious Bazza to the other sofa.

"Can I kill him now?"

"Later. We may have need of him yet." To Cheese, Carlos remarked, "We saw what he did to Rafael's boat and the inflatable from up here. That is why he was punished. Now, we will have to use his little tin thing to get us back to the dive boat and the *Madonna*. We no longer have the instrumentation to take ourselves back, so he will have to take us, and that will be the end of his usefulness and his miserable existence."

"None-o-ya toys are gonna be there dickhead. Cyclone coming. If we don't shut up the shack and get down ta the cave, none-o-us are gonna be alive ta do anything," muttered Bazza through swollen lips.

Marcos went to deliver another punishing blow to Bazza before he was halted by Carlos.

"Wait." To Bazza, "What is this, cyclone? I've heard of it before, but do not remember what it is."

"A hurricane with the wind blowing in the opposite direction. Feel the wind? Last cyclone ta come through here flattened everything. Decimated the coast for hundreds-o-miles either side of the centre when it came ashore."

"No more tricks, and no more following your suggestions I think. We will weather the storm up here. I do not know what you have hidden in your cave, but Marcos and I know everything there is to know about up here. I believe you are exaggerating about the storm to manipulate us once more. It will not work. Get taken for a fool once; suffer the consequences twice. Marcos, take the woman and shut the place up. Keep the gun on her the whole time, do not let your guard down. If either of these two gets the drop on you again you will suffer worse than them, and believe me; they will suffer greatly before they die."

Marcos hauled Cheese to the veranda where she began pulling the shutters closed, and bolting them to the floor with the lockable, galvanised, pad bolts. Cheese lowered the girls' cage to the veranda floor. The light dimmed further with each closed shutter, while the wind escalated and the rain began in earnest. Solar lights on sensors within the shack, lit up as the natural light diminished. Carlos continued to recline comfortably while watching Bazza with a venomous stare. Both the Colombians had changed into Bazza's clothing, ostensibly having forsaken their wetsuits before embarking on the path within the cave, much as Cheese and Bazza had done. Carlos no longer had that polished, suave, countenance that tailored clothing gave him. In Bazza's dungarees, he appeared oafish and evil. Marcos on the other hand, portrayed the muscled physique of a Mr. Universe, in Bazza's shorts and T-shirt.

Bazza scrutinised their every movement, knowing he may be breathing his last. What he cared about most, was the woman he had come to love and admire. He could not bear to see her hurt, yet he had to control every urge to defend her from abuse. Going to her aid like some avenging Don Quixote would only hasten their demise. Bazza's brain was running overtime trying to come up with some sort of plan that might see them survive but drew a blank. He had used up all his luck he believed, and yet, knew that a chance would come sooner or later. He had only to act defenceless and beaten, to lure them into a false sense of complacency.

When Marcos and Cheese returned, Carlos ordered her to

make them all something to eat. Despite having eaten a light meal earlier, Cheese was surprised at how hungry she felt. Marcos prowled about the shack like a tomcat on heat, itching for a resumption of the fight, to end the Australian once and for all. He practised slinging his firearm around like a cowboy in a western movie, touching the barrel to either Cheese or Bazza alternatively, inviting them to take some form of action. Carlos watched the play with wry amusement. He would let Marcos loose on the big baboon soon enough, then he would have some fun with the woman before she joined her friend in the afterlife.

The wind began to howl as the rain pelted the shack with increased force. All about them within the Cathedral, leaves, twigs and ferns fell to the ground after being ripped loose by the wind. Without sunlight, the solar batteries held enough charge to keep basic lighting running for as long as a couple of days. Cheese cooked up a large pan of pasta on the gas stove, to which she added mushrooms from Bazza's last crop, onions, canned spinach, and tomatoes. Accentuated with herbs and seasoning, the dish sent its aromatic flavors around the small confines of the shack, leaving its occupants restless and hungry.

Outside, branches and limbs began thrumming the roof and walls of the shack, whipped into a frenzy by the mounting gale. In the distance they heard the dying cry of a large hardwood on its earthbound journey, crashing into and toppling smaller trees on its descent. Through the wild squalls they heard the tremendous pounding of waves crashing upon the shore in relentless repetition. The walls of the shack shook and trembled with the might of the wind-lashed rain. Torrents streamed against the structure in a deafening display of nature's wrath. Marcos looked about him uncertainly as the shack no longer seemed a safe option. Carlos too appeared worried despite his best efforts to hide any display of uncertainty.

"Bet ya wished ya had listened ta me now huh? Be a lot safer in the cave, but no point in going there now; wouldn't make it. Me shack is made-o-bamboo, chewing gum, and wire. Not going ta stand up ta a full-on cyclone mate. We're probably all gonna die up here."

"Maybe I should have listened to you. Who can know when you are lying or not? You have a very clever mind, *Señor*. You are not the stupid man you would have us believe. Every time I underestimated you, I was left looking the foolish one. I will not make that mistake again. We can always go to the cave after we have eaten."

"Nah, ya can't. Wouldn't make it down the ladder in one piece in this, mate. Wind'd pick ya up and hurl ya inta the next tree. Squash ya like a bug on a windscreen. If ya made it ta the ground, one bit-o-loose iron off the roof or off me dunny which, *ya knocked over*, could cut ya in half. Wouldn't make it ta the cave in this shit. I reckon the cyclone is coming close ta crossing the coast. Winds near the guts could be as strong as three hundred miles-n-hour. I reckon we're fucked mate. Only a matter-o-time fore we're blown away, or torn apart."

"Want me to kill him now boss?"

"He is just trying to trick us again, Marcos. Have a look at the house. Does it look unsafe to you? I think not. He has built the house himself after surviving one of these storms. He would build it to withstand one, no? Relax, Marcos, he is still playing his mind games with us. If he says anything more, cut his tongue off. That should keep him quiet for a while."

Carlos looked at Bazza defiantly, daring him to say more. Bazza merely smiled, then grimaced with the pain it caused. That made Carlos laugh with undisguised pleasure. He truly did enjoy another's pain, especially when inflicted by him or his men. Carlos' laugh was drowned out by a sudden gust that made the Strangler Figs upon which the shack was built, sway dangerously. The bamboo walls and floors creaked loudly in protest to the movement. The roof threatened to let go, groaning against the gale. The rushing wind sounded like a freight train rumbling through the forest. Despite being semi-insulated from the world outside, the area beneath the canopy was battered by high winds, obliterating all other sounds.

It was an eerie sensation as the trees moved noticeably back and forth, sometimes in opposition to one another, causing the shack to squeal and crack as walls separated by as much as a hand's width at times. Door frames skewed and window frames broke as opposing forces twisted the structure into impossible contortions. Cheese barely managed to control her fear to cook a meal which she served up on four plates at the kitchen bench. Carlos motioned for everyone to move to the bench. No one spoke, as the roaring wind dispensed all notions that they would even be heard over the mêlée. Bazza edged his way over, feeling his ribs tenderly to determine the extent of possible internal damage. To his relief, it seemed he had escaped broken ribs and any serious injury.

Marcos and Carlos ate heartily while Cheese picked at the edges of her meal, eating only a little, picking up the occasional piece of pasta, toying with it. Bazza did not eat anything though he was hungry as well. When Carlos gave him a questioning glance, he indicated that his mouth was too sore to eat. That made Carlos and Marcos smile with glee. They wolfed down their food hastily. Marcos leaned over to take Bazza's plate of pasta to eat as well, while Carlos grabbed Cheese's plate impatiently, not wanting to watch her picking away at good food any longer. The Colombians were famished after their ordeal and ate accordingly.

Bazza motioned that he would like to make a cup of coffee, which Carlos flatly refused. He waved a hand at Cheese to perform the task. Cheese obliged readily, pleased to be occupying her mind while the shack seemed to shake itself to pieces. Horizontal rain found its way through the cracks, soaking the walls and floor. Cheese busied herself in the kitchen while Bazza watched and waited. Bazza's attention narrowly focussed on the events inside the shack, dismissing the maelstrom around them. He took the proffered cup of coffee from Cheese without a word or a look. Cheese did not mind, knowing what he was waiting for.

The scene at the table became very subdued while everyone drank their strong aromatic coffee, while the cyclone raged unceasingly beyond the very thin walls. Metal roofing threatened to tear away from the rafters at any moment and the entire tree-house felt like it was about to burst apart. The enormous Strangler Figs swayed and shook like twigs in the face of a top category cyclone with winds swirling around at more than a hundred miles per hour. Throughout the Cathedral and surrounds, could be heard the groaning and creaking of trees before they came crashing to the ground with a resounding thump, that made everything in the shack jump.

Carlos watched the other pair closely, wondering if they were up to yet another one of their tricks, plotting an escape. He was not concerned about dying as a result of the storm. If it was his time, then he would face it with his usual arrogance. He faced many dangers in his life. Human. Beast. Nature. He had swum with the great sharks in his searches for the treasure. He had faced untold numbers of enemies on his rise to riches. He had bested them all. He had survived earthquakes and tsunamis of greater magnitude than the little storm outside the shack. He was looking forward to the excitement of torturing the pair before him. He would devise a few new ways to inflict the torments of Hell upon the troublesome pair, immediately after he had pleasured himself with the woman.

Marcos examined the eyes of everyone at the table with a wariness born of indoctrination. He had been in the boss's employ long enough to know what was expected of him, how to act, and how to pre-empt any plans the enemy may hatch. While the raging storm worried him no end, he felt the tension within the hut growing. Something was brewing besides the coffee, something elusive that continued to evade his detection. He sipped his coffee, peering over the rim of the cup with a deepening suspicion. It felt like time was at a stand-still within the shack, poignantly poised for an as yet unidentified episode.

Bazza took great pleasure in sipping his coffee slowly to make it last as long as possible. Ten minutes had passed since the meal was finished. He knew he did not have much longer to wait. He examined Cheese's features, searching for any tell-tale signs. Cheese looked back into his eyes lovingly, resigned to a certain future. She smiled at Bazza with an almost imperceptible nod. He gave her a look of reassurance. Another five minutes passed before Carlos grimaced. Soon after, Marcos held his stomach as a cramp made itself known. Cheese began to turn a distinct shade of green while Marcos and Carlos began to sweat profusely.

Carlos' eyes became wild and unfocussed while Marcos doubled up with another round of cramps. Carlos waved his gun about frantically trying to aim at something only he could see, while Marcos vomited violently on the floor. Cheese seemingly melted into her chair, unable to control her motor functions successfully. Bazza launched himself at Cheese to throw them both onto the floor just as Carlos let loose a few random shots at the walls and furniture. Carlos then doubled up, racked with a stomach cramp that threatened to loosen his bowels.

Bazza gathered Cheese up in his arms. He slung her over his shoulder as he made his way down the ladder into the maw of the violent weather inundating the entire area into a wind-whipped frenzy. The heavy drops stung his face as he made his way clumsily down the swaying ladder. Twice, he nearly missed a rung with his foot, that might have sent them plummeting the remaining distance to the ground. It was impossible to see anything through the relentless barrage of water and objects being hurled about. They were being battered mercilessly on their descent, while in the shack, Bazza heard more shots being fired randomly. He was not overly concerned that the shots were aimed at them, they would not have been visible through the sheets of water and debris.

Cheese began moaning as Bazza struggled with her writhing body to escape the Cathedral. Instinctively, he made his way out of the clearing without tripping. Leaves, twigs, and a host of other flora slammed the duo as they moved further into the forest. Bazza hoped to make his way along the track to the top road before the Colombians regained their senses and the track became too boggy once more. He could not know how long the Colombians would be out of action, so he wasted no time in creating as much distance between them as possible. Slipping and sliding on the greasy track meant slowing down considerably. Bazza urged Cheese to stop struggling, but his voice was blown away. He could not be heard over the sound of a freight train roaring through the forest. The immensity of the sound enveloped them in a tangible hold. Lightning and thunder added to the increasing mayhem about them.

Bazza strained his ears for any sound like a cracking or falling tree. He had no wish to be crushed to death or worse, trapped beneath a tree waiting to be executed by the Colombians once they caught up. Every muscle in his legs and back quailed with the exertion forced upon them by the steep ascent up the track. For almost every two paces gained, he lost a half pace in his manic effort to flee. Bazza dug deep, to remain strong, to endure, to get past the moment of fatigue. Roaring like a wounded bull, he inched his way up the track, against the slope, against the wall of wind and debris pushing against him. He felt like he was in a performance by Marcel Marceau with the wind pushing him back on the stage in silent, constrained emotion.

Every gruelling step punished his wounded body until he felt he could take no more. He pushed his aching body to the point of collapse when finally, he came across the small path that would lead to the circle of palm trees he called the fairy circle. Bazza knew that very near the circle was a possible refuge. Using his last reserves of energy, he crashed through the undergrowth into a clearing. Barely able to make out his destination through the stinging rain, he toppled forward.

Bazza began to madly dig at the side of a mound, burrowing as deep as he could into the leafy mulch. He had no idea if the structure would support a hole being dug into it, but knew they had little choice but to attempt it. Cheese offered a feeble hand to pat away some of the detritus being excavated from the mound, while Bazza continued to dig as hard as he was able. Finding a solid tree root, Bazza dug furiously beneath the root to enable him to excavate a decent enough hole for them to wait out the worst of the cyclone. He shoved Cheese roughly ahead of him into the opening, following close by. Once inside as far as they could squeeze themselves, Bazza grabbed as much mulch and leaf litter as possible from the sides of the hole to bury themselves within the structure. Although they would be soaked to the bone and by no means safe, Bazza felt they stood a modicum of a chance to survive the cyclone. Before he could produce another thought, the deafening roar diminished into the distance. The wind died to nil and leaves fell softly to the ground.

"We're in the eye of the cyclone Cheese. How're ya feeling, mate?"

"Not good. I feel like my insides want to come out of every orifice.

"Yeah, I know it feels like shit, but it won't last long. Ya didn't have enough ta really make ya blow ya load. Ya did real good. Ya knew exactly what ta do and ya did it. Couldn't-o-done better meself. Yer a bloody bewdy, mate. That's for sure."

"You knew?"

"Course I knew. Soon as I saw them Blue Meanies, I knew what ya were up ta. I had ta feign not being able ta eat, though, otherwise, I woulda been affected as well. Sorry, ya had ta eat a bit yaself, mate. Can ya imagine how those other bozos must feel?"

"I never knew that those Gold Tops could do that to a person."

"Nah, not just Gold Tops love. They were Blue Meanies that I meant ta toss aside. They give ya a bad trip. Worse than LSD. Course, some people like that shit, but if ya aren't used ta it, or don't know ya having it...well, ya cop it full belt. Those mongrels will be seeing shit that isn't there and copping the whole shebang. Stomach cramps, vomiting, diarrhoea, everything. Serves 'em bloody right!"

"Where, where are we Bazza?" screamed Cheese to be heard over the building noise.

"Turkey mound. Only thing I knew of where we might find a bit-o-shelter. We got lucky with there being a tree root in here, otherwise it might have collapsed as I was digging the hole. Rest now, don't talk."

Cheese nodded her understanding. Bazza had more than one reason for wanting her quiet. He did not know how long the mongrels would be under the influence of the mushrooms. While they were reasonably well hidden within the mound, they might still be heard if they were shouting to one another. If they were found again, he didn't like their chances of living to tell the tale. The rain continued to seep through the mound, drenching them with cool water. They were insulated enough beneath the leaf litter to escape the brunt of the storm, but they could not escape the soaking. Sooner or later they would have to try and find some warmth.

Outside the four foot tall mound of leaf litter, twigs, and mulchy earth scratched high by the male turkey to attract a female partner, the wind continued to howl through the trees ripping limbs and boughs off wherever a weakness was discovered. Enormous hardwoods groaned and creaked as they were shunted several yards in all directions by the swirling tempest. Lightning strikes all about them shook the earth while thunder drummed the air mercilessly, vibrating through the ground and up through the bones in their bodies. Neither could accumulate any thoughts as they waited out the worst storm they had ever experienced.

Cheese had been through a tornado at a friend's farm once. It had torn their garage to pieces. While extremely lucky for the house to have survived unscathed, the wind lasted mere moments. Her first experience of a cyclone, made worse by the effects of the hallucinogenic mushrooms was so horrifying that she hoped never to have another. Bazza had been through one or two cyclones which were common in North Queensland during the summer season, but rarely so late and so powerful. He had only experienced the wrath at the fringes of those cyclones, never the centre where the winds are the strongest. The eerie, subdued calm at the eye of the storm seemed totally surreal, like entering into another dimension where all activity around them was dull and muted.

After an hour, the winds diminished to a point where conversation could be heard. Rain continued to pelt down hard upon the canopy where the heavy raindrops gathered until they were released upon the earth below. Branches could still be heard crashing to the ground, but more interspersed than before. The forest soon regained its ethereal quality with only rain to remind them of nature's fury sent to test their wills. Usually, when a cyclone moved on or petered out, it would leave a rain depression in its wake that could last several days or even weeks.

Bazza despaired at the thought that they would have no means of escaping along the track, sodden to impassability by the rain. He did not believe that the Colombians would be able to track them to their hiding place but knew they could not remain there long. They needed to dry themselves before they caught a chill, or worse, pneumonia. Cheese had fallen into a deep sleep, snoring like a coal miner. Bazza feared that she might attract bad company by that sound alone. It amused him to hear a woman snoring so loudly. He had incorrectly assumed that snoring was mostly a man's prerogative. He wondered how their antagonists had fared in his shack. *Hopefully, the shack had been blown to bits and them bastards with it*, he thought. Then he felt guilty about his girls left behind to fend on their own.

CHAPTER NINETEEN

A gunshot interrupted Bazza's thoughts. He could not discern the location of the shooter or the intended target from within the mound. He knew it was too close to be a coincidence, however. He could only assume that Cheese's snoring had indeed given them away.

"Come out of there before I fill it with lead from every angle. Did you forget about my little electronic devices? Did you forget the meal you had aboard the *Madonna*? Did you think I would not bring some of my equipment with me through the cave to follow your path? I was never in a hurry because I always knew I could catch you."

End of the road, thought Bazza as he scratched his way out of their hiding place within the mound. Cheese followed close by as they emerged into the rainy gloom. All about them lay the result of the destructive forces unleashed by Mother Nature. Gaping holes in the canopy foretold of the massive trees toppled to earth by the sheer added weight of water and the power of the wind. The devastation about them caused Bazza to sigh heavily, knowing that his home and everything else he had built his life around would all be destroyed. He did not believe that anything of his could have survived the onslaught of a full-force cyclone. With most of his outdoor carvings having been destroyed already, he did not think it was possible for him to continue with the little savings he had.

Before he could think further, a shot rang out from Marcos' gun. At first, Bazza wondered what he could possibly have been shooting at and why? Both he and Cheese had calmly surrendered. Then he buckled as the pain hit him. The searing, tearing agony travelled along his right thigh, where the bullet entered, sending spasms of agony to his back and other regions where the nerve endings registered the event. Cheese screamed when she saw Bazza crumpling to the ground. Marcos stood over the pair with a malicious grin turning his features into a hideous, grotesque, mask of pure malevolence. Carlos simply stood back to enjoy the show, revelling in the Australian's misery.

Cheese tore a strip off her T-shirt belonging to Bazza's diminishing wardrobe, wrapping it around the thigh to staunch the flow of blood from both wounds. The entry site was only a small hole, while the exit wound was a large tear. Cheese applied the meagre first aid as best she was able to in the circumstances. She looked at the pair of villains with undisguised hostility.

"I wouldn't bother looking at me like that, Ms. Armstrong. Be thankful it was not you who copped the bullet. It was you who put something in our food?"

Cheese nodded, "I just wish it had been poison."

"Then you too might have died. Very clever to eat something first to show us that you were not afraid of eating it. I was watching you very carefully to see if you would put something in our meals. *His,* story I believed about not being able to eat after the treatment from Marcos. You, I would not have believed. Congratulations for tricking us once again. I still feel wretched. What was it?"

"Magic mushrooms they're called sometimes. Gold Tops. I chose a particularly nasty type that Bazza pointed out to me a month ago, he called, Blue Meanies. Works differently on different people. A bit like LSD. The Same type of chemicals and reactions, hallucinogenic."

"Very clever. Don't you think, Marcos?"

"No, boss. I feel like shit and I saw things I never want to see again. Can I kill them now?"

"Patience, Marcos, we still need him to get us out of here to the *Madonna.*"

Bazza chuckled, "Good luck with that, fuckwit."

"Oh, I am sure if we did some things to your little girlfriend here, you would soon be persuaded to take us wherever we want to go."

"That may be, but the *Madonna* won't be in any condition ta get ya anywhere once we find her."

"Chico is very experienced at handling the ship, he..."

"...is dead, and ya ship is fucked. Probably smashed ta bits on the reef it was aimed at before I left. If ya think ya dive boat is where ya left it, guess again. No way ya boat stayed anchored there during a cyclone. She's gone for sure."

"Chico..."

"Killed him and tied him ta the wheel fore I left. Aimed the ship at a reef."

"I do not believe..."

"Why do bad guys always like ta talk? Ya always trying ta explain how clever ya are in the movies, bragging about ya exploits and shit. It's just as well ya keepin' true ta the script, coz it paid off for us. Ya stupid talking and showing off has fucked ya three ways from Sundy. Given us the time ta turn the tables on ya."

"I did not see you eat any of the mushrooms, yet you seem to be delusional. It is, Marcos and I who have the upper hand, my friend. We have the guns and you have..."

"...enough weaponry aimed at ya ta make sure ya never touch anyone again. I only have ta give the signal ta see yiz made inta shish-kebabs."

"You are a very funny man, *Señor*. There is no one around here for many miles. I think I have had enough of your insolence. I will teach you to show me some respect."

At the precise moment Carlos raised his weapon to aim, Bazza's hand raised slightly. From the forest surrounding them came a flurry of native spears penetrating both Colombians. They crashed to their knees. A confused look on their features as they toppled forward to be halted at odd angles by the protruding spears. Locked in an upright kneeling position by the porcupine effect of the crude weapons, Carlos and Marcos watched incredulously as dark human shapes emerged from the surrounding forest to stand in a circle around them. Carlos coughed up blood as he breathed his last. Marcos struggled vainly to raise himself, trying desperately to aim the gun with his useless arm. The more he struggled, the deeper the spears gored and widened the wounds. Finally, all was still as the two men died.

Cheese looked about in fear and confusion at the circle of natives surrounding them, dressed in all manner of traditional and western gear. An elderly man dressed in only a red loincloth came over to them. He knelt before the pair studying them with interest.

"Cheese, say g'day ta, Sergeant Robert Rasta. Boinga Bob to his mates. A descendant-o-the traditional tribe-o-this region known as the Kuku Yalanji. Brought up for a time in 'Merry-Old-England' as a snot-nosed brat, before coming home again. Bout time ya showed up ya bastard. Late as usual."

"Look here old sock, had to battle a cyclone to get here don't you know? Holed up in that God-awful cave of yours while all Hell broke loose. Saw you high-tailing it out of there with this woman draped over your shoulder. What did you say the name of this delectable dish was, Major? Couldn't have heard right the first time."

"Ya heard right. It's a bloody long story, but her name is Cheese, as in cheddar. Got it ya limey prick? Keep ya fucking eyes and ya grubby hands orf her before I snot ya one, gammy leg and all."

"Now see here old bean, that's a bit uncalled for. Followed these mongrels here and saved your life and all that, what ho?"

"Save ya toffy-nosed accent for the tourists, Boinga, and I meant what I said. Ya looking at the future, Mrs. Ottoman there. If she'll have me that is?"

"Was that a proposal, Mr. Ottoman?"

"Um, yeah, I suppose it was."

"Damn strange way you Aussies have of sweeping a girl off her feet, but I will say yes to your proposal, Mr. Ottoman if you will allow us to take care of your leg now before you bleed to death."

"How's me shack, Boinga, can we go back there?"

"Not a hope old man. Done for I'm afraid."

"Shit! Means I'm up ta the 'S' girls now."

"The shack kept those two safe enough during the worst of it, then it all seemed to fall away once they left. We'll have to get you back to my camp and let the women have a look at you. You seemed pretty confident about yourself back then. How on earth could you know we would stop him from killing you?"

"You bloody black fellas might think ya got everything sewed up when it comes ta bushcraft, but ya don't hold a patch on me schnozz, mate. Smelled ya, through the rain, even though me schnozz was busted."

"My dear, Cheese, you would not believe the number of times in Afghanistan that his nose saved us all from certain death. Uncanny, almost like a sixth sense, but without a doubt, saved us many times before we ran into an ambush. He even smelled the lingering remnants of the Mujahedeen at a land-mined road just as we were about to walk on it. As insulting as his statement was, it pains me to verify its complete accuracy."

"You served with him?"

"Served, ate, fought, and bathed with the oaf for a number of years I would rather forget. Been neighbours here ever since. I live with my relatives and friends over the mountain, closer to Cooktown, trying hard to stay on our bit of land before the constabulary move us along again."

"How did you know to come here, or was it purely coincidence?"

"My dear girl, how silly do you think we are to walk through a cyclone purely for our enjoyment? The Major left us a note here which I dug up a couple of days ago. When Major Ott..."

"Will ya kindly cut out the, Major crap and call me, Bazza ya mangy mongrel? Left all that army crap a long time ago ya know?"

"You will always be the Major to me, Sir. I owe you my life so many times over that it can never be repaid. I will never show you any disrespect by calling you anything other than, Major or Sir, Sir."

"Start calling me, Sir, Sir, and I'll have ya guts for garters and ya balls for earrings, ya smelly old bastard, and for fuck's sake, learn how ta tie that loincloth-o-yiz properly would ya? Can see ya worm and ya nuts clear as fucking day."

"Cranky old sausage when you're wounded aren't you? Show some gratitude my dear, Major, or I will take this pretty lady back with me and leave you here. Anyway, as I was telling the lovely lass; I found Major's note buried at the fairy circle which is our secret mailbox to one another whenever he doesn't show up for our usual rendezvous to swap veggies for mushies."

"What about that other dago, did ya round him up like I told ya?"

"Hard to miss that one running around like a mad March Hare I tell you. Whatever did you do to him, Major? Never seen someone in such a mess."

"Tricked the mongrel inta using some Stinging Tree leaves ta wipe his face with. The stupid bastard musta used bark ta try and scrape away the sting. Is he still kicking, or did he croak?"

"After we disarmed him, Aunt Kath got him settled a bit, put on some of her salve to soothe the savage beast, as it were."

"Fuck! That's worse than what I did ta him. No one deserves ya Aunt's bloody salves. Don't ever let her anywhere near ya, Cheese. Not with one-o-her salves at any rate. Ya would sooner chop ya limb orf than have ta put up with the smell-o-her putrid salves. Ya would rather climb back in that cave with all the bat shit and stuff."

"Cave, Major? No caves around here. Only the little one under the waterfall, and I never noticed any bats coming out of there?"

"Long story, Boinga. We might have ta go there for a withdrawal sooner or later. Bout time ya built a proper village ta live in I reckon, and I need some funds ta rebuild me shack."

"Not sure I follow you at all old man. Have you taken a blow to the head, Major?"

"Reckon I wasn't gonna tell anyone and just leave it all there, Cheese, but I think we might take a bit ta give this tribe a home on either my block or yours, and we rebuild our house. Wadda ya say?"

"I say that's a splendid idea husband to be, only, how will you prevent the rape of the land as a result of the discovery?"

"Ah, we'll make out we salvaged it from the ocean bottom somewhere, keep the nosy Parkers away from the actual site. Declare it all proper-n-legal like and have enough after taxes and shit ta do everything we need. Hey, Boinga, that dago ever gonna be right enough in the head ta tell anyone anything?"

"Impossible to say for certain, but given his present condition;

unlikely. I sincerely doubt anyone would believe anything he said at any rate. Would you really give us some of your land to build a permanent community? Do you think the authorities would allow it?"

"I think we could grease enough palms ta make it happen. Hell, we could even salvage that ship-o-his if there's enough left of it, and we might possibly recover some-o-ya funds, Cheese."

"Ship?"

"Yeah, a bonza ship, Boinga, like a floating fucking palace. Worth a mint ta the insurance company I reckon, if it's still in one piece. Should be, I aimed it toward a sandy shoal where it shoulda beached itself and weathered the storm okay."

"I thought you said you aimed it at a reef, Bazza? 'Smashed to bits', you said."

"Aw, I only told *them* that, Cheese. They didn't hafta know everything. I didn't want them forcing us ta go looking for the bloody thing in me little dinghy. Now, how about ya all stop standing around like starched farts and get us outta here!"

THE END

Other Titles by Author

A man undergoes profound psychological changes as a result of isolation, physical pain, and emotional distress. Unfettered by the distractions of everyday life in the city, his mind is left to ferment the negative into more than was ever intended, capable of actions far beyond his perceptions. Ultimately, only a mirror of his brutality will bring his conscience to bear.

Available Now

See author's website for purchase links.
http://lakesidecaravanpark.wixsite.com/josef

Finding the courage to go against the grain of popular convention, one man discovers his true passion for a lifelong kinship. Join Josef as he deigns to venture into the art of woodcarving.

Available Now
See author's website for purchase links.
http://lakesidecaravanpark.wixsite.com/josef

EPHEMERAL IMAGES FROM A TROUBLING DREAM INSPIRE
SAMUEL BORDER TO MEET A GIRL WHO PROCEEDS TO
CAPTURE HIS HEART. THE TRANSIENCE OF THEIR
ENCOUNTER IN NO WAY REFLECTS THE INDELIBLE IMPRINT
HAUNTING HIS MIND, BUT EVENTS INTERVENE TO POSTPONE
THEIR UNION. A COMPULSION TO LOCATE THE WOMAN OF HIS
DREAMS RESULTS IN A TRAGIC ACCIDENT TO HIS YOUNGER
BROTHER, CAUSING SAMUEL TO ABANDON THE SEARCH.
ONLY HAPPENSTANCE MANY YEARS LATER ALTERS THAT
DECISION.
WERE LIFE SIMPLY ABOUT THE PRESENT AND NOT UNDULY
INFLUENCED BY AN EVIL FAMILY LEGACY, SAMUEL WOULD
NOT BE DRAWN INEXORABLY TOWARD HIS DESTINY. IT WILL
REQUIRE ALL HIS INSTINCTS AND COURAGE TO BRING THE
WOMAN HE LOVES BEYOND MEASURE HOME SAFELY.
***WARNING, CONTAINS SEXUAL VIOLENCE AGAINST A
FEMALE***

AVAILABLE NOW
SEE AUTHOR'S WEBSITE FOR PURCHASE LINKS.
http://lakesidecaravanpark.wixsite.com/josef

ABOUT THE AUTHOR

Josef arrived in Australia with his parents and siblings in 1964. A near lifetime of creative pursuits has culminated in his desire to produce entertaining stories. Josef lives with his wife in the tiny outback town of Moulamein, NSW Australia where they own and manage a small caravan park, while they each indulge in their artistic endeavours. Josef chooses to base his stories in Australian settings, populating them with authentic-sounding Aussie characters. While this approach will not appeal to everyone, he stays true to the country he has grown to love.